Sherryl Woods

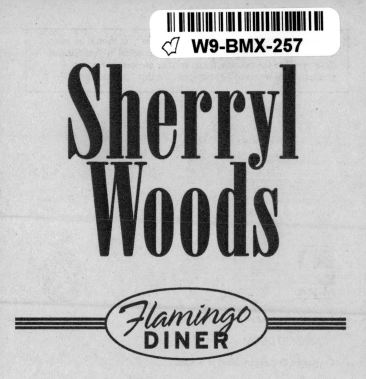

Flamingo DINER

MIRA

ISBN 1-55166-722-3

FLAMINGO DINER

Copyright © 2003 by Sherryl Woods.

Visit us at www.mirabooks.com

Printed in U.S.A.

Dear Friends,

Welcome to the fictional world of Winter Cove, Florida, and especially to Flamingo Diner, which was inspired by my own favorite Florida breakfast place.

Years ago, after moving to Key Biscayne, an island community that is worlds away from downtown Miami yet right across a causeway, I discovered the Donut Gallery. Okay, okay, I know I have no need to be eating doughnuts, but the truth is there are very few doughnuts on the menu anymore. What this tiny restaurant has—aside from the usual scrambled eggs, bagels and sausage—is the pulse of a community. Over the years there I've met everyone from a confidante of President Nixon's to a career lifeguard, from a federal prosecutor to caddies for some of the men on the seniors' golf tour, from the captain of a charter fishing operation to snowbirds from all over the world. Birthdays and babies are celebrated there, deaths mourned.

Over the years, that got me thinking about what would happen if a tragedy struck the family who owned such a place. Would these very diverse people pull together to support them? And in Flamingo Diner they do, just as I know they would at my own favorite spot.

For those of you who've read previous books of mine, you'll quickly see that this one is a bit more serious, because the tragedy that strikes is suicide. My life has been affected twice when very dear friends took their own lives. I've gone through all the stages of grief, wondering what I should have seen, what I could have done. I've been angry with them...for myself and for the families left behind to deal with the heartache. And I've learned, in the end, to remember them when they were joyful and full of life and to be grateful for those times.

I wish all of you happiness and, for those times when you despair, a good friend to listen and a strong family to lean on...and a place just like Flamingo Diner, where people care about their neighbors.

All the best,

Sherryl Woods

Also by SHERRYL WOODS

ABOUT THAT MAN
ASK ANYONE
ANGEL MINE
AFTER TEX

And watch for the newest novel from
SHERRYL WOODS

DESTINY UNLEASHED

Coming June 2004

To all of my friends at Key Biscayne's Donut Gallery,
who are every bit as diverse, warm and wonderful
as the characters in Flamingo Diner.
Thanks for inspiring me
and entertaining me on a daily basis.

1

The July humidity was as high as it possibly could be without rain pouring from the sky. Despite recent power company improvements, another manhole had exploded just down the block in Washington's Georgetown area, shooting flames into the air and shutting off power to several blocks of boutiques and restaurants. Without air-conditioning, Fashionable Memories felt like a steam room in one of those fancy spas their customers were always running off to.

Emma wiped her brow and cursed the fact that today of all days five crates of antiques had arrived from an estate sale in Boston. Normally she regarded the arrival of new treasures with the excitement of a kid on Christmas morning, but today the unpacking seemed a whole lot more like hot, sweaty drudgery. And naturally her boss was nowhere to be found. Marcel D'Avignon, who was about as French as country ham and grits, preferred spending money to the hard work of earning it. He left that to Emma.

In fact, in the five years she'd been at Fashionable Memories, Emma had taken over most of the day-to-day operations of the high-end antiques business, while Marcel concentrated on acquisitions. For a woman who'd grown up in a small Florida town more prone to wicker and plastic, she had an innate ability to spot priceless pieces of old furniture, silver and porcelain and then sell them at a ridiculously high profit to the interior designers and bored Washington society housewives who made up the bulk of their clientele.

Today, with the temperature in the shop approaching ninety, she could probably have gotten a better price for ice. Her friends here still marveled that a woman who'd grown up in Florida could have any complaints about the Washington summers. They didn't seem to understand that back in Winter Cove, power outages from outdated infrastructure weren't kicking off the air-conditioning every couple of weeks.

Just thinking about home made her long to hear the sound of her mother's voice. Rosa Killian had been born in Miami, but her parents had come from Cuba. Rosa had spoken Spanish before she'd learned English, and traces of the accent lingered, along with strong beliefs about family and principles of strict child rearing. Emma had learned at an early age that her father, Don, was a much softer touch than her mother when it came to doling out punishment, especially to the daughter he adored.

Emma sighed thinking about how heartbroken he'd been when she'd announced her intention to leave Winter Cove to attend college in Washington, then stayed on to work for Fashionable Memories. Hurting her father was her only regret about the decision she'd made. Otherwise, it had been the exact right choice for her. She'd come into her own here, away from the watchful eyes of family and neighbors, all of whom thought they should have a say in her life.

She loved Washington and the nearby rolling Virginia countryside. Being at the center of things in a city that hummed with excitement and power filled her with an energy she had never felt in the small Florida town where she'd been born. Winter Cove had its charms, but she'd felt as if she were growing up in a glass bubble with everyone watching everything she was doing, every misstep she made. Here she could make a monumental mistake and there were thousands of people who'd never have a clue about it.

Not that she made *that* many mistakes. She lived a fairly sedate and uneventful life. No messy relationships. No wild nights. Not even a speeding ticket.

Sweet heaven, she was barely twenty-six and she was boring, she thought with a sudden attack of dismay. Wasn't that precisely the fate she'd left home to escape? And wasn't that exactly what Marcel had been saying to her the week before when she'd turned down yet another blind date? She'd argued the point rather emphatically at the time, but she could see now that her boss had pegged her life exactly right. Fulfilling work that she loved was one thing. Having a *life* was something else entirely, and it was time she did something about grabbing one. Otherwise all that independence she'd moved to Washington to claim would be totally wasted.

Spurred on by the thought, she reached for the phone to call her best friend before she could change her mind.

Kim Drake had a social life that a Hollywood starlet would envy. Emma, however, had never felt the slightest twinge of envy, because she knew that the one thing Kim craved—a family—was still as elusive as ever. She called Emma after nearly every date for a postmortem to analyze whether the latest man in her life could possibly be *the one*. So far none had even passed Kim's three-dates-and-he's-out test. Their Sunday morning get-togethers at a trendy Georgetown coffee shop had become strategy sessions for meeting better candidates. Thus far Emma had doled out plenty of advice on the topic to Kim, but followed none of it herself. Today Emma intended to change that pattern.

"Do we know anyone who has a swimming pool?" Kim asked plaintively as soon as she heard Emma's voice.

"I'm sure any number of men in your life live in singles complexes with pools," Emma told her.

"Given the disgustingly boring crop of men in my life at the moment, it's not worth it," Kim said. "I'd prefer to swelter. So, what's up? I thought you were going to be hip deep in dusty antiques today."

"I am, and it's given me too much time to think."

"Uh-oh. What's on your mind?"

"I've decided I need a social life."

"Well, hallelujah! Isn't that exactly what I've been saying for months now? Even Marcel, who's oblivious to most things that don't involve him, thinks you're a hermit," Kim said. "Do you want to go out tonight? I have a date with a Congressional aide. I'm sure he has friends he could call. We could double."

"Which date is this for you and the aide?" Emma asked suspiciously.

"Second, why?"

"That's okay, then."

"What are you talking about?" Kim demanded. She sounded genuinely perplexed.

"If it were your first, then you wouldn't know yet

whether his friends are likely to be awful,'' Emma explained patiently. "If it were your third, you'd probably be breaking up at the end of the evening and that could put a real damper on things for those of us relegated to being witnesses.''

"I am not that predictable,'' Kim protested.

"I could run through the list,'' Emma teased the woman she'd known since their first year of college when they'd shared a dorm room. "We could start with Dirk, freshman year in college. I believe you made a list of his attributes and flaws after the second date and canceled the third. The pattern has been repeated more times than I can count.''

"God, I hate having a friend who knows my entire life inside out,'' Kim grumbled. "Do you want a date tonight or not?''

Emma hesitated. "A Congressional aide, huh?''

"He's mine, but I imagine that's where his pool of available friends comes from.''

Emma hated politics. Living in the nation's capital had given her a jaundiced view of the men—and women, for that matter—who wielded power as if it were their God-given right. They might come to Washington full of high ideals, but it seldom took long for them to learn the art of backroom deal making. As fascinating as it was to watch it all unfold, she had no desire to get too close to that particular fire.

"Never mind,'' she said finally. Another dateless night wouldn't be so bad. She had a great book sitting on her nightstand. "Call me when you're going out with an investment banker.''

"You're too picky,'' Kim said, a charge she made frequently.

"And you're not picky enough," Emma retorted, as she always did.

"But at least I play the game. You can't find gold if you're not willing to sift through all the other stuff. Trust me, the right man is not going to fall from the sky."

"Try telling that to my mother," Emma said, laughing.

The story of the night her father literally fell into her mother's arms on a dance floor was family legend. Don Killian and Rosa had been inseparable from that moment on. That was probably what had fueled Emma's romantic expectations. She wanted that same kind of bolt-from-the-blue feeling to strike her one day. It wasn't likely to happen with a guy who had one eye on the restaurant door to see if anyone important was coming in, and the other checking out his next day's schedule on his handheld computer screen.

"Kim, do you really like this guy you're going out with tonight?"

Her friend hesitated, then sighed. "He's handsome. He's smart. And he's very nice. What's not to like?"

"Handsome is superficial," Emma said, dismissing it. *All* of the men Kim dated were handsome. They were all intelligent, too. Some weren't so nice. She was relieved to hear that this one was. "Nice is fine. Nice can be terrific, in fact, but I worry that you'll decide that's the best you can do. You deserve spectacular. You deserve fireworks."

"I know," Kim said, her good cheer back as quickly as it had faded. "Which is why I keep looking. Stop worrying, Emma. I won't settle for anything less. If I were willing to settle, I'd have married Horace Dunwoodie the Fourth. He was handsome, nice and disgustingly rich.''

"But boring," Emma reminded her.

"My point exactly."

"Okay, then. Now I've got to get back to these boxes," Emma said. "Have fun tonight."

"If I didn't think I would, I wouldn't be going on a second date with the guy. I have less patience than I used to. Some men don't even make the cut after the first date."

"By the way, why haven't you told me his name?" Emma asked. "Come to think of it, I'm pretty sure the last time you told me the name of one of your dates was back in college. In fact, it was old Horace, who followed Dirk. There have been dozens and dozens of nameless men parading through your life since then."

Kim laughed. "Why make you remember somebody who's not likely to last, anyway? This way, if I ever do call a man by his name, you'll know we're at least to the fourth-date stage. If I introduce you, you'll know that picking a wedding date is imminent. If you recall, I had five dates with Horace." She uttered an exaggerated sigh. "I had high hopes for him for a time. It must have been the size of his bank account that blinded me to his obvious flaws."

"At least you have a sense of humor about it," Emma said. "If I had to endure as many bores as you do, I'd be totally depressed."

"There's no point in crying, not when all it does is leave your eyes red and puffy. By the way, did you really call because you're worried about your social life or is something else on your mind?"

"Just a little homesick," Emma admitted. "I

couldn't wait to get away from Winter Cove and Flamingo Diner and my family, but there are still times when I miss it all like crazy.''

"Then you should have called home, instead of calling me," Kim chided. "Do it now and tell your folks hi for me. Are they doing okay?"

"They sounded good when I spoke to them over the weekend. I need to get down to Florida, though. I really do miss them."

"Then go," Kim said, suddenly serious. "Take it from someone who's lost a parent, you don't get a second chance. I'll come with you. It's been a long time since you've taken me down there for a visit. There's not a restaurant here in town that can make *arroz con pollo* as good as your mom's."

"We'll do it," Emma promised. "The weather starts to break down there in October."

"October's good. We'll talk about the specifics when I see you Sunday morning. Bye, sweetie."

Emma hung up feeling better than she had before she'd called, even if she was facing another dateless night alone with a good book. There were worse fates. She could list at least a hundred of them while she was checking in the rest of the new inventory.

But before she could get back to work, the phone rang. Wiping the sweat from her brow, she picked it up and tried to inject a gracious note into her voice. "Good morning, Fashionable Memories."

"Sis, is that you?"

"Andy?" Her sixteen-year-old brother was a quiet, well-mannered kid who was not in the habit of making long-distance calls to chat with his big sister. "Is everything okay?"

"I guess."

"You don't sound very sure. What's happened?"

"Can you come home, Emma? Please."

If hearing her brother's voice had been a surprise, hearing him plead for her to come home sent a shudder of alarm through her. "Andy, what is it? Is Mom sick? Dad?"

"No."

"Then what? You don't call out of the blue and ask me to fly down to Florida unless there's a reason. Talk to me."

He sighed. "I guess it was a mistake to call. I'll see you."

"Wait!" Emma shouted, suddenly afraid he was about to hang up on her before she could get to the real explanation for his call. "Andy?"

"I'm here," he said.

"Come on, talk to me. You obviously didn't call just to chat. Something's going on. Spill it. If Mom and Dad are okay, is something up with Jeff?"

Her other brother was in college in a town not far from Winter Cove, but was home for the summer. It was a point of friction with her father that this year Jeff had refused to work at Flamingo Diner, the family business, choosing instead to work at a clothing shop at the mall. He'd had a dozen valid excuses for the decision, but the unspoken reason was his inability to get along with their father. He thought Don Killian was too controlling, the family business too confining. The truth was, Jeff hated Flamingo Diner even more passionately than Emma had.

"Jeff's okay, I guess. He's not around much."

"Are you disappointed about that? I know you like having your big brother around during the summer."

"He's not as much fun as he used to be," Andy

said. "Besides, he and Dad fight all the time, so it's better when he's gone."

Emma was running out of ideas to explain her brother's unexpected call. "Tell me about you," she said finally. "Are you having a good summer?"

"I guess," he said without enthusiasm.

"Got a girlfriend?"

"Not really."

She searched her memory for the name of the pretty girl Andy had had his eye on. "What about Lauren Patterson? I know you like her. Have you asked her out?"

"No."

His refusal to answer in anything more than monosyllables was getting to her. "Come on, sweetie," she pleaded. "Help me out here. I know you called for a reason. Tell me."

"I did tell you. I asked you to come home," he said.

He sounded angry, maybe even a little frantic. It was so unlike her easygoing brother, Emma was more alarmed than ever. "Okay, I hear you," she said carefully. "Why is it so important to you that I come home?"

He hesitated. "It's Dad," he said finally. "He's acting really weird."

If Andy was an even-tempered kid, it was a trait he'd inherited from their father. Don Killian never raised his voice. When he was angry or disappointed, he managed to convey it without shouting. Jeff had always been able to push him to his limits, but Andy and Emma rarely ruffled his feathers.

"Weird how?"

"He and Jeff are getting into it all the time, but

that's pretty much par for the course,'' Andy said.
"Now he's getting on my case all the time, too. It's
not like I do anything bad, but he jumps all over every
little mistake and he does it in front of the customers.
He's been snapping at Mom a lot, too.''

"Mom and Dad are arguing in Flamingo Diner?''
Emma asked, genuinely taken aback. They'd always
prided themselves on running a neighborhood restaurant where the customers were considered guests.
They'd done everything they could to ensure that the
regulars who'd been coming since they opened the
doors nearly thirty years ago felt welcome. Family
squabbles—what few there were—were to be kept at
home.

"A lot," Andy said. "And Dad looks kinda sad,
too. I'm scared they're gonna get a divorce or something.''

"Oh, sweetie, that's not going to happen," Emma
reassured him. "Mom and Dad are as solid as any
two people I've ever seen. They have a strong marriage. I talked to them both over the weekend and
they sounded great.''

"Sure," he scoffed. "You talked to 'em for how
long? Ten, maybe fifteen minutes? Anybody can put
on a good show for that long.''

Stung by the suggestion that she no longer knew
what was going on with her own family, Emma
thought about her last conversation with her parents.
It had been brief, but surely she would have sensed
any unusual tension. "Andy, I think you're reading
too much into a couple of little arguments.''

"It's more than a couple," he insisted. "I'm telling
you that something's not right. I even asked Mom

about it, but she brushed me off just like you're doing. She says everybody has bad days.''

"Well, then, there's your answer. If she's not worried, why should you be?''

"It's not one day," he said, his voice rising. "I knew you wouldn't believe me. Jeff didn't, either. He says Dad's always been short-tempered, but he hasn't been, not with me and never with Mom."

"I'll call Mom—how about that?''

"She won't tell you anything," Andy said. "You need to be here and see for yourself. They can't hide it if you're here for a whole week, or even for a weekend. Please, Emma."

"I was just talking to Kim about trying to get down in October," she said.

"That's too late," he said. "You need to come now."

Emma heard the urgency in his voice, but none of what he was saying made any sense. She'd picked up on none of the weird vibes he claimed had become commonplace.

"I'll get home as soon as I can," she promised finally.

"This week?''

"No, but soon."

Andy sighed heavily. "Yeah, whatever."

"I will get there, Andy. Meantime, try not to worry."

"I know. I'm just a kid. If the grown-ups are having problems, they can fix them." He sounded like he was reciting something he'd already been told, probably by Jeff.

"That's true, you know. Mom and Dad have been

married a long time. I'm sure they've had their share of ups and downs. They'll weather this one too.''

"Whatever," he said again.

"I love you," Emma said, her heart aching for him. It was obvious he'd blown a few incidents out of proportion. He wasn't used to being criticized by their father, so he'd taken whatever their father had said to him to heart. "Everything will be okay, Andy."

"You wouldn't say that if you'd been around here," he said, sounding defeated.

Before she could try one more time to cheer him up, she heard the phone click and realized Andy had hung up on her.

"He's exaggerating," she told herself as she placed the phone back in its cradle. "He has to be."

There was just one problem with that theory. Andy was the most conscientious, levelheaded kid she'd ever known. And he was scared. There had been no mistaking the fear in his voice.

Maybe she could get home sooner than October. She pulled out the calendar of auction dates and other appointments that were already scheduled for her and Marcel. July and August, the supposedly dead days of summer, were crammed with commitments. Early September was even worse. Maybe by the middle of September, she concluded, penciling in her trip on a weekend that looked clear at the moment.

But even as she went back to unpacking the new inventory, she couldn't shake the feeling that she ought to find some way to make that trip sooner.

2

There weren't a lot of big-time criminals in Winter Cove, and that was just the way Police Chief Matthew Atkins liked it. After working in the worst sections of Tampa for nearly ten years, he'd been more than ready to come home to Winter Cove, where arguing with citizens over parking ticket fines seemed to fill the bulk of his days.

Because most of the people in town had known him since he was in diapers, they seemed to think he owed them a favor. Hell, maybe he did. They'd all done their part to make sure he stayed out of any serious trouble, even after his no-account father had headed off to jail and his mother had all but disappeared into a bottle of booze.

No one in town had been kinder to him than the Killians. Rosa Killian had seen to it that he had something to eat and Don had given him not only work, but a strong sense of the man he could become despite his background. Together, the two of them had taught him that a marriage didn't have to be volatile and that there was no place for violence in love.

Flamingo Diner had become Matt's refuge, a place to go in the morning before school for a healthy meal and in the afternoon to avoid home and the steady parade of men who passed through his mother's life.

It had given him a surrogate family, not only the Killians, but all of the regulars who came there each and every day for food and gossip before work. He'd also met tourists from all over the world, which had broadened his view of life and reminded him that what he'd endured at home wasn't the way it had to be.

The diner had also been the place where he'd fallen in love. Emma Killian with her huge brown eyes and cloud of dark hair had been sweet and sassy, and completely oblivious to the fact that Matt was head-over-heels crazy about her. She'd treated him with the same easygoing affection she showed her brothers. Even now, thinking about the torment of it made him sigh.

Of course, it was just as well. It had been clear from the start that the one thing in life Don wouldn't give Matt was his approval for the often reckless, troubled young man to date Emma.

And, Matt was forced to admit, Don had been right. Not only was he four years older than Emma, but at that point he hadn't proved that any of her father's lessons had stuck. He'd had his father's quick temper and his mother's lack of self-esteem. It had been a dangerous combination. Back then, he'd needed to leave town and find his way in the world, to make something of himself before he could possibly have anything to offer a woman.

It had taken him a year of working odd jobs in Tampa before he'd been drawn into police work. During his training, he'd learned to defuse his own temper at the same time he'd learned how to defuse a tense domestic standoff.

Now he was back home with a respectable job, more than ready to settle down and raise a family, and Emma was still out of reach. And since it had been nearly ten years since he'd seen her, his feelings for her were more nostalgic than real. She was like an illusion, one he couldn't seem to shake. Every time some other woman caught his attention, every time he considered making a commitment, an image of Emma popped up and forced him to reconsider. It was not only pathetic, it was damned annoying.

As annoying as it was, though, it had been motivation enough to get him to say yes when he'd been approached about the police chief's job in Winter Cove a few months back. It hadn't hurt that the mayor had sent Don Killian to Tampa to do the asking.

Over the years Matt had come back to Winter Cove from time to time, so there had been little in Don's practiced pitch that surprised him. He'd seen for himself that the sleepy little Central Florida town was growing, that its downtown was turning trendy with sidewalk cafés and the sort of unique little boutiques that appealed to tourists. The trailer parks and orange groves on the outskirts of town were slowly dying out and being replaced with golf courses lined by expensive townhouses. There were Sunday concerts by the lake during the cooler spring months, a winter arts festival, and an old-fashioned strawberry festival that now drew thousands, but somehow managed to maintain its small-town appeal.

Don had mentioned all of that when he'd come to Tampa to see Matt. He'd handed over a fancy, four-color brochure touting Winter Cove's charms along with a packet of promotional material and statistical information put together by the mayor's staff.

"Pretty slick stuff," Matt had noted, watching closely for Don's reaction.

"Bunch of damned nonsense," Don had replied succinctly. "You'd think Habersham would know better. This isn't the kind of thing that'll get you to come back to Winter Cove."

Matt had grinned. "What do you think will get me back there?"

"A chance to prove that you've made something of yourself," Don told him without hesitation. "Not that you need to prove anything to anybody, but I've known you a long time, son. You've had a chip on your shoulder thanks to those folks of yours. This is your chance to get rid of it once and for all, especially now that your mother's moved on to Orlando."

That had been news to Matt. He'd made it a point not to stay in touch with her. "When did that happen?"

"A few months back." Don had regarded Matt intently, then added, "When your daddy got out of jail."

Matt had felt as if he'd been sucker punched. "She's back with that lying, scheming, abusive son of a bitch?"

"Hiding out from him, more than likely," Don replied. "He's come through town once or twice asking questions about her and about you, but he's been smart enough not to stick around. He knows people in Winter Cove haven't forgotten what he did to your mother and to you."

Clyde Atkins had been a mean drunk. He'd have gone on using Matt's mother for a punching bag, if Matt hadn't stepped in between them one night. Not yet thirteen and scrawny, Matt had been no match for his bigger, angrier father, but the resulting commotion had drawn the attention of neighbors and the police.

A whole slew of charges had been filed against Clyde, and this time they'd stuck. Matt had seen to it that his mother didn't withdraw them at the last second as she had in the past. And even if she had, his own bruises, carefully recorded by the police the night of the incident, would have been enough to convict the bastard.

Until that moment when he'd learned of his father's release from jail, Matt thought he'd put all of that behind him, but the swell of anger and bitterness in his chest had told him otherwise. His father had made his childhood a living hell, and his mother hadn't done much to help. He'd spent every day since trying to live down the reputation he'd inherited from the two of them.

He met Don's understanding gaze. "You think I should take the job, don't you?"

"I think you should give it some serious thought, for your own sake and for the town. Winter Cove can use a man with your experience, but more than that, it can use a man who knows what the town was, as well as what it can be. Personally, I don't want to see us drift too far from our roots. We're already dangerously close to doing that."

Matt had frowned at that. "I'd be coming to keep law and order, not to block change."

"Sometimes it's the same thing," Don told him.

"Haven't the changes been good for your business? Aren't you busier now than ever at the diner?"

"True enough, but I don't know everyone who walks through the door the way I used to," Don had lamented. "Especially not in mid-February when all the snowbirds are tying up traffic and taking up tables where my regulars like to sit. One of these days we're going to have a fistfight over that. I can see it coming. Habersham's likely to be in the thick of it, too. The mayor's got his favorite table in the corner where he can be seen by everyone. Three sweet little old ladies with blue hair and stretch pants were sitting there when he came in the other morning and he stood there glowering down at them. I thought he was going to have a stroke, especially when one of them responded to his intimidation tactics by beaming up at him and inviting him to join them.''

Matt chuckled. ''And you want me around to personally keep the peace in your restaurant?''

''I want you around because Rosa and the boys and I miss you,'' Don had said. ''We consider you part of the family and you haven't been home nearly enough.''

The fact that he hadn't mentioned Emma spoke volumes in Matt's opinion. Or maybe Don had just been wise enough to know that any reference to Emma would have been taking unfair advantage of old feelings.

Matt hadn't been able to resist the opening, though. ''You didn't mention Emma. How's she doing these days? Is she still in Washington?''

''Yes, more's the pity,'' Don said with a shake of his head. ''I don't understand what she sees in the place, much less in that man she's working for. He's got sneaky eyes, if you ask me. And you'll never convince me that Marcel D'Avignon is his real name. More likely, Marty Birdbrain, straight out of rural West Virginia. Maybe I should get you to check him out.''

Matt would have liked nothing better than to investigate any man in Emma's life, even if theirs was

only a working relationship, but something told him
Don was only half-serious. "Say the word and I
will," he'd told him.

"And have her come down here and tear a strip
out of both our hides? I don't think so," Don said
with obvious regret. "And if she didn't, Rosa surely
would. No, Emma's got a good head on her shoulders.
I just have to have faith that she can look out for
herself and not let the man take advantage of her."

"Does she get home much?"

"Not nearly often enough." Don had given him a
knowing look. "But maybe you could change that."

His words were tantamount to a blessing and gave
Matt the hope he'd never had before where Emma
was concerned. The slimmest possibility that Don
could be right had been an added incentive for him
to take the job once it was offered.

Maybe if the mayor had sent someone else, maybe
if Matt hadn't handled way too many domestic dis-
turbance calls on his last shift, he might have been
able to turn the offer down flat. As it was, he'd
jumped at the chance to explore going back to Winter
Cove in a respectable position. The salary and bene-
fits had hardly mattered. Don had pegged him exactly
right. Matt had wanted a chance to prove something
to the people of Winter Cove. And he'd clung to the
likelihood that sooner or later, he'd catch a glimpse
of Emma and see if he'd finally outgrown his infatuation.

His first few months on the job had gone smoothly
enough. Even without a visit from Emma, he had no
regrets about his decision to come home. Don had
been right about the number of strangers around, but
there were still a lot of familiar faces, and Matt had

made it his business to get to know the strangers, as well. Little went on around town that he didn't observe or hear about.

Like the scene he'd witnessed in Flamingo Diner that morning. It wasn't the first time Don had lost patience with Andy lately. Nor was it the first time he'd snapped at Rosa, but each troubling incident took Matt by surprise. Years ago Don would never have taken that tone with any of them. In fact, over the years, whenever Matt thought of the Killians, all he remembered was the laughter and Don Killian's gentle, persistent way of teaching all of them the right way to do things. The little displays of temper, mild in comparison to what Matt had lived through in his own home, were still worrisome because they were so totally out of character.

But as much as Matt loved the family, as much as he'd always been made to feel as if he were part of it, he wasn't sure if it was his place to step in and ask Don if anything was wrong. Maybe he didn't want to admit that his mentor might have flaws. Besides, people had their bad days. Even he could be short-tempered, snarling at anyone who crossed his path. But until the last few weeks, he'd never witnessed Don saying an unkind word to anyone, especially a member of his own family.

Matt wasn't the only one concerned, either. Since that morning, half a dozen people had stopped him on the street and asked if he knew what was on Don's mind. Having everyone know about every little mood swing was both the blessing and the curse of a place like Winter Cove. There was something comforting about knowing how many people cared, but it could be disconcerting, too. Matt was still getting used to all the teasing questions about his own social life, which was nonexistent at the moment since he'd recently broken off a brief flirtation with a local investment adviser because she'd been more serious than he was.

Fleetingly, he considered calling Emma and filling her in on this new tension at the diner, but he knew in his gut that his motives weren't entirely pure. Why stir her up over something that she wasn't here to fix? As genuine as his concern was, it was a pretty pathetic excuse to hear the sound of her voice and see if it still had the power to make his knees weak.

He uttered a rueful chuckle. Here it was after midnight, and unable to sleep, he was cruising along the lakefront dreaming up ways to make contact with a woman he hadn't seen in a decade. Even more absurd was the fact that he was still carrying a torch for a woman he'd never even kissed, a woman who'd been little more than a girl the last time he'd seen her.

He sighed. He really did need to get a social life. The next time Jessie Jameson offered to fix him up with her granddaughter, he just might take her up on it. Everyone knew that Jessie Three, as the younger woman was known around town, was always up for a good time. Maybe that was what Matt needed, a little uncomplicated sex and a few laughs.

In the meantime, he could definitely use a distraction. Catching a burglar in the act would be good. Even a traffic violation. But the streets of Winter Cove were quiet at this hour. Few people were stirring.

He was almost relieved when he finally spotted something out of the ordinary, a glint of something metallic at the edge of the lake, picked out by his headlights as he rounded a curve. It could be nothing more than a piece of debris that had washed ashore, but it also wouldn't be the first time that some crazy kid had taken the curve at excessive speed and wound up in the water.

Feeling a sudden sense of urgency he screeched to a stop, grabbed his flashlight and ran across the grassy slope toward the edge of the water. As he got closer, there was no mistaking the fact that what had caught his eye was the chrome of a bumper. The car itself was almost fully submerged. Unless the accident had happened minutes earlier, unless the driver had managed to break a window and swim free, there was little chance anyone had survived.

Matt radioed for help, then, still clutching the waterproof flashlight, he waded into the water, preparing himself for the sudden drop-off that would then level out at about six-feet deep. The lake wasn't as dangerously deep as many of the nearby canals, where cars could disappear completely, but it was deep enough to kill, especially if the driver didn't have the presence of mind or the tools to free himself.

Keeping one hand on the car as a guide, he sucked in a deep breath and went beneath the surface, praying as he'd never prayed before that he'd find a broken-out windshield and no one inside.

Shining his flashlight he caught a glimpse of the car's color, the same dark blue as Don Killian's five-year-old sedan. Matt's pulse kicked up a notch. He told himself it couldn't be Don's car. Don would never be out at this hour, not when he had to be up before dawn to do the baking at Flamingo Diner. Nor would Jeff or Andy have taken Don's car. They both had their own, bought and insured with their own money at their father's insistence. Matt had gone with Andy to look at pickups just a few weeks ago, right after he'd gotten his license.

Sucking in another deep breath, Matt dove back below the surface and made his way toward the front of the car. The beam of the flashlight cast an eerie glow through the water-filled interior. There didn't seem to be anyone in the back seat, or even on the driver's side, and for an instant a wave of relief washed through him. Maybe the car had been stolen and then ditched, he thought as he broke through the surface of the lake and gasped for air.

Even though his theory was a good one, Matt knew he couldn't take chances that the driver of that car was still trapped inside, especially if there was even the remotest chance it was Don Killian. Even as he heard the wail of sirens in the distance, he dove back beneath the surface and shone his light slowly from back seat to front. Logic told him that if the driver had been able to free himself, he would be in the back, seeking the last little pocket of air as the car filled with water. Unfortunately the damn lake water was murkier than it should have been and all he could make out were shadows and the faint shape of something large and solid on the passenger side of the front seat.

Matt was a strong swimmer but his lungs were near to bursting when he made the discovery. As desperately as he wanted to take a closer look, he forced himself to the surface again.

By then the shoreline was swarming with policemen and rescue workers, including a team of divers.

"There's someone in there," he said, coughing up water. "Front passenger side."

Not ten minutes later, the divers were back, hauling the victim out of the water, their expressions grim. At Matt's questioning look, they shook their heads.

"Too late," diver Dave Griffin told him. "We'll have to wait for the medical examiner's report, but I'd say he's been down there awhile." His expression turned sympathetic. "Sorry, boss. I know you two were close."

Matt felt his heart clench. "Then it's…?" He couldn't bring himself to complete the thought.

"Don Killian," Dave said. "Damnedest thing, too. He was all strapped in. It was like he never even tried to get out."

Matt's head shot up and he stared at the dive team leader. "He was strapped in?"

"Snug as could be," Dave confirmed.

"I could have sworn he was on the passenger side," Matt said.

"No. Driver's side. It just looked like he was on the other side because of the way his body was leaning toward the console."

Why the hell wouldn't Don have made some attempt to free himself? "Could Don have been dead when the car went into the water?" Matt asked, knowing that Dave wouldn't have the answer. It was something the ME would have to decide.

"No visible wounds," Dave told him. "He was strapped in too tight to have hit his head on the windshield. Can't rule out a heart attack or a stroke, though."

What the hell did he have on his hands? Matt wondered. An accident? That seemed like the obvious answer, but given Don's behavior lately and that secured seat belt, he couldn't rule out suicide.

Whichever the case was, he dreaded having to be the one to tell Rosa, Jeff and Andy that Don was gone.

One thing was for certain, until he had conclusive proof otherwise, he intended to give the family the small comfort of thinking that Don had died in a tragic accident.

3

Suicide was such an ugly word. Maybe that was the reason it was seldom spoken above a whisper, Emma thought as she arrived in Florida, still dazed by the call that had come in the predawn hours. The officer who'd called her in the middle of the night had been very careful to describe her father's death as an accident. Emma wished she believed him.

In fact, she desperately wanted to be convinced that her father *had* somehow missed a curve that he'd driven every day of his life for thirty years or more. Ever since she'd hung up, she'd prayed that the medical examiner would find evidence of some sudden condition that had sent him careening off the road or that the police would find dents in the car to indicate he'd swerved after being hit by another driver. At the very least, she wanted the ME to find absolutely nothing to disprove the idea that her father's death had been an accident.

But remembering Andy's call only two days earlier made her think otherwise. She didn't want to believe that the weird behavior her brother had described had anything at all to do with her father's death, but she couldn't dismiss the possibility, not as easily as she would have liked to.

So far, she hadn't mentioned anything to the police

about her concerns. She excused her silence by telling herself it wasn't as if she actually knew anything. Besides, it would be better if they formed an unbiased opinion based on the evidence.

If only she'd been able to talk to her mother, but Rosa had been too distraught to take her calls. It was hours later and Emma still hadn't spoken to her. Rosa had been sedated and Jeff and Andy were nowhere to be found when Emma had called to let her family know when she would be arriving. She'd been assured by Helen Lindsay, her mother's best friend, that someone would be at the Orlando airport to pick her up and drive her to Winter Cove, but she had no idea who it might be.

The flight had been endless, giving her far too much time to sort through the scant information she had, too much time to twist the facts inside out and come up with theories about how and why her father had died.

An accident, she repeated firmly. It had to be. She was still telling herself that when she walked into the luggage claim area. With her gaze intent on the luggage carousel, she almost missed the tall, lanky man in faded jeans and a snug-fitting, white T-shirt who pushed away from a railing, but something about the lazy, sexy way he moved caught her eye. In fact, on any other occasion, she would have given his muscular body an appreciative once-over, noting the details to share with Kim the next time they talked. Now they barely registered and she tried to make sense of the fact that he was moving directly toward her.

"Emma?"

She took off the sunglasses she'd been wearing to hide her red-rimmed eyes to get a better look. Finally recognition dawned and with it came a vague sense of relief at finding a familiar face amid the crowd of strangers. "Matt Atkins? What on earth are you doing here? I thought you were working in Tampa."

"I'm back in Winter Cove now, as the police chief, no less. I'm surprised your family hadn't told you."

"Who would have thought..." she began. A grin almost formed then faded as it dawned on her that he knew, had to know, about her father, that in fact that was what had brought him here. This wasn't an accidental meeting, after all. Tears, never far away over the last few hours, welled up again. "You're here because..." She couldn't finish the thought.

"I came to take you home," he confirmed quietly, clearly as uncomfortable with mentioning her father's death as she was.

Before she knew it, Emma was in his arms, gathered close against all that solid, reassuring strength. After feeling cold and empty since the call had come, it felt good to feel so much heat and energy, to feel alive.

"I'm sorry," he whispered as he held her tight. "You can't imagine how sorry."

Emma couldn't answer. The words wouldn't come. Instead, the tears just continued to fall, soaking his shirt, ruining what little was probably left of her makeup, and not doing a damn thing to wash away the hurt.

Matt didn't seem to mind. He let her cry herself out, until she finally gave him a watery half smile and apologized.

"Don't you dare apologize," he said, his own voice thick with emotion. "Your dad is...*was* like a father to me. I owed him more than you'll ever know. I'm sick about this."

Emma pulled a wad of tissues from her pocket and blotted ineffectively at her face. "What happened? Do you know? Has the medical examiner made any sort of ruling?" she asked. "Did Dad have a heart attack?"

Matt's mouth formed a grim line. "Let's get your bags and get out of here. We can talk on the drive home."

Emma wanted to argue, but what was the point? The answers wouldn't be one bit different ten minutes from now, an hour from now…a lifetime from now. And in the end, what difference would they make, really? Her father—the man who had made up stories to chase the monsters from a little girl's bedroom— would still be dead.

They were twenty minutes into the ride when she decided she was ready to know everything Matt knew. "Matt, tell me what happened."

"I wish I could. The ME doesn't have anything conclusive yet. Maybe by the end of the day, maybe not for a few days till all the toxicology reports come in."

"Toxicology reports?"

"To see if there were any drugs or even alcohol in his blood."

"Don't be absurd. Dad rarely drank and he certainly never took drugs."

"Not even medications?" Matt asked.

Emma realized she didn't know. He could have been on a dozen different prescriptions and no one would have thought to tell her. She sighed. "I don't know." She regarded him evenly. "What do you think happened? Did he miss the curve?"

"That's what I want to believe," he said tightly, but he wouldn't look at her.

She heard the same doubts in his voice that had echoed in her head for hours now. "Matt, there's something else, something you're not telling me, isn't there?"

"Not now, Em. Let's wait for the reports."

"I need to know, dammit!"

He gave her a look filled with sympathy. "I know you do. We all do, but what good is it to have speculation? You need facts, not theories."

She drew in a deep breath and asked the question that had plagued her all the way home. "Could he have driven into the lake on purpose?"

"Don't go there, Emma."

"Is it possible?" she asked again.

"Anything's possible, but he didn't leave a note, at least not that we've found so far. There wasn't one in the car, at the diner or at the house."

"Then you did search for one?" To her that was damning proof that Matt thought there was something odd about the way her father had died.

"Of course."

"So you believe suicide's a possibility, don't you?" she asked, pushing the point because she had to.

"It's one of them," he admitted with obvious reluctance. "Why would *you* think that, though?"

"Andy called me a couple of days ago. He was really worried about Dad. He said he'd been acting weird for a while. He wanted me to come home." She blinked back tears. "I told him no."

Matt reached for her hand. "And now you're blaming yourself," he concluded. "Don't. What good will that do? We don't know what happened last night, Emma. Until we do, cut yourself some slack."

"Have you talked to Mom yet?"

"Not really. She…" He sighed. "She was in no shape to be questioned last night."

"Andy or Jeff?"

"Andy's scared. He's not making much sense right now. He's blaming himself."

"And me," she said, half to herself. "He must be blaming me."

Matt shook his head. "Not aloud, anyway. He's too caught up in his own guilt. He thinks if he and your father hadn't fought at the diner yesterday, everything would have been okay. He's sure your father was still upset, too upset to be behind the wheel of the car."

"What do you think?"

"That's grief talking. I was there when they fought. It was nothing, just the usual father-teen spat, but Andy's not ready to hear that yet. As for Jeff, all I got from him was attitude."

Emma regarded him with surprise. The way she remembered it, her younger brother had idolized Matt. "Jeff was giving you attitude?"

"I asked him to stay with your mom while I came to get you. He told me I wasn't his boss, that somebody else could do it, that he had things to do."

"Jeff said that?" Emma was genuinely shocked. "What things does he have to do that could possibly be more important right now?"

"He's angry and confused. It wasn't personal," he said, making excuses for Jeff. "He's just taking it out on the only person available. He can't very well yell at your mom. He'll be okay." He glanced sideways at her. "You're going to have to step in and take charge, you know. Your mom's in denial. She kept telling me I was making it up, that I was lying to her just to hurt her for some reason. I think a part of her is absolutely convinced that your father will walk in the door any second now."

Emma regarded him ruefully. "I felt the same way when one of your officers called me. I kept telling him he had to be mistaken, that my father couldn't possibly be dead."

"I'm sorry I had a stranger call," he said. "I wanted to do it myself, but I had my hands full with your mother at that point and I thought you needed to know right away so you could make plans to get down here."

"It's okay. I doubt the news would have gone down any easier, if you'd been the one delivering it. If Jeff refused to stay with her, who's there now?"

"Helen hasn't left, though your mother won't see her. She won't see anyone. She's locked herself in her room."

Though it was out of character for her normally strong mother to hide out, Emma couldn't really blame her. If she'd been able to hide and pretend this hadn't happened, she would have. "I just don't understand how this could happen. I can't believe he's really gone. I'd just spoken to him over the weekend. He sounded great, as upbeat as ever. Andy said he was faking it."

"I have to admit, I agree with Andy. Your father has been a little short-tempered lately," Matt explained. "No, I take that back. He's been *very* short-tempered. People have been commenting on it. That scene with Andy yesterday morning wasn't the first. He's even been snapping at your mother over nothing."

Hearing Matt echo what Andy had tried so hard to tell her made it that much worse that she hadn't listened to her brother.

"That's so unlike him. He'd rather strip naked and run through Winter Cove at high noon than lose it in front of the customers," she said.

"I know. We all thought it was out of character," Matt said. "I kept thinking I ought to talk to him, but I wasn't sure it was my place. If..." His voice trailed off.

"Say it," Emma demanded. "If he killed himself, what?"

Matt frowned. "If that's what happened, then I'm as much to blame for letting this happen as anyone in the family. We all knew something wasn't right, but this was your dad. He always worked things out for the rest of us. I suppose none of us believed he wouldn't be able to work out whatever was going on with him."

Emma fell silent, thinking. What could have been weighing on her father's mind to change his personality so dramatically? There had been no hint of a problem in their conversations; or, as Andy had accused, had she simply been oblivious to it? Had she been so caught up in her own life that she'd ignored some sign? She'd certainly been eager to ignore the warning signals Andy had described. She couldn't help feeling that she'd let down not only Andy, but also her father.

She was still tormenting herself with what-ifs when Matt pulled the car to a stop in front of the Spanish-style stucco house with its red-tile roof where Emma had lived practically her whole life. Before she could get out, he tucked a hand under her chin and forced her to face him.

"This is not your fault," he said emphatically. "Or your mom's. Or your brothers'. There's still every chance in the world that this was a tragic accident. Remember that."

"I'll try."

Slowly, he released her. "Just in case, I'll be around to remind you," he promised.

Tears welled up in her eyes and she reached for his hand, clinging to it for one last reassuring second before she went inside to face the reality of her family's unthinkable tragedy.

Rosa refused to get out of bed, refused to eat. She feigned sleep every time anyone came into her bedroom. If she was asleep, no one could say anything about Don. No one could tell her he was dead. She could pretend that it was all a terrible nightmare and that when she woke up, he would be right there beside her. He would hold her, maybe make love to her, and their day would begin as every other day had begun, with a mad rush to get to Flamingo Diner before the first customers began arriving at 6:00 a.m.

But as the sun began to set and shadows filled the room, she could no longer deny the harsh reality that she'd awakened to just after one in the morning when Matt had come knocking on their door. She'd shouted at him to stop his lies, that Don was not dead, that he knew that curve in the road, that he would never drive so recklessly that he'd wind up in the lake, but Matt hadn't changed expressions even once. He'd just led her to a chair, then hunkered down beside her and held her hand, pleading with her to tell him who he could call, what he could do.

Rosa hadn't known how to answer. For nearly thirty years, whenever there had been any kind of trouble in her life, she had turned to her husband. Who else could she possibly call? Who else could offer consolation and support and love? She had the children, of course, but they were young. They would need *her* support, even Emma, who would be devastated that her beloved father was gone. She needed to be strong for all of them, but she wasn't strong, not without Don beside her.

Finally Matt had awakened the boys and told them the same awful lies about Don. He'd called Helen and asked her to come over. He'd made sure Emma was notified. He'd done all the things Rosa should have been doing, but had been too paralyzed to do. And she'd hated him, because he'd made it real.

That's why she'd retreated to her room, so she could pretend that it had been nothing more than an awful nightmare.

A light tap on the door startled her. She thought everyone had given up, had decided to let her grieve in private.

"Mama?"

It was Emma. Rosa sat up in bed, flipped on the light, drew in a deep breath, then called out for her daughter to come in.

As the doorknob turned, Rosa realized she wasn't ready for this, would probably never be ready for this. From the moment her children had been born, they had looked to her and to their father for answers. Now there were no answers, at least none that made any sense. She doubted there ever would be again.

While Emma was in with her mother, Matt watched Jeff warily. The kid was on edge. He hadn't said a word, but Matt knew Jeff was craving something that would take away his pain. Maybe he'd turn to alcohol, maybe drugs. Either way, Matt could have told him that the pain would still be there. He'd made his own share of mistakes along those lines. He knew the signs and he knew there were no easy answers.

"I'm going out," Jeff announced to no one in particular.

"Where?" Matt asked.

"None of your business."

"Your brother needs you."

"Andy's fine."

"Oh, really? He didn't seem that fine to me when he left the house."

Jeff's belligerent expression faltered. "He's not here?"

"No."

"He was right here. Why'd you let him leave?"

"Frankly, I thought you'd go after him. I thought maybe you'd see that he was hurting. We're talking about your kid brother, Jeff. He needs you."

"He's probably outside," Jeff said, half to himself, as he headed for the back door.

Matt considered leaving it to Jeff to look out for his brother, but he didn't entirely trust him not to run off. He followed Jeff outside. He had a pretty good idea where Andy had gone. Years ago Don had built his sons a tree house in a sprawling banyan tree in the backyard. Matt had spent many an hour up in the hideaway with the younger boys.

With its twisted trunk and gnarled branches, the tree had inspired Jeff and Andy to claim that the tree house was haunted. At night, the fantasy had been especially easy to believe. It had been years since Matt had climbed up into that old tree, but that was the first place a distraught Andy would think to go.

Sure enough, even from the ground, Matt could hear Andy's choking sobs. Jeff deliberately made as much noise as he could crashing through the higher branches until he emerged on the rotting platform that had once been the scene of their greatest childhood adventures.

From below, Matt could see that Andy deliberately looked away, as Jeff carefully picked his way over to sit beside him, legs dangling over the edge. Matt moved to a spot just out of sight, there if they needed him, but willing to let the brothers work through this painful time on their own.

Sitting on the back step, Matt barely resisted the urge to light up a cigarette as memories flooded through him. As kids, they'd thought they could see the world from up in that tree, but it had turned out that the world was a much bigger place than they'd ever imagined. It wasn't half as idyllic, either. The past twenty-four hours had proved that.

He listened for the sound of voices and was relieved when Jeff finally spoke.

"It sucks, doesn't it?" Jeff said.

"I don't get it," Andy said, his voice choked. "Dad never drove fast. He couldn't have missed that curve."

"Well, he did," Jeff said angrily.

"Do you think…? Was it because I messed up yesterday morning? I was trying to get up the nerve to ask Lauren Patterson on a date, and I wasn't paying attention to the customers the way I should have been. He got really mad at me. Maybe he was still mad. Maybe he shouldn't have been driving."

"People don't have accidents because their kid messed up," Jeff said, poking his brother lightly in the ribs with his elbow. "Otherwise, every mom and dad in the world would be dead before their kids get out of their teens."

Below, Matt bit back a grin. There was a world of wisdom in Jeff's words and more than a hint of cynicism.

"Then why did it happen?" Andy asked again. "I don't get it."

"Dammit, Andy, give it a rest. Dad's dead. That's all that matters," Jeff said bitterly.

Silence fell then and once again Matt felt an urge to light up the one cigarette he kept in his pocket as a safety net.

"Jeff?"

Andy's voice was soft and scared, the way he used to sound in the dark of night when he thought there were monsters hiding under the bed. Matt had spent enough nights at the house to recognize it.

"Yeah, kid?"

"What's going to happen to us?"

"We'll stick together," Jeff said finally. "You, me, Emma and Mom. We'll figure things out."

"Do you think Emma will stay?"

"Sure," Jeff said.

"I called her and told her things were all messed

up around here and she wouldn't come home," Andy said. "What makes you think she'll stay now?"

"She will, that's all. She'll have to."

Matt wondered if Jeff was right. Would Emma stay? He'd heard the guilt and self-recrimination in her voice earlier and guessed that she would hang around, if only because of that. But he hated that it had taken something like this to get her home.

"Well, I don't want her to," Andy said heatedly. "I don't want her here. She wouldn't come when I asked her to and it's too late now."

He scrambled down from the tree house and ran. Matt stepped in his path and caught him.

"Don't take this out on your sister," he told Andy quietly. "She's hurting, too. You all need to stick together now."

Andy uttered a curse Matt had never expected to hear cross the boy's lips.

He leveled a look straight into Andy's eyes. "What would your dad think if he'd heard that?"

"Well, he's not here, is he?" Andy retorted, then brushed past Matt and went inside.

Matt sighed. Whatever had happened at the lake the night before, this family's world was never going to be the same again.

4

Emma was stunned by her mother's appearance. No matter the time of day or the occasion, Rosa had always taken such pride in herself.

"No one wants to be greeted by someone looking haggard and disheveled when they come in the door for breakfast," she'd told Emma more than once, when Emma would have settled for a hastily combed ponytail, a pair of jeans and a wrinkled T-shirt to work at the diner. It didn't matter to her mother that grease and spills were likely to ruin clothes faster than playing outside in the dirt.

Rosa always wore bright colors, skillfully applied makeup and a ready smile, even at 6:00 a.m. And even after a tiring, ten-hour shift at Flamingo Diner, she usually looked as energetic and tidy as she had when she'd greeted the first customer in the morning. Somehow she never spilled anything on herself.

Tonight, though, her thick, dark hair was in disarray, her cheeks were pale and she was wearing the rattiest old robe in her closet, the one she usually wore when she scrubbed the floors. Emma was as shocked and dismayed by that as she was by the lost look in her mother's red-rimmed eyes.

"Oh, Mama, I can't believe it," Emma whispered, crossing the room to take her mother in her arms.

Rosa, whose figure she herself had always referred to as pleasingly plump, felt fragile to Emma, as if all the familiar strength had drained out of her overnight.

"Neither can I," her mother said, clasping her hand. "I'm so sorry, Emma. I should have been the one to call you, but I couldn't find the words. I didn't want to believe it had happened. I still don't."

"Neither do I, Mama."

Rosa's gaze drifted away, as if she were looking at something Emma couldn't see. "I keep waiting for him to come home," she murmured, half to herself. Her gaze once again sought Emma's. "He should be here by now. Don't you think so?"

Alarmed by her mother's refusal to accept reality, Emma squeezed her hands. "Mama, he's not coming back. You know that."

Her mother regarded her with a bewildered expression. "But that can't be. He had an appointment after we closed and he said he'd be home right afterward. I've been waiting and waiting."

"Daddy's gone," Emma said quietly but firmly. "He's dead."

The unexpected sharp slap of her mother's hand against her cheek shocked her.

"Don't say that," her mother said furiously. "He's not dead."

Emma was too shaken to respond. Her mother had never hit her before, had never really lost her temper. As kids, they'd always known when Rosa was angry. Patches of color would flare in her cheeks and her eyes would flash, but her words were always cool and reasoned. There had been times when Emma had wished that she would simply yell at them, because that icy disappointment in her tone had been devastating.

Touching her cheek gingerly, Emma stood up and moved away, wanting to cry, but terrified that once she started, she'd never be able to stop. Obviously her safe, secure world was never going to be the same again, not with her father dead and her mother so distraught that she would actually slap one of her own children.

"Emma, I'm sorry. I shouldn't have done that," Rosa said, sounding as shaken as Emma felt.

"It's okay, Mama. You're not yourself right now. None of us are."

"It is not okay. I just…" She shook her head, as if to clear it. "I can't think straight. I don't want to think at all. Could you get me another one of the pills the doctor left? They're in the bathroom."

Emma retrieved the bottle and read the label. She had no idea what sort of medicine it was. "What are these?" she asked as she brought them into the bedroom.

"Sleeping pills," her mother said. "They're good. They keep me from remembering."

"I thought you hated taking pills," Emma said, worried by the eagerness with which her mother was reaching for the plastic bottle.

Her mother frowned at her. "I've never been in this situation before. The doctor prescribed them. It won't hurt to take them for a few days, just to get through this." She swallowed two and drank some water.

"You mean the funeral?" Emma asked.

"All of it," her mother replied. "I want to sleep

through all of it. I don't want to wake up until the nightmare ends.''

Alarmed, Emma reached for the bottle, but her mother held fast. "You can't hide from this, Mama. None of us can. There are decisions to be made."

"Then you make them," her mother told her, sliding beneath the covers and turning her back. It was like watching a turtle slowly retreat into its protective shell.

"What about Jeff and Andy? They're going to need you. I need you."

"You're strong, Emma. You'll do just fine. Maybe Kim can fly down and help you."

"Kim has to work, Mama."

"Then you'll manage. I know you will."

This was the second time someone had told Emma she was going to have to handle things. She wasn't ready for that kind of responsibility. Panicked by the prospect, she said urgently, "No, Mama. You're the strong one. We're counting on you."

"Don't," her mother said flatly.

Emma stood where she was and stared at her mother's back, feeling more shut out and alone than she ever had in her life. Her mother was overcome with grief, totally in shock. That's what it was. It had to be. Rosa Killian wasn't the kind of woman to turn her back on her family, on her responsibilities. All her life she had taught her children to be caring and generous with their support for friends in need. This retreat from reality wasn't like her at all.

Was it possible that her mother had guessed it hadn't been an accident? Was that what she really couldn't face? Sooner or later, they would have to talk about it, all of it, but obviously not tonight.

Leaning down, she pressed a kiss to her mother's damp cheek. "I love you, Mama."

She waited for her mother to say, as she always did, "I love you back," but there was only silence.

Outside the door to her mother's room, Emma leaned against the wall and let the tears flow unchecked down her cheeks. She was beginning to fear that when her father's car had gone into the lake, she'd lost not only him, but both of her parents.

Matt couldn't make up his mind whether to go or stay. After Andy had charged past him, he'd considered leaving, but something told him that Emma was going to need him after she saw her mother. Rosa wasn't herself. Not that anyone could blame her, but she was deliberately shutting everyone out, her kids included. Jeff and Andy had never needed her more, but she hadn't reached out for them after Matt had delivered the news about Don. When Matt had refused to deny the news of Don's death, she'd simply gone into her room and closed the door behind her. He doubted it would be any different with Emma. His heart ached for her, for all of them.

He'd been ready for the tears when he'd met Emma at the airport, but not the underlying vulnerability. The Emma he remembered had been strong, resilient, like her mother. She'd had a biting wit and a confidence that came from knowing that she was well loved. He'd figured the years would only solidify those traits. But if confidence had failed Rosa at a time like this, it was only reasonable that it would have failed Emma, too.

After all, this was hardly a normal circumstance.

For all he knew, Emma could take on the world under most conditions.

He found the coffee in the kitchen cupboard and started to brew a pot, then decided tea would be better. Hadn't he heard somewhere that tea was supposed to be soothing? Or was that just herbal tea? God, why didn't he know these things? Why wasn't he better prepared to help this family he loved get through this crisis? In his years on the police force, he'd somehow mustered the courage to deliver bad news, but he'd rarely been left to deal with its aftermath. With friends involved, however, he couldn't walk away. He felt like he owed it to Don to stay and cope with the fallout from his passing.

He was still standing in the middle of the kitchen, boxes of tea spread out on the table, when Emma walked in. Her face was streaked with tears, her expression shattered. Matt would have reached for her as he had at the airport, but there was something about her rigid stance that told him she wouldn't welcome his embrace a second time. In fact, she looked as if she were holding herself together by a thread. He didn't want to do anything to shatter what was left of her composure.

"I was going to make…" He hesitated, then shrugged sheepishly and gestured at the boxes of tea and coffee he'd dragged from the cupboard. "Something."

Her lips curved into a fleeting smile. "Couldn't make up your mind?"

"It's a little late to be drinking coffee. I thought tea would be better, but I don't drink the stuff, so I wasn't sure what kind to make. So, can I get you a cup of something? You tell me."

"Chamomile tea would be wonderful," she said, slipping into a chair at the table.

Matt noted the exhaustion in her eyes. "Would you rather go to bed? You've had a tough day. You don't have to entertain me. I can take off."

"No, stay, please," she said urgently. "I don't want to be alone just yet. I won't be able to get to sleep."

"Okay, then," he said, pouring hot water over the tea bag, then setting the cup in front of her.

He pulled out a chair across from her. "How'd it go with your mother?"

"She's in bad shape. She doesn't want to deal with any of this. She says I should do whatever I want." She regarded him with despair. "How can I make the kinds of decisions that need to be made? I have no idea what sort of funeral to arrange. She's our mother. He was her husband. These are her choices to make. I don't know if they have burial plots, a particular funeral home they prefer. How could I know that? I thought it would be years and years before I needed to know details like that."

"She's still in shock," Matt said. "She'll be better in the morning. Then you can all make the decisions together. You need to include Jeff and Andy in this, too. They're feeling lost right now, too."

"I'm sure they are, but they have each other at least. I was the one who always relied on Mama. She was my role model." Emma looked at him, a mix of hope and doubt on her face. "Do you really think she'll be better in the morning?"

Matt wanted to believe it. He knew Emma needed to believe it, so he reminded her, "Your mother's a strong woman."

Emma shook her head. "I always thought so, but she's retreated to someplace I can't reach her." She touched her cheek. "She slapped me."

Matt stared, spotting the faint trace of pink in Emma's pale complexion. "Why on earth would she do that?" he asked, genuinely shocked.

"I told her that Dad was dead, that he wasn't coming back. I insisted that she face the truth and she slapped me."

He reached for her hand. "I'm sorry. I really am. You know she's distraught. She'll feel awful tomorrow."

"She apologized. As for tomorrow, I'm not sure she'll feel anything. She seems determined to sleep through everything." She regarded him with a look filled with hurt and confusion. "What do I do if she's not better? Do I make the decisions without her?"

"Nothing has to be decided right away," Matt reassured her. "If she's not up to it in the morning, you, Jeff and Andy can talk things over and decide what you want. I'll help in any way I can, too. I can talk to the funeral home, make the arrangements, whatever's necessary."

"It's not your responsibility," Emma said.

Matt met her gaze evenly, refusing to be shut out. "I loved him, too, you know."

Her expression instantly apologetic, she squeezed his hand. "I know you did." She sighed heavily, then glanced around. "Where are Andy and Jeff? Have you seen them?"

"Andy's in his room. Jeff's outside, unless he decided to take off after I came back in."

"He's in the old tree house, I imagine. They used to love that place. I was barred from ever going up there." She gave him a faint smile. "I used to sneak up when they weren't around. In fact, I had my first kiss up there."

"Oh, really?" Matt said, feeling an unmistakable trace of envy for the lucky boy. "Who was it?"

"Owen Davis," she announced, her voice a conspiratorial whisper.

"You're kidding me," he said, shocked. "You had a thing with Owen Davis? Did your father know about it?"

Emma chuckled at his reaction. "Of course not. He would have been appalled. Owen was not only two years older than me, he rode a motorcycle. He was every girl's fantasy of a very dangerous guy."

"More than me?" Matt inquired, wondering just where he'd shown up on her personal radar.

"You weren't dangerous," she said as if the idea were ludicrous.

"Your father thought I was."

"Don't be ridiculous. You were one of the family."

Matt wasn't sure whether to be pleased that he'd been so readily accepted in her view or insulted by her complete lack of appreciation for the qualities he'd shared with Owen Davis. If he'd had any idea she was drawn to dangerous boys, maybe he would have made his move back then despite Don's disapproval. He decided to leave that particular discussion for another day. It wasn't possible to change the past, anyway.

"So," he began, forcing a teasing challenge into his voice, "was Owen a good kisser?"

Her expression turned nostalgic. "At the time I thought he was a fantastic kisser," she admitted.

Matt barely contained a curse at the response. He was being ridiculous. Here he was jealous of a boy Emma had kissed more than a decade ago. Obviously it had never led to anything. He doubted they'd even been in touch in years.

"Have you seen him lately?" he asked anyway.

She stared at him blankly. "Why would I have seen him?"

"You said yourself he was a fantastic kisser."

"A short-lived opinion. I grew up and discovered that really good kissing involves more than some guy sticking his tongue down your throat," she said, chuckling. "Owen would not even make my list of top ten kissers today. Probably not even my top hundred."

Top *hundred?* What the hell had she been doing up in D.C.? More important, he wondered if he would make the cut. Under other circumstances, he would be tempted to find out. He would be tempted to sweep her into his arms and demonstrate the many nuances of a great kiss. He'd had a lot of years to practice just in case an occasion like this ever arose. He looked up and caught her staring at him curiously.

"What are you thinking?" she asked, her voice vaguely breathless, as if she had a very good idea where his thoughts had wandered.

"You don't want to know," he said grimly, deciding to make that coffee after all. If he was going to sit here discussing Emma's past escapades with the hundred greatest kissers in her life, he was going to need something a whole lot stronger than tea. Liquor was out of the question, given his exhaustion and the fact that he'd have to drive home soon.

"Matt?"

"What?"

"Did I say something to upset you?"

"Of course not. You can say anything you want to me."

"I always thought I could," she said, sounding suddenly uncertain.

"You still can," he insisted, even if listening killed him. He would go through the tortures of hell, if it would distract her for a while from the reality of her father's death.

"You're a good guy," she said.

She said it the way she might say it to an older brother. It grated on Matt's nerves. He'd worked damn hard to become a good guy, and now he didn't want to hear it. How ironic was that?

"That's me, all right." He poured himself a cup of strong coffee, then sat back down. "Tell me about your life in Washington. You work in an antiques store?"

"Fashionable Memories," she said at once, her eyes brightening. "It's a great place."

As she began to talk, the years fell away and Matt could remember sitting in the backyard by the pool, listening to her spin her dreams for the future. He was pretty sure that back then there had been more talk of Hollywood or piloting a jetliner than selling antiques.

"When did you develop this fondness for old things?" he asked. "I thought you wanted to be an actress or maybe a pilot."

She laughed. "How on earth did you remember that? I'd almost forgotten. I guess by my senior year in high school I'd figured out I wasn't cut out for the silver screen, since I never once got chosen for the school play. As for being a pilot, once I understood how much technology was involved, I realized I was more interested in seeing the world than in actually flying a plane.''

''It's still a big leap from either of those careers to selling antiques,'' Matt said.

''While I was in college, I used to wander around Georgetown when I had some free time. There was this great thrift shop next door to a coffee shop I liked. I started poking around in there, looking for things to decorate my dorm room. One day I found a piece of porcelain. Even under all the grime, something about it made me think it might be valuable. I paid a few bucks for it, cleaned it up, then took it up the street to Fashionable Memories. Marcel bought it from me for a hundred dollars, then sold it for twice that. He told me he'd buy any other treasures I stumbled across. Next thing I knew, I was haunting thrift stores and going to flea markets and garage sales all over town. He suggested I start taking some appraisal courses. When I graduated, he offered me a job.''

She grinned at him. ''Believe it or not, that's the short version.''

''And the long version?''

''You don't want to hear it. I go on and on about the thrill of the hunt, about trying to discover the history behind a particular piece, about feeling connected to the past. It's pretty boring stuff.''

Matt gazed into her shining eyes and felt that familiar spark of desire, that tug of longing to know everything that went on in her head. She had the kind of enthusiasm that was contagious. ''I can't imagine anything you have to say ever being boring,'' he said honestly.

"Then one of these days before I go back to Washington, I'll take you with me to explore a few thrift shops around this area. I guarantee I'll have you pleading for mercy by lunchtime," she promised, barely stifling a yawn.

Matt laughed. "I'll hold you to that." He stood up. "I really do need to get out of here and let you get some sleep." He searched her face. "Think you can now?"

She nodded slowly, looking vaguely surprised. "Actually, yes. Thank you."

"For what? Making you sleepy?"

She stood up and touched his cheek. "No, for distracting me for a little while."

"My pleasure. I'll be back in the morning. If you need anything in the meantime, my home number's on the back of this card." He handed it to her, noting the beginnings of a smile tugging on her lips. "What?"

"Matt Atkins, Chief of Police," she said with a shake of her head. "I guess we really are all grown-up now."

He shrugged. "So they say." For the last few hours, he'd felt like a teenager again, awkward and uncertain in the presence of a girl on which he'd had a secret crush forever.

When she reached up to give him a kiss on the cheek, he turned so that her lips brushed his. It was just a fleeting, unexpected caress, but it was enough to send fire shooting through his veins.

When he looked into Emma's eyes, he saw by her startled reaction that the kiss had done something to her, too. Then her gaze turned shuttered, as if she'd suddenly remembered that her father had just died, and Matt cursed himself for being a jerk. The woman was in mourning and he was sneaking kisses just to prove something to himself.

And what had he proved? That he could coax a reaction from her? That he still felt a powerful pull where Emma Killian was concerned? Or simply that he was about as sensitive as a sledgehammer?

He considered apologizing, then decided that would make way too much of what had been little more than a friendly peck on the lips.

"Get some sleep," he ordered brusquely instead.

"You, too. You must be exhausted."

He had been, but then he'd met Emma at the airport and he'd caught a second wind. "I'm used to long hours."

"But not to finding a friend drowned in the lake, I imagine," she said quietly, a quaver in her voice as if the haunting image had lodged in her head.

"No, not to that," he agreed. "Don't focus on that, Emma. It doesn't do any good."

"How can I not?" she asked wistfully. "I'm afraid when I close my eyes that's what I'll see. It's just been words up till now, but I'm afraid if I try to sleep, I'll see what you saw."

To be honest, Matt shared the same fear. The scene was indelibly inscribed in his head. Even without having been the one to pull Don from that car, he'd seen him in the murky water, still and lifeless. If it had been horrifying for him, how much worse would it be for Emma? Thank God he'd been the one to discover Don, and not someone in the family who would be haunted by the image forever.

"Come on, then," he said, making a decision.

Swearing to himself that this was not a totally self-serving act, he led the way into the living room and pulled Emma down on the sofa beside him.

"What are you doing?" she demanded, but she didn't resist. "Matt, you don't need to stay. You need to go home and get some sleep."

"I can pretty much sleep in any position, especially after being up more than twenty-four hours straight," he said, gently tugging her until her head was resting against his shoulder. "Now, go to sleep. I'll be right here, if you start to have nightmares."

"I can't let you do this," she protested sleepily, but her eyes were already drifting closed.

Eventually he felt her relax against him, heard her breathing ease. Then, and only then, did he turn off the light and let himself fall asleep.

5

"**W**ell, if this isn't just fucking terrific!"

Emma was awakened by the sound of Jeff's disgusted voice. "What's going on?" she mumbled sleepily. She squinted and caught a glimpse of her brother's outraged expression. "Jeff? Is everything okay?"

She felt something shift beneath her and realized that she was resting not against a pillow in her own bed, but against Matt's chest. At her sudden movement, he groaned and stirred.

"Dad's dead, and the two of you are making it in the living room," Jeff accused. "Yeah, looks to me like life's just peachy, at least for you."

"We are not making it," Emma said calmly, straightening her blouse as she stood up. Jeff was clearly looking for someone on whom to take out his anger. She refused to let him goad her into such a ridiculous fight.

"You could have fooled me," Jeff said. "Dad thought you were such a saint. I guess now that he's gone, the truth's out."

Emma fought against the tide of hurt that crashed over her at the reminder that her father was dead. Somehow during the night, wrapped in Matt's arms, that reality had slipped away. She opened her mouth, but nothing came out. It was Matt who filled the silence.

"Don't speak to your sister that way," he ordered curtly, scowling at Jeff. "You owe her an apology."

"For what? Telling her the truth?"

"Nothing happened here, Jeff," Matt said quietly, "and you know it. We're both fully clothed. And don't you think if we were making it, as you put it, we'd have gone someplace a little more private and comfortable? Your sister was upset. I stayed. End of story."

Emma saw the anger and confusion in Jeff's eyes and knew that what he was really upset about had nothing to do with finding her in Matt's arms on the living room sofa. He might be twenty, but he was still a scared kid who'd just lost his dad. She could certainly relate to that. Her father's death had shaken her world to its very foundation, and she was six years older and had been on her own for some time now.

Determined to fix things between them, she crossed the room and hugged Jeff tightly. At first he simply stood there, rigid and unresponsive.

"Have you shed even one tear?" she asked him, rubbing his back as she'd seen her mother do when Jeff was little and came home fighting tears after some schoolyard incident.

"I'm not crying over him!" he retorted furiously, every muscle still tense. "I'm not. He was on my case all the time. Why should I be sorry he's dead."

"Jeff, he was our dad. Sure you fought. All kids fight with their parents, but there's no denying that you've lost someone very important to you. It's natural to feel some anger, because this is the last thing any of us were expecting to happen, but you also have a right to be sad.''

His lip quivered then, but he fought it. When tears welled up in his eyes, he turned away. ''I am not crying,'' he said staunchly.

She bit back a grin at the brave words. ''Okay, then, how about going into the kitchen and starting breakfast while I take a shower?''

''Alone?'' he asked, the bitterness back in his voice as he scowled in Matt's direction.

''Yes, alone,'' she said, giving him a smack on his arm. ''Stop acting like such a jerk. You know perfectly well nothing's going on between Matt and me. Matt's been like a big brother to all of us. Now, go.''

She turned to find Matt staring after Jeff, his expression worried. Or was that some other emotion in his eyes? Sorrow, possibly?

''You're going to have to keep an eye on him,'' he warned, turning back to her at last, his expression composed. ''He's furious and he hasn't figured out what to do with all that rage yet.''

''I don't think any of us have,'' Emma responded, admitting for the first time aloud that she, too, was furious. This should never have happened, and if her father was gone because he'd chosen to die, it would be a thousand times worse.

''Yes, but you're not a twenty-year-old boy who's still finding himself. I've been there,'' Matt reminded her. ''I know what the choices are and exactly how easy it is to make the wrong one.''

''You never made any bad choices,'' Emma said.

Matt regarded her with a rueful grin. ''Oh, yes, I did, but your dad was around to steer me back onto the right path. Jeff won't have that kind of guidance.''

Emma deliberately met his gaze. "He'll have you, won't he?"

Matt looked momentarily taken aback that she was placing her faith in him, but then he nodded slowly. "I'll do what I can, but it won't be the same. And based on the way things have gone here this morning, I'm not sure he'll listen to me."

Emma sighed. "No, it won't be the same, but it will be more than good enough. Jeff idolized you once. When he calms down, he'll turn to you. I'm counting on that."

Their gazes remained locked for what seemed an eternity before Matt finally looked away. When he looked back, there was a once familiar spark of mischief in his eyes.

"You know, Jeff did have an interesting idea a minute ago," he said mildly.

"Oh?" she said, instantly suspicious.

"You know that shower you're about to take? We could cut expenses and save on water, if I were to join you."

Emma laughed at the outrageous suggestion, though the sound of her voice seemed a little unsteady, even to her. More than once since she'd returned there had been this little shock of awareness with Matt, something that proved he no longer fit neatly into that surrogate big brother slot she'd always kept him in.

"In your dreams, Atkins," she said tartly, trying to mentally push him back where he belonged.

He murmured something as she left the room, something that sounded a little like, "You've got that right."

* * *

Matt spent the day at the Killians' fielding calls from the medical examiner, who still had precious little information to offer about Don's death beyond ruling out a heart attack or stoke, from his colleagues and from concerned residents of Winter Cove who wanted to express their condolences to the Killians. None of the family, though, were up to taking the calls themselves. Matt made note of everyone who called, so Rosa and the family would know how many people in Winter Cove truly cared.

Emma was clearly overwhelmed. Andy had once again retreated to his tree house and Jeff had taken off for parts unknown right after breakfast, mumbling something about a girl named Marisol expecting him. As for Rosa, she had refused breakfast, then sent Emma away, insisting that she had no intention of taking part in the planning of her husband's funeral.

"Do whatever you want," she had told Emma.

That had been her final word. Nothing Emma or even Matt had said could persuade her to reconsider. Nor would she see any of the steady stream of visitors who appeared at the front door bearing casseroles, fruit baskets or homemade cakes and pies. The dining room table was beginning to sag under the weight of all that food and Emma was starting to sag under the weight of her burden.

"I don't know what to do," she said, regarding Matt helplessly. "Should I just go ahead and make the arrangements? Obviously they'd never made any plans for something like this."

"You tell me what day and time you want the service and I'll do that," Matt told her. "Why don't you call a couple of your mother's friends and ask them to come over here and talk to her? Maybe it would be easier for her to talk to one of them than it is for her to face you.''

"Why on earth would she feel that way?" Emma asked.

"Think about it," Matt said. "She must have the same questions that have occurred to you and me. If she suspects Don's death wasn't an accident, she must feel as if she let down not only Don, but all of you.''

Emma nodded at once. "I'll call Helen. Mama turned her away this morning, but I'll plead with Helen not to give up this time. Helen's been through this kind of thing herself." She sighed. "I take that back. Her husband died after a long illness. It's not the same thing at all, is it?''

"She was still left to cope with her grief," Matt said. "And make no mistake, your mother is grieving.''

"Matt, are we ever going to know what really happened at the lake?" Emma asked. "Or are we going to live with this uncertainty?''

"Will a ruling from the medical examiner that it was an accident satisfy you?''

Emma's expression went from thoughtful to sad. "That's what I want more than anything, but to be honest, it won't erase the doubts. I need to know what really happened. If there's any chance at all it was a suicide, I need to know why he did it.''

"Then you intend to pursue this?" he said wearily. "I figured as much.''

"Will you help?''

"I'll do what I can. But Emma, until we know something more, I don't think you should share your doubts with your family.''

She nodded. "I agree.''

He studied her intently. "You going to be okay here? If so, I'll run on over to the funeral home."

Emma looked torn. "I should go with you."

"Please, let me spare you this part. I'll go over everything with you afterward, and if something's not the way you want it, we'll change it."

"Thank you," she said finally, her relief obvious.

He tucked a finger under her chin. "You'll get through this. You all will," he said emphatically. "It'll just take a little time."

Emma gazed down the hallway toward her mother's closed door and sighed again. "I hope so. I really do."

Matt intended to do everything he could to see that she had all the support she needed to get through the tough days ahead.

Rosa would not go to the funeral of a man who'd betrayed her, betrayed all of them, by taking his own life.

There, she thought with a touch of defiance, she'd admitted it. She knew in her heart that Don's death hadn't been an accident. The police could say whatever they wanted, but he wasn't a careless driver. Besides, there had been too many signs that he was unhappy. She hadn't wanted to see them, but now they were impossible to ignore.

Not that she was about to say a word to a living soul. How could she? What he'd done was a sin. It was horrible enough that she believed it, without admitting it to the whole world and destroying his reputation.

Still, she couldn't bring herself to go to his funeral. She'd been telling Emma that from the moment the arrangements were made, but Emma hadn't listened. Now it was less than two hours until the service, and she still hadn't budged from her bed. She knew she was upsetting her daughter, but this was the way she felt.

Suddenly the door to her room burst open and Helen came striding in, trailed by Emma. They were both dressed in black. Emma's complexion was so pale, her eyes so haunted that for an instant Rosa felt guilty for causing her more anguish.

"Rosa Killian, I am ashamed of you," Helen said, scowling down at her. "I never thought of you as a coward."

Rosa didn't have the strength to counter the charge. Maybe that's exactly what she was, a coward. Maybe she didn't want to face all those stares, all that conjecture. Maybe she didn't want to face the fact that her husband was really dead. So what? She had a right to hide out if she wanted to. When it came to being a coward, her husband had just set her a fine example.

"No argument?" Helen demanded. She got a firm grip on the covers and ripped them out of Rosa's grasp. "Get up at once. This day is going to be difficult enough on your children without them having to go through it without their mother. Stop being so damned selfish!"

Rosa stared at her. Helen never cursed. That she had done it now spoke volumes about just how upset she was with her friend.

"I can't do it," Rosa said simply, huddling where she was, wishing she'd taken another of those sleeping pills.

"I didn't think I could do it when Harrison died,

either, but I managed. You were there. All my friends were there. And my children needed me. I concentrated on that and somehow I got through the day.''

''Maybe you're just braver than I am.''

''Don't be ridiculous. Emma, tell her how strong she is.''

''You are, Mama. You're the strongest woman I know,'' Emma said quietly.

''Perhaps I was, once,'' Rosa conceded. ''Not anymore.''

''Inner strength doesn't disappear,'' Helen chided. ''It just gets buried for a while. It's there when we need it.''

Rosa looked into her friend's eyes, then into her daughter's. They were both expecting more than she had to give. ''I honestly don't know if I can do this.''

''You can and you must,'' Helen insisted. ''You take a shower and fix your hair. I'll find you something to wear.'' She turned to give Emma a reassuring smile. ''It will be okay now. Just give us a half hour.''

''Are you sure you don't need me?'' Emma asked, her gaze on Rosa.

Rosa thought of the burden she'd left on her daughter's shoulders for days now and forced herself to shake her head. ''Helen's right. It'll be okay. Could you make me a cup of strong tea with some sugar?''

Looking relieved, Emma nodded and left the room.

''You should be proud of your daughter,'' Helen said. ''She's heartbroken, but she's doing what needs to be done. And Matt's been a godsend. He's been right by her side. Do you suppose that after all this time…?''

''I can't even think about that now,'' Rosa said, cutting her off.

"Maybe it would do you good to think about something besides yourself," Helen retorted.

Guilt rushed through Rosa. "I have been selfish. I know that. I just can't face this. I can't face any of it."

"You can," Helen repeated. "We'll be right beside you. All of your friends are just waiting for you to reach out to us. Jolie and Sylvia are heartsick that you haven't let them in. After today, we'll be right here as you start to pick up the pieces of your life. I can tell you from experience, you do it one day at a time. You'll have good days and bad ones, but you will go on. And eventually life returns to what passes for normal."

There was only one thing wrong with Helen's promise, Rosa thought as she went to get ready. Without her beloved Don, she had no life.

Matt remained by Emma's side throughout the funeral, but he kept his eye on Jeff. During the service Jeff stayed dutifully beside Andy, but the instant it was over, he began drifting away from the crowd. Matt made his way toward him and clamped a firm hand around the back of his neck.

"You about ready to head back to the house?" Matt asked, keeping his tone friendly enough.

Heat flooding into his cheeks, Jeff regarded him angrily. "What's it to you?"

"Your mom and Emma will be expecting you," Matt said. "Are you going to let them down?"

"The whole damn town's going to be hanging out at the house. Who needs it?" he retorted. "This whole funeral thing is a crock."

"It's a ritual," Matt corrected. "It's a way for people to say goodbye, a way they can offer comfort to those left behind. Doesn't it feel good to know how many people loved your dad?''

''They weren't here today because they loved him,'' Jeff said scathingly. ''They were here to gawk at us, to watch us bawling our eyes out.''

''You don't really believe that,'' Matt argued. ''People were here because they care about all of you. Your family's a real part of this community. Flamingo Diner isn't just another restaurant. It's a home away from home for a lot of people. Maybe you can't appreciate that now, but someday you will.''

''If you think this town is so great, why'd you leave?''

Matt smiled. ''For the same reason you did, I imagine. I needed to figure out who I was and how to make something of my life. Once I'd done that, I came back.''

''You came back because you've always had the hots for my sister,'' Jeff retorted.

''If that were the case, why wouldn't I have moved to Washington? That's where she lives these days,'' Matt reminded him mildly.

Jeff apparently had no answer for that. But it didn't stop him from saying, ''I know what I know. I've seen the way you look at her.''

''Your sister's a beautiful woman. Any man who doesn't take a second look has to be blind.''

Jeff shook his head in disgust. ''And Dad always thought you were a straight shooter. You can't even tell the truth about a little thing like this.''

''Maybe because any feelings I might have for any woman are private,'' Matt replied. ''That's a lesson you should learn, kid. Never kiss and tell. Now let's get on over to the house.''

''I have other plans with my friends.''

''They can wait,'' Matt said, his gaze unyielding.

Jeff tried to stare him down, but he was no match for a cop's steady gaze. ''Yeah, whatever,'' he said finally.

He started to walk away, but Matt clapped a hand on his shoulder.

''One more thing,'' he said. ''If these were your real friends, they would have been here today.''

''Like I told Andy, they didn't even know my dad.''

''But they know you, and they could have come out of respect,'' Matt said pointedly. ''That's what real friends do. Maybe you ought to think about that before you get too tight with these people.''

''Lay off, okay?'' he said, still defiant. ''I'm not a kid and you're not my boss.''

''Maybe not,'' Matt agreed, keeping his gaze perfectly level. He knew how disconcerting that could be when someone had something to hide. ''But you step out of line, and I can make you regret it. Your mom and your sister and brother don't need that kind of grief right now, know what I mean?''

''Whatever,'' Jeff said, but he looked just a little shaken.

''I'll see you at the house, right?'' Matt called after him, still not letting up.

''Yeah, yeah, yeah,'' Jeff said with a one-fingered salute.

Matt forced himself to ignore the gesture. ''It's a ten-minute drive,'' he told Jeff. ''I'll give you fifteen before I come looking for you.''

"I said I'd be there," Jeff said.

Matt nodded slowly. "I'm trusting you to keep you word."

"Yeah, whatever," Jeff said, but when he climbed into his car, he turned it toward home.

6

Rosa should have felt gratified. There had been so
many people at the funeral, so many sincere expressions of sympathy. Every word spoken to her had
been filled with very real dismay over her loss. Even
the mayor had come by the house to offer his condolences. Though Rosa listened skeptically, for once
his remarks seemed to be genuine, rather than cal-
culated for maximum political benefit.

"Don Killian was a tremendous asset to this community," Owen Habersham said, clasping Rosa's
hand in his. "Whenever I had a problem, I knew I
could come to him for clear thinking."

Rosa had always felt the same way about her husband, had thought he felt the same about her. So why
hadn't Don come to her with whatever devastating
problem had been on his mind at the end? She'd always believed there was nothing they couldn't discuss, nothing they couldn't work out.

The early years of their marriage had been filled
with trials—business struggles, a miscarriage, the loss
of his parents, then hers—but they had met each test
together. Even before they'd married, there had been
a few serious ups and downs. One rift had almost
broken them up permanently, but they'd mended it
and been stronger than ever.

She sighed at the irony in the mayor's comment. If her husband had been thinking clearly, would he have killed himself? She was ashamed of his actions, even more ashamed that she hated him for them. One act, one instance of craziness, had destroyed everything she'd felt for him, all the love in her heart. It had turned her into a liar and a hypocrite. She was keeping her suspicions—her certainty—that Don had purposely driven into that lake from the police and, more important, from her family. She simply couldn't bring herself to add to the devastation that Emma, Jeff and Andy were already feeling. And even now she felt a tremendous sense of loyalty to Don. She wanted to protect his reputation, which was more than he'd seen fit to do when he'd decided to drive into the lake.

Hearing so many people say such nice things should have been gratifying, but it wasn't. She felt like a fraud, as if she didn't deserve their sympathy because she was so horribly angry with the man they were bent on praising. Worse, she felt she didn't deserve any compassion because it was plain to her, at least, that she had let Don down in some real, meaningful way. Why else would her husband take his own life?

"Excuse me," she said to the mayor, when she could take it no longer. Hurrying from the room, ignoring those who spoke, she made her way to the comparative quiet of the kitchen.

Helen, who'd rarely let Rosa out of her sight, rushed after her. "How are you holding up?" she asked.

"Can you get these people out of here?" Rosa pleaded. "I'm not sure I can handle it if one more person tells me how wonderful Don was."

"He was wonderful," Helen replied, her tone chiding Rosa for thinking otherwise even under the current circumstances.

"I always thought so," Rosa said, feeling the rage once again begin to build in her chest. "But wonderful people do not suddenly decide to kill themselves one day. They do not abandon their families and leave them with a million questions."

Helen gasped. "Rosa, what on earth are you saying? Don's death was an accident. No one's said otherwise."

"I know better," Rosa said. "He drove into that lake on purpose. Nothing else makes sense."

"Stop that. Stop it right now!" Helen said. "You can't be saying such a thing. You can't even think it."

"I don't think it. I *know* it," Rosa insisted, then sighed. "But you're right, I can't say anything to another living soul." She gazed at her friend. "But I have to talk to someone, Helen, or I'll go crazy."

"Then you can talk to me," Helen said decisively. "If you need to work through this, then you can say whatever you want to me and it will go no further."

Rosa nodded. "You knew Don. How could he do such a thing?"

"If—and I'm not saying I believe it for a minute—if he committed suicide, then something terrible obviously drove him to it. Anyone can reach a breaking point."

"Of course they can," Rosa agreed. "But what was Don's breaking point? Can you tell me that? Was he having an affair? Did some other woman dump him or threaten to tell me what was going on? Was he sick? Was he trying to spare us months of suffering? Or was he just tired of everyday life with me and the children?''

"I don't know," Helen said, looking utterly helpless. "I wish I could give you answers, but I can't. I can't even accept the possibility that you might be right. You may have to resign yourself to not knowing."

"I can't live with that," Rosa said angrily. She searched her friend's face and voiced just one of her fears. "Helen, do you think he was involved with another woman? Someone at the diner, maybe?"

"Don't be ridiculous," Helen scolded. "Don would never have an affair right under your nose. He would never have an affair, period. He loved you. If there's one thing I do know, it's that."

"How do you know that?" Rosa scoffed. "I never thought he'd kill himself, either."

Helen obviously had no answer for that. She merely returned Rosa's gaze, her expression distraught.

"I know one thing," Rosa declared. "I am not setting foot in that diner ever again, not when there could be someone there who was sleeping with my husband."

"Rosa, you're talking crazy now," Helen said impatiently. "Listen to me. There was no other woman. I am as sure of that as I am that the sun will rise tomorrow morning. You love that diner. You're its heart and soul. People come there for a kind word from you. They can get a decent omelette or pancakes anyplace, but they can't see their friends or be welcomed like one of the family anyplace else in Winter Cove. Besides that, it's your livelihood. Who'll run it, if you don't?''

Rosa faltered at that. Don had always taken care of
the finances. She had no idea what sort of money they
had, but she doubted it was much, not with Jeff in
college and Emma out only a few years. Don had
believed in building up the equity they had in Flamingo Diner. Every spare penny had been put back
into the business. That equity ought to be worth something. And it was on a prime piece of real estate now
that downtown Winter Cove was turning trendy.

"I could sell it," she said slowly.

"You wouldn't," Helen replied with shock.

"Why wouldn't I?" Rosa challenged. "Emma and
Jeff aren't interested. That leaves Andy, but why
should I tie him down to a business he might not even
want? Why not sell it and invest the money?" She
was already warming to the idea. In fact, she could
move back to Miami to be closer to her sisters. No
one there would stare at her with pity the way so
many of her friends had today. Of course, she wasn't
as close to her sisters as she was to Helen, Sylvia and
Jolie, her three best friends.

"And do what?" Helen asked. "How would you
spend your days?"

Right now the only thing that appealed to Rosa was
sleeping through them. "I'd find plenty to do," she
said confidently. "Especially if I went back to Miami.
I could work in my uncle's restaurant. I could have
Sunday dinners with my family, go to Mass at the
church where I had my First Communion."

And best of all, there were few memories of Don
in Miami. They had met there, but the courtship had
been brief and tumultuous. Then, immediately after
the wedding, they'd moved to Winter Cove and

opened Flamingo Diner, using every penny of both their savings to invest in their future.

Helen was staring at her as if she didn't even know her. "Would you honestly rip Andy out of school here, just before his senior year? Would you be that selfish?"

Rosa felt Helen's jab hit its target. She couldn't do that to Andy. It would destroy his chances of getting into a good university with the football scholarship they were counting on. She sighed heavily, filled with regret.

"You're right," Rosa admitted reluctantly. "I'd have to wait." She met Helen's gaze and added defiantly, "But it's still something to consider."

"If I learned nothing else when Harrison died, I learned that it is not wise to make any sort of major decision when you're grieving," Helen told her. "Whatever you do, don't make any hasty decisions. Promise me."

Since Rosa didn't feel capable of deciding what clothes to put on, much less what to do about the future, she nodded. "I promise."

"That's good, then," Helen said, linking her arm through Rosa's. "Now let's get back out there. This will be over soon."

"Not nearly soon enough," Rosa said grimly.

Matt hovered in the background as the gathering at the Killians' finally began to wind down. People had been coming and going for a couple of hours now, sharing stories about Don, reminding Emma and her mother of how much Flamingo Diner meant to them. He could see from the weariness in Emma's eyes and the distance in Rosa's that the words weren't really registering. As for Jeff and Andy, they had disappeared back into the tree house. Matt had reassured himself on that point the second he'd realized they were gone. As long as Jeff focused on getting Andy through his grief, he couldn't be somewhere else getting into the sort of mischief that could ruin his life.

Matt glanced around at the few remaining guests, most of whom were longtime friends. He wondered if any of them had any inkling of what had gone wrong in Don's life. If they knew, would they eventually share what they knew with the family, stirring up the doubts about Don's death that were already plaguing Emma?

If it was a suicide, then finding a motive wasn't really his job, but Matt felt compelled to investigate, because Emma wouldn't be at peace until they had one. She was going to push this, no matter where it led.

He spotted Gabe Jenkins and Harley Watson huddled together in a corner and wondered if they knew anything about what had tormented Don in his last weeks. Gabe was a cranky old geezer on his good days, but he and Harley somehow managed to get along, and Don had always found a few minutes to sit with them once the breakfast rush had died down at the diner. Matt doubted they'd exchanged any deep, dark secrets, but after knowing each other for a lot of years, there was no telling what they talked about. Matt wandered over, hoping to pick up some tidbit of information on the sly, but they were on to him at once.

"Might's well come all the way over here, if you expect to hear what we're saying," Gabe told him irritably.

Matt grinned at having been caught. "I thought I'd wait to see if you were talking about anything interesting. I don't want to be bored to death listening to you two moan about your prostates."

Harley gave him a dark look. "We're talking about life and death, if you must know. Can't figure out how Don missed that curve. He drove along the lake twice a day at least, sometimes more. He knew the road. Was there any evidence that he was hit by another car?"

"None," Matt admitted.

"He was smart, too," Harley added. "I'd bet there was one of those gizmos in the car that can crack a windshield in an emergency. Why do you suppose he didn't use it?"

Nothing in the report Matt had gotten just that morning indicated that there was a tool to shatter glass inside the car, but he agreed with Harley that it was the kind of thing Don would have, given the number of canals around Central Florida. He needed to check on that.

He tuned back in to what Gabe was saying.

"I just don't get it. He had a great business, a terrific family—what more is there?"

"Nothing I can think of," Matt agreed.

"You think the mob was after him?" Gabe asked with more enthusiasm than usual. "Maybe they ran him off the road."

"Are you crazy?" Harley retorted. "What's the matter with you, old man? Have you been watching *The Sopranos* again?"

"Only sopranos I know sing in the choir at church," Gabe responded. "But everybody knows the mob likes to pokes its nose into all sorts of places asking for protection money. Maybe Don wouldn't pay up.''

''Protection from what?'' Harley demanded. ''What kind of crime do we have in Winter Cove? Matt here sees to it that we don't have a lot of criminals on the loose.''

''He does his part,'' Gabe agreed with a nod in Matt's direction. ''Doesn't mean he doesn't have a little help. You never know.''

''I know,'' Harley retorted, scowling fiercely.

''You don't know everything.''

Matt decided it was time to step in before the two men came to blows. ''I think we can safely assume that there was no mob involvement in this. I know a little bit about organized crime.''

Gabe nodded enthusiastically. ''It's rampant in the big cities, am I right?''

''I wouldn't say rampant,'' Matt countered. ''But it does exist. I just don't happen to think it's made its way to Winter Cove, certainly not to the point where our residents are likely to be the target of a hit that's made to look like an accident.''

''Maybe it wasn't an accident at all,'' Gabe suggested. ''Maybe he killed himself because they were after him.''

''Oh, give it a rest, you old coot,'' Harley said, regarding him with disgust.

''You got any better ideas about why a good driver like Don would wind up in the lake?'' Gabe asked, clearly annoyed that his theory hadn't been taken seriously. He turned to Matt. ''You think there's something funny about the way he died, too, don't you?''

Matt refused to answer. He didn't want to send

their already wild imaginations into a frenzy. Who knew where that could lead?

Gabe regarded him with disgust. "Okay, don't say it, Matthew. I can see the truth written all over your face. That's what brought you sneaking over here to listen in on our conversation. You don't think it was an accident any more than we do." Before Matt could respond, Gabe turned to Harley. "I suppose you've got a theory."

"A woman," Harley said without hesitation. "When a man goes off his rocker, there's always a woman involved, believe you me."

"And you would know, wouldn't you?" Gabe retorted. "What's it been? Three marriages? Four?"

Harley frowned. "Five, if you must know, so yes, I think I know a thing or two about what a woman can drive a man to do."

"Don had Rosa," Gabe reminded him. "You ever seen two people more in love?"

"They'd been together a lot of years," Harley persisted. "Sometimes a man gets to a certain age and decides to take a look around. Don was a friendly guy. A lot of women who came in the diner probably took a second look at him."

"Any one in particular?" Matt inquired casually, even though he couldn't imagine Don ever looking at anyone besides Rosa.

Harley looked pleased as punch that someone was taking him seriously. "Maureen Polk, maybe. She's been looking to get married again. She's even cast her eye in my direction."

Gabe rolled his eyes. "Just shows the sort of taste she has. Don would never give a woman like that the time of day."

"Anyone else?" Matt asked.

Harley's expression turned thoughtful. "You know he was huddled with that Sawyer girl an awful lot."

Gabe hooted. "Are you crazy? Jennifer Sawyer is young enough to be his daughter. She went to school with you, didn't she, Matt?"

Matt nodded slowly, unwilling to comment. His own relationship with Jennifer hadn't been common knowledge. He'd seen the financial consultant at Flamingo Diner just about every morning, but few people had suspected that they hadn't simply bumped into each other there by accident. When Jennifer had wanted their relationship to go public and Matt had broken it off, he'd managed to avoid her. In all that time, Matt couldn't recall Don paying any particular attention to Jennifer. Besides, Don wouldn't so much as innocently flirt right under Rosa's nose, much less start a torrid affair with a woman half his age. Matt wouldn't believe it of him, not without hard proof. And for a while there, Jennifer hadn't had time to be involved with another man. He could swear to that.

Harley's expression turned sour. "Don't either of you think that Don was above such a thing. There's not a man on the planet who can't be tied up in knots by a female, and that's the truth. You talk to her, Matt. I'm willing to bet that Sawyer woman knows something."

"Bet what?" Gabe demanded at once. "Put some money on the line and make it interesting."

"The only place I bet is the racetrack," Harley retorted piously. "And Gabe Jenkins, you should be ashamed of turning this into some sort of sleazy way to make a couple of bucks."

Gabe did have the grace to look abashed by the criticism. "Sorry," he mumbled.

Matt regarded them both sternly. "I hope neither of you let Rosa or Emma hear your wild ideas. This has been difficult enough for them. Right now Don's death is considered an accident, period. Are we clear on that?"

"Absolutely," Harley said at once, obviously horrified that Matt would think he might share his speculation with the family.

"She won't hear a word from me, either," Gabe assured him.

Satisfied, Matt left them and went in search of Emma. She'd left the room a half hour earlier and hadn't reappeared.

He found her out by the pool, sitting on the edge, her bare feet dangling in the water, her cheeks streaked with tears. The vulnerable expression in her eyes when she looked up tore at him.

"Mind if I join you?" he asked.

She shrugged.

Matt kicked off his shoes, ripped off his socks and rolled up his pants legs before dropping down beside her. The pool was bathwater warm. On any other occasion, he'd have been tempted to search for a spare bathing suit inside the house and jump right in.

"A swim would feel good about now," he said just to make conversation.

"Believe me, I thought about jumping in with my clothes on, but I figured everyone would panic and think I was trying to drown myself," Emma retorted with a wry glance in his direction.

"Emma, no one would make comparisons with

what happened to your father. As far as most of the people here are concerned, he died in an accident.''

She gave him a skeptical look. ''I saw you huddled with Gabe and Harley. They were good friends of Dad's. Do they think it was an accident?''

''Gabe and Harley are bored. They're always looking for excitement,'' he said carefully.

''In other words, they think there's something off with the way he died, too,'' she said. ''What do they know?''

''They don't know anything,'' Matt insisted. ''They're just speculating.''

She started to get to her feet. ''I need to talk to them.''

''Not now,'' he insisted, catching her hand and pulling her back down beside him. ''I know everything they know and it's nothing we can do anything about right this second. I'll follow up on it tomorrow. You need to get some rest.''

''As if I can,'' she said wearily. ''Do you think any of us will be able to look at anyone else ever again without wondering if there's some dark secret at work? If my dad could kill himself, is there anyone who's not susceptible to suicide as a way out?''

''You,'' Matt said with certainty. ''And I wish you would stop saying that your dad killed himself. We don't know that.''

''I do,'' Emma said. ''I don't want to believe it, but I can't ignore what my heart is telling me. As for me not being likely to kill myself, I don't see how you can say that. Everyone always said Dad and I were a lot alike.''

''And you were, but you have your mother's

strength. Problems don't daunt you. You pitch in and look for solutions.''

Emma seemed surprised by his analysis. ''What makes you say that?''

Matt grinned. ''Remember the time you broke your brother's bike? You'd borrowed it without permission, then ended up smashing it into a tree. I've never seen such a mess, but when I came along you weren't crying or wringing your hands. You looked me straight in the eye and asked me if I could sneak back to the house and get some tools and help you put it back together.''

She leaned into him for a second. ''You were definitely my hero that day.''

Matt gazed into her eyes and barely resisted the desire to sigh. If only he could have stayed her hero.

Then again, maybe he was getting a second chance now, though he wondered how she'd feel if she knew he'd carried on a brief, but torrid affair with the woman Gabe and Harley thought might also have been linked to her father.

''You're doing the same thing now,'' he told her, forcing himself to focus on the present, not the past. ''You're trying to fix this, doing what needs to be done, even though your heart is breaking.''

''I suppose,'' she said. ''But it's one thing to come home and organize a funeral, to get meals on the table, and try to lift everyone's spirits. It's quite another to know what to do next.''

''You'll figure it out. When the time comes, the answer will come to you.''

She regarded him skeptically. ''What if I don't like the answer?''

He knew what she was really worried about. She

was terrified that she was going to be needed here indefinitely, when her life—the life she loved—was elsewhere.

"Then you'll come up with a better one," he said confidently. "Or if there's only one solution, then you'll make peace with it."

"You make it sound so easy," she said, sounding wistful.

"Not easy," Matt corrected. "I know nothing about this is easy, but I have every confidence that you're up to the challenge." He glanced over and saw the sad, lost expression on her face, and decided that what Emma needed more than anything right now was to get her mind off the future. He elbowed her gently in the ribs to get her attention.

"Last one to the other end is a rotten egg," he taunted, already shoving off the edge of the pool.

She stared after him in shock. Then a grin slowly spread across her face and she, too, pushed off.

Emma was a strong swimmer, more than strong enough to be a match for his greater height and head start. They touched the far end of the pool at the same instant and came out of the water laughing.

"You're crazy," she said, but her eyes were sparkling for the first time since she'd returned home.

Matt figured that ruining his best suit pants in all that chlorine was a small price to pay to see Emma happy. It might be a very temporary fix, but at least it was a reminder to both of them that life went on, that laughter was still possible even in the face of tragedy.

Just then she reached up, her hand cool against his cheek. "Thank you," she said quietly.

"For?"

"This. Everything."

Matt turned his head and pressed a kiss to the palm of her hand. "Anytime, darlin'. Anytime."

Still soaking wet and dripping all over the tile floor in the kitchen, Emma ran smack into her mother, who regarded her with a horrified expression.

"What on earth were you thinking?" Rosa demanded. "We've just buried your father and you're jumping into the pool with your clothes on. What will people say?"

Before Emma could reply that she didn't give two figs what anyone thought, she sensed Matt stepping up behind her.

"It's my fault," he told her mother. "I fell in and Emma had to rescue me."

Rosa scowled at both of them as if they were fourteen again. "As if I'm likely to believe that. Emma, go change your clothes. Jack Lawrence wants to talk to us. Matthew, go up to my room and find something of Don's to put on before you go home."

"Yes, ma'am," Matt said meekly, then winked at Emma as he passed by.

Emma stood where she was, shivering in the air-conditioned room. "Why does Mr. Lawrence need to see us tonight?"

Rosa sighed. "It's about your father's will."

"Can't that wait?"

"He says not."

Emma touched her mother's pale face. "Are you up to this?"

"No, but it appears I have no choice. Now, hurry and change, please. Let's get this over with. Jeff and Andy are already waiting."

Emma changed clothes quickly and ran a comb through her damp hair. She said a quick goodbye to Matt in the hallway, then drew in a deep breath before joining her mother and brothers in the living room.

Jack Lawrence, her parents' lawyer, had a sheaf of papers in front of him and a somber expression on his face that made her catch her breath. He nodded when Emma walked in, then began to speak in what she assumed to be the tone he deliberately chose for sad occasions. No normal human being talked in such a low, falsely soothing monotone.

"As you know, I have been this family's attorney for many years now. As soon as I heard the terrible news about Don, I began gathering the information I knew you would need to move on with your lives. I have his will here, which is simple enough. If it's all right with all of you, I'll dispense with a formal reading and just explain it."

"Please," Rosa said, as if she would agree to anything that shortened the proceedings.

"Okay, then," the attorney said. "Everything is left in your name Rosa, with provisions that it be divided equally among Emma, Jeff and Andy after your death."

Emma glanced at her mother and noted that she'd clenched her hands so tightly that the knuckles were white.

"What exactly are our assets?" Rosa asked. "Don had insurance policies."

The attorney looked uncomfortable. "I've looked into those. Because his death hasn't…" He stopped, censored himself, and tried again. "Because Don's death hasn't officially been ruled an accident, they won't pay. Not yet, at any rate. Of course, once there's an official ruling, I'm sure that money will come to you."

Emma watched her mother's face as the attorney spoke. She showed no reaction to his pointed remark about the death not having been ruled an accident. Once again she wondered if her mother shared her suspicions about it being deliberate. Was that why she'd been so angry, why she'd refused to see her friends? Because she didn't want to voice her fear that her husband had committed suicide?

"I see," Rosa said, her voice weak and clearly strained. "What do we have?"

"There's your joint checking account. A small retirement account. This house and, of course, Flamingo Diner. Rosa, I'm sure you have a better sense of your cash flow than I do, but as long as the diner stays operating, I imagine you'll be just fine financially. The mortgage payment is a little higher than I anticipated, but you've been managing for months now, so there's no reason to assume you won't be able to continue to do so."

Her mother's complexion paled. "We can't possibly have a high mortgage payment on the diner. We took out that loan nearly thirty years ago. We should be within months, maybe a year, of paying it off."

The attorney looked taken aback by her claim. "Rosa, I'm afraid there's been some mistake. According to the records I have, the loan won't be paid off for another fourteen years. Don refinanced and took out a fifteen-year note on the diner just a year ago."

Emma reached for her mother's hand, found it to be cold as ice. "How can that be?" she asked.

"Surely my mother wouldn't be mistaken about something like that."

"All I know is what the bank reported to me," Jack said defensively. "The loan on the house should be paid off about the same time. It was refinanced last year as well."

"Oh, my God," Rosa whispered, looking shocked. "What did he do to us?"

Emma, Jeff and Andy watched helplessly as their mother ran from the room, listened as the door slammed shut behind her. Her sobs echoed through the stunned silence.

"I'm sorry," Jack said, looking at Emma. "I had no idea she didn't know." He gathered his papers together, then met Emma's gaze. "Let me know if there's anything I can do, anything at all."

Emma doubted she would be calling on him. For the moment, he'd done quite enough to further shatter their once secure world. As for her, any last hope she'd had of being able to go back to Washington in the near future was pretty much dashed to bits. Far worse, with the revelations about the financial mess her father had created and hidden from her mother, any slim shred of hope she'd clung to that her father's death had been an accident had been snapped in two.

7

Emma wished with everything in her that she could follow Jack Lawrence out into the night and never come back. She dreaded going back inside to face the million questions her brothers were bound to have. How could she calm their fears when she had so many of her own? As for her mother, she had no idea how to deal with her at all.

When she finally drew in a deep breath and went into the dining room, she walked into the middle of a heated argument between Andy and Jeff.

"Leave it to the old man to throw us a curve," Jeff said angrily. "Did you see mom's face? She didn't know about those mortgages. I'll bet dad was throwing all that money away on some woman."

"He was not!" Andy said, obviously near tears. "Don't you dare say that."

"Andy's right," Emma said quietly. "I won't let you talk about our father that way."

"Then you explain where all that money went," Jeff retorted.

"I don't know," Emma said. "But I do intend to find out."

Andy ignored her and turned to Jeff. "Are we broke?"

Fearful of what Jeff might say, she stepped in.

"No. As long as we have the diner, we'll never be broke."

"What are we going to do?" Andy asked, still looking to his brother. He swallowed hard, then squared his shoulders and said bravely, "I can drop out of football this fall and work another job. I can put off college for another year, too."

Emma wasn't surprised that Andy was immediately willing to make sacrifices. It was his nature, but she couldn't allow him to do it.

Before she could say a word, though, Jeff spoke up. "Don't be ridiculous," he said fiercely. "This is not your problem to solve."

"Then who will?" Andy asked.

"We'll all pitch in, I guess," Jeff said, sounding less certain.

"Even Emma?" Andy asked as if she weren't sitting right there. His skepticism was plain.

Emma sighed. Until now, things had been so hectic that she'd been able to avoid the fact that her brother was furious with her for not coming home sooner. Clearly, she had some fence-mending to do with Andy.

"Of course, I'll pitch in," Emma said emphatically.

"You planning on sending a check from D.C. every so often?" Jeff asked bitterly, then added mockingly, "Big deal."

So, it was two against one, she thought. Maybe she deserved their attitude. She returned Jeff's angry gaze with an unflinching look. "What would you like me to do?"

Jeff faltered at that. "Honestly, I don't give a rat's ass what you do," he retorted, heading for the door.

"Jeff!"

Emma's impatient, slightly frantic voice carried after him, but he ignored her. She turned to Andy.

"Why don't you go ahead and say it," she suggested quietly.

He squirmed uncomfortably. He was not the kind of kid who enjoyed confrontation.

"Well?"

"Say what?" he asked.

"I know you're angry with me. I know you think if I had come home sooner things might have turned out differently."

"That's right," he said, his voice climbing. "If you'd been here, Dad might not be dead. It's your fault, Emma." His voice caught on a sob. "I hate you! I hate you!"

She stopped him as he tried to run from the room and held him tightly. "I wish I'd been here," she told him, her own tears streaking down her cheeks. "I wish I'd listened to you." He had no idea how much she regretted the choice she'd made to wait to come home.

But unlike Andy, she wasn't convinced that there was anything she could have done to stop any of this.

Matt spent a restless night with images of Emma dancing in his head, her wet clothes plastered to her body, her eyes sparkling as she'd laughed for the first time since she'd returned home. He knew better than to turn that shared moment of laughter into anything more than it was, but his heart seemed oblivious to his head's very rational advice. Damn, but the woman got to him. It would kill him to see her walk away again, and that was exactly what she was going to do, no question about it. There was no point in him getting any wild ideas about the future.

Rather than going to Flamingo Diner, which was supposed to reopen this morning, he deliberately picked up two apple-filled doughnuts and a cup of coffee and headed straight for the station, telling himself that he was at least eating fruit for breakfast. He was at his desk a full hour earlier than usual.

Cramer Dillon, the overnight desk sergeant, regarded him with surprise and followed him into his office. It never occurred to Cramer to wait for an invitation.

"Thought Flamingo Diner was going to open today," the longtime sergeant said, eyeing the doughnuts with a mix of curiosity and longing.

"That's the plan," Matt agreed.

"Thought the Killian girl would still be here from D.C.," he added as if Emma's presence were of particular significance to his boss.

"She is," Matt replied.

"Thought you always had a thing for her," Cramer said.

Heaven save him from people with long memories and absolutely no sensitivity. Matt scowled at him. "Don't even go there."

Cramer hadn't reached the ripe old age of sixty-two and worked with several chiefs by being easily intimidated. He deliberately plucked up one of the doughnuts and took a bite, his expression thoughtful.

"A smart man would be there this morning," he told Matt. "It's bound to be a tough day."

"Don't you have paperwork you ought to be doing?" Matt asked, struggling to resist the advice because it would be too damn easy to follow it.

"Nope," Cramer said easily. "I'm all caught up. It was a quiet night. I've got nothing better to do than sit around here and be your conscience." He wiped his mouth on a napkin and reached for the second doughnut, his gaze on Matt direct and unrelenting.

The weight of all that expectation finally got to him. Matt sighed and stood up. "It's no wonder no woman ever stayed married to you. You are such a nag."

Cramer grinned. "Who needs marriage when I've got Gwendolyn to go home to at night, and I don't hear no complaints from her."

Matt laughed. "Gwendolyn's a basset hound, in case you haven't noticed, and she looks mighty sad to me."

"That's not my doing," Cramer retorted. "That's genetics. Now get on over there and do the right thing. I caught a glimpse of the Killian girl at her dad's funeral yesterday. She's turned into a real looker. A smart man wouldn't let her get away a second time."

"What makes you think you know the right thing to do, when it's clear that the rest of the world botches it up all the time?" Matt asked.

"I had a mama who taught me right from wrong," Cramer said. His expression suddenly sobered as he met Matt's gaze. "And you had Don and Rosa Killian to teach you the same thing. I imagine those lessons stuck well enough, even in your hard head."

"Low blow," Matt murmured, but he dutifully headed for the door. "If anyone calls, tell 'em—"

"I'll tell 'em what I always tell 'em this time of day, that you're in your other office scoping out what's going on around town.'' He winked at Matt. ''While you're over there, give Emma a kiss for me.''

''Any kissing that goes on, I'll take the credit for it, thanks all the same.''

Cramer laughed. ''Whatever works.''

''By the way, have you filed that report on Don's car?''

''Of course I have.''

''I imagine you read it, too, correct?''

''Does a hound dog hunt?''

''Was there a glass breaker in there?''

''Right in the console. One of them kind that shatters glass and has a blade on the other end for cutting through seat belts,'' Cramer said, then turned pale. ''Holy Mother of God, are you thinking what I'm thinking?''

Matt didn't respond. But he left for the diner with his heart a whole lot heavier than it had been earlier.

Emma must have fried ten pounds of bacon. For a woman who hadn't cooked anything beyond the bare essentials since the day she'd walked out of Flamingo Diner to go to college, finding herself in front of the once familiar gas stove trying to meet the demands of a breakfast crowd should have been frightening. Instead, she found herself relieved to not have to think. Keeping her eye on the steady stream of orders required all her concentration. She didn't have time to acknowledge Jeff's sullen attitude or Andy's fumbling attempts to keep the orders straight as he delivered them to the packed tables. At least he was acknowledging her presence this morning.

The attorney's words the night before had left the entire family shaken. Rosa hadn't left her room since.

Andy still looked as if he wanted to cry. Jeff was back from wherever he'd disappeared to the night before, but he hadn't exchanged two words with Emma. And Emma had had to face the fact that she couldn't go back to Washington while things were in such a state of uncertainty.

At the front door the night before Jack Lawrence had looked her in the eye. "You're going to have to open the diner again soon," he said. "Or it will be too late."

Still not fully comprehending just how dire things were, Emma had merely nodded. "We're already planning to open tomorrow."

"That's good then. If I were you, Emma, I'd hire a good financial planner who can look over all of this and get you back on track."

On track. His words echoed now. When—how— had they gotten off track? Her father had always been so savvy about finances, so conservative. Emma knew her mother's head had to be reeling with the same questions. She would never forget the dazed expression on her mother's face as the reality of their situation had sunk in. It was as if this final blow had been too much.

After the others had gone to bed—or out, in Jeff's case—Emma had wrestled with her options. She had only one, really. The work she loved was in Washington, but her family was here and they needed her. Holding back tears of anger and frustration, she had called and broken the news to Marcel that she wouldn't be back.

"Sweetheart, you can't do this," he'd protested with satisfying dismay. "It's not just that I need you.

You'll perish in that abysmal little town. You need to be doing the kind of work you love."

"And one of these days I will," she insisted. "It just can't be now."

"Please, don't close this door, Emma. Stay another week or two, till things are back on an even keel, then come back to Washington."

"I don't think things here can be fixed that fast," she'd told him honestly. If she and Matt and the ME all reached the same conclusion, that her father's death hadn't been an accident, she was determined to find out what had driven him to commit suicide.

"Take a month. I can manage for that long," Marcel assured her. "Then get back up here where you belong. Your job will be waiting. The customers ask about you every day. You've gotten to know them. They trust you. Even that sourpuss designer Noreen Winchell told me what an asset you are to the store and how much she relies on you to help her find the perfect objet d'art for her clients."

As pleased as she was by his coaxing words, as badly as she wanted to say yes, Emma knew that two weeks or even a month wouldn't be nearly long enough to make things right for her family. The handwriting had been on the wall after the meeting with the attorney.

"Thanks, Marcel. I appreciate the offer, I really do, but I think you should be looking for someone to replace me." She'd put the phone down before Marcel could argue, before she could be tempted to accept his very persuasive offer.

Five minutes after she'd hung up on Marcel, Kim had called. She'd checked in several times since

Emma had gotten to Florida, but this call was no coincidence. Emma knew it.

"Marcel just called me. Don't do this," Kim pleaded. "I know you feel responsible for making things right, but nothing will be right, if you're miserable. Don't be a martyr. Your mom, Andy and Jeff can manage."

"They can't," Emma said. "Mama's fallen apart. Jeff's on the verge of doing something crazy. Andy's barely speaking to me. I have to fix this."

"Some things people have to fix for themselves," Kim replied. "Sweetie, this is not what your father would have wanted."

"I never thought I'd say this, but I don't think any of us know anymore what my father wanted," Emma admitted, venting her frustration to the friend who'd known her for so many years. "We're facing a whole slew of unanswered questions."

"Maybe you just have to let them go," Kim responded quietly. "Maybe the only thing to do is to move forward."

"How can I do that? Did I mention that Andy's thinking of dropping football, which would mean no college? I can't get through to Jeff. And Mama won't leave her room. Somebody has to take charge."

"If you left, they'd have to pull it together," Kim pointed out. "If you stay, they can just leave it all to you. Do you really want to be a martyr? Do you want to wake up ten years from now, or even a year from now and realize you sacrificed some of the best years of your life for people who probably won't even appreciate it?"

"That's not fair," Emma said, hurt by the suggestion that she was playing martyr, rather than doing the right thing.

"None of this is fair," Kim agreed.

A part of Emma knew that Kim was right, but the part of her that was terrified more tragedy would strike if she didn't step in won out. "No matter what you think, I have to do this," she told her friend. "Believe me, I wish it didn't have to be this way, but I've thought it over. It's the only choice. I'll be back in Washington as soon as things here are in order. If Marcel doesn't have a job for me then, I'll find something else. I'm not giving up on my dream, just postponing it."

Kim sighed. "I know that tone," she said, sounding resigned. "You're not going to change your mind. I guess I'll just have to start flying down there every few weeks so we can have our Sunday breakfast chats."

Emma's chuckle was only slightly forced. "Only if you can pitch in and cook while we're talking."

"God forbid!" Kim replied. "You'd never recover from the lawsuits."

Overnight, Emma made peace with her decision. Everything she'd said to Kim and Marcel had been true. This morning before leaving to open the diner, Emma had stopped in her mother's room and told Rosa she intended to stay, at least until the business was on solid ground again. Because she hated the decision she was being forced to make, because she knew she couldn't defend it for long, she had cut off her mother's halfhearted protests. Staying was the only choice. For now.

That was what she kept clinging to, the fact that this was only a temporary solution. Kim was wrong about one thing. She wouldn't let this drag on forever. Her life was on hold for a few months, a year max. Wasn't that a small sacrifice to assure that her family regained its footing after this tragedy?

Besides, she was worried sick about her mother. Even this morning, Rosa had spoken mostly in mono-syllables, a sharp contrast to the woman who'd always chattered about anything and everything. And not once in the seven days since Emma's dad's death had Rosa even mentioned Don, at least not in Emma's presence. If Emma or her brothers mentioned him, Rosa immediately left the room, her expression shuttered. The reaction had only gotten worse since their meeting with the lawyer.

"Emma, dear," Jolie Vincent said, catching her attention. "How is your mother?" She shook her head. "What a silly question. How could she be anything other than devastated? This has been a terrible shock to all of us. I wish she'd let us help."

Not trusting herself to speak, Emma nodded. She knew the woman was trying to be kind, but it was still too soon. She was afraid of kindness, afraid she would burst into tears and never stop. More than that, she was angry, furious with her father for leaving them with so many unanswered questions, furious with him for leaving them at all. What had he been thinking? What kind of pain or pressure had driven him to take such a drastic step? She couldn't stop thinking about it, couldn't stop herself from laying out all sorts of scenarios that might drive a strong, decent man to suicide.

Despite Emma's silence, Mrs. Vincent didn't take the hint. Her expression sympathetic, she said, "You don't have to say a thing. It's too soon. But I hope you know that everyone who comes in here loved your father like family. We love all of you. If you need anything, all you have to do is ask. We all feel that way. And I have no intention of giving up on your mother, either. Sooner or later, she'll be ready to accept our support.''

Emma blinked back the tears that threatened. ''Thank you,'' she managed to reply, her voice thick, her hand suddenly unsteady.

Before she realized what was happening, the spatula was taken from her, the bacon flipped onto a waiting plate. She looked up into Matt's concerned face.

''Take a break,'' he ordered.

''I can't,'' she protested, gesturing toward the order tickets that lined the overhead spinner.

''Of course you can. I'll hold down the fort. I've probably scrambled more eggs in here than you have.''

A flash of memory made her smile. There had been a weeklong period years ago when her father had been trying to teach Matt to cook. Everyone's eggs had been scrambled. He couldn't flip a fried egg without breaking it to save his soul.

''Yes, I remember,'' she said. ''But can you fry one?''

He grinned. ''I guess we'll find out. Now go for a walk, get some air.''

''Don't you think people will wonder why the chief of police is moonlighting as a short-order cook?''

''Maybe they'll conclude they don't pay me enough and give me a raise.''

''I should have known you had an ulterior motive,'' she teased, surprised that she could still find something to laugh about. It didn't surprise her that

Matt had been the one to remind her. He'd always had a wicked sense of humor.

He'd also had a penchant for getting into trouble, at least until her father had stepped in. She wondered just how much of the devil-may-care kid was left in the respectable chief of police. Last night's unexpected dip in the pool suggested he still had a sense of mischief. Maybe one of these days when she had five spare minutes to consider anything except the family's dire straits she'd check out how deep that mischievous streak ran. Maybe she'd try to figure out what the changes between them really meant, whether this simmering attraction held any real possibilities.

Relieved to have a break, however brief, she went outside and sat on the bench that had been installed for customers who were waiting for a table inside. She'd been there only a few minutes when Jeff came out to sit beside her. Emma studied her brother intently. At twenty he looked a lot like their father with thick brown hair, brown eyes and a killer smile. He also looked as if he'd like to start breaking things. The tension emanating from him was palpable.

Emma reached for his hand, but he jerked away.

"I hate this place," he muttered, his tone fierce. "And it's worse than ever now. I'll never get away from it."

"Of course, you will," she told him. "You'll go back to college in another month."

"How? There's no money. Dad blew any chance of me graduating when he drove into the lake. For all I know he did it on purpose."

Even though she'd suspected as much herself, Emma didn't like hearing it from her brother. "Jeffrey David Killian, don't you dare talk like that. We don't know what happened.''

"We know he's dead, don't we?" he said defiantly. "I hate him for dying. Look at you. You're trapped here, too. We can't go off and leave Mom and Andy. Mom's a basket case. And Andy's going to stress out completely from trying to step in and fill Dad's shoes. You heard him yourself. He's already talking about not playing football this fall, so he can help out more. A football scholarship was going to be his ticket to college.''

"I won't let him quit the team," Emma reassured Jeff. "It will all work out. I promise." But even as she uttered the words, she wondered if it was a promise she could keep.

"How?" Jeff asked, his tone filled with disdain. "You counting on winning the lottery? That's what it's going to take to get us out of this mess. After I got home last night, I went over the books myself. I thought the attorney had to be lying. Dad was always good with money. Sometimes he was so tight with a dollar, he could make it squeal.''

Emma almost smiled at that, but the rest of Jeff's words wiped out her amusement. "I looked all over for those books myself," she said. "Where did you find them?"

"Dad had everything locked away in his desk, but I broke the lock." His tone was defiant as if he expected her to criticize him. When she didn't, he went on. "I don't know what the hell was going on with him, but he was bleeding this place of every penny. If anything, it's worse than what the attorney said.''

Emma stared at him in shock. "You have to be

wrong. Dad wouldn't do that, not to Mom and the rest of us.''

"Stop defending him. I may not have my business degree yet, but even I can read the numbers, and they don't lie. We'd be better off selling what little bit's left. This location's worth a lot, probably enough to pay off the mortgage and leave some left over. Mom and Andy could sell the house and move into a smaller place. If you and I worked, we could help them out.''

"No," Emma said flatly.

"No what? You won't help out?"

"No to all of it." She tried to imagine her mother's life without Flamingo Diner. She couldn't. Despite Rosa's refusal to set foot in the place this morning, the restaurant and its customers were as essential to Rosa as breathing.

And it worked both ways. For a lot of their customers, the diner was where they came to socialize with their neighbors, to catch up on local gossip, to share family news with people who cared. And though everyone had been subdued this morning, most avoiding the topic of her father's passing, usually not a birth or a death in the tight-knit community went unremarked. Celebrations were to be shared. There had been more impromptu birthday parties and baby showers than Emma could count. Tragedies brought quick and heartfelt sympathy.

"We can't sell," Emma said emphatically. "It's going to be difficult enough for Mama to go on without Dad. She's going to need the diner."

"If it's so important to her, then why isn't she here this morning?" Jeff asked. "She knows what's at stake."

"Because it's too soon. Sweetie, we lost our dad, and that's a terrible thing, but you and I have been away for a while now. We've made lives for ourselves separate from theirs. It's going to be harder for Mom and Andy. They saw Dad every single day. They counted on him."

"And he let them down. He let all of us down," Jeff said, his bitterness back. He stood up suddenly. "I've got to get away from here."

Emma felt a sudden tingle of alarm at the urgency in his voice. She wanted to hang on to him, but settled for asking him where he was going.

"Anywhere. Just away from here."

He was gone before she could think of anything to stop him. Filled with worry, she stared after him. Jeff had always been a good kid, but she couldn't help thinking about Matt's warning that there was no telling what he might do in his current mood. Emma sighed. Her family was coming unraveled and she had absolutely no idea what to do about it. Her mere presence wasn't going to be enough. She needed expertise that she didn't have.

For a fleeting moment, she thought of seeing a grief counselor, but that wasn't her way. Matt had been right about her tendency to look for solutions—solid, practical solutions—not the touchy-feely comfort a counselor would offer.

Jack Lawrence had suggested a financial planner, but Emma didn't want to expose their financial circumstances to an outsider, not even to one in Orlando or Tampa, who'd never heard of the Killians. Maybe she could get Jeff to sit down with her and explain what he'd discovered in the financial records. Maybe that would also help him to focus his energies on something positive.

First, though, she had to keep him from running off every time things got uncomfortable. Not that she could blame him, she thought with a sigh. Truthfully, there had been a lot of moments in the last week when running away had struck her as a damn fine idea.

But if that wasn't an option, she concluded with a sigh, then she would concentrate on getting to the bottom of this whole, entire mess. She would poke and prod until she knew exactly what was going on in her father's life, if not in his mind, on that night that his car had ended up in the lake.

8

The delegation of women marched into Rosa's room on an obvious mission. These were her friends, people she had known for years, people with whom she had shared some of the most intimate secrets of her life. Today she rolled over and turned her back on them.

"Go away," she said, her voice muffled as she buried her face in her pillow. "I don't want to see anyone."

"Rosa, you have to get up and out of that bed," Helen insisted. "What you're doing is not healthy."

"When did you get your degree in psychiatry?" Rosa grumbled.

"It doesn't take a degree in psychiatry to know that you're hurting and that you're trying to hide from your friends. We want to help you," Jolie added, backing Helen up as she always did. For all of her flamboyance when it came to her attire, she was a traditional woman who tended to follow everyone else's lead.

"No one can help me," Rosa said bleakly.

"Not if you won't help yourself," Helen agreed, her tone brisk. "Tell me one thing, do you feel one bit better with your head buried in that pillow?"

"How would she know?" Jolie asked. "She hasn't

taken her head out of it long enough to know the difference.''

"Maybe we should just leave her be," Sylvia countered sympathetically. Sylvia was the sort of good-hearted, generous woman who could smother a person with kindness without meaning to. She was always trying to make things right, trying to smooth over the ruffled feathers among them. "It's only been two weeks since Don died. Everyone has to adjust to a loss like that at their own pace."

Rosa felt the salty sting of tears and fought it. She would not cry over a man who'd deliberately abandoned her. He didn't deserve her tears. If Don had died a sudden death, like from a heart attack, she didn't think she'd feel like this, as if she were drowning in a sea of unanswered questions, as if she couldn't show her face, not even to her best friends. If there had been anything ordinary about his passing, she could have accepted the outpouring of sympathy, shed her tears and moved on, knowing that what had happened was God's will.

But *this,* this hadn't had anything to do with God. It had been a sin, a sin committed by a man who'd always been devout, a man who had to have understood that the choice he was making was unacceptable in God's eyes.

"Please, Rosa, talk to us," Helen pleaded. "We love you. We can help, if you'll just let us in."

"No one can help," she said flatly. How could anyone relieve her of this twisted mess of anger, guilt and despair? Add to that the effort it was taking to protect her children from her suspicions. The strain of it was beginning to tell.

"We could send Father Gregory to talk to you," Jolie offered.

"No!" Rosa said vehemently. She would have to confess the truth to him, and then what? How could she bear to listen to her priest go on and on about Don's unnatural act? Maybe the church was more liberal about such things these days, but Father Gregory was not. And until this had happened, Rosa would have agreed with him, but when it was her husband who'd committed suicide, she realized that the issue wasn't as black-and-white as the priest would have everyone believe.

Don Killian had been a good man his entire life, right up until the moment he had killed himself. She was ready to admit that now. One instance of despair or insanity didn't change the past. It didn't negate it. The past merely made that one out-of-character act almost impossible to understand.

She sighed. She still didn't understand. She doubted she ever would.

That's why she was holed up in her room all alone. She wasn't in hiding, not exactly. She was methodically going over every day, every minute of the weeks leading up to Don's suicide, trying to find an answer. But even now, after hours and hours of self-examination and recriminations, she had nothing, not a single clue that would explain his unnecessary death. Worse, she couldn't talk about it, not even to these women who'd been her friends for so many years. It was bad enough that she'd told Helen what she thought had happened that night.

"What can we do?" Sylvia asked. "Would you like us to fix you some lunch? I could make that chicken salad you love."

"I'm not hungry," Rosa said, then added politely, "but thank you. I just want to be left alone."

"Then we'll go," Sylvia said determinedly. "Won't we, girls?"

"Of course," Jolie agreed, giving up the fight.

Helen was not so easily swayed. "I don't think you should be alone."

"It's not about what you think," Jolie told her firmly. "We'll come back another day."

"Fine," Helen said with obvious reluctance. "But we'll be back tomorrow. And the day after that."

Rosa almost smiled at her friend's fierce tone. "I know," she said, reaching for Helen's hand and giving it a squeeze, as she accepted Jolie's and Sylvia's hugs.

Despite the lack of welcome she'd shown them, despite the way she kept putting them off, she trusted that they wouldn't desert her. They would be there when she was ready, and in the meantime, they would keep prodding her, reminding her that she was alive and that she had obligations. They wouldn't let up until she was back on her feet. She might not totally appreciate that today, but she knew the day would come when she would thank them.

After her friends had gone, Rosa lay back against the pillows and let her mind drift. She wanted to go back to a happier time, but recent memories kept intruding. Images of Don chatting with the customers plagued her. It wasn't the daily visits with the men that bothered her, but the time he spent with the women.

Had one of them been more than a friend? Had he showered extra attention on Maureen Polk after her divorce? Had he laughed a little too hard at Jayne Dixon's corny jokes? On the days when he'd lingered at Flamingo Diner, ostensibly to give the stove a more thorough cleaning or to arrange the supplies in the storeroom, had one of those women or someone she hadn't even thought of stayed behind to help? Had his natural tendency to be supportive to everyone taken a romantic twist that, in the end, had tormented him? Rosa didn't want to believe it, but it wasn't out of the realm of possibility. Men Don's age strayed. It happened all the time.

If Don had been unfaithful, he would have suffered unbearable guilt. She knew that, too. And that could have explained his short-tempered outbursts. She couldn't even bear to think about the humiliation of coming face-to-face with someone who might have slept with her husband. Had that already happened? Had someone been secretly laughing behind Rosa's back? Or had the woman—if she even existed—had the good grace to avoid Rosa and the rest of Don's family?

Rosa tried to think of someone who'd stayed away from the funeral, perhaps out of guilt, but no one came to mind. Everyone they knew well had been there. Most had come by the house. Would her husband's lover have the nerve to walk into Rosa's home and offer condolences? Would Don have gotten involved with a woman who could do such a thing?

Her husband had been an outgoing man, a caring man. He'd always shouldered the customers' problems as if they were his own. Just look at how he'd taken Matt in years ago, guiding him away from trouble and onto a respectable path.

There wasn't a young person who'd grown up coming into Flamingo Diner that Don hadn't taken an interest in. He'd counseled dozens of kids to stay in school, to steer clear of drugs. He'd listened to outpourings of teenage angst without judgment, offering advice when it was sought. He'd mended many a fence between stressed parents and belligerent kids.

So why hadn't he been able to solve whatever problem he'd had in his own life? Whatever had been bothering him had to have been so huge, so overwhelming that he could see no other way out than suicide. Rosa couldn't imagine anything that devastating, not even an affair he was desperate to hide.

Rosa rolled over and punched the pillow in frustration. This was getting her nowhere. Maybe she did need to get out of bed and go back to the diner and look each and every customer in the eye, see if she could read something in their expressions, detect some hint of guilt.

Not today, though. Maybe not even tomorrow.

She closed her eyes and forced herself to go back in time, to the night Don had proposed. A smile settled on her lips at the memory. He'd been so romantic, so dashing in his dark suit and crisp white shirt when he'd picked her up for dinner.

A snapshot of the two of them taken that night had always sat on the nightstand beside the bed, but she'd shoved it into a drawer on the day Matt had told her Don was dead. She reached for it now and dared to look at it, feeling the familiar swell of love and pride, then the oppressive sense of unbearable sorrow and loss.

"Oh, Don," she whispered, gently touching the cool glass covering the photo. "How could you do this? We were supposed to be happy forever."

That night they had certainly believed their love would last forever.

He'd taken her back to the nightclub where they'd met, a huge, noisy place with a Latin floor show and an orchestra for dancing. He had two left feet when it came to the intricate steps of the tango, but he'd tried, making her laugh, making her fall even more deeply in love.

Even though he was a native of Central Florida with very little experience with the Cuban culture, he'd embraced it during his years at the University of Miami. He was the only non-Latino man she'd ever met who could discuss Cuban politics with her exiled parents and, even more astonishing, do it in fluent Spanish. They had adored him.

"Te amo," he'd whispered that night on the dance floor, when the music had turned to something slow and sultry.

Rosa remembered how her breath had hitched, how her heart had stood still as she'd gazed into those deep blue eyes. "I love you, too."

"Enough to marry me?" he'd asked. "I want to take you with me when I go home after graduation. I want to make a life for us, have children." He'd tucked a finger under her chin, his gaze unwavering. "Grow old together."

The music had faded into the background, the noisy chatter of the other customers dimmed. It was only the two of them, their senses alive, their hearts pounding.

"Yes," Rosa had whispered, then more exuberantly, "Yes!" She'd felt as if she were soaring, as light as a feather floating on the wind. There hadn't been a doubt in her mind that Don Killian was her destiny.

The trouble with her parents that followed had been a shock. They loved Don, but they didn't want their daughter to marry him, didn't want her to move away from Miami. They found flaws in him that she'd barely even noticed and made them seem monumental. They'd pointed out that he wasn't close to his family, that he gambled a little too much, that he drank.

"A glass of wine," she'd retorted about the drinking. "And so what if he doesn't get along with his family? He'll have us now."

The gambling had been harder to explain away. She'd confronted him about it and eventually convinced him to give it up. Her parents had remained skeptical. There were daunting battles and one terrifying moment when Rosa feared they had won, feared that the honorable man she loved would walk away from her because they didn't have her parents' approval.

He had come back for her the next day, though, and they had eloped and never looked back.

Eventually her parents had made peace with the decision. Their respect for Don had overcome their doubts about the two of them, but they had never once left Miami to come to visit. Because of that, they had missed out on so much, Rosa thought now, trying to imagine a day when she had grandchildren. Could she bear not to see them, not to watch them grow, not to spoil them?

She and Don had gone back to Miami a few times, but the visits were short. The children barely knew their maternal grandparents when they lost them one

after the other. Andy had never even met his grandfather, who had died the year before he was born.
And Jeff had been only seven when his grandmother
had died. Only Emma had memories of both of them.
Fond enough memories, Rosa assumed, since a doll
they had given her still sat in her room.

If only they were here now to comfort her, Rosa
thought wistfully, but maybe wherever they were,
they were giving comfort to Don, comfort she hadn't
been able to give him here on earth.

This time when the tears began to fall, Rosa didn't
try to hold them back. Hot, scalding tears slid down
her cheeks as she thought of all the wasted years, time
they could have shared. He'd promised they would
grow old together, and now she would have to do that
alone. She might be able to forgive him for a lot of
things, but not that. Never that.

The walls were starting to close in on Emma. She'd
forgotten how exhausting it was to work ten hours
straight at the diner. Even though she thoroughly enjoyed people, the sheer volume of customers started
to get to her midway through the noon rush. This time
there had been no savior in sight in the form of Matt.
With Jeff nowhere to be found, Andy had done his
best to help out, but he wasn't as fast as his father
had been or as glib as his mother. Nor could he handle
waiting tables and working the register as deftly as
Jeff.

Emma had been all too aware of the muttered complaints about the service, especially from the scattering of tourists who knew nothing of the family's current struggles.

At the end of the day, she and Andy looked at each

other, then sighed with relief when they locked the door behind the last of the customers.

"How about a soft drink?" Emma asked, hoping to coax him into spending a few minutes with her.

"Please," he said, slumping down in a chair, looking as despondent as Emma had ever seen him. This normally upbeat kid was drawn and tight-lipped.

When she'd put his Coke in front of him and taken a sip of her own, he met her gaze.

"We're not going to make it, are we?" he asked.

"Don't be silly. Of course, we are," she insisted. "This was just an incredibly busy day."

"People were complaining."

"I know. I heard them."

"Can we hire more help?" he asked. "A couple of my friends might pitch in."

Emma considered the idea, then dismissed it. They had to economize any way they could. They would have to manage on their own. "I don't think so. We need every penny."

Andy nodded, looking even more defeated.

"I'll talk to Mama, tonight," Emma promised. "If she came back, it would be a huge help."

"What about Jeff?"

"Of course, we could use him, too, but I have no idea where he is." She gazed into her brother's eyes. "Do you?"

Andy shrugged. "Probably with that girl he's been seeing."

That Jeff had a steady girlfriend was news to Emma, but she had been out of touch with him for a long time. "Is it anyone we know?"

"I've never seen her," Andy admitted. "Neither

have Mom and Dad. Jeff doesn't say too much about her.''

Emma couldn't help wondering why Jeff would be so secretive if the girl was someone special to him. "Do you have the impression it's serious?"

Andy hesitated, looking torn. "I probably shouldn't say anything. It's not like I really know."

"Know what? Andy, we're on the same side here."

"Are we?" he asked, his skepticism plain.

It was obvious he still didn't entirely trust her, Emma thought with regret. He might never trust her again the way he once had. "Of course we're on the same side. We both want what's best for Jeff."

"Then I don't think it's this girl," Andy said.

"Why not?"

"I'm pretty sure they get together just to smoke pot and have sex. Jeff hasn't said that exactly, just that she's pretty wild and she's hot, stuff like that."

"I see," Emma said wearily. Jeff wouldn't be the first guy to choose a girl who liked to have fun over one who was more respectable or more appropriate. He was only twenty, after all, probably a long way from wanting to settle down.

It was just that right now, when he was filled with so much rage, a girl like that might tempt him into doing something that could ruin his life. They could end up arrested or, in some ways even worse, married.

"You're not going to tell him I said anything, are you?" Andy asked, looking worried.

Emma forced a smile. "I know you're still mad at me, but you know perfectly well that I never tattle." She reached across the table and ruffled his hair. "I never told anyone it was you who broke Mama's little porcelain statue of the Virgin Mary, remember?"

Andy flushed. "I'm still saying Hail Marys for that one. I should probably just confess to Mom."

"Up to you," Emma said. "But you might feel better, if you did, even if it was years and years ago. She loved that statue."

"Because it was Abuela Conchita's," Andy said, his regret apparent. "She brought it from Cuba."

"Tucked inside her bra," Emma said, adding the footnote that always went with the story.

They fell silent then, sipping their soft drinks, trying to gather the strength necessary just to mop the floor and head home.

"Emma?"

"What?"

"Would it be better if we just sold this place like Mama and Jeff said?"

"Is that what you want?"

Andy regarded her with a forlorn expression. "I always thought I'd go to college and then come back and run it after Dad retired. I like working here. I like listening to what's going on around town. There's something special about Flamingo Diner, don't you think?"

Emma tried to see what Andy saw, but she wasn't entirely sure she did. She knew she hadn't run across anyplace like it in Washington, but she hadn't really looked. When she went out for a cup of coffee, she didn't expect to have the shop owner greet her by name or ask about her work. All she wanted was decent coffee.

She could see, though, how people might come to a place like this and feel as if they were part of an extended family. For many of the seniors who stopped by, there was a comfort in knowing that Don or Rosa or one of the other regular customers would worry if they failed to show up, that someone would inevitably check on them.

Ever since the funeral, the customers had returned the favor, offering support of all kinds. At first Emma had been taken aback. She'd grown used to keeping her personal business to herself. But after a few days, she had taken comfort in the genuine outpouring of warmth and concern.

She met Andy's gaze at last and slowly nodded. "Yes," she said. "Flamingo Diner is a special place, and if it's where you want to spend your future, then we'll do whatever it takes to make that possible."

Her brother's expression brightened at once. "I wouldn't really need to go to college, if I'm just going to run this place. I could learn everything I need to know right here. Jeff could teach me some of the business management stuff he's learned."

"You're going to college," Emma said flatly. "That's what Dad wanted for you and a business degree certainly won't hurt when it comes to keeping this place in the black."

He laughed then, the sound music to her ears. It was the first unrestrained display of real emotion he'd allowed himself in front of her since he'd told her he hated her.

"You sound exactly like Dad," he explained.

"Well, he was right about most things."

The laughter immediately faded. "Not lately," he said, sounding bleak. "He'd changed, Em. I told you that when I called you. Nothing I ever did was right. If there was any kind of mistake, he was always sure it was my fault. He didn't ask, he just blamed me. It wasn't like that before. He told me when I screwed up, but he was patient about it, you know? Lately, though, it was like everything was the end of the world.''

That certainly didn't sound like her father. Emma had never known him to be either harsh or unfair. ''Sweetie, there's no question that he had something terrible weighing on him. I wish I'd listened to you and come home. Maybe he would have told me, but if he didn't tell Mom, then I imagine he wouldn't have said anything to me, either. Whatever that something was, it made him do and say things he didn't mean. You have to forgive him.''

''Have you forgiven him for dying?'' Andy asked pointedly.

Emma wished she could say with conviction that it hadn't been his choice to die, but she couldn't. All she could manage to say with honesty was that it was normal to be angry when someone died. She reached for her brother's hand. ''We'll just have to work harder to get past the anger and hurt.''

And in the meantime, it wouldn't hurt to go looking for answers she knew were out there, because without them, forgiveness was going to be a whole lot more difficult.

9

Matt was sitting behind his desk when Emma came striding into his office, looking as if she were about to embark on a crusade for truth and justice. Despite her pallor, despite the evidence that she'd lost a few pounds she couldn't spare since coming home, she still looked beautiful to him. But it was the shadows in her gorgeous dark-brown eyes that almost did him in. He could almost hate Don Killian for putting them there and for putting him in the position of having to give her news she most likely didn't want to hear, despite her claims to the contrary.

"You have a minute?" she asked, sitting down opposite him without waiting for a reply.

"For you, always. What's up?"

Now that she had his attention, she seemed to be at a loss for words.

"You're here about your father," he said, relieving her of the need to tell him.

She nodded, her expression grim. "Do you know anything more?"

"Anything conclusive beyond a doubt? No. I spoke with the medical examiner earlier. I think he's going to come out with a ruling, probably later today, that it was an accident."

A faint spark of hope filled her eyes, then faded.

"But you don't believe that, any more than I do, do you?"

"I'm sorry, Emma, but truthfully, no."

"Did you tell the ME that?"

Matt met her gaze. "I thought about it."

"And?"

"What would be the point? It wouldn't change anything. It would only make your mother, Jeff and Andy even unhappier than they already are. I wish you could accept it and move on, too."

She returned his gaze, looking torn. "I wish I could let it go. I really do," she said. "But I can't. I need answers. What convinced you it was a suicide?"

Matt told her about the tool found in the car's console that would have allowed Don to free himself and escape from the car. "The console wasn't even open. To me, that was a dead giveaway, especially in light of the fact that there was no evidence that he'd suffered any injuries in the crash or that he'd had a heart attack or stroke. He died from drowning."

"In other words, he just sat there and waited to die." Emma swiped at the tears on her cheeks. "It must have been so horrible for him. Why would he do such a thing?"

Matt had been waiting for that question. Emma wasn't the first person grieving over a sudden loss who had come to him for answers. He'd never had them before. He most assuredly didn't have them now. He fell back on platitudes and statistics. "People who commit suicide are usually under a great deal of pressure. They don't see any other way out. Sadly, it's a permanent solution to what most likely is a temporary problem, but they can't accept that."

She frowned at him. "I could have read that in a book."

He shrugged. That was exactly where he'd read it the first time he'd had to handle a suicide. In that case it had been a jumper, who'd refused to listen to any of the officers trying to intervene. At least with that man, they'd had a slim chance. Don had made sure no one could even try to talk him out of it. He'd driven to the lake alone, late at night, making certain that his nearly submerged car wouldn't be discovered until it was too late.

"It's the best I can do," he told Emma. "I wish I had something concrete to tell you about your father."

"But you knew him, Matt," she protested. "You've been back awhile now. I imagine you've been in and out of the diner a thousand times. Surely you noticed something aside from the fact that he was short-tempered. Was he worried about something? Distracted? Anything at all unusual?"

As he had a hundred times recently, Matt thought back over the weeks leading up to Don's death, but there was still only one clue. "The way he was snapping at your mom and Andy is the only thing that sticks out in my mind. I wish there were something more I could tell you, Emma."

"If he was treating my mom and my brother like that, why didn't you say something? Why did you just let it pass?" she asked, her voice rising.

Matt understood her anger. "In retrospect, I wish I had confronted him, but at the time, I thought it was just a bad patch. People hit them all the time."

"This one was so bad, he killed himself," Emma retorted. "And you did nothing! How could you?"

The accusation stung more than she could possibly realize. Matt wanted to rush around the desk and hold her, tell her that no one had guessed Don was so desperately depressed that he would end his own life, not even Rosa, who had known him better than anyone. Because his own sense of guilt ran deep, he didn't say a word, didn't try to defend his decision to give Don a little space to work things out on his own.

Finally Emma sighed. "I know it's not your fault, Matt. I do. But it's awful knowing that he was so desperate and felt he couldn't turn to anyone. Maybe if I'd been here—"

"Stop that right now. Thinking about what might have been won't do you or anyone else any good. I know, darlin'. I've never felt more helpless or guilty in my life than I did the night I found that car. I've gone over and over that day and the days before it trying to come up with something I could have done differently, but your dad wasn't the kind of man to open up about his problems. He solved everyone else's, but whatever issues he had, he kept to himself."

"I know," she whispered, swiping furiously at the tears tracking down her cheeks. "And I also know it's too late to fix things, but I still need to know what drove him to it. Maybe then I'll be able to find some peace. Please, Matt. Help me find some answers. Where can we start?"

Matt suspected Don had deliberately set out to make the cause of his death seem ambiguous. He'd left no note offering a tidy explanation. Maybe he'd thought he was sparing the family, rather than causing them even more anguish. Maybe it had been a matter of the insurance money, thinking it would help them move on with their lives. If his death were ruled a suicide, whatever policies he had would be null and void. He wondered if Emma understood that.

He also knew that anything else Emma discovered, no matter how it stacked up, would never be conclusive proof of anything. The best Emma would ever have would be circumstantial evidence and speculation.

"Will it really help?" he asked, hoping to convince her to let it go. "No matter what we find, it will still only be conjecture. And, in the end, it won't really change anything, except the fact that there will be no insurance money."

She paled at that. "I hadn't considered that. We need that money."

He heard the edge of panic in her voice. "If you need it that badly, then let this drop. Accept the medical examiner's ruling."

She seemed to weigh his words for an eternity, then shook her head. "As badly as I want to do that, I can't. I think it's important that we understand what was going on in his head, even if we can't ever say for sure what drove him to kill himself." She looked more lost and vulnerable than he'd ever seen her look before. "Please." She picked up a tote bag she'd brought in with her. "I have these."

She pulled out what looked like accounting books.

"You think there's something in there?" he asked, surprised. The diner had been in business a long time in a prime location. It was always crowded with customers. By every standard he could imagine, it most certainly had to be a financial success. Some sort of business problem would be the last thing Matt would have suspected.

"I don't know," Emma admitted. "The attorney told us some things, then Jeff looked over the records and he says the numbers don't make sense, that dad was bleeding the business dry. He'd taken out a new mortgage on the house, too. There had to be a reason for it. He'd never been reckless with money. If anything, he was conservative."

A shudder washed over Matt as he realized why she'd sounded so desperate about the insurance money. He didn't like the direction this was taking. Suicide was always messy and left families with a million and one questions, but what Emma was suggesting hinted that more had been going on. Blackmail? Gambling losses? Another woman? Whatever it was, it could get ugly. Did she really want to take the chance that her father's reputation might be tarnished forever, even if the only people who knew were members of his own family? And the odds of keeping the truth secret would diminish with every clue they unearthed. The mere fact that they were conducting an investigation would tell people that he and Emma, at least, didn't believe the accidental death ruling.

"You might not like what I find," he warned her. "It's not just the insurance we're talking about. Your father's reputation could be ruined if I discover that he was mixed up in something illegal or immoral."

She regarded him with a familiar stubborn set to her jaw. "I don't believe for a minute it was anything illegal or immoral, but whatever it was, I have to know the truth."

"What about your mom? Would she want this? As devout as she is, would she want to know that Don committed suicide?"

Emma faltered at that. "I don't know," she admitted, sounding shaken. "In a weird way, even though we haven't discussed it, I think she already suspects it. I think that's why she's been hiding out in her room." She regarded Matt wistfully. "Couldn't we do this quietly, then decide what to tell her?"

"She'll hear about it if we're asking questions, Emma."

"Not if she doesn't leave the house, and she's showing no signs of going out."

"And is that what you want? Do you honestly want her to continue avoiding everyone?"

"No," she conceded.

"Then you have to sit down and tell her what you're doing, you have to explain the insurance implications, because once I start looking under rocks, you won't be able to turn back. The truth will come out, whatever it is. And you won't be able to hide it from Rosa or Jeff and Andy. They're hurt and confused now, but at least their memories of your father haven't been destroyed. At least whatever financial mess your father created would be solved. Think it through, Emma. Maybe it's best to leave it alone. Pick up the pieces and move on."

Her hands were clenched together so tightly that her knuckles were white. Matt noticed that, as well as the strain around her mouth. He wondered idly if a kiss would put some color back in her cheeks, maybe soften her lips into a smile. And then he felt like a complete jerk for allowing his thoughts to even stray in that direction when she was in such obvious pain. She didn't need a momentary distraction. She needed much more from him.

"I've been thinking about this for days now. I can't

move on without answers,'' she said finally. ''No matter what it costs.''

Matt nodded, knowing he had no choice. He had to help her. She would do this alone, if she had to, and he didn't want her making whatever discoveries were out there without someone supportive at her side.

''Then we'll find the answers,'' he told her.

She seemed relieved by his response, as if she'd doubted it. ''Where should we start?'' she asked.

''The books are here. Let's start with those,'' he said. ''Unfortunately, I don't know a thing about accounting procedures or numbers. Do you?''

Emma shook her head. ''I can do the day-to-day stuff, but my boss has an outside accountant do the books.''

''Then I know someone who does have some expertise,'' he said. ''Would you mind if I show them to her?'' When Emma looked uncertain, he added, ''She'll be discreet. She's known your folks for years.'' Besides that, it would give him a chance to check out a few of the things Gabe and Harley had said at the reception following the funeral. He'd hesitated about going to see Jennifer before, because of their history. He didn't want to give her any reason to think he'd had a change of heart about the two of them.

Surprise registered on Emma's face. ''Who is it?''

''Jennifer Sawyer. She was in school with me, so she's a couple of years older than you. She's a very successful financial planner, and she's been a regular at the diner since we were kids.'' He deliberately didn't add that, according to Gabe and Harley, she'd been spending an inordinate amount of time huddled with Don Killian before his death. Granted, it had been very public huddling, but who knew where that might have led?

"Of course. I remember her," Emma said, her expression brightening. "She hasn't been in since I got back, though. May I come with you?"

Matt would have preferred to go alone. He didn't want Emma picking up on any of the vibes between him and Jennifer. Not that he was either ashamed of the relationship or had any reason to hide it from her, but it would only complicate things. Besides, there was every chance that he'd have better luck getting information from Jennifer if he handled it alone. And if there were any ugly secrets to be uncovered, he wanted the chance to pretty them up before telling Emma.

But these were Emma's accounting records and Don had been her father. She had a right to come along. Hopefully he wasn't leading her straight into a quagmire.

"Of course," he told her, standing up. "Let's go."

"Shouldn't we call first?" she asked, sounding oddly hesitant now that they were about to move forward.

"She'll be there," he said wryly. "She doesn't go anywhere during the day where she can't keep her eye on the stock exchange ticker tapes." It hadn't been the reason he'd stopped seeing her, but it had put some other men off, men who'd wanted to be her first priority.

"Okay, then," Emma said with obviously forced enthusiasm. "Let's do it."

Matt tried to make small talk en route to the office building where many of the brokerages in town maintained suites. Jennifer's financial planning firm was in the penthouse, a testament to her success.

When he'd parked down the block from the building, he turned to her. "We don't have to do this," he reminded her quietly one last time. "Or I can go in alone."

"No," she said, clutching the record books more tightly. "I'm coming."

On the twelfth floor, the elevator doors whooshed open quietly to admit them to a carpeted suite with dark paneled wood on the walls and Sawyer Financial Services in gold block letters behind a very impressive reception desk.

"Hey, Matt," Corinne Fletcher said, brightening when she saw him. "What brings you by? I thought…" Her voice trailed off and her eyes widened. "Emma Killian, is that you?"

Emma seemed momentarily taken aback when the very pregnant Corinne lumbered awkwardly around the desk and embraced her. She blinked hard and then a slow smile spread across her face. "Cori? Corinne Holt?"

"It's Fletcher now." Her own smile dimmed. "Oh, Emma, I am so sorry about your dad. You know how we all adored him. I'd expected all my kids to grow up in Flamingo Diner under his watchful eye just the way we did. I can't even count the number of times he sat down with me and gave me advice. He always had time to listen, even when I was going on and on about my parents or some boy. You were so lucky to have a dad like that."

"I know. Thanks," Emma said, her eyes turning damp.

Matt immediately stepped in. "Cori, can you get

us in to see Jennifer? We have some questions we thought she might be able to help us with.''

Cori looked oddly uncomfortable. ''Actually she's out of town right now. I'm not expecting her back till next week. Can someone else help you?''

Matt glanced at Emma, who shook her head. ''No, we'll wait for her,'' Matt said. ''Set up an appointment for Monday afternoon. Is that okay for you, Emma?''

''Sure. Anytime after three should work.''

Cori went back behind the desk and scanned the page of a date book. ''She has a three o'clock, but I can change it.''

''Thank you,'' Emma said.

''Will you be staying in Winter Cove?'' Cori asked her. ''I'd love to get together if you are.''

Emma nodded. ''At least for the time being, and I'd love to see you. Maybe we can have dinner sometime?''

''I'll check with my husband and compare schedules, then call you,'' Cori promised. ''You're staying with your mom, right? I have that number.''

''Then I'll wait to hear from you,'' Emma replied.

Cori looked from Matt to Emma, then back again. ''You want to join us, Matt?'' she asked, her tone about as innocent as that of the scheming operator of a full-service matchmaking enterprise.

Matt glanced at Emma. ''Sure, as long as Emma doesn't object.''

''Of course not,'' she said with something that almost sounded like relief.

After they'd left, he called her on it. ''Was there some reason you weren't looking forward to getting together with Cori and her husband on your own?''

She frowned at the question. "What gave you that idea?"

"Oh, I don't know, maybe the fact that you looked as if I'd saved you from a fate worse then death when I agreed to come along."

"Maybe I just wanted your company," she replied.

He leveled a look straight into her eyes. "Did you?"

He heard her breath hitch, saw the pulse fluttering at the base of her neck, the quick rise of color in her cheeks. Clearly she hadn't been expecting him to call her on her claim.

"It's dinner, Matt, not an invitation to have sex," she finally said testily.

"Too bad," he murmured, then grinned. "I'll try real hard to remember that."

"See that you do," she said sternly, but there was an unmistakable twinkle in her eyes.

That little spark was more than enough to give a man hope.

Emma spent a lot of time weighing Matt's argument that she needed to be honest with her mother about what she was doing. She finally concluded that he was right, it wouldn't be right to keep Rosa in the dark, especially since it could cost her mother whatever insurance money there was. If Rosa objected too vehemently, there was still time to call off the investigation.

When she took a supper tray into her mother's room, she carried a bowl of cold, spicy gazpacho along for herself.

"I thought I'd eat with you," she announced, not

waiting for her mother's response before pulling a chair over beside the bed.

Rosa watched her warily. "What's on your mind, Emma?" she asked eventually.

Emma barely resisted the urge to snap a response asking what on earth her mother thought would be on her mind these days. Instead, she said quietly, "I've done something I wanted you to know about."

Rosa's hand froze in midair. Slowly she placed the spoonful of soup back into the bowl. "What have you done?"

There was no point in dancing around it, Emma decided. "I took the diner's books to Matt and asked him to help me figure out what was going on with Dad."

Rosa's already pale complexion turned ashen. "Oh, Emma, you didn't. Why would you do such a thing?"

This was going to be the hard part, telling her mother that she suspected her father's death wasn't an accident. She drew in a deep breath. "We need to know, Mama."

"Maybe you do."

"We all do," Emma insisted. "I don't want to hurt you. I don't want to make this harder on you than it already is, but the truth is that I don't believe Dad's death was accidental."

She waited for a shocked gasp, some hint of outrage, maybe even another slap, but her mother merely closed her eyes. A tear trailed down her cheek. In that instant she looked as if she'd aged ten years.

"You suspect the same thing, don't you?" Emma said at last. "I thought so."

"I can't talk about this," her mother said, shoving

away her tray. "Please, Emma. Leave it alone. Think of your brothers."

"That's exactly who I am thinking about. Them and you. Look at you. You've been holed up in here for a couple of weeks now. Jeff's run off to who knows where. Andy's worrying himself sick."

"And you're trapped here in Winter Cove," Rosa said sharply. "That's the real problem, isn't it? Once you find out what happened with your father, you'll be able to place the blame on me or someone else and then take off again."

The accusation was as stinging as the slap she'd anticipated. "That's not it," she insisted. "I'm happy to stay and help out for however long you need me, but none of us can go on forever wondering about that night and why it happened. It's this huge elephant sitting in the middle of the room and we're all trying to ignore it. I think even Andy and Jeff suspect that something's not right."

"Surely not," her mother said. "They're young. They adored their father, even Jeff, though he'd never admit it."

"I know and this won't ruin that. It will just make it easier for them to understand why he's gone."

"Will it really?" her mother asked bitterly. "How will you explain that there's no insurance money for Jeff to finish college, for Andy to go next year, or to pay off the mortgages your father took out on the house and the diner?"

Despite her mother's emphasis on the money, a vague suspicion crept into Emma's head and refused to be ignored. "Mama, do you already know why Dad would commit suicide? Do you think he did it for the money?"

"Of course not. If I had known he was that upset over something, don't you think I would have insisted he get help? Don't blame me for any of this."

"I wasn't blaming you. It's just that it wasn't like him to refinance the house and the diner without talking it over with you."

"Well, he didn't," Rosa snapped. "I would never have let him do such a thing and he knew it."

Emma sighed. "I just thought maybe you had some idea what was going on in his head, maybe without even realizing it was important. You two always talked about everything."

"Well, not this time, and I don't want to know, either." There was real fear in her voice.

"What are you afraid of, Mama?" Emma asked.

"I'm not afraid. I'm angry."

"At Dad?"

"No, at you for taking a step like this without asking me first. You're just going to make it worse, Emma."

"How?"

"I don't know. I just feel it in my gut."

"I'm sorry, but I'm doing what I think is best," Emma said unrepentantly. "And now that I've talked to you, I'm more convinced than ever that I'm right. Whatever you're thinking has to be worse than the truth."

"You can't know that."

"I do. I knew Dad. So did you."

"No," Rosa said sadly. "I only thought I did." She rolled over, turning her back once again on Emma.

That hurt as much as anything that had happened in recent days. She and her mother had always been able to talk, had always understood each other. Now her father had managed to drive a wedge between them.

Ever since the suicide, Matt had driven by the lake every evening, passing the spot where he'd found Don's car. There was a makeshift memorial there, a growing pile of flowers and markers left by the grieving citizens of Winter Cove. A similar memorial had appeared in front of the diner the day the news had spread, but out of respect for the family's feelings, someone had cleared it away before the restaurant opened for business again. Now this place, rather than the cemetery, was where people left their tributes to a man who'd done so much for the community.

In all his past trips, Matt had never actually spotted anyone at the site, but tonight there were two shadowy figures there. Rather than leaving something behind in remembrance, though, it looked as if they were digging through the display. Thoroughly disgusted by the apparent vandalism, he slammed on his brakes and turned on his flashing lights.

"Dammit, I told you, we shouldn't be doing this," a crotchety voice grumbled. "We're about to be hauled off to jail."

"Oh, shut your trap," the other man answered. "It's not as if we're committing a crime."

Matt groaned as he recognized not only the voices, but the sparring. Gabe Jenkins and Harley Watkins, he concluded as he took a more leisurely stroll in their direction.

"Nice night," he observed when he could look the two men in the eyes.

Gabe regarded him suspiciously. "You stopping by for a chat?"

"That depends," Matt said. "What are you two up to?"

"Nothing," Harley responded flatly, casting a quelling look in Gabe's direction.

"That's right, not a thing," Gabe said dutifully.

"Looked to me as if you were poking around for something in Don's memorial," Matt countered. "Did one of you lose something?"

"No," Gabe said, just as Harley said, "Yes."

Matt bit back a chuckle. "Which is it?"

"I lost something. He didn't," Harley said.

"What?" Matt inquired. "I'll help you look."

"A contact lens," Harley said readily. "I was bending over, putting a handful of flowers down, and the dang thing fell right out of my eye."

Gabe stared at him as if he'd grown two heads.

"I don't recall ever seeing you wear glasses," Matt said.

"Because I have contacts," Harley said patiently. "Had 'em for years now, practically from the minute they were introduced on the market."

Matt nodded. "Is that so? Soft or hard lens?"

"Hardheaded, more likely," Gabe muttered.

Harley scowled at him. "Are you determined to blow this? I'm doing the best I can here."

Matt leveled a look straight into his twenty-twenty eyes. "Blow what, Harley?"

Gabe heaved a sigh. "We might's well tell him. It's not like we're committing a crime or something. Maybe he'll appreciate the help."

Matt nearly groaned. He'd been afraid it might be something like that. "What sort of help?"

Harley shot a sour look at his friend, then said, "We got to thinking this morning that somebody might have left a clue out here."

"A clue?" Matt repeated slowly.

"Are you deaf, boy? Or just stupid? You do know what a clue is, don't you?"

"Indeed, I do," Matt said. "But why here? And why did the two of you decide to come looking for it, instead of just telling me?"

"Didn't want to waste your time on a wild-goose chase," Gabe said. "We figured we'd scope things out, then fill you in."

"What exactly did you think you might find?"

"Maybe a note from somebody who was feeling too guilty to send flowers to the funeral," Harley explained. "Or maybe some little memento."

Matt couldn't really argue with the theory. He just didn't want these two to start getting ideas about conducting their own investigation into Don's death. Who knew what sort of mischief they might get into. If they needed more excitement in their lives, they should take up bingo.

"Next time you guys get a bright idea like this, bring it to me," he told them sternly. "Otherwise I'm liable to haul you in for interfering in police business, obstructing justice or any other charge I can dream up and make stick."

"So that's the thanks we get for wanting to do the right thing?" Gabe grumbled.

"No, the thanks you get is me not hauling you in tonight," Matt said. "I won't go so easy on you next time, if you keep this up. What makes you think you have any business digging around in Don's death?

The ME's ruling came out this afternoon. The case is officially closed. It was an accident.''

"As if you believe that any more than we do," Harley scoffed.

Matt groaned. If these two were convinced otherwise, then half the town probably was, as well. "Could you manage to keep your opinions to yourselves?"

"Well, of course, we will. We don't like seeing the family upset," Gabe said.

"Then leave it alone."

"Silence never solves anything," Gabe retorted. "We figured if we could come up with some sort of explanation for why Don did what he did, it might be easier on the family in the long run."

There was a lot of that kind of thinking going around these days, Matt thought. "I don't disagree," he told them. "But let me do the investigating, okay?"

The two men eyed the pile of flowers and stuffed toys with regret, but they did turn away to leave.

"You're not leaving, are you?" Matt finally concluded with a sigh.

"Seems like a waste to have three of us standing here and not poke around a little," Harley said.

"Okay, fine," Matt said, resigned. "Now that I'm here, I suppose I could use some help, but you only touch things I tell you that you can touch. Got it?"

Their expressions immediately brightened. "Got it," Harley said enthusiastically.

"What do you want us to do?" Gabe asked.

"I'm going to pick things up one by one," Matt said. "I'll look 'em over, then hand 'em to you. See if you see anything I missed, then set it down over there.'' He gestured to a bare patch of ground where the memorial could be rebuilt with few people the wiser. Just on the remote chance there actually was a clue, it might be best if no one knew there had ever been a search conducted out here.

Matt began plucking up the wilting bouquets of flowers one by one, feeling like a bit of an idiot for going along with this crazy scheme of Gabe's and Harley's. Then, again, he would have felt like even more of an idiot if there was some clue out here and he'd ignored it, especially when only a few brief hours ago he'd promised Emma to do whatever he could to find answers.

Most of the tributes hadn't been signed. There were bunches of daisies and carnations, a scattering of single roses. A few stuffed toys had cards that had been written in the awkward style of a very young child. There was even a spatula tied with ribbons and a white apron with ''We'll miss you,'' written in marker across the front. All of these were touching, but essentially the sort of thing Matt would have expected to find.

But there was one bouquet, buried almost at the bottom of the pile, that intrigued him. It was more lavish than the others, the kind that normally would have been sent to the funeral home. That it was now covered by so many others suggested it had been here almost from the day the news of Don's death had broken.

There was a pale green ribbon wound around the expensive basket filled with browning lilies and limp white roses. Attached to it was a small florist's card with one word written in bold script. Though it had almost been washed away by one of the recent afternoon showers, he could still make it out: "Why?"

Matt sighed. Why, indeed?

10

Emma was on her way to deliver a plate of eggs and bacon to Gabe Jenkins and a bowl of raisin bran to Harley Watson. A hush fell over the two men as she approached. Since they were never silent for more than a few seconds at a time, she regarded them with suspicion. When they avoided her gaze, she knew immediately something was up.

"Okay, guys, what's going on?" she demanded, setting their food on the table.

"Nothing," Gabe said, looking increasingly guilty.

"Absolutely nothing," Harley agreed.

Emma wasn't buying it. A quick glance around the restaurant reassured her that things were temporarily under control. She pulled out a chair and sat down. "I don't believe you," she said flatly, looking into one pair of hooded eyes and then the other.

"Well, if that isn't a fine thing to be saying to a loyal customer who's been coming into this place since you were knee-high to a grasshopper," Gabe said with indignation.

"It's because you've been coming in here so long that I can read you like a book," Emma retorted. "What are you two up to?"

"Nothing," Matt said sternly, arriving just in time

to overhear her and inject himself into the middle of things.

His comment promptly tripled her suspicions. Emma whirled on him. "Did I ask you?"

He grinned, completely unintimidated. "Nope, but I happen to know the answer, and I love to share."

"Nothing is just what we told her, too," Harley chimed in as if he were eager to reassure Matt on that point. "She doesn't believe us."

"No, I don't," Emma said emphatically, then decided on a tactical retreat. She smiled sweetly at the entire lot of coconspirators. "But with Matt sticking his nose into things, I suppose I'll never get you to cough up the truth. I might as well go back and scramble some more eggs."

"Good idea," Gabe said, holding out his plate. "These are cold."

She frowned at him. "Whose fault is that? Eat them, anyway."

Gabe shook his head sorrowfully. "It ain't like the old days in here, when the customer was always right."

Emma gave him a phony smile as she stood up to leave. "*Most* of our customers still are," she said as she headed back behind the counter.

"Girl, I have pictures of you when you had gap-teeth and pigtails," Gabe called after her. "You want me showing them around?"

Emma laughed. "Most everyone in here has already seen me at my worst, and they're still coming around. I'm not scared of your threats."

A few minutes later, she glanced across the diner and saw that Matt was giving the two men a serious lecture about something. Something was definitely up with those two, and Matt was not only in on it, he didn't want her to know about it. Well, she had ways of getting the truth out of him. He might think she was unaware of the crush he'd had on her years ago, but she wasn't. She'd simply been too young to know what to do about it.

The good news was that unless she was very much mistaken, the sparks were still there. Kim's efforts to turn her into a femme fatale hadn't been a total waste—she knew how to exploit that sort of weakness and, in this case at least, she wasn't above doing it.

After Gabe and Harley left, along with most of the other regulars, Matt wandered over to the counter. With her back to him, Emma discreetly unbuttoned the top button of her blouse, checked the effect, then dared to undo one more button. Then she grabbed the coffeepot and took Matt a refill. When she leaned down to pour, he was certain to get an eyeful of her adequate, if not ample cleavage.

When she stood up, though, he was chuckling, not speechless.

"It's not going to work, you know," he said.

She plastered an innocent expression on her face. "I have no idea what you're talking about."

"I'm not going to crack and spill my guts to you, just because you're putting on a little show for my benefit."

Emma flushed. She obviously needed a little more practice if she was going to get this femme fatale stuff right. "I am not doing any such thing," she retorted with what she considered to be an appropriate level of indignation.

He reached across the counter and skimmed a finger along the opening in her blouse. "Then this isn't just for me?"

Emma swallowed hard and tried to ignore the deliciously wicked sensation set off by his touch. She hadn't been counting on that. Then, again, Matt had taken her by surprise more than once since she'd returned.

"Absolutely not!" she insisted, lying through her teeth.

He made a great show of looking all around the now empty diner. "Then who is it for?"

"I was just a little overheated," she claimed. "Since everyone else had gone, I thought I'd unbutton my blouse and cool off a little. I didn't think you'd object. You've seen me in a lot less."

"On the beach or at the pool," he reminded her. "And as I recall your mother was pretty strict about the amount of skin you could show off even there."

"But I'm all grown-up now. Mama doesn't have a say about how I dress."

"Then you think she'd approve of this?"

"It's just a couple of buttons," she said blithely. "Why not?"

"Liar! She'd have a stroke if she thought you were blatantly trying to seduce information out of me."

"Oh, please, I am not trying to seduce you," she claimed. "Your ego is out of control, Matthew."

She began to jerk away, but he tucked a finger under the edge of her blouse, his knuckle barely touching her bare skin, and held her perfectly still. A part of her wanted to command him to slip that finger just a little lower, but she didn't dare. She was already risking far more than her reputation. She was taking a huge chance with her ability to cling to her composure.

His gaze locked with hers. "In that case," he said very softly, his eyes flashing dangerously, "allow me to fix this."

Before she knew it, both buttons were neatly back in place and she was once again looking as prim and proper as she usually did. He'd accomplished the task so deftly, she was sure he had to be an expert. The thought grated.

Worse, she was feeling anything but prim and proper, as he'd so clearly intended. She wanted to blame the fire licking through her on anger, but she was too honest to attempt the lie, even to herself. She'd played a wicked little game with Matt, and he'd won. She hadn't been anticipating that, had pretty much thought she was immune to him. If the past few minutes had taught her anything, it was that the days of thinking of him as a big brother were over.

As for thinking of him as a potential lover, that was the last thing she needed. She wanted him for an ally. She wanted him to be her friend. She wanted to go back to the way it had been a few minutes ago, before every sense in her entire body had danced a little jig at his touch.

Desperate to recapture their easygoing relationship, she moved away and carefully set the coffeepot down before turning back to face him, her expression neutral.

"Why did you want Gabe and Harley to clam up?" she asked, deciding on the direct course of action, since subterfuge had pretty much blown up in her face.

"What makes you think I wanted them to keep silent about something?"

"Matt, I've known those two my whole life, and you just about as long," she said impatiently. "I can recognize a conspiracy when I see one."

"What would Gabe, Harley and I have to conspire about?"

"That's what I'm asking you," she said, exasperated by his display of obviously phony innocence. "Does it have something to do with my father?"

"Don't be crazy."

"Does it?" she repeated, regarding him with an unflinching look.

"Okay, okay." Matt sighed heavily. "I found those two poking around at the memorial people have put up where we found your dad. They were conducting their own investigation."

"Dear God," Emma said, trying to imagine Gabe and Harley playing sleuth. The thought boggled the mind. With their vivid imaginations and blundering ways, they were bound to end up in trouble at the least. At worst, they could mess up some really solid lead.

"I hope you convinced them to cut it out," she said.

"No, I deputized them," Matt said sarcastically, then shook his head at her. "Come on, Emma. Of course, I told them to butt out."

"Will they listen?"

"I doubt it."

Now it was her turn to sigh.

"They just want to help," Matt pointed out. "They're feeling pretty helpless right now and this is the one way they could come up with to show their support to you and the family.''

''I know how they feel. I've been feeling pretty helpless myself,'' she conceded. ''So did the three of you turn up anything interesting last night?''

Matt described finding an expensive bouquet amid all of the smaller tributes. ''I can't help wondering why someone wouldn't have sent that to the funeral.''

''Maybe it was from someone who didn't know him all that well,'' she said, but Matt was already shaking his head. ''Why not?''

''Because of the card,'' he explained. ''There was something almost plaintive about it. All it said was, 'Why?' That suggests that there's someone out there who wants answers just as much as you do.''

Emma's heart began to thud dully. ''A lover?'' she asked, barely able to squeeze the word out past the lump in her throat.

Her mother hadn't said as much, but Emma had guessed it was one of the things Rosa was afraid of. Emma had always thought her parents' marriage was on rock-solid ground, but maybe it hadn't been. No one, not even a daughter, could ever know what really went on in a marriage, unless the people were prone to public arguments.

And lately, they had been, she recalled with dismay. She forced herself to meet Matt's sympathetic gaze. ''That would explain why Dad was so short-tempered.''

''Do you honestly believe your father would have cheated on your mother?'' he said with satisfying skepticism.

''I don't want to believe it,'' Emma said.

"Then don't. I certainly don't, and we don't have any evidence pointing in that direction."

Cautious relief stirred inside her. "Thank you for saying that."

"I'm saying it because it's true. Emma, don't jump to conclusions and don't think the worst. Let's take this one step at a time and see where it leads us. Maybe we'll know more after we meet with Jennifer on Monday."

She nodded. She could wait a few more days, especially if the news was likely to be bad.

"That reminds me," she said, relieved to be able to change the subject. "Cori called last night. She wondered if Sunday evening would be good for us for dinner."

Matt nodded. "Works for me. How about you?"

"Actually, it's the best night for me, too. Cori's cooking. I'll tell her it's fine. She said seven o'clock, if that works for us."

"I'll pick you up at six-thirty, then," Matt said.

"I could just meet you there," she said, her thoughts drifting back to that earlier instant of sizzling awareness. It would be really smart to avoid a situation in which that could be repeated.

Apparently Matt guessed exactly what she was thinking, because his gaze locked on hers. "I'll pick you up," he repeated, then added, his eyes twinkling, "Just keep your blouse buttoned, okay?"

Emma frowned at him. "I'll wear a turtleneck."

He laughed. "No need to go quite that far on a hot August night. I can remain reasonably civilized when I have to."

But what if I don't want you to? Emma wondered, barely managing to keep the thought to herself. What if what she really wanted was for Matt Atkins to make her feel totally alive for just a few blissful hours in the midst of all this mind-numbing uncertainty?

"Or not," he said quietly, his gaze unwavering.

Emma barely contained a sigh. It was almost as if he'd read her mind...the one she'd obviously lost.

Matt was pretty sure that little scene in the diner with Emma had cost him ten years off his life. Didn't the woman know any better than to play a game like that with a man? A less scrupulous man would have taken what she was offering and not given it a second thought. Hell, *he'd* almost grabbed her and plundered that sweet mouth of hers without thinking.

Matt shuddered at the memory of just how close he'd come to forgetting every rule he had where Emma was concerned. As a girl, she had driven him crazy without doing a thing besides bestowing an occasional smile on him. As a woman, she had an arsenal of weapons that could tempt a saint, which apparently was precisely what she'd thought she was doing. If he couldn't get a grip on his hormones, these visits to the diner were going to kill him.

Not that he would stay away to save himself. She needed him and he'd promised to be there for her. Of course, maybe he could speed things along, spending some of his own time investigating whether there really was a motive that might explain her father's suicide. Determined to do just that, he pushed back from his desk at the station and headed for the door.

"You going someplace?" Cramer inquired as he passed.

"I've got a few things to look into," Matt said.

"I'd go by Sweet Smell of Success, if I were you."

Matt spun around, his gaze narrowed. "Why would I want to go by a florist's?"

"You want to know who sent those flowers to Don's memorial by the lake, don't you?" Cramer asked, his expression totally innocent.

"Are you clairvoyant or something?" he asked testily. "Or have you been hiding out in the bushes by the lake?"

Cramer chuckled. "I had dinner with Gabe and Harley last night. They couldn't wait to tell me about their big investigation."

"Heaven help me," Matt muttered.

"It's going to take more than heavenly intervention to keep those two under control. If I were you, I'd lock them up in protective custody."

"Maybe I'll just assign you to keep them out of mischief," Matt retorted.

"As if," Cramer said, then apparently spotted the serious gleam in Matt's eyes. "Oh, no. They're my friends."

"Who better to keep an eye on them?"

"I don't spy on my friends."

"It's not spying. It's police business."

"My police business is right here," the desk sergeant reminded him. "Stacks of paperwork to do while I'm subbing on the day shift." He shuffled an inch-high accumulation as if that would prove his point.

"You can have that finished by lunchtime," Matt said. "Besides, I don't think Gabe and Harley are likely to get into too much trouble during the day. It's evenings I'm worried about."

"I'm off at three."

"Which means you're free to spend your evenings

with those two old coots,'' Matt said, liking his plan
better and better. ''Make sure they don't know you're
watching them, either. Take 'em to dinner. Take 'em
bowling. Do whatever you can think of. I want 'em
safe and out of my way. I don't want to have to deal
with their hurt feelings.''

''Who's paying for all this?'' Cramer asked suspiciously. ''Does the department have a budget for
this sort of thing? I'm sure as heck not spending my
money on those two.''

Matt reached in his wallet and pulled out some
twenties. ''Have a ball.''

Cramer grabbed up the money, looking considerably more cheerful. ''Don't worry about a thing, boss,
I've got it covered.''

''See that you do.''

Satisfied that he'd neutralized his rogue sleuths for
a day or two, Matt set off for the florist shop with the
too cute name. He wasn't sure what instinct of Cramer's had zeroed in on this particular shop, but he
trusted the desk sergeant to know a thing or two about
what was going on around town.

When he entered Sweet Smell of Success, a bell
tinkled merrily over the door and Valencia Freeman
floated out of the back room in a bright orange caftan.
A smile spread across her round face when she saw
him.

''Matt Atkins, I was wondering when you'd turn
up here. Are you after information or flowers for
Emma?''

Matt bit back a curse. Was there anyone in this
town who wasn't aware of his feelings for Emma?
Then again, Val was supposedly known for her psychic abilities. She told fortunes when she wasn't mak-

ing up pretty bouquets of rosebuds and lilies. He had a feeling her sideline was more lucrative than her primary business, since a lot of people wanted to know what the future held. He, however, was more interested in the past, at least today.

"Information," he told her.

"About those flowers I made up for Don's memorial by the lake, I assume."

He wasn't surprised that she knew that, too. "Yes. Who bought them?"

"As much as I'd like to help you, I can't say."

"You're not bound by confidentiality rules," he pointed out.

"Perhaps not, but what sort of businesswoman would I be if I didn't respect my customers' wishes?" she asked.

Matt regarded her with a penetrating look. "Did someone ask you to keep quiet about those flowers?"

"To be honest, no," she conceded. "I was just trying to make a point."

Matt frowned at her.

"Okay, okay, the fact of the matter is that I have no idea who ordered those flowers," she admitted. "I found a note tucked under my door when I opened that morning. There was a hundred dollar bill with it and a request that the flowers be delivered to the lakefront."

"Did you save the note?"

"Of course," she said.

Matt was holding on to his patience by a thread. "Val, may I see the note?"

She regarded him with obvious reluctance, then relented. "I'll get it, but it won't do you a bit of good. It was written on a computer, then printed out. No handwriting, just a standard font, Times Roman, if I'm not mistaken.''

For all of her carefully contrived offbeat attire and the fortune-telling that went on in the back room, Val was a hardheaded businesswoman. It took her less than a minute to lay her hands on the piece of paper in her well-organized files. She handed it to Matt.

Val's description had been perfect, right down to the font of the type. He knew because it was the standard setting on his own computer and probably about a thousand others right here in Winter Cove.

''Mind if I hang on to this?'' he asked, already tucking it into one of the little evidence bags he carried in his pocket.

Val shook her head. ''What if I said yes?''

''I'd argue with you, threaten to get a warrant. You'd be sensible and turn it over. I just bypassed all that,'' he replied.

''I'd argue the legalities with you, but I don't have the time right now. I have a client coming in for a reading in ten minutes and it will take me at least that long to fix up a bouquet of flowers for you to take to Cori, when you and Emma go for dinner.''

Matt groaned. ''I do not want to know how you know about that. I do not believe in all this psychic mumbo jumbo you preach.''

Working with nimble fingers, Val tucked white tulips and calla lilies into a dark green vase in an arrangement that was both simple and elegant. Even Matt could appreciate the beauty of it.

''You shouldn't be so quick to dismiss what I see,'' she told him as she handed him the flowers. ''For instance, these are for Cori, but they're Emma's favorites. She'll be impressed.''

"Why should that matter to me?" Matt grumbled defensively.

Val laughed. "Because you're in love with her," she said at once. "And trust me, it doesn't take a psychic to read that one. It's written all over your face every time the two of you are in the same room. Has been for years." She patted his hand. "I'm not going to tell you how Emma feels. I think I'll let you figure that one out yourself."

For a moment, Matt considered threatening to have her subpoenaed to pry the information out of her, but she was probably right. It was better if he reached that particular conclusion entirely on his own, based on hard evidence he'd gathered himself. Sunday night would be a good time to start.

"Thanks for the flowers," he said. "How much do I owe you?"

"They're on the house," Val said. "I'm a sucker for a man in love."

Matt rolled his eyes and headed for the door. He was almost out when something occurred to him. "Did Don buy flowers from you?"

"From time to time," she said, her expression suddenly sad. "I had a standing order for Rosa's birthday, for Mother's Day and for their anniversary." She lifted her gazed to meet Matt's. "And before you ask, he never bought flowers for anyone else in here. I wouldn't have sold them to him if he'd tried, but Don Killian loved his wife and no one else. I'd stake my professional reputation on that."

This was one time when Matt wasn't the least bit inclined to question Val's certainty. "Yeah," he said softly. "Me, too."

He hoped to hell they were both right.

11

Rosa knew she couldn't hide out at home forever, but the prospect of walking into Flamingo Diner, where she'd spent more than two decades working side by side with her husband, was intolerable. She was afraid of coming completely unglued at the memories of Don standing at the stove, of Don grabbing her around the waist and kissing her thoroughly to the delight of their customers, of Don with Emma or Jeff or Andy in one arm, while he flipped pancakes with his free hand.

And then, more recently, of Don snapping at Andy and at her, of the startled looks on the faces of the regulars as his temper flared again and again. At the time she'd suffered pangs of mild embarrassment at the incidents. Now they loomed as monumental evidence of his distress, distress she had ignored with apparently tragic consequences.

Here in the shadows of her room, she could blank out everything but the good memories. The pills the doctor had given her to help her sleep kept her in a blessed state of semiconsciousness. Her mind drifted as the hours passed, recapturing a mental snapshot of Don in the pool with the kids, of Don surprising her on their tenth anniversary with a trip to Paris, of the pride on his face at Emma's college graduation. At first with each image came a fresh flood of tears, hot, scalding, angry tears. Now, though, she remained dry-eyed. Increasingly, especially since her conversation with Emma about her belief that Don's death was, in fact, a suicide, Rosa felt completely dead inside.

The children had given up trying to get her to come to the table for meals. Emma brought breakfast in before she left in the morning. An hour later, Andy took away the tray, the food untouched. Dinners came and went the same way. Rosa was too drained to care about the worried expressions on their faces or about the fact that she hadn't seen Jeff at all and everyone seemed to be avoiding any mention of his name.

How had her life come to this? She was forty-six years old, and for the first time in nearly thirty years, she was on her own. She had always thought of herself as strong and capable, but she didn't think she could bear facing the future alone. If only she could wake up and discover that all of this was nothing more than a terrible nightmare.

When her bedroom door opened, she blinked against the light that spilled into the room, then turned her back on it.

"Mama, you have company," Emma announced, her tone determinedly cheerful as if she were about to deliver unwanted medicine to a reluctant child.

"I don't want to see anyone," Rosa mumbled. "Tell them to call ahead next time."

"No, Rosa, that won't do," Helen said briskly, flipping on lights as she crossed the room. "Jolie and I are here now, and we're not leaving until we've seen you. We brought cheesecake from Henderson's Bakery. It's strawberry, your favorite."

"I'm not hungry," Rosa insisted. That she wasn't

even interested in her very favorite cheesecake spoke volumes about the depths to which her spirits had sunk.

"Well, I don't know how that can be," Jolie said. "Emma says you're not eating enough to keep a bird alive. Emma, can you bring some plates and forks?"

"Of course. Right away," Rosa's traitorous daughter replied.

"Don't bother," Rosa called after her. "Helen and Jolie will be leaving."

"I'll wait a few minutes, then," Emma said, sounding defeated. "Maybe you'll change your mind."

Rosa heard her sigh as she closed the door behind her. Ignoring the wave of guilt that washed over her, Rosa retreated into sullen silence, but neither Helen nor Jolie seemed to be bothered by her attitude. Jolie sat staring at Rosa expectantly. Helen bustled around the room tidying up the piles of magazines Rosa had barely glanced at. Helen even snatched away the pillows on the bed and began to plump them, seemingly unconcerned about Rosa's muttered protest or the fact that she was now awkwardly propped against the headboard.

"Are you quite through?" Rosa inquired tartly. Struggling to sit up, she scowled at her best friends.

Rosa knew that on some level they understood her loss. Helen had lost her husband when he was only forty-six. Jolie had been divorced for more than twenty years and had an active social life that involved flitting from man to man in search of some elusive quality. In general, though, they led rich, fulfilling lives. If they'd been envious of what Rosa had with Don, they'd certainly never shown it. They had both bounced back in a way that Rosa simply could not envision herself doing.

They were also as stubborn as any two mules on the face of the earth. Rosa had known from the instant they walked in tonight that they were out of patience. They were tired of letting her get away with hiding out here in her room. This time they weren't going away until they got whatever they'd come for. She might as well find out what they were after. Maybe then, they'd leave her in peace.

"Why have you two come to pester me?" she inquired testily.

"Because we're your friends and we've been worried sick about you," Jolie said. "You haven't taken our calls. You haven't seen anyone. It's not like you to shut yourself away from the people who love you. I don't care what happened, we're your friends. You should have more faith in us."

Rosa shot a look at Helen, who merely shrugged. "What are you saying? What is it you think you know?" Rosa asked Jolie.

Jolie didn't back down at her angry tone. "There's been some talk—okay, a *lot* of talk—that some people don't think Don's death was an accident."

Rosa covered her face. "Oh, God."

Jolie reached for her hand. "It's okay. We loved him and we loved you. How he died doesn't matter."

"Of course, it matters," Rosa practically shouted.

Helen frowned at her. "If all that talk is right— and we don't know that any of it is—do you think that people are going to think of you differently now? Is it pity you're afraid of? If so, you should be ashamed of yourself. You know us better than that. We love you. We want to help you the way you've

always been there for us. Not only that, we're grieving over Don, too.''

"I am not grieving," Rosa said fiercely. "I hate
him for what he did.''

Jolie gasped at her harsh declaration. "You do
not.''

"Of course, she doesn't," Helen chided. "She
hates that he abandoned her. That's what it is.''

"Don't try to put words in my mouth," Rosa retorted heatedly. "I meant exactly what I said. I hate
him." Her voice caught. "I do. I hate him.''

For a while now she had remained dry-eyed when
the memories crept in. Now the sobs she'd held back
burst forth as if a dam had broken. She drew her
knees up to her chest, wrapped her arms around them
and rocked back and forth.

In an instant her friends were beside her, reaching
out, murmuring comforting words.

"That's it," Helen soothed. "Let it out, Rosa. You
can't begin to heal until you let the pain out. That's
what you told me when my Harrison died.''

"I'm just so furious with him," Rosa whispered
between choked sobs. "How could Don do such a
thing? How could I have missed the signs that things
were that bad with him? There must have been signs.
He was moody and irritable, but we all get that way
sometimes. We don't go out and kill ourselves.''

"We don't know that's what Don did," Helen repeated.

"I'm not blind," Rosa said. "I can't ignore what's
staring me in the face.''

"What if you're right?" Jolie asked. "I've been
reading up on suicide on the Internet. Suicide is a
choice, a selfish one at that. Maybe it's not a rational

choice, but nobody else could make him do it, certainly not you.''

''But if I'd known he was depressed and desperate, I could have stopped him,'' Rosa whispered. That was where the guilt that had tormented her since Don's death came from. She had known Don Killian better than any other human being on earth. Had she been wearing blinders for weeks or even months? How could she not have known he was on the edge of despair? Why hadn't she seen it and done something to prevent what happened? How could she live with the fact that she had let her husband down so badly?

''I don't think so,'' Helen said. ''I've done a little reading, too, and I've talked to some people who know about such things. When someone wants to be stopped, there are warning signs, cries for help, maybe even failed attempts. But when someone's desperate and totally serious, they make sure they do it right the first time.''

Rosa refused to believe that. Don had been her husband, her best friend. If he was desperate, she should have known. How could her own children even bear to look at her, knowing how she had failed both Don and them? Don had always been the provider, the one with the business acumen. She had been the one who kept the family on an even keel. They'd balanced things perfectly. But the one time it had really counted, she'd let the family down. Maybe that was why she'd been hiding out from Emma, Andy and Jeff, because she didn't want to face their censure.

Helen dug in her purse and pulled out a slip of paper and handed it to Rosa.

''What's this?'' she asked without looking at it.

''There's a grief counseling group that meets at

Saint Luke's. I think you should consider going. It's one thing to listen to me and Jolie, but you need to talk to other people who've suffered a huge personal loss.''

''Absolutely not,'' Rosa said emphatically. ''I will not spill my guts to a bunch of total strangers.''

Helen rubbed her back. ''You're forgetting one thing. You have something in common with these strangers. They've all been through what you're going through now. Wouldn't it help to hear their stories, to know you're not alone? My experience isn't the same as yours. Neither is Jolie's. But some of this group will know exactly what you've been going through. They'll understand your fear that Don chose to die. More important, they've faced the loss and they've recovered.''

Rosa shuddered at the prospect of exposing her still-raw wounds to the scrutiny of strangers. ''I can't.''

''You *won't*,'' Jolie corrected, her disapproval plain. ''Rosa, you're my dear friend and I love you, but I thought you were made of tougher stuff than this.''

''Jolie's right,'' Helen said. ''But if you won't do it for yourself, think about Emma and the boys. Maybe they'd like to go. They're suffering, too, you know. Emma's been protecting you from worrying about Jeff and Andy, but it's time you did. You're their mother. You've shut them out, forced them to shoulder the responsibility for the restaurant and to deal with their grief, while trying to hide it from you. The Rosa Killian I know would never do such a thing if she weren't in terrible pain. It's time to get some help. It's time to be strong for your children.''

"They're not children," she said, even though it was a cop-out. She knew how badly Emma, Jeff and Andy were hurting. It didn't matter how old they were, losing their dad had been devastating. And even in her current state of denial, she was aware that Jeff, in particular, was in danger of doing something totally reckless. Maybe he already had, which would explain why Emma and Andy had been avoiding any mention of him.

"Rosa," Helen chided.

"Okay, I'll think about it," she said at last.

Helen and Jolie regarded her with satisfaction, clearly convinced that she would not only think about it, but do it. She probably would, too, at least eventually.

Rosa frowned at them. "Oh, don't look so pleased with yourselves," she grumbled, then called out, "Emma! Get those plates and forks in here. And bring one for yourself. It's time for cheesecake."

And tomorrow maybe, just maybe, it would be time to get back to living, or at least what passed for living in a world that no longer made any sense.

Sunday mornings at Flamingo Diner had always been Emma's favorite time. Her father had made huge cinnamon rolls that filled the place with their sugary scent. Customers, who rushed every other morning, lingered over coffee and their newspapers or stayed to chat with neighbors and catch up on local gossip.

Emma wasn't the baker her father had been, but she was determined she was going to revive this tradition which had been in limbo since her father's death. She arrived at the diner at 5:00 a.m., half-asleep and in desperate need of caffeine. She brewed the first of what would probably be dozens of pots of coffee and read over the recipe, trying to remember her father's tips on making the cinnamon rolls.

She was rolling out the dough when she heard a key in the front door and looked up to see her mother hesitating just outside the door. A smile broke across Emma's face as she went to meet her.

"Mama, you didn't tell me you were coming in this morning."

"I didn't want to say anything in case I changed my mind," Rosa said, finally stepping inside and closing the door behind her. She sniffed the air. "You're making cinnamon rolls."

"I'm *trying* to make cinnamon rolls," Emma corrected. "I'm not so sure if I have the dough right."

Rosa reached for her hand and gave it a squeeze. "Let me take a look."

Emma regarded her with surprise. "I thought Dad did all the baking."

"He did, but it was my mother's recipe. I was making these rolls long before I met him." She studied the dough, sifted a little more flour over it and began to roll it out with sure, steady strokes.

Emma sat back and watched her. "Why did you let Dad take over?"

Her mother's expression turned nostalgic. "Because he enjoyed it so much, and I liked talking to the customers. Over time we learned to divide things up so that we were both happy." A tear spilled down her cheek. "At least I thought we were."

"You were. All those years weren't a lie."

"It feels that way, though."

Emma didn't want her mother to dwell on the sad thoughts. She'd done more than enough of that. She reached for her hand. "I'm glad you're back, Mama. It hasn't been the same around here without you."

Her mother paused, her hands falling idle. A visible shudder washed over her. "I'm not sure I can stay," she whispered. "I heard you leave the house early and thought maybe I could come and help you get set up, you know, before everyone starts coming in."

Emma held back a sigh. It was a start. She reached out and gave her mother a hug. "Stay as long as you can."

Her mother worked in silence for a few more minutes, spreading a coating of melted butter on the dough, then sprinkling a heavy dusting of cinnamon and sugar on top.

Eventually she glanced Emma's way. "I'm sorry I've let you down."

"Oh, Mama, you haven't let us down. I know how hard this must be on you."

"But I'm not alone in being miserable, and I've been acting as if I were. You and the boys are hurting, too. My heart aches for you, but I've been so lost in my own pain, I haven't been able to think about anyone else's. Helen and Jolie told me they were disappointed in me."

"They shouldn't be. You're coping the best way you can. We all are."

Her mother gave her a wry look. "Including Jeff? Do you honestly believe he's coping? I know he hasn't been staying at the house. I've listened for him to come in, but it's been days now, hasn't it?"

Emma hesitated, then nodded.

"Has he been in here to help?"

"No."

Rosa shook her head. "I imagine he's with that girl he's been seeing, Marisol something."

"You've met her?" Emma asked, surprised.

"I've seen her. She usually waits for him in the car, when he stops by here to ask your dad…" Her mother's face fell and her voice faltered. For an instant, she closed her eyes as if steadying herself. "Well, I guess I don't have to worry about that anymore. He knows not to come to me for money, especially when he won't explain what he needs it for."

"I thought you and Dad gave him money for expenses at school. Isn't he expected to earn his own spending money?"

"Of course, he is, just as you were. But Jeff could always get around your father. I think it went back to the days when your father struggled to make ends meet when he was in college and we were dating. He wanted to spare Jeff that. He wanted his whole college experience to be as carefree as possible."

Emma tried to ignore the stirring of resentment. She'd understood the rules when she'd left for college. She'd worked hard for her spending money, grateful that her tuition, room and board and books had been covered. How could Jeff have taken advantage of her father this way?

"I thought Jeff had a job off campus," she said. "What was he doing with that money?"

Her mother shrugged. "I wish I knew," she said as she put the tray of cinnamon rolls into the oven.

As the kitchen filled with their delicious aroma, Emma thought of the hint Matt had dropped that Jeff could be headed for trouble. At the time she'd dismissed the possibility that he could be talking about drugs, but was the idea really so outrageous? Did she dare ask her mother? Or would the mere suggestion that Jeff was involved with drugs be too much for Rosa in her already fragile state?

"Do you think I should ask Matt to look for Jeff?" she asked instead.

Rosa shook her head. "He'll turn up. I know he quit his job at the mall. Or maybe he was fired. I didn't press him about it. If he hasn't been working here, he'll be out of money soon." She went to the sink to wash her hands, then met Emma's gaze. "Don't give your brother a cent unless he earns it. And see that Andy doesn't, either." She dried her hands. "Now I've got to go. You'll be opening soon."

"Are you sure you won't stay, just for a little while?" Emma asked. "People ask about you every day. They'd love to see you."

"Not today, sweetie." Rosa touched her cheek. "Have I told you how grateful I am that you decided to stay? I know you think Washington is your home now, but this is where you belong. I hope you come to realize that one day soon."

"My staying now is not a problem," Emma lied, thinking of how desperately she missed Washington and her job and friends there. She couldn't bring herself to commit to staying forever, not when the promise would be a lie.

"Of course it is," her mother said. "It's a sacrifice and I know it, but it won't be for too much longer, Emma. I promise you."

"I'll be here as long as you need me," Emma reassured her. "And I'll find those answers about Dad before I leave, so we can finally understand what happened."

"You always do the right thing. Your father loved that about you," Rosa told her. "He lost patience with Jeff and Andy, but never with you. From the day you were born, he said you'd never give us a moment's worry and you haven't."

"I left," Emma reminded her. "I know that disappointed him."

"He would have loved it if you'd stayed here, that's true," Rosa said, brushing the hair back from Emma's face as she had a million times when Emma was a girl. "But he was so proud of you for standing up to him, for finding something you loved and going after it. He had Flamingo Diner, so he understood all about fulfilling a dream."

Emma was surprised. "Really?"

"The only thing he really wanted for you was your happiness, wherever that took you. He understood that the diner was his dream, not yours."

"Thank you for saying that. I was so afraid that me being gone was one of the things weighing on him."

"Absolutely not!" Rosa sighed heavily. "I suppose we're all afraid that it was something we did that made him..." she hesitated "...careless," she said at last. She met Emma's gaze. "Helen and Jolie told me about a group at Saint Luke's. It's for those who are grieving a loved one. Would you want to go with me?"

"It might help," Emma conceded without enthusiasm. "Of course, if you need me to, I'll go with you."

Her mother gave her a sad smile. "But you'd rather not, am I right?"

"I don't think that's where I'll find the answers I need," Emma admitted.

"I'm not sure I will either, but I have to start somewhere," Rosa said. "You have a good day, sweetie. I'll see you at home."

Emma pulled her mother into her arms and hugged her tightly, noting that she'd lost weight. She was no longer plump. In fact, she felt almost fragile. "I am so glad you came in this morning, Mama. I'm glad we had a chance to talk."

"Me, too. I was thinking of cooking a special dinner for you and Andy tonight."

Emma thought of her plans with Matt to go to Cori's. She could cancel.

"What?" her mother said. "Do you already have plans?"

"It's not a problem. I can change them."

"Don't you dare. You deserve to have some fun. Maybe Andy and I will go out for pizza. I owe him some undivided attention."

Emma studied her closely. "Are you sure?"

"Absolutely." She grinned. "I'll even wait up so I can sneak a peek at your date."

"It's not a date," Emma protested. "It's Matt."

Her mother looked startled at first, then pleased. "I always thought there was something between the two of you."

"Mama, I told you, it's not a date."

"He's a good man. Your father always liked him."

"That's the thing," Emma explained. "He's part of the family." She wasn't about to mention how she'd momentarily forgotten that when he'd touched her.

Her mother just laughed. "That's how it was with

your father and me, too. My mother and father loved
him before I did. I was in lust,'' she admitted, blush-
ing. ''What I didn't understand at the time was that
they thought he was terrific company for them, but
not marriage material for me.''

''Why?''

''He wasn't Cuban,'' Rosa said simply.

''That's why they never came to visit?'' Emma
asked.

''Yes. They got into the habit of staying away
when we were first married. Even though they mel-
lowed later, the rift was already there. It broke my
heart that we never fully mended it.''

''I always wondered about that,'' Emma said. ''I
loved going to visit Abuela Conchita, but there was
always some sort of tension I didn't understand.''

''Families aren't easy sometimes,'' Rosa said. ''In
many ways, we've been lucky. Your grandmother and
grandfather Killian were here for you for many years,
even though things were once strained between them
and your father. Until now, we haven't suffered any
tragedies. Business has been good. We've been
blessed. It's time I tried to focus on that.''

''We'll make it, Mama. We just have to take one
step at a time. You took a huge one this morning.''

''And now I have to go,'' Rosa said, glancing at
the clock. ''I'm sure Gabe and Harley will be on the
doorstep any minute now. I'm not ready to face
them.''

Emma walked her to the door and watched her until
she reached her car, then waved and went back inside.
She flipped the sign on the door to Open and turned
on the burners on the stove. When she had bacon and

sausage sizzling, she took the first batch of cinnamon rolls from the oven and put in another tray.

When the door opened for the first customer, she turned, expecting to see Gabe and Harley, but it was Matt who stood there, freshly showered and sexy as sin in a tight T-shirt and jeans.

"I called Andy and told him to sleep in this morning," he said. "I told him I'd help out in here."

Emma couldn't seem to tear her gaze away from him. "Why did you do that?"

"I had a hunch you were going to start baking cinnamon rolls this morning, and I figured you'd give me one free if I helped out."

Emma bit back a smile. "Things must be tough if you can't afford to buy your own breakfast."

"Oh, I could pay," he told her, moving closer, crowding her just a little. "But I thought it might be a lot more fun trying to coax one of those sinful rolls away from you."

Her breath hitched. "Oh?"

His thumb touched the corner of her mouth. "You have a little bit of sugar right here. Have you been sneaking samples?"

Emma grinned. "Of course. What's wrong with that? Isn't that exactly what you're hoping to do?"

"Um-hmm," he murmured, his gaze steady and disconcerting.

"The cinnamon rolls are on the counter," she whispered.

"I know, but I thought I'd start here," he said, touching his lips to the corner of her mouth. "And I'm pretty sure I saw a little bit of sugar over here." His tongue flicked lightly against her lower lip.

"Matt?" His name barely squeezed past the giant boulder suddenly lodged in her throat.

"Hmm?"

"What are you doing?"

"Sweetheart, if you don't know, I must not be doing it right."

"But why?"

"Because I woke up this morning with you on my mind."

She stared into the depths of his eyes and swallowed hard at the desire she saw there. "Oh."

He laughed. "Oh, indeed."

The door opened just then and Harley and Gabe came in, already bickering. They fell silent the instant they spotted Emma in Matt's arms.

"Well, will you look at that?" Gabe muttered.

"About time," Harley said.

"Ain't that the truth," Gabe said.

Matt winked at Emma. "Guess I'd better get to work. I'm pretty sure the bacon's burning."

Emma blinked and sniffed the air. Sure enough, she could smell it. Matt was already heading off to handle the problem, which left her to face Gabe and Harley and their knowing smirks.

She picked up two mugs and the pot of coffee and headed their way. "One word and this can be on top of you, instead of in your cups, okay?"

"My lips are zipped," Gabe said, still smirking.

"Mine, too," Harley agreed. "Long as you know that we approve."

"There is nothing for you to approve of," Emma said. "What you saw, or think you saw, was nothing."

"Whatever you say," Gabe said, giving Harley a sharp poke in the ribs.

"Yeah, Emma, whatever you say."

She gave the two old busybodies a satisfied look, then marched back behind the counter and tried to catch her breath. It took everything in her to keep from touching a finger to her lips, where she could still feel the sensation of Matt's mouth, warm and gentle against hers. She'd always thought of Winter Cove as a boring little place where nothing happened, but all of a sudden that image was changing. Her life, at least, was getting damned complicated.

12

Matt wasn't sure what had gotten into him that morning. Okay, he'd awakened fully aroused with Emma very much on his mind, but that wasn't an entirely new experience. Never before had he gone over to Flamingo Diner and kissed her just because he felt like it. He wouldn't have dared to as long as Don was alive. Was he taking advantage of his friend's death in a way that was totally inappropriate? Maybe.

He had to admit, though, that he had no regrets. Emma hadn't exactly kissed him back, but she hadn't slapped him silly, either. He wouldn't have blamed her if she had. Instead, though, he'd managed to put some color into her too pale cheeks. Maybe tonight, after dinner at Cori's, he'd see what he could do about bringing that color back. He recalled her claim of having once been attracted to bad boys. Perhaps it was time he showed her that he had a dangerous side of his own.

Assuming she gave him the chance. He glanced toward the passenger seat and noted that Emma was staring straight ahead, her spine so rigid it looked as if she had a yardstick running up her back. She looked unyielding and pretty much as if she were biting her tongue. He figured holding in all that anger couldn't be healthy.

"Okay, go ahead and spit it out," he said.

She scowled at him. "I have no idea what you're talking about."

"You're still ticked off about that kiss this morning." He studied her intently. "Or are you only upset that Gabe and Harley walked in before it could go any further?"

"Go to hell," she retorted.

Matt laughed. "There you go, Emma," he said approvingly. "Say what's on your mind."

"Okay, then, why did you kiss me this morning and then go running off before I had a chance to tell you what a pig I thought you were? What gave you the right to come into my place of business and kiss me where anyone could see? You know how people in this town love to talk. Gabe and Harley won't keep their mouths shut. You know they won't."

"So? It was a kiss, Emma, a tiny little peck at that. I didn't have you sprawled across the counter."

A riot of color bloomed in her cheeks. "Thank heaven for that."

"I'm not saying there won't come a day when I go for that," he warned her, his gaze steady. "I've decided I've been patient long enough. I'm going after what I want and what I want is you."

She stared at him with obvious shock. "Don't you dare even think about it," she said heatedly. "Matt, nothing can happen between us."

Irritated by her certainty, he pulled off the highway, cut the engine and turned to look at her, barely managing to keep a tight rein on his temper. "Because you don't want it to, or because you do?"

She opened her mouth to reply, then snapped it shut again.

He stroked a finger down her cheek, felt the quick rise of heat, saw the shudder that washed over her. "Tell the truth, Emma."

Frowning, she met his gaze. "Okay, you're right. Maybe I am attracted to you, but I don't want to be, and you shouldn't want me to be, either," she insisted. "Everything's such a mess. I'm not thinking straight. Why start something when it's doomed?"

"How about because we're two consenting adults, who are perfectly capable of keeping things in perspective? I've wanted you for a long time, Emma. Since we were teenagers, in fact. And now I think you want me. The signs are there, in the way you look at me, in the way you touch me." He looked into her eyes. "Tell the truth, am I misreading anything?"

She regarded him miserably. "No."

Relief flooded through him, despite how obviously unhappy she was about her feelings for him. "Okay, then."

"Matt, I need you to be my friend," she said plaintively.

He regarded her with surprise. "This doesn't change anything," he reassured her. "I will always be your friend. That's a given."

"No, that's impossible. Sex always changes things between a man and a woman."

"Not with us," he insisted. "I'm not going to stop being your friend, not ever. And I'm not going to rush you about the rest. If it's meant to be, it'll happen. I'm just giving you fair warning about where my head is."

She gave him a familiar wry look. "As if your head has anything at all to do with this."

He grinned. "Yeah, well, I did consult it."

"And?"

"It didn't have anything important to add to the discussion."

She laughed then, breaking the sizzling tension between them. But when he touched her again, just a light stroke of his knuckle along her jaw, the laughter died and the tension came back.

"Fair warning, okay?" he said.

She nodded slowly. "Fair warning."

"Now I'd better get to Cori's before dinner gets cold. I hear pregnant women lose their sense of humor somewhere around the third trimester."

"Aren't you being a little sexist?" Emma asked.

"I'm being a lot sexist," Matt conceded. "But some things are fact, and that's one of them. You'll see one of these days."

She regarded him with a startled look, as if the prospect of having a child had never once occurred to her.

"You are planning to have children, aren't you?" he asked.

"I guess I've been so busy I haven't given it much thought," she admitted.

"Then you're obviously not involved with anyone who's making you think about happily-ever-after," Matt said, barely able to contain the note of glee threatening to creep into his voice. He didn't want her to hear him gloating.

"No, I'm not." She ventured a glance in his direction. "What about you? Do you want kids?"

"Three or four, at least," he said, surprising himself. He'd always figured he was lousy father material given his own father's lack of skill in that department. But since Emma had come home, he'd begun to dream. He was pretty sure he was willing to risk it, since any kids would have her to make up for his shortcomings. And he had had Don as an example for a lot of years. Until recently, he would have said that could make up for any bad traits he'd inherited from his own father.

He grinned at her suddenly wary expression. "Don't look so panicked. Maybe we should both remain noncommittal until we get through this evening. I hear Cori's first two kids are spoiled brats."

Emma regarded him with obvious surprise. "This isn't her first?"

"Nope, her third. And because she and her husband both work, they tend to give the kids whatever they want to make up for the lack of attention."

"Do you see much of them?"

"Not really."

"Then how do you know all this?"

He hesitated, trying to decide if he should admit that there had been a brief time when he and Jennifer Sawyer had spent time with the Fletchers. He doubted Cori would bring it up. She was too eagerly pursuing this little matchmaking plan. He concluded that bringing it up himself would only muddy the waters between them. He settled for another part of the truth. "They used to come in Flamingo Diner every Sunday morning. The kids ran wild, while Cori made a pretense of trying to contain them."

"What about her husband?"

"He read the paper and ignored them."

"They haven't been in recently," Emma said.

"Because the last time they were there, one of the regulars told them they should leave the kids at home unless they could keep them under control. They left in a huff."

"I'm amazed Mama didn't step in and try to smooth things over," Emma said.

"If you ask me, your mother's the one behind the suggestion. It was Jolie who made it, and she didn't look one bit sorry after the words left her mouth. She even took a little bow when the cheers went up after Cori and her family took off and peace once again reigned."

"I had no idea," Emma murmured. "Maybe we'd better check the food for arsenic tonight."

Matt grinned. "Only if she offers you a doggie bag to take home to your mother."

After what Matt had told her to expect, Emma was pleasantly surprised by Cori's family. The children were on their best behavior, offering polite responses to questions and behaving with impeccable manners at the dinner table.

After the meal, Emma followed Cori into the kitchen to help with the dishes.

"The food was wonderful," she told her old friend. "You've become a fabulous cook."

"At least I have a more diverse repertoire than the hot dogs and hamburgers I used to specialize in for all our parties back in high school."

"You seem really happy."

Cori smiled, her hand resting on her huge belly. "I am. I love my husband and lately I actually love my kids. I owe your mom and Jolie for that. I kept trying to pretend that they weren't turning into little hellions, but Jolie called me on it. I haven't taken 'em out to eat in public since, and we've been working on the behavior problems. They're both hyperactive, but I don't want to resort to medicine to keep them under control.''

"They were angels tonight, so whatever you've been doing has worked."

"We still have good days and bad, but they're really good kids at heart. Maybe if I weren't working, it would help, but I love working for Jennifer, or at least I did until lately, and we need the money. I've just stopped using that as a cop-out for not spending time with the kids. The truth was, I didn't enjoy it, so I didn't do it, and things went from bad to worse. Now I'm working hard to make sure they know I love them.''

She looked Emma in the eye. "Enough about me. What's going on with you and Matt?"

"We're friends," Emma said.

"A good place to start," Cori said, grinning as if she didn't believe for a second that that's all it was. "But there's enough electricity in the air when you two are in a room to light all of Winter Cove during the holidays, and you do know how we love to decorate around here.''

"I can't think about any of that right now," Emma said, repeating what she'd told Matt in the car.

"Maybe it shouldn't be about thinking."

Cori's words echoed in Emma's head as she and Matt drove home a short time later. It wasn't the first time she'd been reminded that Matt could make her feel alive. Would it be so wrong to let him? Would it be so terrible to spend a few hours in the arms of a man who made her feel attractive and sexy and desirable?

She'd been reminded all too vividly lately that life could be short and unpredictable.

"I can practically hear the wheels turning in your head," Matt said, glancing at her as he pulled to a stop in front of her house. "What's on your mind?"

"Cori said something earlier, something that made me take a fresh look at things."

"Oh?"

"She said I think too much."

"About?"

"You and me."

"I see," he said softly. He reached for her hand and brought it to his lips. "Anytime you want to stop thinking, just say the word. My place is only a few miles away."

Was that what she wanted? To go home with Matt? She'd never slept with a man simply for the pleasure of it. In fact, the pitiful truth was, she'd slept with only two men, because she'd always believed that making love should be reserved for someone who truly meant something. Ironically, Matt probably meant more to her than either of the men she'd convinced herself she loved. He'd been in her life longer, too, and in recent weeks he'd proved himself to be steady and dependable, unlike either of the lousy choices she'd made in the past.

If she had to think this hard, though, could it possibly be right? Both of her prior relationships had developed out of some sort of spontaneous combustion the first time she'd met the men. She might not have slept with them right away, but she'd known it was inevitable from the first instant she'd looked into their eyes.

When she looked into Matt's eyes, she felt a kind of longing, a sense that there was something wonderful awaiting them. It was quieter, less intense, but it held the promise that it would last, rather than burning itself out.

In the end, maybe that was what scared her the most, the possibility that she and Matt might find something so deep, so irresistible that she would never escape Winter Cove again.

She lifted her gaze to meet Matt's. "I wish this were easier."

"It would be, if you'd turn off your brain," he teased. "Then again, I don't want you to do something you'll wind up regretting. I'm a patient man, and you're worth waiting for." He released the hand he'd been holding and put both of his hands on the steering wheel, as if to prevent himself from reaching for her.

"I should go in," she said. "There's a light on in her room, so Mama's probably waiting up."

Matt nodded. "I'll walk you to the door."

Even as she protested, he was around the car and opening her door. He took her hand to help her out, then pulled her toward him.

"One last thing," he murmured, covering her mouth with his.

Emma let herself drift into the kiss, let it take over her senses. If the kiss in the diner had riled her, this one overwhelmed her. Matt definitely knew how to take a simple good-night kiss and turn it into something spectacular, she thought in the one instant before her senses scrambled and her mind shut down completely.

When he pulled away eventually, she was thoroughly shaken. He rubbed a thumb across her lower lip, sending sweet little waves of desire washing over her.

He put his hand at the base of her spine and steered her toward the front door on unsteady legs.

"Good night, Emma."

Still dazed, she merely nodded.

"See you in the morning."

"Uh-huh."

"Lock the door when you go inside."

"Uh, sure."

He laughed, looking downright pleased with the fact that he'd rendered her all but speechless.

Emma stepped into the foyer at last, then watched as Matt strode back to his car, whistling an annoyingly cheery little tune.

So much for quiet longing, she thought as he drove away. Once he put his mind to it, Matt's kisses packed enough heat to spontaneously combust and burn down everything between here and Orlando. If she didn't watch her step, she was going to go up in flames, too.

When she heard the car, Rosa went to the bedroom window hoping to see Jeff coming home at last. Instead, she caught a glimpse of Matt kissing her daughter as if there were no tomorrow. She couldn't help grinning, even as she felt a vague trace of envy that Emma was just starting out on a romantic adventure, while her own days of romance were over.

Matt was a good man, and he'd been in love with

Emma forever. Nothing would please her more than to see the two of them finally together, especially if it would keep Emma here in Winter Cove. She knew this was the last place Emma wanted to be, but she'd never really given it a chance as an adult. Maybe Matt could strip the blinders off and make her daughter see all that the town had to offer.

If only that had happened sooner, she thought as she listened to Emma start up the stairs. Maybe having Emma home again would have been enough to give Don a reason for living. She, Jeff and Andy hadn't been enough, but his daughter had always held a special place in his heart.

Emma tapped lightly on Rosa's door. "Mama, are you still awake?"

"Come in," she called out, moving away from the window, so Emma wouldn't guess how much she'd seen. She noted the flushed cheeks and bright eyes, though. They would have been a dead giveaway, even if she'd missed the actual kiss. "Did you have a good time?"

"I really enjoyed Cori and her kids," Emma said.

Rosa raised an eyebrow. "Really?"

Emma laughed. "You probably wouldn't recognize them now. Apparently, Cori took Jolie's criticism to heart. They both behaved like little angels all during dinner."

"And here I'd given up on miracles," Rosa said.

"I told her to bring them back to the diner next Sunday. Maybe you can come by and see for yourself."

"We'll see," she said evasively. "How is Matt? You should have invited him in."

The flush in Emma's cheeks deepened. "He, um, had to go."

"Too bad."

Emma gave her a searching look, then groaned. "You saw the kiss, didn't you?"

Rosa chuckled. "I wasn't spying on you, I swear, but yes, I saw it. Looked pretty intense from up here."

"It felt pretty intense down there." She regarded Rosa with confusion. "Who would have thought it?"

"Any female with her libido intact," Rosa retorted dryly. "Matthew is considered quite a catch in Winter Cove. Haven't you noticed that the clientele at the diner is running heavily toward single women in their twenties these days, especially around 7:00 a.m. when he's usually in there? Not that he's ever anything but casually friendly toward any of them. Matt's a single-minded kind of guy."

Emma regarded her curiously. "Meaning?"

"I don't think he's ever had eyes for anyone but you. Not that he doesn't flirt from time to time and there was one woman he went out with a few times, but his heart's been yours forever."

"I always knew he had a little bit of a crush on me," Emma admitted. "Are you saying you think it's serious?"

"That kiss looked pretty serious to me."

Emma held up her hands and backed toward the door. "No, I can't think about that. A fling might be one thing, but anything more, no."

"Emma, wait!" Rosa commanded.

Her daughter stopped in the doorway.

"Whatever you do, don't use him just to get through a difficult time. Matt doesn't deserve that."

Emma sighed, looking guilty. "I won't, Mama. I guess that's why I didn't go home with him tonight, even though a part of me wanted to."

"People do a lot of crazy things at a time like this. Just look at Jeff and that girl. I know he's turned to her, even though I can't imagine anyone more unsuitable. There's nothing wrong about reaching out for a little comfort, not for him or for you," Rosa told her. "In your case, though, the important thing is to be totally honest, with Matt and with yourself."

"I'm trying to be," Emma assured her.

"I know you are. You're too kindhearted to do anything else. So is Matt."

She felt somewhat reassured as Emma went off to bed. Things would turn out okay for her daughter. At least maybe Rosa could protect her from having her heart broken. One broken heart in the house these days was already one too many.

Jeff's girlfriend had blue hair, a pierced nose and a tattoo on her arm. Her jeans were two sizes too big, her tank top too small, exposing a wide band of flesh at her waistline. Emma could hardly take her eyes off of the girl. What on earth had she been thinking? Or had Jeff simply brought her into the diner first thing Monday morning for the shock value, knowing that Emma would be appalled?

More than likely, that was exactly it. She glanced in his direction, caught the defiant stance, the challenging glare in his expression. Emma kept her own gaze steady and vowed she would be polite, even if she choked on every word.

"So, Marisol, where are you from?"

"California, you know, the Valley. But I've got a

great-grandpop who lives here in Winter Cove. That's why I came to Florida to go to college, so I could spend some time with him, you know, before he dies."

Emma's head reeled. This was a Valley girl? Times surely had changed from the days when they were perky, perfect cheerleaders with blond hair and empty heads, Emma thought. Though she wasn't quite prepared to label this girl completely empty-headed just yet.

"Do you go to school with Jeff?" she asked, as the girl slouched on a stool at the counter, oblivious to the stares of the other Flamingo Diner patrons.

"Uh-huh," she replied, snapping a wad of bubble gum.

"What's your major?"

"Like Jeff, I was going to do the business thing, till I figured out that it's all a bunch of capitalist bullshit. American business is destroying the world."

Emma bit back the sharp response that popped into her head. "Oh, how is that?"

"This globalization stuff sucks, you know what I mean?" Marisol said, looking as bored as if she were trying to explain the obvious art of tying shoelaces to a two-year-old.

"No, I can't say that I know what you mean," Emma said. "Why don't you explain it to me?"

Marisol blinked. "Now?"

Emma propped her elbows on the counter and looked the girl straight in the eye. "Why not?"

"Because it's, like, way too complicated, that's why."

"Let me guess, though. You've been involved in

those protest marches where everything gets reduced to three or four words on a poster, right?''

''Sure. Those people get it.''

Emma looked at Jeff. ''Do you get it?''

He shrugged.

''I didn't think so,'' Emma said wryly, then gave up the battle before she antagonized both of them. ''What can I get the two of you for breakfast, assuming you don't mind eating food from American farmers and prepared by an American capitalist?''

The girl blinked rapidly. ''Are you, like, making fun of me?''

''Absolutely not,'' Emma said. ''So, what's it going to be? Egg? Pancakes? French toast? Jeff, are you having your usual?''

''French toast,'' he said, sliding onto the stool next to the girl's. ''A double order.''

''I'll have what he's having,'' Marisol said.

Emma barely resisted the desire to explain that the toast wasn't really from France, but decided she'd already pushed the boundaries of polite conversation. She was all for kids being passionate and outspoken about issues, but it would be nice if they actually understood those issues.

She turned away to place the order with Andy, who seemed far happier working the grill than waiting tables. Then she grabbed the coffeepot to make her rounds of the tables, where at least half the customers avoided making eye contact, probably for fear they'd burst out laughing at Jeff's idea of the perfect date.

Helen snagged her hand as she passed by. ''Your mother would have heart failure if she were in here right now,'' she told Emma in a hushed voice.

''I believe Mama has already gotten an eyeful of

Marisol," Emma said. "Maybe that's the real reason she's been hiding out at the house."

Helen chuckled. "At least it's not serious between that girl and Jeff, right?"

"Lord, I hope not," Emma said. "I can assure you that I intend to corner him and ask just that before he takes off with her again."

"Careful," Helen warned. "He's at that impulsive, rebellious age. If you act too scandalized, he'll probably elope with her just to prove he's his own man."

Wouldn't that be a fine addition to the family tree? Emma thought, then chided herself for making a snap judgment based on a very brief meeting.

She left the two of them alone at the counter until they'd finished their breakfast. Marisol chattered incessantly. Jeff looked sullen and bored. Emma had to brace herself to approach them and interrupt their fun time.

"Jeff, are you planning to go by the house to see Mama?"

He looked shocked that she'd ask. "No way."

"Do you expect to come back here to help out anytime soon?"

He flushed at that. "Looks like you and Andy have things covered."

"Barely," she said tightly. "And I have an appointment this afternoon at three. I'd appreciate it if you could be here at two to help Andy close up."

He seemed startled by her stern tone. Without glancing at Marisol, he nodded. "Yeah, sure. I can come by for an hour or so."

Emma looked at his too dull complexion and into his too bright eyes and knew that he'd probably forget between now and then. "Is there a number where I can reach you?"

"Mari's got her cell. You could call that, I guess," he said grudgingly. "Is that okay with you, Mari?"

The girl shrugged. "Whatever."

Jeff gave Emma the number. "You don't need to call, though. I won't forget."

"Okay, then," she said quietly. "I'm counting on you."

"All right, all right, I get it," he said, grabbing Marisol's hand and half dragging her toward the door.

Emma watched them go, her gut twisting into knots. If her brother wasn't high now, he had been very recently. Odds were good, he would be again.

And she had absolutely no idea how to help him.

13

Emma was almost frighteningly pale and quiet when Matt went by the diner to pick her up for the their meeting with Jennifer Sawyer. He'd heard about her confrontation with Jeff that morning and wasn't the least bit surprised to see that the kid hadn't come back to help out as promised. If he ever had the chance, he intended to try once again to explain to him what it took to be a real man.

"You okay?" he asked Emma.

She gave him a wan smile. "I've had better days."

"I heard about Jeff and his girlfriend stopping by."

"I'm not surprised. You don't see girls like that on every street corner here in Winter Cove. Her appearance was the talk of the diner."

"That was mentioned, but what most people were concerned about was Jeff being belligerent and giving you a really hard time."

"Yeah, there was that, too," she said, sounding defeated. "I don't know what to do about him."

"Have you told your mother he's out of control?"

"Actually, I think she knows, but she's as much at a loss as I am. I don't think she can cope with anything besides her own grief right now." She held out a piece of paper. "At least now I have a phone number where I can reach him in an emergency."

"Give it to me," Matt said, taking out his cell phone and punching in the numbers before she could protest. When a spacey-sounding girl answered, he said, "Let me talk to Jeff."

"Who is this? Emma?" Jeff demanded when he came on the line. "Stop bugging me, sis."

"This isn't your sister. This is your worst nightmare," Matt said, trusting Jeff to pick up on his identity. "You promised Emma you'd be at the diner at two. Where the hell are you?"

"I got tied up," Jeff replied, sounding a little less belligerent and a lot less sure of himself.

"Well, get untied and get over here," Matt said. "You've been slacking off long enough. Emma and Andy are leaving with me now. When they get here in the morning, this place better shine from top to bottom."

"Hire a damn cleaning crew," Jeff retorted.

"That would be you," Matt told him. "And lose the drugs before you get here, because if I so much as get a hint that you have 'em on you, you're going down. Am I clear?"

He heard a startled gasp, then the soft click as the phone cut off. When he met Emma's gaze, she was obviously shaken.

"You know about the drugs?" she asked. "I thought you believed it was just a threat."

"It's more than that, Emma. I haven't seen him light up or pop a pill, but I've seen all the signs that he's using," Matt confirmed. "And if I wasn't sure of it before, I am now. He definitely wasn't expecting me to call him on it. Hopefully, the fact that I did will scare the hell out of him. Until now he's probably thought he had it under control, that he was pulling the wool over everyone's eyes.''

''I just don't understand,'' Emma said. ''He knows better than to use drugs. Dad taught us that from the time we were old enough to understand.''

''And your father's gone now,'' Matt responded quietly. ''What better way for Jeff to rebel than to do something totally self-destructive that he knows would have hurt your father?''

''But the real person he's hurting is himself,'' Emma said.

''You and I can see that. He can't. I sure as hell couldn't when I was his age.''

''You used drugs?'' she asked, clearly shocked.

''I experimented once. Your dad caught me with a marijuana joint and read me the riot act. He was so damn disappointed in me. I think that's what really did it. I never wanted to see that look in his eyes again.''

''Do you think you'll have the same impact on Jeff? Will he show up?'' Emma asked.

''If he's half as sensible now as he was when he was a kid, he will,'' Matt said grimly. ''I'm not joking around, Emma. I've cut him some slack in the past because of your folks and lately because of the situation, but I haven't been doing him any favors. He needs to wake up and understand that there are consequences.''

Matt turned to Andy, who was listening, wide-eyed, to the entire exchange. ''Come on, kid. We'll drop you at the house.''

''I could stay here and help Jeff,'' he offered, his brow knit with worry.

''No,'' Emma said flatly even before Matt could.

"You need time off, too. Doesn't football practice start soon? You should be getting in shape. When was the last time you went for a run?"

"I told you before, I don't have to play," Andy said, his expression earnest. "Really, Emma, it's no big deal."

Emma ruffled his hair. "And I told you before, that while I'm here, I intend to come to every game and cheer like crazy. You'd better be on the field making the kind of big plays Dad was always bragging about."

Andy's eyes immediately filled with tears. "How can I?" he asked, his voice choked. "I always counted on Dad to be there."

Matt gave the boy's shoulder a squeeze. "He'll still be there," he told him gently. "Your dad would never miss one of your games." He grinned. "And now he'll be able to whisper in your ear and tell you where the holes are in the defense."

Andy chuckled as Matt had hoped he would. Matt met his gaze. "It's going to be okay, you know. You'll get your college scholarship. Jeff will get straightened out. Your mom will be her old self. And Emma will go back to Washington, if that's what she wants."

"I guess," Andy said doubtfully. He looked at Emma. "Maybe you're right. Maybe I should jog home. The run will do me good."

She brushed his cowlick out of his eyes. "You do that. I'll see you later."

"Where are you guys going?" Andy asked as he laced his sneakers more snugly.

"To see a friend," Matt replied.

"We won't be long," Emma added. "If you beat

us home, tell Mama I'll be there in time to make dinner.''

"Am I invited?" Matt inquired hopefully.

"I'm not sure if we have enough food in the house for a bottomless pit, but yes, you're invited," she said.

They were all heading for the door when Jeff rolled up, alone. He avoided meeting Matt's gaze and looked at his sister.

"Sorry, Emma," he said, sounding almost sincere.

"No problem," she told him.

"Emma's fixing dinner tonight," Andy chimed in. "Can you come by the house when you finish here?"

Jeff looked from his brother to Emma and then to Matt. "Sure," he said at last, as if reaching a decision on where his best interests lay.

Matt gave him an approving nod. "We'll see you later, then."

Jeff's arrival and his concession to come for dinner weren't much, but the relief in Emma's eyes made Matt glad he'd forced the issue. He had a hunch that Jeff had a long and difficult road to go before he got his act together. Rosa needed to step in and play hard-ball with him, but as long as she wasn't up to it, Matt would do what he could. In the end, though, it might take all of them together to make Jeff see that he was in danger of ruining his life.

Rosa almost missed the light tap on her front door. Most people rang the bell. She hesitated at the bottom of the stairs, not sure she was ready to face whoever was on the other side of that door. She'd grown too comfortable letting Emma run interference for her.

Then she thought of just how much she'd left to

her daughter to handle. Emma had stepped in and taken over too many responsibilities that should have been Rosa's. It was time Rosa started taking a few of them back.

Drawing in a deep breath, she opened the door and found Sylvia on the steps, a covered cake dish in her hands.

"This is a first, you coming here without Helen and Jolie right on your heels," Rosa said, smiling at her. "Or are they on their way?"

"No, it's just me. I brought another cheesecake." She met Rosa's gaze. "It's a bribe, actually."

"Oh?" Rosa said, eyeing the cake warily. "Come on in and tell me what you're after. A donation of some kind? I will not cochair another fundraiser, not in a million years, so you can forget that."

Sylvia grinned. "I don't want your money or even your time, at least not that way."

"Oh?"

"I want you to go with me to Saint Luke's."

Rosa felt her heart constrict. "You want me to go to that survivor's group," she said flatly.

Sylvia nodded. "Helen told me about it and..." She looked uncomfortable. "I hope you don't mind, but she said why she and Jolie want you to go, you know, because of Don. I agree with them and, well, I thought it might be easier the first time if you didn't have to go alone."

"I told Helen and Jolie—"

"I know what you told them," Sylvia said, regarding her earnestly. "But you need this, Rosa. Helen and Jolie won't push you to go, but I will. The meeting is in a half hour, so we don't have much time."

Rosa couldn't have been more surprised if Sylvia

If offer card is missing write to: The Best of the Best, 3010 Walden Ave., P.O. Box 1867, Buffalo NY 14240-1867

NO POSTAGE
NECESSARY
IF MAILED
IN THE
UNITED STATES

BUSINESS REPLY MAIL
FIRST-CLASS MAIL   PERMIT NO. 717-003   BUFFALO, NY

POSTAGE WILL BE PAID BY ADDRESSEE

THE BEST OF THE BEST
3010 WALDEN AVE
PO BOX 1867
BUFFALO NY 14240-9952

MIRA® BOOKS,

The Brightest Stars in Fiction, presents

The Best of the Best™

Superb collector's editions of the very best books by some of today's best-known authors!

2 FREE BOOKS

and a FREE GIFT!

YES! I have scratched off the gold star to reveal my prize. Please send me the 2 FREE *"The Best of the Best"* books and FREE gift for which I qualify. I understand that I am under no obligation to purchase anything further, as explained on the back of this card.

▲ Scratch off the gold star to reveal your prize!

385 MDL DRST   **185 MDL DRSP**

FIRST NAME   LAST NAME

ADDRESS

APT.#   CITY

STATE/PROV.   ZIP/POSTAL CODE

Visit us online at **www.mirabooks.com**

® and ™ are trademarks of Harlequin Enterprises Limited. ©2002 MIRA BOOKS

DETACH AND MAIL CARD TODAY!

had come over announcing that she intended to run for mayor. She was a wonderful friend, always the first one to pitch in and help, but she wasn't aggressive. Rosa blamed that on her overbearing husband. Frank wasn't abusive, but he was a control freak and Sylvia's meekness made her life easier.

"I know you all think I'm weak because I don't fight with Frank over every little thing," Sylvia said, as if she'd read Rosa's mind. "But the truth is, I pick my battles, and the ones I pick, I win."

"And you've decided that it's worth fighting with me over this?" Rosa guessed.

Sylvia beamed at her. "Exactly."

Maybe it was because she was so startled by Sylvia's determination, or maybe it was because in her heart she knew her friend was right, but Rosa finally nodded. "I'll get my purse."

She started away, then turned back and squeezed Sylvia's hand. "You're a good friend and I love you. I hope you know that."

"Well, of course, I do," Sylvia said, her cheeks pink. "You have no idea how much you, Jolie and Helen mean to me, too. I love my husband, I really do, but it's different with a man. They're just not wired the way we are."

Rosa grinned. "Tell me about it," she said as she went to get her purse.

Sylvia was silent on the ride to Saint Luke's. The big Spanish-style stucco Catholic church with its red-tile roof sat on a low-rise overlooking the lake. A separate building housed classrooms for elementary school children and another building had meeting rooms for Sunday school classes and the adult education programs the church offered. The grounds were

well tended and filled with blooming hibiscus and
bougainvillea, which added bright splashes of pink
and purple.

It was a serene setting that Rosa had always found
to be the perfect counterpoint to the hectic rush of her
life. This, though, was the first time she'd come here
since Don's death. Even now, she wasn't sure she was
ready for an encounter with the priest. In fact, given
his stance on the subject of suicide, she was almost
surprised he even permitted survivors to join the
grief-counseling group on the premises.

"Sylvia, who runs this group? Not Father Gregory,
I hope."

"Hardly. No, it's a psychologist. I spoke to her
yesterday and told her I was planning to bring you
today. She seems very nice."

Rosa nodded, relieved that she wouldn't be facing
the priest today.

When they reached the meeting room, Sylvia hesitated. "I should let you go in alone. I don't belong
here. I can take a walk and meet you later at the car."

"No, please," Rosa said. "Come with me, just this
once. I can't walk in there alone."

"Of course, you can," Sylvia argued, then relented. "But I will come this time, if it will make it
easier."

There were fewer than a dozen people gathered
around a coffeepot when they went inside. An attractive dark-haired woman in her forties separated herself from the others and came toward them. "Which
one of you is Sylvia?" she asked, smiling.

"I am. And this is my friend, Rosa."

"Welcome." She held out her hand, clasping
Rosa's just a second longer as if to reassure her that

everything would be okay. "I'm Anne Porter. I'm the psychologist and the only one here who uses a last name. We try to give each other at least an illusion of privacy, though Winter Cove is small enough that some of our participants do know each other outside of this room. What we say in here goes no further, though. That's the one and only rule we have."

Rosa nodded, relieved to know that these people, at least, weren't likely to be gossiping about her behind her back.

Anne gave her a reassuring smile, then clapped her hands. "Everyone have coffee? Then let's get started."

The group gathered in a small circle, four women, two men and a teenaged girl, not much older than Andy. Rosa and Sylvia added their chairs to the circle.

Anne glanced at Rosa and Sylvia to include them. "We go around the circle and everyone talks about whatever's on their mind, whether it's a hurdle they've finally been able to overcome or a problem they encountered," she explained. "If you don't feel like talking, that's okay, though we do encourage everyone to speak. Everyone here is at a different stage in the grief process. Since Rosa is new, would each of you tell her a little bit about yourselves and your situation, when it's your turn? Okay, then, who wants to start?"

"I will," a woman who appeared to be in her late twenties said. "I'm Nancy, and I'm here because my mother committed suicide six months and fifteen days ago."

To Rosa's surprise, Nancy had managed to get the horrible words out without a hitch in her voice.

She gave Rosa an understanding look. "You have no idea how long it took me to be able to say that without bursting into tears. Not a day goes by that I don't miss her. And for a long time, not a day went by when I didn't hate her for leaving me and my sisters and her grandchildren too soon. You see, she had cancer and she thought she was sparing us all the suffering. That's what she said in her note. She had no idea that we would have given anything for just one more day with her. My sister Ellen still hasn't forgiven her because she didn't even wait long enough for Ellen's baby to be born. She said in her note she didn't want to spoil that happy time for my sister, but, you see, she did it, anyway."

"I'm sorry," Rosa whispered, suddenly overwhelmed by all the things that Don was going to miss…weddings, grandchildren, baptisms, holidays.

"So am I," Nancy said. "I understand why she did what she did, even though I hate it. I'm working on forgiveness now, but I'm not there yet."

"You will be," Anne reassured her. "Who's next?"

One of the men raised his hand, looking uncomfortable. "I suppose I will." He glanced at Rosa with dark, haunted eyes, then looked down at the floor. "I'm Larry. My wife died in an accident." He sighed heavily. "Only the police don't really believe it was an accident. The official version is that she deliberately drove into a canal. There were witnesses who saw it happen and the medical examiner concurs. He says she didn't have a stroke or a heart attack or any other discernible medical emergency."

His words hit Rosa with the force of a sledgehammer. It was all she could do not to gasp with recognition as he described the awful uncertainty over his wife's death.

He hesitated, his expression shattered. "If what they say is true, it's my fault. I'd told her that morning that I was leaving her for another woman."

This time Rosa's gasp of dismay escaped. She understood his guilt all too well, had been living with the torment of believing herself responsible for Don's decision.

"Larry, it was not your fault," Anne said firmly, turning to share the same sympathetic look with Rosa as if she'd read her mind.

Larry wasn't readily convinced. "How can you say that?" he asked heatedly. "It was because of me, because I wanted out of our marriage."

"But you'd been unhappy for a long time, hadn't you? You'd even talked about divorce before, correct?" Anne persisted. "What had stopped you?"

"She'd always talked me into staying, into giving it one more try," he said.

"How had she done that?" Anne prodded.

"By threatening suicide," he said in a voice barely above a whisper.

"In other words, she emotionally blackmailed you into staying," Anne said, putting it in the harshest possible terms.

He nodded.

"But she'd never tried to kill herself, had she? And you'd encouraged her to get help, isn't that right?"

"She was supposed to be seeing someone, a doctor. He'd given her antidepressants," he said. "I honestly thought she was better, that she was well enough to take it."

"Then you did everything you could," Anne said.

He didn't look the least bit relieved by her reassurances. "God knows, I tried," he said. "Now, not only do I have to live with all this guilt, but also with the anger, because her dying cost me the relationship with the woman I'd been seeing. We broke up this week. I couldn't seem to look at her without thinking about what had happened and finally she couldn't take it anymore."

"So your wife got what she wanted, didn't she?" Anne asked.

Larry looked startled by the question. "How can you say that?"

"You're no longer with the other woman." When he started to speak, she held up her hand. "I don't know if this woman is the right woman for you, but if she is, are you willing to sacrifice your future happiness because of something you couldn't control? Or are you going to forgive yourself and move on? Maybe fight to get her back?"

He nodded slowly, but he still looked miserable. "I hear what you're saying, but I'm just not there yet."

"You will be," Anne promised him. "It takes time. Who's next?"

It was the pale, slight teenager who spoke, after giving Rosa a shy smile. "I'm Lauren. I'm going to be a senior in high school this fall, and I'm here because my boyfriend committed suicide just before Christmas last year."

Once more Rosa wasn't able to prevent a horrified gasp. "You poor child," she murmured.

"Teen suicide is a growing problem," Anne told her. "Think back to when you were that age. Every problem was magnified a thousand times. Everything seemed to be life-or-death important, whether you had a date for the prom, whether you failed a test, whether you got into college. Teenagers don't have the same perspective that we do. They don't understand that problems are temporary, that things usually work out for the best.''

Lauren nodded, her expression serious. ''That's what happened to Christopher. His parents had scrimped and saved forever so he could go to an Ivy League college. All they ever talked about was college and how much better his life would be if he had such a good education. When midterm grades came out, he was failing chemistry. Everyone told him he could make it up and still get a B or at least a C in the class, but he panicked. His other grades started slipping, because he was struggling so hard to catch up in chemistry. He felt like this huge failure, and nothing I said could get through to him. He just kept saying how disappointed his parents would be.''

She regarded them with tears streaking down her cheeks. ''The awful part is that I knew his dad kept a gun in the house and I knew Christopher was depressed and talking about finding a way out, but I didn't realize he really meant it. I thought maybe he was going to drop out of school or something. Then one of his teachers called his folks to ask if they knew why he was suddenly having trouble in school. They confronted him and it was pretty awful. That night, he went into his room, called me, and then shot himself before I could call 911 to get help over there.''

''Oh, Lauren, what a terrible thing for you to go through,'' Rosa said, her heart filled with sympathy for what this young girl was dealing with. If it was impossible for her to deal with Don's decision to take his own life, how on earth could this young girl cope?

"I'm okay," Lauren said staunchly. "It's just that now I panic when anyone starts talking crazy. I've called 911 so often, they recognize my voice. And I'm terrified that one of these days, they'll think I'm just scared for no reason and not respond, and it'll be the one time something bad happens."

Rosa knew that Matt would not permit the police to ignore a cry for help, even one from a teenager who tended to overreact. The girl had every reason to fear for her friends. She'd learned from bitter experience what the danger signs were and she'd never risk ignoring them again.

As the others told similar stories, many of them about anger over a loved one's dying, even of natural causes. Rosa felt as if a terrible weight was lifting from her shoulders. She was not so different, after all. She was going through the same stages of denial and anger and grief as these people. They weren't freaks. Nor had they deserved to lose their loved ones in such a tragic way.

And neither had she. She could almost accept that now.

She glanced up and saw Anne regarding her expectantly.

"Rosa, would you like to tell us a little bit about yourself?"

"I'm Rosa," she began softly. Sylvia reached for her hand and gave it a reassuring squeeze. "I think— no, I'm almost certain—my husband committed suicide two months ago. And…" She looked into all those sympathetic eyes and her voice faltered. "And I don't know why." She looked toward Larry. "In my husband's case, the police do believe it was an accident. That's the official report. It would be so easy to accept that. For one thing there's insurance money that we desperately need right now, but I can't let that matter, not when I know in my heart it wasn't an accident. There's too much evidence to the contrary, and it's breaking my heart that I ignored the signs and never saw this coming.''

''What really matters is that you lost the most important person in your life,'' Anne said quietly. ''You need to grieve for him. Have you done that?''

Rosa shook her head. ''Not really. I've been too angry.''

''Been there,'' several voices reassured her.

''It gets better,'' Nancy said. ''I promise you.''

The others nodded.

''I don't think I would have made it without this group, though,'' Larry said. ''Keep coming, Rosa. I know it's hard to expose your feelings in front of a bunch of people you've never met before, but it helps. And we've all been there.''

''Thank you,'' she said, and meant it. She turned to Sylvia. ''Thank you especially. I wouldn't have come today if she hadn't pushed me,'' she told the others.

''I just did what any friend would do,'' Sylvia said, looking embarrassed by the praise. ''You're going to be okay, Rosa. I honestly believe that now.''

Rosa nodded. ''So do I.'' She faced the group. ''And I will be back next week,'' she said with renewed determination. She was finally going to take the steps necessary to get her life back.

Cori looked as if she wanted to cry. Emma felt a sinking sensation in the pit of her stomach the instant she saw her. She reached out and gripped Matt's hand.

"Jennifer's not here, is she?" she asked Cori.

"I told her it was really important, but she said she had another commitment and that it was important, too." Cori regarded them apologetically. "I honestly don't know what's gotten into her lately. She's not herself. She hasn't been for weeks and weeks now."

"You said something like that at your house last night. What's going on?" Emma asked her.

"I can't explain it exactly. She's been way stressed out, snapping at me in a way she never had before, refusing to take calls. Then she vanished without a word. I had no idea where she'd gone or when she'd be back till she finally called in the middle of last week. All I had was a note saying she'd be in touch and to put off all appointments until she told me to start scheduling them again."

"When did she leave?" Matt asked.

"I guess the first time was a couple of months back, out of the blue. She didn't have a vacation planned. She just left. I found a note on my desk saying there'd been some sort of emergency and that she'd be out of touch indefinitely. This from a woman who usually has a cell phone attached to one ear and one eye on the stock ticker from the second the stock exchange opens every day." She looked at Matt. "You know how she is."

Emma looked at Matt. "What are you thinking?" she asked.

He hesitated.

"Come on, Matt. Tell me."

"I'm thinking that the timing is damned weird, that's what I'm thinking."

Emma's breath caught. "You think her leaving is tied to my father's death, don't you?"

He met her gaze. "Don't you?"

"That's a huge leap," she said, not wanting to believe that there was any significance to the timing.

Cori stared at Matt. "You can't be serious. Jennifer and Emma's dad? That's absurd. Of all people, you should know that."

Emma regarded Cori curiously. Why did she think Matt would have some special insight into Jennifer's behavior? Was there something he hadn't told her about his relationship with Jennifer? Were they something more than old classmates? She couldn't read anything in his expression, but more than once now she'd picked up on hints that there was something he was hiding where Jennifer was concerned.

"Was Don ever here?" Matt asked, his face carefully averted from Emma.

"Well, sure, but..." Cori's voice trailed off. She called up the date book on her computer and scanned back a few weeks. "Emma, look at this. Your dad died on the night of the seventeenth, right?"

Emma pushed aside her suspicions about Jennifer and Matt and concentrated on Jennifer's schedule for the date her father had died. Emma's father had been on her calendar for a four o'clock meeting. And two days later, two days after his death, Jennifer had canceled all of her appointments and left town. It was getting harder and harder to ignore the coincidences.

She tried to imagine her father involved with a woman half his age, but the image wouldn't come. Besides, if this were about an affair, would Jennifer have had his name on her office calendar where Cori could readily find it? Wouldn't she have been far more discreet? And if Emma's father had somehow lost his mind and gotten mixed up in an affair with the investment adviser, where did Matt fit into the equation? Were they rivals of some sort? Had Jennifer thrown Matt over for Emma's father? Or could it have been the reverse? Could the woman have broken things off with Don in order to be with Matt? Was that what had driven her father over the edge? Was that why Matt was being so nice to her, because of his own guilty role in the breakup?

Obviously she was letting her imagination run wild. She could only worry about one part of that, Emma told herself. She had to concentrate on Jennifer's relationship with her father. She had to find out whether it was professional or romantic.

Unfortunately, the only person who could answer those questions was Jennifer herself and she'd gone missing.

"Reschedule us to see her tomorrow," she told Cori flatly.

"No," Matt countered. "Don't put it on the calendar. If she's trying to avoid you, Emma, she'll just take off again when she sees her date book. Cori, you call me when she comes in. I'll get Emma and we'll come over as soon as we hear from you."

Cori nodded slowly. "There has to be some mistake, Emma. I can't believe it's anything like what you're thinking."

Emma attempted a reassuring smile. "I'm trying really, really hard not to think at all."

14

Outside Jennifer's office building, Matt turned toward his car, but Emma caught his hand.

"Can we go for a walk?" she asked. "I need to clear my head."

"Sure," he said at once, worried about her pallor and the lost, desperate look in her eyes. "Anyplace in particular you want to go?"

"Around the lake," she suggested.

Matt hesitated, wondering if she truly wanted to walk all the way around the lake to the spot where her father's body had been discovered. As if she'd suddenly realized what she was suggesting, she lifted her gaze to capture his.

"Just halfway," she said, indicating her awareness that reaching the north end would not improve her mood.

Matt nodded. "Sounds good to me," he said, shortening his stride so that she could match it.

She didn't say a word until they'd walked the two blocks to the lake and then started around the south end, where there were hot dog and ice cream vendors and rowboat rentals. Her eyes lit up when she spotted the boats.

Looking more lighthearted than she had in weeks,

she gestured toward the boats. "How about it? Are you game?"

"You and me out on the lake just before sunset?" he said. "What's not to like?"

She grinned. "I'll get the ice cream."

Matt paid for the rental, then watched as Emma came back with two cones, trying desperately to keep up with the melting ice cream on both of them.

"Here," she said, shoving one in his direction. "It's getting all over me."

He grinned. "I could help with the cleanup."

She shot a scolding look in his direction. "I think I can manage. That's what napkins are for."

"My way's more fun," he teased, earning a blush.

"Are we going out on the lake or not?"

He gestured toward the boat. "After you." He helped her step into the boat and get settled, then sat across from her.

"We're not going anywhere," she pointed out.

He held up his ice cream. "I only have one hand. Unless you intend to help with the rowing, we have to wait."

"I can help," she said, reaching for an oar. "Try to keep up, so we don't go around in circles."

Matt laughed. "As if I'll be the problem," he scoffed.

They set off across the lake, their strokes working nicely in tandem. He considered it a good sign.

Eventually Emma handed him her oar. "You take over," she said, turning her face up to the warm, fading sun and closing her eyes.

Matt took the oar, but let the boat drift, unable to take his gaze off of her. She was without question the most beautiful woman he'd ever known, even more so because she was so totally unaware of it. Though she was far too pale, the sun had managed to put a hint of pink into her cheeks and brought out the fiery highlights in her dark hair.

"Matt," she murmured eventually.

"Hmm?"

"We're not going anywhere."

He'd had the same sense for weeks now, but that wasn't what she was talking about. He decided to pretend it was. "Where do you see us going?" he asked quietly.

Her eyes snapped open. "Us?"

He grinned at her reaction. "You know, you and me."

"Is there an us?"

"That's what I'm asking you," he said. "I'd like there to be. I'd like to have the right to pull you into my arms right now and kiss you till your head spins, to take you home with me and make love to you till dawn."

Her eyes widened and the muscles in her throat worked. "You would?" she asked with a catch in her voice.

"That can't be a huge surprise."

"No," she agreed. "It's not a *huge* surprise. You saying it, though, is something of a shocker."

"Years ago you intimidated the daylights out of me, or should I say your father did," he said wryly. "Now that we're all grown-up, I've decided it's time to stop being the strong, silent type. Something tells me this could be my last chance. Once you go back to D.C., I might never get another one unless I come chasing after you."

"I see." She regarded him with a worried expression. "Matt, I don't know what to say."

"I guess that's an answer in itself," he said, fighting to hide his disappointment. He hadn't really expected her to fall straight into his arms, but he'd hoped for more than speechlessness. He knew the feelings were there. He also knew she didn't want to acknowledge them, that she did want to go back to Washington and that she most likely did not want him chasing after her.

She reached for his hand and rubbed her thumb over his knuckles. Matt's body responded as if her touch had been far more intimate.

"I don't want you to misunderstand. My life is in such a state of turmoil right now, you know that," she explained. "What if we make a mistake? We could lose something really precious, our friendship."

"What if it's not a mistake?" he asked reasonably. "Then we'd lose something even more amazing, because we never even tried." He risked a look directly into her eyes. "Unless you're just not interested in me that way."

Her gaze held his and he knew at once that that was the last thing he needed to worry about. Desire smoldered in her eyes, right along with uncertainty. He could capitalize on the desire and in all likelihood there would be no regrets, but it was the uncertainty that stopped him.

"Sorry," he told her sincerely. "My timing sucks."

She smiled sadly. "On the one hand, your timing does suck," she agreed. "On the other, it couldn't be better. When we came out here, I felt completely lost and alone." Her eyes locked with his. "And now I don't."

"Then I'm glad I said something."

"So am I."

"The offer's good anytime," he told her. "I live to cheer you up."

She laughed, just as he'd intended, and the tension lifted.

"Something tells me that sleeping with you would go a bit further than merely cheering me up," she said.

"I certainly hope so."

"Will you settle for dinner tonight?"

"Being with you is never settling," he told her honestly. "And if you play your cards right, I'll even help with the dishes."

"Help?" she said. "Forget that. You'll *do* the dishes."

"Anything to keep that smile on your face."

She gave him a wicked grin. "Then try stealing a kiss over dessert."

"Now *that* would definitely be my pleasure."

Rosa sat back and listened to Matt and Emma bickering as they prepared dinner, saw the color bloom in her daughter's cheeks, and caught the way Matt managed to touch her every chance he got. So that's the way it was, she thought, feeling a little wistful as she remembered when she and Don had been the same way.

"You know, you two would get a lot more work done, if you'd cooperate," she advised them finally.

Two pairs of startled eyes turned to her, almost as if they'd forgotten she was in the room.

"We are cooperating," Emma said.

"Oh, please," Matt countered. "Telling me to do it your way or to get out of here is not cooperating."

Rosa shook her head. "So do you actually expect dinner to be ready sometime tonight?"

"A half hour," Emma predicted, just as Matt said, "Ten minutes."

Rosa rolled her eyes. "Maybe I should take Andy and Jeff out for dinner. How'd you get Jeff over here, by the way?"

"Better not to ask any questions," Emma advised.

"In other words, Matt pulled rank," Rosa guessed. She looked him in the eye. "Thank you. Think you can talk him into sticking around?"

"I'll work on it," Matt promised.

"So, Mama, you seem to be in an especially good mood tonight," Emma said, studying her curiously. "What happened today?"

A part of Rosa wanted to keep the whole survivor's group thing to herself, but Emma deserved to know. "I went to one of those meetings at Saint Luke's. Sylvia took me."

Emma dropped her paring knife on the counter and came over to kneel in front of Rosa and take her hands. "That's wonderful. It helped, didn't it? I can see it on your face."

"More than I'd ever thought it would," Rosa agreed. "It's not a miracle cure, but listening to the other people there made me realize that I'm really not alone." Though she selfishly wanted this just for her own recovery, she couldn't help wondering if Emma wouldn't benefit from it, too. Last time she'd mentioned it, Emma hadn't shown much enthusiasm, but maybe she'd feel differently now that Rosa had broken the ice.

"Would you like to go with me next time?" she asked.

Emma hesitated, then glanced toward Matt, before finally shaking her head. "I'm doing okay right now. If that changes, I'll consider it."

"Just because you're not letting your father's death immobilize you the way I did doesn't mean you're okay," Rosa told her. "I realize now that talking really can help."

Emma nodded, and once more looked toward Matt in a way that spoke volumes. "I know," she said. "Matt's been a godsend in that regard. He listens to me. More than that, he's helping me investigate why dad did what you and I both think he did. Taking action is going a long way toward helping me get all of this into perspective."

Matt was helping her daughter in other ways, too, Rosa suspected. She couldn't say that her daughter looked wildly happy and in love. How could she be this soon after her father's death? But she was coping, and Rosa had a hunch that real happiness was lurking just around the corner for her, if she'd let it happen. And there were signs that she might. Emma hadn't mentioned Washington or her life there in days now. Maybe she was reaching a point where she'd be ready to accept the possibility that her future was right here in Winter Cove.

Maybe a blessing would come from Don's death, after all. Emma staying here and falling in love with a fine man like Matt would certainly be one.

"It's been two weeks since I heard from you," Kim told Emma accusingly when she caught up with her by phone late that night. "I miss our Sunday morning get-togethers."

"So do I," Emma said.

"I wish I'd been able to be there for you, but getting away from work on short notice is impossible. Plus I have virtually no leave time left and my boss is a stickler for the rules."

"I know that," Emma told her. "Not that I don't wish you'd been around, but I understand."

"You doing okay?"

"I'm coping," she said. "There's so much I want to talk to you about, but it seems as if there's never time to even pick up the phone. If I'm not at the diner, Matt and I are trying to make some headway in trying to figure out why my Dad died."

"Matt, huh? You mention him a lot. Something tells me there's a lot more going on there than an investigation."

Emma hesitated, uncertain how to answer.

"My God, there is, isn't there?" Kim said. "I was teasing, but I got it exactly right. You've got a thing going with the sexy police chief."

"It's not a thing," Emma denied. "Not yet, anyway."

"He wants it to be, or you do?"

"Both of us do, actually."

"Oh, really? Then why hasn't it happened?"

"I'm the holdout," Emma admitted. "How can I start something with him when I might not be around long enough to finish it? Matt and I have been friends forever. If we do something crazy and it blows up, we could ruin that friendship."

"In this case, I think friendship is highly overrated,

when you could be having hot, steamy sex. You do think it will be hot and steamy, don't you?''

Emma had tried hard not to think about what she'd been avoiding. That was precisely the problem. She suspected that making love with Matt would be incredible. Each time he touched her, she felt things she hadn't felt before, wicked, wonderful sensations. And then she immediately felt guilty, because feeling so alive seemed wrong under the current circumstances. But this was Kim, and she could tell her anything.

"Oh, yeah," she admitted. "I imagine it would be incredible."

"Then I really don't see what's stopping you," Kim said. "It's not as if you're making a lifetime commitment to the man."

Emma remained silent.

"Oh, sweetie, that's it, isn't it? You're afraid you'll fall in love with him and wind up spending the rest of your life in Winter Cove."

"Me being here is temporary," Emma said flatly. "I'm coming back to Washington as soon as everything settles down."

"And you can't make yourself think of Matt as some sort of fling?"

"Having a fling with Matt would be wrong," Emma told her. "He wants more."

"Has he said that?"

She thought of the crush he'd been unsuccessfully hiding for years. "No, not in so many words, but—"

"But nothing. Go for it. He's a big boy. I'm sure he can handle it, if things don't work out."

"And me? How am I supposed to handle it, if it turns out that the two of us are better than I ever dreamed of?"

"You'll follow your heart," Kim said confidently.

"Even if that means staying here?" Emma said, not happy with the obvious choice.

"Even then," Kim said. "You'll be so deliriously happy, you won't even notice where you're living."

"Trust me, I'll notice."

"Only if he's not doing something right," Kim said. "And something tells me that's not going to be a problem. Sweetie, people can fit into more than one place, but true love is not something to toss aside lightly."

"Who said anything about true love?" Emma asked defensively.

"You didn't have to say the words for me to hear it in your voice. This Matt is special."

"Yeah, he is," she said. "Okay, enough about me. What's going on in your life? Anyone made it past the second date yet?"

Kim sighed heavily. "I haven't even met someone worthy of a second date lately. I'm thinking of giving total celibacy a try."

Emma started to laugh, but the laughter died when she realized that Kim was serious. "Why don't you come down here for a few days, even if it can only be for a weekend? It sounds to me like you need a break someplace where there's no pressure."

"And I could get a firsthand look at Matt," Kim said thoughtfully, her voice brightening. "I'll do it. As soon as I've made the arrangements, I'll be in touch, that is, if you're really serious, Emma. You sure this isn't a bad time for company?"

"I'm serious and it's never a bad time for you," Emma said. It wasn't that she was especially eager for Kim to cross paths with Matt, but her friend could provide a nice little buffer between them. That would keep Emma from having to make the decision that was seeming more and more inevitable with every day that passed.

Matt was half-asleep when the dispatcher called him at home.

"I've got a woman on the line who says she'll only talk to you. Want me to patch her through or tell her to call back in the morning?"

"Patch her through," he said at once.

"Matt?"

The voice sounded familiar, but whoever it was was so clearly shaken he couldn't be sure he was hearing right. "This is Matt," he said quietly. "Who's this?"

"Jennifer."

He sat up in bed. "What's the problem?"

"I think someone's been following me."

"Where are you?" he asked, already reaching for his jeans.

"I'm home now, but I think they're outside. I don't want to overreact. This could be my imagination playing tricks on me."

"They?"

"I'm pretty sure there are two men," she said. "Could you come by and check it out? I would have asked for a squad car, but I didn't want to look foolish, if it's nothing. I'm sorry if I woke you."

"Not a problem," he reassured her. "I'll be there in ten minutes."

And if it turned out to be the two men who'd immediately popped into mind, he was going to hang them both without benefit of a trial.

He made it to Jennifer's street in less than seven minutes, then cut his lights as he turned onto the block. He noted that halfway down, one house had every light on, inside and out. It didn't take a genius to figure out that Jennifer wanted to scare off the prowlers. Unfortunately, he figured if he was right, Gabe and Harley were too dense to take the hint.

He circled the block slowly. Sure enough, directly behind Jennifer's, he spotted Gabe's car. It was empty, which meant the two old coots were probably creeping around her yard. He was surprised they hadn't been spotted and reported by half the neighborhood.

He parked his car so he was blocking Gabe's, then went to look for them. He could hear them bickering before he reached the edge of the lawn.

"I'm telling you somebody was driving around with their lights off," Harley told Gabe. "We need to get out of here. There's nothing going on here, anyway."

"I say we stay," Gabe insisted. "She's bound to do something to give herself away."

"Such as?" Harley scoffed. "You think she's going to toss her diary down so we can read it?"

"There you go," Gabe said. "Maybe she has one of those fancy date book things. We get our hands on that, we can see what she's been up to."

"How the hell do you propose we do that?" Harley asked, sounding disgusted. "You plan to break in while she's got every light in the place on and, more than likely, a shotgun laying across her lap?"

"If we have to," Gabe said stubbornly.

Matt sighed heavily and stepped out of the bushes.

"Don't even think about it," he warned. Both men jumped as if he'd pulled a gun on them.

"Dammit, Matt, are you deliberately trying to give us a heart attack?" Gabe demanded.

"That's what you deserve," Matt retorted. "What the hell were you thinking creeping around out here? You're acting like a couple of aging, Peeping Toms."

"We're investigating," Gabe said, clearly offended by the possibility that their actions might be misinterpreted.

"I thought I told you to leave the investigating to me," Matt said, wondering how the devil they'd gotten away from Cramer. He was supposed to be preventing exactly this kind of rogue investigation.

"Have you found anything?" Harley asked.

"Not yet," Matt conceded.

"Then you need us," Gabe said.

"What I need is the patience of Job," Matt countered. "Go home, while I try to explain to Jennifer that she has nothing to worry about."

Gabe regarded him indignantly. "You can't go and tell her something like that. I still say she knows something about Don dying the way he did."

"If she does, I will find out about it, but not if the two of you go blundering around here and get her guard up. Now go, before I drag you up to the house, so you can apologize in person."

"You wouldn't," Harley said.

"Try me," Matt said. "Let's go."

He walked with them until they were safely settled into Gabe's car, pulled his own car out of their path, then followed until he was reasonably certain that they were actually headed home. Then he drove back to Jennifer's and rang the bell.

"Matt?"

"It's me," he reassured her.

She peeked out, then opened the door. "Did you find them?"

"It was nothing for you to worry about," he assured her. "Just a couple of old guys who got lost."

She didn't look as if she believed him. "Are you sure about that?"

"Very sure. I don't think they'll be over this way again."

"There's something you're not telling me," she said, regarding him with suspicion. "I could always read you, you know."

"I'm telling you the truth," he insisted, though maybe not the whole truth. She didn't need to know the rest.

She didn't look entirely reassured. "If you say so," she said skeptically. "Can you come in for coffee?"

He hesitated, then decided maybe this was the best chance he'd have to get some of the answers that he and Emma were after. "Sure, for a few minutes," he said, then followed her into the kitchen.

The coffee was already brewed, the kitchen filled with the aroma of an expensive blend. He could see the bag of imported coffee beans on the counter. One of the reasons they would never have worked—aside from the fact that he was still crazy about Emma—was Jennifer's expensive taste. She would have hated living on a cop's salary and he would have hated being with a woman who insisted on buying her own luxuries.

"Late at night to be drinking so much caffeine," he noted. "You planning on being awake awhile?"

"I'm not sleeping that well lately, anyway. I thought I might get some work done."

"I thought you just got back from vacation," he said. "That's what Cori said, when I came by the office."

"It wasn't exactly a vacation," she said, avoiding his gaze.

"A business conference?"

"No."

"What then?"

She lifted her gaze to meet his. "Does it matter?"

"It might."

"I needed to get away. That's it."

"Where'd you go?"

"I have a place in the mountains in North Carolina. I bought it last year, after you and I split up. It was sort of a reward for not falling apart when I realized you still had the hots for Emma Killian after all these years. I went up there for a while." She regarded him with a hint of defiance. "Satisfied?"

"Far from it." He met her gaze. "Did you happen to buy some flowers before you left?"

She regarded him with what looked to be genuine incredulity. "Flowers?"

"A funeral arrangement, to be specific."

She looked shaken by the question. "No. Why on earth would you think that?"

"Somebody sent a rather lavish arrangement to the lakeside memorial for Don Killian."

"It wasn't me," she said at once. "I left...I left before I even heard about his death."

Now Matt was the one who was startled. "You did?"

She nodded. "I didn't know anything about it, until

I picked up my mail in North Carolina a few days later and got the Winter Cove paper. The funeral was already over by then.''

Something didn't sound quite right, but he couldn't put his finger on it. "You had your mail forwarded? Why?"

"Because I knew I was going to be gone for several weeks," she explained with exaggerated patience. "Why else does someone have mail forwarded?"

"Why such a long vacation?"

"I told you, I needed to clear my head. I had a lot going on."

"Such as?"

Her expression turned hard. "Am I under investigation for something?"

Matt sighed. "No, not really. I'm just looking for answers."

"About?"

"Why Don killed himself," he said bluntly, watching closely for her reaction to his claim of suicide when all published reports had called the death an accident.

She didn't disappoint him. Shock registered in her eyes. "I thought it was an accident. That's what the paper said."

"That's the official ruling, yes," Matt agreed.

"But you have doubts?"

"I have doubts," he confirmed. "How about you? What was your gut reaction when you heard the news?"

"I didn't have one, except for sorrow. I took the report at face value."

"Really? Even though he'd had an appointment

with you late in the afternoon on the very day he died?''

Bright patches of color appeared in her cheeks. ''You think I had something to do with his death?'' she asked angrily. ''That's why you and Emma made an appointment to see me? Dammit, Matt, I was afraid it was something like that. Are you crazy?''

He ignored the indignation. It seemed genuine, but she could be faking it. He'd never been able to read her all that well. ''We made the appointment because I thought you could give us some help looking over his accounting records, yes. It wasn't till today when you deliberately tried to avoid us that I began to think you might be more involved than we realized.''

''Well, I'm not,'' she said fiercely. ''I can't imagine why he would do such a thing.''

Matt leveled a look straight into her eyes. ''Then you won't mind meeting with me and Emma tomorrow to take a look at those books, will you?''

Her expression faltered, but she'd set a neat trap for herself. If she truly had nothing to hide, then there was no reason to avoid seeing them.

''What time?'' she asked, evidently resigned.

''I think we'll play that by ear. Just stick close to your office.''

''I can't spend the whole day in there waiting around for you to show up,'' she protested. ''My schedule's packed. I have a lot of appointments to catch up on. Not all of them are in the office.''

He regarded her with an unrelenting stare. ''Make it work, Jennifer. You'll have your phone, your computer and the stock ticker. What more could you possibly need?''

"You're being unreasonable. That's almost like house arrest or something."

"I could bring you down to the station and let you cool your heels there till Emma's free. Would that be better? I'm pretty sure our stock ticker's on the fritz."

She sighed. "I'll be in my office."

"Good choice," he said, shoving aside his untouched cup of coffee. "Have a nice night."

She gave him a sour look and didn't offer to walk him to the door. Matt figured he'd pushed her just about as hard as he could given the fact that he had absolutely nothing to indicate that she was in any way involved with any crime. But she wasn't being totally forthcoming. He'd stake his badge on that.

15

Rosa sat at the kitchen table drinking a cup of coffee, waiting for Jeff to wake up and come downstairs. It was the first morning in weeks now that she'd felt halfway normal. She attributed that to having all of her children at home and to the impact of the meeting she'd attended at Saint Luke's. It was the first day she'd awakened and hadn't resented the brilliant blue sky and bright sunshine.

She'd almost finished reading the morning paper when Jeff wandered in, yawning. As he reached past her to grab the milk and pour himself a glass, she noticed that his eyes were clearer than they had been in a while.

"Good, you're up just in time," she said, smiling at him.

"Just in time for what?" he asked suspiciously.

"I thought we could go over to the diner and give Emma and Andy a break. They've been carrying the whole load for too long now." She looked directly into his eyes as if she were anticipating a protest and added, "I could use the moral support, Jeff."

She waited as he automatically opened his mouth to argue, but then clamped it shut again.

"Sure," he said finally.

"Thank you. It means a lot having you back home."

He seemed genuinely startled that she'd even noticed his absence. He gazed at her curiously. "You seem different, Mom, like you're getting your act together. Has something happened that I don't know about?"

"Actually, yes. I met some people yesterday, Jeff, people who'd lost loved ones...." She hesitated, not willing to get into the whole suicide thing with him. Instead she said, "The deaths were as unexpected as your father's. It helped. Maybe you should come along next time I go."

"No way," he said at once. "I don't give a damn about all that touchy-feely crap."

"I felt the same way before I went, but it's not like that at all," she insisted. "These are real people who've been through what we're going through. They understand in a way nobody else can."

"If it helps you, go for it," he said. "But I want no part of it."

"You're so angry, Jeff. It's not healthy."

"Are you telling me you're not angry?" he asked incredulously.

"I was," she said. "No, that's not right. I'm still angry, but I'm facing it. I'm doing something about it. You need to do that, too. If you won't let me help, there has to be someone else you can turn to. Matt, maybe."

"As if he'd help me," Jeff scoffed.

"Somebody else, then. Somebody besides Marisol. I don't want to say anything against the girl—"

"Then don't," he said, cutting her off.

"Jeff, she's wrong for you. Can't you see that?"

"She's been there for me," he insisted.

Rosa accepted the claim at face value. "Okay, then. Who you rely on is up to you."

He frowned, clearly not happy about her disapproval. "If we're going to the diner, let's go," he said brusquely. "I've got someplace I need to be in a couple of hours."

"Where?"

"Just someplace."

"With Marisol, I imagine," she said.

"You imagine right," he said. "I'm out of here. I'll wait for you in the car." He slammed the kitchen door behind him.

Rosa stared after him. She was glad he had someone he could turn to, but did it have to be a girl who promised to be nothing but trouble? True, she was judging her on superficial things, her hair, her clothes, her tattoos, but those were indicative of her lifestyle and her self-esteem in Rosa's opinion.

At least Jeff was home now and willing to work at the diner. Maybe she'd just have to be grateful for that and worry about the rest later.

Gabe and Harley regarded Matt sheepishly when he walked into Flamingo Diner and headed directly to their table.

"Did you two go straight home last night?" he asked as he pulled out a chair and straddled it facing them.

"You told us to, didn't you?" Harley replied.

Matt rolled his eyes. "Since when have you listened to anything I had to say?"

"We listen," Gabe retorted. "Sometimes we're forced to ignore you in the interest of a higher good."

"Oh, please," Matt said.

Gabe was about to say something else, when Harley shushed him and turned to Matt. "Did you learn anything from the Sawyer dame after we'd gone?"

Matt regarded him incredulously. "What have you been doing? Watching old Humphrey Bogart movies? Jennifer isn't some *dame*. You've known her since she was a kid. She's still young enough to be your granddaughter."

Harley managed to look chagrined. "Okay, okay. Did you learn anything from Ms. Sawyer? How's that? Is that politically correct enough for you?"

"Better," Matt said. "And whatever I learned from her is none of your concern."

"We're partners," Gabe protested.

Matt stared at him, barely managing to smother a laugh. "I don't think so. If anything, you two are the thorns in my side, the banes of my existence, the weeds in the cabbage patch."

Harley scowled at him. "We get it. You don't have to be insulting. We're just trying to help, you know."

"I do know," Matt agreed. "Which is why I haven't locked the two of you up before now, but don't think I won't if you pull another fool stunt like the one you pulled last night. You're lucky she didn't shoot you."

The two men fell silent, their expressions thoughtful. Matt had a hunch they weren't pondering their misbehavior. More likely, they were trying to think of ways they could get away with more. Suddenly Harley's expression brightened.

"Well, will you look at that?" he said, gazing past Matt. "Rosa's back."

The word quickly spread as Rosa came into the

diner, a sullen Jeff trailing along behind. Matt caught her gaze and gave her a thumbs-up. He knew what a huge step this was for her, for the whole family.

He watched Emma come out from behind the counter to give her mother a hug. Then, her chin lifted high, Rosa grabbed a coffeepot and began making her way around the tables, offering refills as if this were a perfectly ordinary day. The bright patches of color in her cheeks suggested she wasn't entirely comfortable with the old routine, but she was doing it. He admired her courage.

When she finally reached their table, Harley grabbed her free hand and gave it a smacking kiss. "Welcome back, beautiful. These tired old eyes surely did miss seeing you every morning."

Rosa laughed and pulled her hand away. "You're still full of it, Harley Watson."

Matt met her gaze. "No, he's not. You are beautiful," he said quietly. "And everyone here has missed you. You back to stay?"

"That's the plan," she said, looking around the crowded diner with a nostalgic expression on her face. "Today was hard, even with Jeff beside me, but it'll get easier, and this is where I belong. I just got a little lost for a while."

"You have friends here," Gabe told her, his expression serious for once. "Don't ever forget that, Rosa. There's not a person in here who wouldn't do anything at all to help you get through this bad time."

"I won't forget that," she said quietly. "Not ever again." Her gaze caught Matt's. "Think you can get Emma out of here? I don't need her hovering over me all day as if she expects me to fall apart."

He grinned. "Consider it done." She had no idea

how easy it would be, once he told Emma about the promised meeting with Jennifer. "Give me five minutes and we'll be out of your hair."

He crossed the diner, marched behind the counter and reached for the ties on Emma's apron. "We're out of here," he announced.

She frowned at him. "Are you crazy? I can't leave Mama alone here."

"In case you haven't noticed, Jeff came in. He may not be happy about it, but he's already pitching in at the grill to relieve Andy." Not that Andy had budged, Matt noticed. He just looked pleased to have his brother working alongside him. Matt looked Emma squarely in the eye. "Come on, Emma. Your mother wants you gone. I've been assigned to see that you go. Are you going to get me into trouble with her?"

"An intriguing thought," she said, looking as if she might challenge him.

"Don't go getting any ideas." He tucked a hand at her waist and nudged her in the direction of the front door.

"What if I don't want to go?"

He met her gaze. "Are you honestly going to deny your mother the chance to prove that she's up to handling this place again?"

Emma hesitated for an instant and Matt knew he'd won. She would never willingly interfere in her mother's recovery. She'd been waiting too long for some sign that Rosa's heart was mending. The aching sense of loss might never go away, but it could be held at bay long enough to go about the business of living.

"Let's go," she said, then regarded him with eyes

suddenly twinkling with mischief. "But you'd better make it worth my while."

"Careful, sweetheart. You just might get more than you bargained for."

She laughed. "Now *that* really is an intriguing thought. Do you seriously think you're up to it?"

Matt's blood raced so fast, it was all he could do to think coherently, but he kept his gaze locked with hers. "Only one way to find out."

He caught her hand and dragged her from the restaurant. "Your place or mine?"

She faltered then. "Um, Matt, I was only teasing."

"Oh, really?" he asked innocently. "That's the kind of teasing that can get a woman in trouble."

She reached up and touched his cheek. "Not with you," she said confidently.

He took her hand, turned it and pressed a kiss to her palm. "Don't count on it, darlin'. Even I have my limits."

And he was damn close to reaching them.

Coming back to Flamingo Diner had been easier than Rosa had anticipated. These people were her friends, and they did everything they could to make her first day back seem like a celebration. It had been weeks since Don had died, changing her life forever, but today had felt like the first real day of the rest of her life. If she could get through today without coming unglued, then she really was going to be okay.

Not that the day had been without its bittersweet moments. A snowbird, who apparently hadn't been in town at the time of Don's death, inadvertently caused a moment of painful silence when she'd asked after him. Helen had stepped in and quietly saved the day, explaining that he'd died, but not the circumstances. The woman's genuinely heartfelt condolences had more than made up for her blunder.

In fact, it was Helen's reassuring presence, along with Jolie's and Sylvia's, that had made the day bearable. They'd stayed so long, nursing first coffee, then iced tea, then sodas, it was a wonder they weren't floating. After sending Jeff on his way and locking the front door, Rosa sank down at their table with her own glass of tea.

"You did great," Helen said.

"Better than I would have," Sylvia added.

Rosa gave her a grateful look. "Only thanks to you. If you hadn't made me go to that meeting at Saint Luke's, I'm not sure I would have been brave enough to come here today."

"Tomorrow will be easier," Jolie promised her. "I'll never forget the first time I had to face everybody after my divorce." She grinned at Sylvia. "It was the annual Fourth of July barbecue at your house, remember?"

"I remember," Helen said. "Rosa and I had to come by and drag you over there. You said you were going to be a fifth wheel, that you didn't want to be around all those couples. And then Mick Henderson came on to you in the first ten minutes and everything was just fine."

Jolie blushed. "Okay, so I needed to get my confidence back. Getting dumped doesn't do much for a woman's self-esteem."

"And Mick Henderson does?" Rosa teased. "The man chases any female with a pulse."

"But that day, he chose me," Jolie retorted, then lowered her voice and confided, "I let him kiss me."

Rosa glanced at Sylvia and Helen, then all three of them started laughing.

"What?" Jolie demanded.

"Did you actually think that was a secret?" Helen asked.

"Well, of course," Jolie began indignantly, then faltered. "It wasn't?"

"The only thing Mick enjoys more than flirting is talking about it," Sylvia told her. "We knew, and frankly, we couldn't have been happier. It proved you were ready to start living again."

Rosa frowned at them. "Don't get any bright ideas about trying to prove the same thing with me." She glanced at Jolie. "Unless, of course, Mick is a better kisser than I imagined."

"He thinks it's his civic duty to console widows and divorcées, so he's had a lot of practice," Jolie said. "Draw your own conclusions."

Rosa shuddered. She wasn't ready to consider kissing another man, not even to prove to herself that she was still alive. "I think I'll pass, anyway," she told her friends. "It's going to be a very long time before I even look at someone new." Her eyes filled with tears. "The only man I ever wanted was Don. I thought I was the only woman he wanted, too."

"You were," Helen said fiercely. "You have absolutely no evidence to the contrary, so stop making yourself crazy."

"And even if—" Jolie began, only to have Helen cut her off with a sharp look.

"Even if nothing," Helen said emphatically. "Don Killian was faithful."

Rosa thought about Emma's revelation that she was investigating what had made Don feel desperate

enough to kill himself. There was no telling what
she'd turn up.

"Emma's trying to find out why her father died,"
she told the others. "I'm not sure if I want to know.
It seems so pointless now. He's dead, so what does
it matter why he died?"

"For one thing, it might end all this wild speculation you're engaging in," Helen said. "I think she
should try to find the answers. It's always better to
know the truth."

"Always?" Rosa asked doubtfully.

Jolie nodded slowly. "Always. I didn't want to
know that my husband was cheating on me. Out-
wardly I ignored all the signs, but inwardly I tortured
myself with doubts every single night he didn't come
home from work on time. Maybe if I'd faced facts
sooner and forced the issue, we could have worked
things out. Instead, I suffered in silence, getting more
and more resentful every day. That gave him just the
excuse he needed to turn to other women, and pretty
soon he wasn't home at all anymore. We hadn't had
a real marriage for at least two years before he finally
walked out for good."

She clasped Rosa's hand. "So, yes, I think it's better to know. You can deal with the truth. You can't
fight shadows."

But sometimes, Rosa thought, shadows were the
only thing left to protect the heart from breaking.

For the first time in weeks, Emma felt hopeful that
her family was going to be okay. Her mother had
come back to Flamingo Diner and even Jeff had
pitched in. He'd looked resentful as he'd taken over
from Andy at the grill, but he'd done it without com-

plaint. That was something, anyway. She'd even seen him smile a time or two at Andy's determined attempts to joke with him. Andy was such a sweetheart, how could anyone resist him? She'd noticed Lauren Patterson paying a lot more attention to him lately, too.

If things really were turning around for everyone here, then it wouldn't be long before she could start thinking about going back to Washington. She glanced at Matt and felt a momentary twinge of sorrow that she would be leaving him behind.

The pull between them had grown stronger day by day, more powerful than any attraction she'd ever felt for another man. And she was going to leave without ever knowing what it would be like to spend a night in his arms. Suddenly that seemed wrong, as if she were cheating them both of an experience that might be life altering.

It wasn't as if she were after a quick, experimental roll in the hay. This was Matt. She'd cared about him forever and he about her.

That was the justification. There were just as many persuasive arguments in favor of maintaining the status quo. She'd been over those countless times, in her head and aloud to him. Now, though, none of that seemed to matter.

Matt was pulling into a parking place in front of Jennifer Sawyer's office building, when she finally spoke.

"Matt, don't park," she said.

He turned to stare at her. "What? I thought you were anxious to see Jennifer and find out what she knows."

"Not today," she said, reaching her decision. "I

have something more important to do.'' Her gaze locked with his. ''If you have the time.''

He swallowed hard. ''Time? For what?'' he asked, his voice choked and a hint of uncertainty in his eyes, as if he were afraid to read too much into her words.

''To take me to your place,'' she said, her own heart in her throat. She hadn't once considered the possibility that he might turn her down, that he might want to protect his heart more than he wanted to make love with her.

''I think you'd better spell it out for me,'' he said. ''What exactly are you suggesting?''

''I want you to make love to me,'' she said bluntly.

There was the faintest tremble in his hands before he clutched the steering wheel more tightly. ''I see. Any particular reason you decided you want that here and now?''

''I'm not sure I can explain it.''

''Try,'' he said, his tone urgent. ''I want to be sure you know what you really want.''

''Okay,'' she said and searched for the right words. ''Mama came back to work today. Her life is getting back on track. Jeff's at least trying to do the right thing, for today, anyway. Andy's getting ready for his senior year. He's even got a girlfriend. And once you and I go inside that building and talk to Jennifer, we may finally have the answers I've been searching for about why my father died.''

Matt nodded. ''I'm with you so far, but what does that have to do with you and me?''

''I just realized that everything's starting to settle down and soon, there won't be any reason for me to stay here. I can go back to Washington and pick up the pieces of my life.''

He frowned at that. "So what? You want to have a little fling with the local cop so you'll have something to remember when you're back in D.C.?" he asked, his voice heating up.

Emma stared at him in shock. "No, absolutely not," she said, reaching out to grasp his arm. She felt the muscle clench and knew she'd gone about this all wrong. She'd picked the wrong time, the wrong place, everything. "Oh, Matt, please don't think that."

"Then what should I think?" he asked, his expression stony.

"That my feelings for you have grown over the past few weeks, much more than I ever anticipated. I don't want to leave here with any regrets. I want to give us a chance, a real chance."

"And then, what? You'll leave anyway?"

Emma faltered. "I...I don't know exactly."

He pulled back out of the parking space, still not looking at her. She had no idea if he was going to his place or not. She held her breath until they turned onto his street, then pulled into his driveway and he cut the engine.

He did face her then. "Emma, I have been in love with you for more years than I can remember," he said, not sounding especially happy about it. "It started as a boy's infatuation with a girl who was way too young for anything serious. I tried to get over it during the years we were separated, but I couldn't. Now you're here and nothing has changed for me. I still love you. I still want you. Every sensible brain cell in my head tells me I should turn you down flat and send you back to Washington without touching you."

He met her gaze. "But I can't. So if you don't

really want this, Emma, now's the time to back down, right here, in the driveway while I can still take you home.''

She was shaken by the powerful emotion behind his words, shaken by the awareness that what was about to happen was something huge for him, while for her it was filled with uncertainty. She had never expected to be loved like that. She'd wanted it, yes. How could any daughter of Don and Rosa Killian, who'd grown up surrounded by so much powerful passion, not want it for herself? To realize she could reach out and grab it for herself made her heart beat wildly.

She met Matt's gaze with an unwavering look. ''Take me inside,'' she said in a steady voice that belied the racing of her pulse.

''If we do this, I will fight to keep you here,'' Matt warned. ''I'll pull out all the stops to persuade you that this is where you belong. I won't let you walk away and leave me without doing everything in my power to make you stay.''

For one tiny instant, Emma hesitated, then smiled at him. ''You know how much I enjoy a good battle.''

''Even knowing you're destined to lose this one?'' he asked, his lips finally softening with the faint beginnings of a smile.

''Awfully sure of yourself, aren't you?''

''Awfully sure of us,'' he countered with confidence, his smile spreading.

To Emma's amazement, despite all the inevitable drawbacks to having a relationship with a man whose ties to Winter Cove ran deep, she was almost beginning to share his faith. The reaction was both scary and exhilarating.

16

Matt understood the risk he was taking as he poured a beer for himself and a glass of red wine for Emma. He knew that he wanted forever, and Emma wanted this one afternoon, but he thought, in time, he could convince her to stay here with him. And if he failed, at least he would have memories—real memories this time—to last a lifetime. Maybe it was pathetic to be willing to settle for so little, but it wasn't as if he had a choice. Going or staying would be her decision. He could only do whatever he could to influence it.

He handed Emma the glass and looked deep into her eyes. "To us, Emma."

"To us," she said without hesitation. "And to wherever today takes us."

Matt smiled, oddly relieved. "An open mind. I like that. Of course, I like almost everything about you, other than your stubborn determination to live nearly a thousand miles away. Then again, this afternoon is all about working on that."

"Really? I thought it was about sex," she taunted.

"Thus the persuasive element," he retorted.

She carefully set her glass down on the kitchen table. "Then I guess you ought to come here and kiss me."

"You sure about that?" he asked, watching her expression for signs of doubt.

"How many outs are you planning to give me, Matt?"

"As many as it takes to make certain this is what you want. I don't want this afternoon to be tainted by regrets or blame."

"I didn't come here lightly. I knew exactly what I was doing," she told him, her gaze unwavering. "Something's happening between us. It's foolish to deny it." She touched his cheek, let her hand linger. "I just don't want you to be hurt, if it can't be something more than this."

Hurt? He would ache like hell when the time came for her to go, but if it was the price to be paid for here and now...

"In that case..." He tossed his still-full beer can in the general direction of the sink. "I guess you've answered my question," he said, pulling her into his arms and covering her mouth with his.

It was a no-holds-barred kiss, the kind he'd been having dreams about for what seemed like a million years. And it lived up to all his expectations as it turned greedy and demanding with Emma melting in his arms, her body pliant, her tongue wicked, her mouth hot. It wasn't just about sex. Never that with Emma. It was about exploring and discovering a whole new facet of her, about staking his claim so that she could never forget him, no matter how hard she tried.

Matt could have taken her then and there, on the kitchen table, without a second thought, but this was Emma. She deserved romance and foreplay and finesse.

But as she ground her hips against his arousal, he realized that what she deserved and what she wanted were two entirely different things. He figured he could accommodate both with a slight adjustment to his own plans. Thank God for the condom he'd stuck in his wallet the day after she'd hit town, when he'd known—okay, hoped—that this moment would eventually come.

"Make me feel, Matt," she pleaded, shoving his T-shirt up until it was half-bunched around his armpits and her hands were sliding restlessly over his bare chest.

He stripped the shirt over his head before she accidentally choked him with it, then took his own sweet time about removing hers, letting his knuckles graze bare skin as heat rose in her eyes.

"Is this what you want?" he teased, his fingers skimming lightly over the tips of her breasts, making the dark nipples peak against the delicate peach lace of her bra.

"More," she murmured, her head thrown back.

"This?" he asked, kissing a trail down the side of her neck, then closing his mouth over her breast and sucking hard.

"Oh, yes."

"I can make it better," he said, easing off the bra. He skimmed his tongue over the sensitive peak, even as he undid the snap on her jeans and worked his hand inside her panties to skim through moist heat to find the already tight, sensitive bead of her arousal. With no more than a stroke, he had her crying out and shuddering in his arms.

Even as the tremors faded, he opened his own jeans, slid on his condom and entered her hard and fast, taking her breath away, and sending her off into another orgasm that had her writhing against him.

Thoroughly aroused by her abandon and responsiveness, he managed to hold on to his own control by a thread, his gaze locked with hers. Only when he saw her slowly falling back to earth did he begin to move again, taking his time, tormenting them both with the sweet agony of waiting between strokes, until she was pleading with him and his own body was hot and on the verge of exploding.

"Look at me," he commanded, waiting until her eyes were open and filled with passion before he thrust hard and deep, once, twice and then again, sending them both into a shuddering release that shattered any hope he'd ever had of forgetting Emma. A man could forget a lot of things, a lot of women, but not a woman who had taken him to a place he'd never been before.

"You're mine," he whispered against her cheek. "Mine."

A sigh eased through her. "I know."

A tension Matt hadn't even known he was feeling eased then. "Maybe we should go into the bedroom," he suggested.

"Why, when this was so incredible?" she asked, a twinkle in her eyes and a dare in her voice.

"Because sooner or later you're going to realize that this table is hard and that the neighbors can see in the kitchen windows," he said. "Besides, I have big plans for the rest of the afternoon and I don't intend to share them with the rest of the world."

"Big plans, huh?"

"Very big plans," he confirmed.

She reached for him, skimmed a finger along the length of his arousal. ''Yes, I can see that.''

''Umm, Emma,'' he said. ''You might not want to do that just now.''

''Oh?''

''It's going to make it that much more difficult to get to the bedroom.''

She regarded him with a wicked glint in her eyes. ''Maybe we don't need to go just yet,'' she said, her hand tightening around him.

Matt gasped. ''Maybe not,'' he said, then buried himself inside her one more time.

Emma stretched languorously and tried to recall exactly why she'd ever hesitated about letting Matt make love to her. Heaven knew, he was good at it. She'd never felt like this before in her life, as if her entire body were humming. There had been men who could make her feel like a woman, but none had made her feel like the decadent, passionate woman who'd come apart in Matt's arms time and again through the afternoon and on into the night.

Was that because he knew her so well? Or simply because he was the kind of man who paid attention to a woman's needs and knew how to fulfill them before taking his own pleasure? Was it genuine intimacy or merely skill? The latter was something she could deal with. Real intimacy, born of years of friendship, scared her to death.

She decided, for the sake of her own peace of mind, that it was skill. After all, it had been years since they'd spent much time together. She certainly didn't know Matt, not his heart and soul, the way two adults should know each other if there was anything truly meaningful between them. And if she didn't know him, how could he possibly know her? So it was definitely skill, she concluded, satisfied with the logic of it.

Then she rolled over and saw him studying her with an intense look that surely could see straight into her heart. "You scare the daylights out of me," she admitted, even as she curled back into all that reassuring strength.

Surprise lit his eyes. "Why would you be scared of me?"

"You make me feel things I'd never expected to feel. It's almost as if we've been together forever, when the truth is that we hardly know each other."

"How can you say that? We've known each other since we were kids."

"That's different from knowing each other as adults," she said. "You went away when I was just a teenager. By your own admission, you were still a little wild and reckless then. Now you're a thoroughly respectable member of community, the police chief, no less."

He grinned. "Disappointed in me?"

"Not a chance," she said, realizing it was true. All the changes in Matt had been for the better. But this wasn't all about him. "I've changed, too. I'm hardly the same innocent teenager I was when you last saw me. I realized when my father died that I was still naive about a lot of things. If I didn't know my own dad, if I couldn't see through the facade he was obviously putting on for me when we talked on the phone, how could I possibly claim to know anyone?"

"You answered your own question," Matt told her, his touch gentle as he brushed a stray curl from her cheek. "Your father was putting on a show for your benefit. It was meant to fool you. It fooled a lot of people."

"Or maybe I just heard what I wanted to hear, because if I'd realized how much pain he was in, I would have had to deal with it," she said with a hint of the self-loathing she'd been feeling. "Maybe I was blind, because I wanted to be."

"Don't talk crazy. All these years haven't changed who you are," he insisted. "You were a kind, generous girl and you've grown into a kind, generous woman. You love your family. If you'd had any inkling about what was going on with your dad, you would have come home to help."

"Andy tried to tell me. I dismissed it. He's still angry with me about that."

"He'll get over it," Matt reassured her. "He knows what happened isn't your fault."

"How can you be so sure of that?"

"Because I do know you."

"What do you think you know about me?" She honestly wanted to know.

"That you're funny and sweet, stubborn and sexy." He grinned. "That last one I suspected years ago, but confirmed only last night."

"Good thing you waited," she said, thinking of how her father would have reacted years ago if Matt had made a move on her. He'd been tough enough on the boys she had dated, all of whom had come from respectable families.

"Yeah, your father would have strung me up if I'd laid a finger on you," Matt said. "I got that message loud and clear." A shadow crossed his face. "I'd like to think he'd be happy about seeing us together now.

In a way this time we have to rediscover each other is a gift from him.''

Unexpected tears welled up in Emma's eyes and spilled down her cheeks. ''I can't regret what's happened between us, but I wish something else had brought us together.''

Matt wiped the tears from her cheeks with the pad of his thumb. ''Me, too, darlin'. Me, too.''

Emma sighed and settled against his chest, listening to the steady, reassuring beat of his heart. In an odd way, this truly had been her father's gift, and not entirely in the way Matt thought. True, her father's death had brought her back to Winter Cove so that she could discover this sublime feeling of being cherished, but it had also brought a man into her life who was strong and steady, qualities she'd always counted on in her father.

With Matt's arms around her, she didn't feel nearly as alone and frantic as she'd felt when she'd arrived weeks ago. Maybe if she hadn't just learned the bitter lesson that nothing lasted forever, she'd be a little more willing to see where these new feelings took them.

As it was, Emma was grateful for right here and right now. Tomorrow would have to take care of itself.

Matt didn't want to make too much of what had happened between him and Emma. He knew she didn't trust him or herself when it came to love or commitment. How could she when a man she'd idolized had ripped his entire family apart in one instant of insanity? Don's selfish, desperate act would have repercussions for years to come with the people he'd left behind. They might be functioning far better now than they had been right after his death, but Emma, her mother and her brothers would bear the scars forever. They would question everything, every relationship. Finding the faith to trust in love wouldn't come easily to any of them.

If Matt could keep Emma right here, in his bed, he might be able to block out reality for a time, but sooner or later it was bound to intrude and then what? Would he lose her? Would he have to watch her go back to her old life in Washington? In the time she'd been back he'd gotten used to building the rhythm of his days around glimpses of Emma. Would he have to say goodbye with a smile because that's what love required, letting go? He didn't even want to contemplate it.

Instead, he rolled her onto her back and buried himself inside her yet again, taking his time, trying to imprint himself on her memory, the way she was burned into his. When she erupted into a spasm that rocked them both, he captured her cries with his mouth and tried not to let her see his fear.

When the last shudder had died away, she sprawled beneath him, limp as a rag doll, an expression of pure contentment on her face.

"Oh, my God," she murmured with little energy. "I think you've stolen all my muscles and melted my bones. I doubt I'll ever move again."

Matt grinned. "That could be good. At least I'd know where to find you at the end of the day."

"Unless you're a lousy cop, you'll always know where to find me."

"Not necessarily. I don't know my way around D.C.," he said, putting his greatest fear on the table.

Her expression turned shuttered. "Can we not talk about that right now?"

"Because?"

"Because you want answers that I can't give you." She touched a finger to his lips. "You deserve them. I know that. I just don't have them for you."

"How about I paint a scenario for you?" he asked.

"A self-serving scenario?"

He shook his head. "A mutually beneficial scenario."

"Is there such a thing?"

"I think so. I do have your best interests at heart, Emma. I know you loved Washington. I know you think you belong there, but I'm not so sure that's true. Not anymore."

"Because we've been having sex for most of the last twenty-four hours?" she scoffed.

"No, because your life has changed dramatically. You're not the girl who was desperate to run off to a big city to prove herself. You've done that. You're an accomplished woman who needs more than a career to fulfill her. If you're honest, you'll admit that. Jobs are a dime a dozen. Even careers can change half a dozen times in a person's lifetime and each one can be rewarding in its own way. But the one constant that really matters is having people in your life to share that with—family, friends, and, most important of all, someone who loves you, who aches for you, who understands you even when you don't understand yourself."

Her expression hardened. "And you think you're that person for me?"

"I know I am," he said with confidence. "Because when push comes to shove, I will let you go."

"How damned noble of you," she said, a real bite in her voice.

"Not really," he said, ignoring the note of bitterness and risking more disdain by adding, "Because I know you'll come back. I'm counting on it."

She wrapped a sheet around her and climbed from the bed, her posture as regal as a queen's. "Don't," she said, dragging the sheet behind her as she strode into the bathroom.

"I'm right," Matt murmured, mostly to himself after she'd slammed the door. "I have to be."

"Of all the unmitigated gall," Emma grumbled as the hot water sluiced over her body, stirring every nerve ending as if it were more of Matt's deft touches. "One night of incredible passion doesn't mean I'm his forever. What kind of man leaps to that conclusion in this day and age? Independent women can have sex every night of the week, if they want to. With a different man each night, for that matter."

Not that she'd ever been one to do that, but Matt didn't know that. For all he knew, she could be up in Washington sleeping with any male who caught her fancy and never giving any one of them a second thought. She sighed heavily. As if she'd ever do a thing like that. Who was she kidding? Not Matt, and certainly not herself.

Last night had been the start of something amazing, or it could be, if she'd allow it. Apparently she was at least willing to consider the possibility, because after she'd showered she didn't dress or take off as she'd originally intended. She borrowed one of Matt's shirts and wandered downstairs, lost in thought.

She was making coffee when the doorbell rang.

She tried to ignore it. This wasn't her home and Matt might prefer that whoever it was not discover her wandering around downstairs half-dressed while he was still upstairs taking a shower. The scene left little to the imagination.

Still, it might be important, and it would serve him right if people started gossiping about the police chief. He was the one who'd have to live with it, not her. She would be gone from Winter Cove the very second she felt her family was back on its feet.

"Let 'em talk," she muttered en route to the door.

Even though she figured the fallout was going to land on Matt, she took care to make sure that his shirt covered her adequately, before opening the door.

"Surprise!" Kim said, a grin spreading across her face as she surveyed Emma's scanty attire. "I guess you decided to take my advice, huh?"

Emma stared at her friend in shock. "What are you doing here?"

Kim ignored her testy tone and stepped right past her, curiosity written all over her face. "You invited me, remember? I played on my boss's sympathy, got an extra day off, if you can believe that, and here I am. So where is he? I can't wait to meet the guy who's finally managed to get you looking all tousled and sexy."

Emma ignored the comment. "I thought your boss was a tyrant. I thought you were going to call and let me know when you could get away," she protested. "You weren't supposed to just show up, especially not here. You've caught me completely off guard."

Kim laughed, obviously unrepentant. "Yes, I can see that. Otherwise you'd never be answering a man's front door dressed only in his shirt. Who were you expecting? Your mother, perhaps?''

"Heaven forbid," Emma said fervently, wondering why that particular thought hadn't even crossed her mind before she'd flung open the door.

"You say that as if you don't think she knows where you are or what you're up to. Who do you think sent me over here?" Kim inquired, barely containing her smile.

Emma sank down on the sofa and groaned. "I never called home last night."

"Apparently Matt is considerably more considerate. He called."

Emma groaned again. Things were going from bad to worse. Her mother would make way too much of this.

"Oh, stop worrying," Kim admonished. "Your mother is pleased as punch. She thinks this means you'll stick around Winter Cove a little longer." Kim's gaze searched hers. "Is that what it means?"

"If I have any say over it, it does," Matt said, standing in the doorway wearing nothing but a pair of jeans, his hair still damp from his shower.

He looked so impossibly sexy he took Emma's breath away. Any woman who walked away from a man like that deserved to live out the rest of her life in lonely isolation.

"It doesn't," Emma said very firmly. She had to make him see that he was wrong about them, about the future, pretty much about everything except how good they were in bed together.

He gave her a peck on the lips, then said mildly, "We'll see," before walking over to grasp Kim's hand and introduce himself.

"You're not going to hurt her, are you?" Kim demanded protectively.

"Not the way you mean," he assured her, then turned his gaze on Emma. "But if she persists in ignoring all reason, I could be tempted to shake her."

Emma rolled her eyes. "I'm going to get dressed," she said, then thought better of leaving the two of them alone together. Kim was not above plotting with the enemy, if she considered it to be in Emma's best interests. If only Emma had left after her shower, rather than deciding to stick around and have this out with Matt, she wouldn't even be in this predicament right now. She would be safely back at home and Kim would be nowhere near the man who was trying to turn Emma's world upside down. She scowled at them. "Then, again, maybe I'll finish making coffee," she said. "You two coming?"

Matt grinned at her, clearly perfectly aware of what she was up to. "Maybe Kim and I should stay in here and get to know each other. It seems to me we might have a lot in common."

"You have nothing in common," Emma declared fiercely. "Nothing!"

"We have you," Kim noted, watching the byplay with obvious amusement.

"Like I said, a lot," Matt said.

Emma gave up, crossed the room and sank onto the sofa. She realized her mistake at once. Matt's shirt might cover her decently while she was standing, but seated, she was way too exposed. Matt couldn't seem to tear his gaze away from her very bare thighs. She frowned at him.

"Then compare notes to your heart's content," she

said airily. "I'll be right here. I'll be sure to correct you when you get it all wrong."

"Spoilsport," Kim accused. She winked at Matt. "We might as well go into the kitchen, if she's going to listen to every word we say."

Matt nodded. "I'll make breakfast."

"You can cook?" Kim asked, taking his arm and leaving the room without so much as a backward glance toward Emma, her supposed best friend.

"Not as well as Emma, but she has the day off," he said. "Second day in a row. I think she's getting the hang of it."

"It's about time," Kim said, then added something in an undertone that Emma couldn't hear as they disappeared from view.

Emma sat for a minute and seethed, then reluctantly followed them to protect her own interests.

Ever since her father's death she'd been feeling as if her life were teetering on the edge of a precipice. A few days ago, she'd almost started to believe she was finally pulling back from the brink. Now, in just the past ten minutes, she was pretty sure Kim and Matt had reached some sort of pact to see to it that she leaped straight on over the edge.

17

Rosa would have given anything to have Sylvia's comforting presence beside her as she attended her second group session at St. Luke's. It wasn't as easy this time. She was trying to respond to Anne's gently probing questions as honestly as she could, but she felt exposed, her emotions raw.

"What kept you shut up in your room for weeks after Don died?" Anne asked.

"Grief," Rosa said at once, then faltered under the psychologist's steady gaze. "Okay, anger."

"Dig deeper," Anne coached. "Why were you so angry?"

"Because he left me," Rosa said. "He vowed to be with me forever, through good times and bad, and then he abandoned all of us. He *chose* to leave us."

Anna nodded. "That would make most people angry," she agreed. "Everyone here understands that, right?"

The others nodded.

"Was there anything else that made you angry?" Anne asked.

Rosa faltered. Wasn't her outrage at the abandonment enough? Wasn't it justified? "I'm not sure what you mean." she said, not quite meeting the psychologist's steady gaze.

"If he committed suicide, what does that say about the relationship the two of you had?" Anne pressed.

The question ripped away the tender scab over her still raw wounds. "That I wasn't enough for him," she whispered. "That his children and I didn't matter."

"And?"

"Isn't that enough?" she said furiously. "I spent my whole marriage being there for him. I was always the one he turned to, the one everyone around me turned to when there was a problem." Her words were spilling out faster and faster, along with scalding tears. "But this time, when it mattered most, my own husband couldn't turn to me. What does that tell you? It says all those years I spent with him were wasted, that I was useless." As the words tumbled out, she felt her sense of self-worth disintegrating with them.

"No," Anne said gently, but firmly, regarding Rosa with compassion. "It tells me he wasn't himself, that he was lost and didn't know how to find his way back. It was about him, Rosa. His feelings, not you."

"No," Rosa said, not ready to let herself off the hook. "It says I wasn't capable of helping him."

"Absolutely not," Nancy said fiercely, interrupting the exchange. When Rosa whirled on her, she said more quietly, "Don't you see? Anne's exactly right. His suicide wasn't about you at all. It was about him and whatever misguided idea he had that drove him to it. Until you can accept that, you won't be able to move on. I know because for a long time I tried to take responsibility for my mom's death. I thought if I'd been stronger, she wouldn't have felt the need to save me from her suffering."

The others nodded.

"I know how you feel," Larry said.

"Because of how you see yourself, your husband's death was a blow to your self-esteem, Rosa," Anne explained. "You see yourself as a problem solver, don't you?"

Rosa nodded, beginning to understand what they were trying to say. "So I've been trying to make this my failure, when it wasn't at all," she said slowly, feeling the first tiny whisper of relief. "It's not my fault if I couldn't solve Don's problem, because he didn't even share it with me."

"Exactly," Anne said. "And even if he had, in the end it would still have been his problem to solve, not yours. Maybe you could have fixed it together, maybe not, but the choice to die was his alone. We're all accountable for our own actions."

"So in my case, guilt and grief and anger got all twisted together with a major blow to my self-esteem, to the way I've always seen myself," Rosa concluded.

"And none of that is wrong," Anne reassured her. "Your emotions are what they are. It's just important that you sort it out, grieve for your husband, express your hurt and anger, then move on with your life. This was one incident, Rosa. It was a terrible tragedy, but it doesn't define your marriage and it certainly doesn't define who you are."

Rosa sighed heavily, feeling as if she'd been through a wringer. At the same time, an awful weight was slowly lifting from her shoulders. She'd always been so proud of her knack for helping others sort through their difficulties. When Don had died, it had made her question everything about herself as a woman, as a wife and as a friend. She'd gone into seclusion, not so much because of what he'd done, but because of what his act said about her. It had shattered her understanding of who she was. She'd been afraid no one would ever turn to her again, that no one would ever trust her judgment because she hadn't been able to help her own husband.

Rosa left the session feeling both drained and exhilarated, as she went to meet Helen, Jolie and Sylvia for an early dinner intended to celebrate her return to the real world.

The timing couldn't have been better. Not only was she emerging from the darkness, but she had news about Emma to share, as well. If last night was any indication, Emma and Matt were getting a whole lot closer, which meant maybe Emma would stay right here in Winter Cove. If only Don had lived to see that, Rosa thought with a momentary twinge of sorrow. Maybe that would have been enough to make a difference. The bond between father and daughter had always been such a strong one.

Rosa walked into the Italian restaurant that Jolie had chosen because she had her eye on the owner, a recently divorced man who looked a lot like Dean Martin and who oozed Continental charm. Jolie actually stuttered when he kissed her hand. If Jolie had her way they would eat here every night of the week, which meant Rosa would gain twenty pounds from all that pasta. If it kept Jolie's eyes sparkling, though, it was worth every ounce.

Rosa found the three woman already giggling from their glasses of red wine. They were almost finished with the first bottle by the time she joined them.

"I'm cutting you off now," she said, laughing as she poured the remainder of the bottle into her own glass. "I could hear you when I walked in the front door."

"We've been toasting Jolie," Helen explained. "Gianni asked her to have a drink with him later."

"Really? I suggest you make it coffee," Rosa teased as Jolie blushed becomingly. "Strong coffee."

"You sound as if you're in a good mood," Helen observed. "How was your session?"

"I had a breakthrough," Rosa confided and proceeded to tell her best friends all about it. She reached for Sylvia's hand. "I owe it all to you. I would never have gone if you hadn't pushed."

"You would have come around on your own eventually," Sylvia said. "But I'm really glad if this group has helped to speed up the process. We missed seeing you like this."

"Amen," Helen agreed. She lifted her glass. "Welcome back, Rosa."

"Welcome back," Sylvia and Jolie echoed.

Rosa felt her heart swell with emotion as she raised her own glass. "To good friends."

Her marriage had meant the world to her, as did her children, but these women brought something special and irreplaceable into her life. She was just starting to understand how much their friendship mattered. That they hadn't given up on her, even when she'd been pushing them away, spoke volumes about how deep the friendship ran.

"To best friends, always," Helen chimed in.

"Through thick and thin," Jolie added.

All three of them turned to Sylvia and were stunned to see her eyes brimming with tears.

"What?" Rosa demanded at once, the toast forgotten.

"I'm getting a divorce," Sylvia whispered.

All of them stared at her in amazement, but it was Helen who finally spoke, her glass lifted in a toast. "About damned time."

Sylvia laughed even as her tears fell. "It really is, isn't it?"

Emma would have given anything to be able to avoid going back to her house with her best friend. Kim could see right through her, and she was obviously brimming with questions about the state of Emma's relationship with Matt. Emma wasn't sure she had any answers. If anything, last night's incredible lovemaking had only confused things. Just as she had feared, the prospect of leaving town—going home, she thought determinedly—was no longer nearly as attractive as it had been.

"How about a walk around the lake before we go home?" Emma suggested once they'd finally left Matt's after a breakfast that could have qualified as a late lunch. He'd offered to drop them off at the diner or the house, but Emma had declined, saying she needed the fresh air. But even after reaching her car, which had been left in the diner's parking lot, she was still too restless to go home and face Kim's barrage of questions.

"Are you hoping I'm so out of shape that I'll be too breathless to ask you anything?" Kim inquired, giving her a knowing look.

"Hardly. I'm well aware of the amount of time you spend at the gym. I know you do more than ogle all the bare-chested men."

Kim nodded. "As long as you're not trying to put me off, a walk around the lake would be lovely."

To Emma's relief Kim kept silent as they made their way past picnickers lounging on the grass and children sailing miniature boats on the water. When she spotted an ice-cream vendor, she turned to Emma with an expression of pure delight on her face.

"How about a sundae? I'll buy."

Kim's love of ice cream was second only to her love of men. "I'll treat," Emma said. "You're my guest."

"I got the distinct impression earlier that you weren't especially happy about that," Kim said after she'd placed their order with the vendor.

"Just with your timing," Emma said.

"Because I caught you in a compromising position?" Kim teased. "Frankly, I was relieved. I was beginning to worry you were a saint or something."

Kim took the strawberry sundae she'd ordered and handed the hot-fudge sundae to Emma.

"I'm hardly a saint," Emma said, paying the vendor, then turning back to Kim. "Just a confused mortal."

"Over here," Kim commanded, leading the way to a bench in the shade. After they were seated and she'd rolled her eyes heavenward in pure rapture after her first taste of ice cream, she met Emma's gaze. "Tell me about this confusion. What's that about? Aren't you crazy about the guy?"

Emma nodded slowly. "I think I might be falling in love with him."

"Well, hallelujah!"

"No," Emma said miserably. "How can I love him? I don't want to stay here."

"Then get him to move to D.C., if it's that important to you. Judging from the way he looked at you, he'd follow you to the moon and back without asking questions.''

''I can't ask him to do that. He loves it here, as much as I love Washington. He's found a place for himself as chief of police.''

''Then stay.''

''And do what?''

''Start your own antiques business,'' Kim said readily, as if it were as simple as a snap of her fingers. ''You get the career you love in the place he loves. Ta-da! Compromise. It's a wonderful thing.''

''You make it sound so easy.''

''It's as easy—or as complicated—as you want it to be,'' Kim replied. ''If I had a man as gorgeous and nice as Matt madly in love with me, I'd do anything necessary to make it work.''

Emma gazed into her friend's wistful face and realized just how lucky she was to be facing this particular dilemma. ''You'll find your dream man,'' she reassured Kim, then thought of how it had happened for her. ''Or he'll find you.''

''I know,'' Kim said with forced gaiety. ''I just wish he'd hurry the hell up. I don't want to be too old to enjoy the fireworks.''

Emma thought of the way her parents had been together until recently. ''I don't think you ever get too old for that,'' she said quietly. ''My folks certainly didn't.''

Kim's expression sobered at once. ''How is your mom? She seemed good to me, but I was only in the diner long enough to find out where you were.''

''She's getting stronger every day, I think,'' Emma said. ''Coming back to work was a huge hurdle, but now that she's back, I think it's going to be good for her.''

"And Andy?"

"He's still trying to be the man of the family, taking on too much and being way too willing to give up his own life to help out. It took everything in me to persuade him he had to play football this season, especially since he's still not all that happy with me.'' She grinned. "But now that the girls are all hanging around practice, his interest in the game has been revitalized.''

"I can just imagine,'' Kim said. "He's a handsome kid. The girls must fall all over him.''

"All except for the one he really wants,'' Emma said, thinking of his awkward attempts to even hold a conversation with Lauren Patterson. Even though she'd been paying more attention to him lately, he still got tongue-tied whenever he tried to respond. Lauren, thankfully, seemed to have enough self-confidence for both of them. Emma was reasonably certain the girl didn't intend to give up.

"Good. Every man needs a challenging woman in his life,'' Kim said. "What about Jeff? I know you've been worried about him.''

Emma frowned. "Wasn't he at the diner this morning?''

Kim shook her head. "I didn't see him. Andy was cooking and your mom was waiting tables.''

"Damn! I thought Matt had finally gotten through to him. If Matt finds out Jeff's taken off again, there's going to be trouble.''

"It's not exactly Matt's call, is it?'' Kim asked.

"It is if Jeff is doing drugs, which is what we've all been afraid of. The signs are there, and Matt called him on it once. I think that's the only warning Jeff's likely to get.''

''Do you honestly think Matt would arrest your brother?''

''He's the police chief first,'' Emma said. ''Besides, the way he sees it, he'd be doing Jeff a favor by getting him away from that crowd he's hanging with.''

''What's wrong with them?''

''I haven't met anyone but his girlfriend and she's a real piece of work. Maybe I'm wrong about her. Maybe I'm basing my impression on appearances, but everything tells me she's not good for him. Even Mom and Andy think she's a bad influence.''

''Let me get a look at her,'' Kim said. ''Being one myself, I'm very good at spotting females who are trouble.''

''If only Marisol were the same kind of trouble you claim to be,'' Emma said with heartfelt sincerity, ''I wouldn't be so worried about my brother.''

''Maybe we should forget about Jeff, since talking about him only upsets you,'' Kim said. ''Let's get back to Matt.''

Emma frowned. ''Just thinking about *him* upsets me.''

Kim grinned. ''Forget about you. What about me? Does he have any sexy friends?''

Emma laughed. ''You'll have to ask him that yourself.''

''He's a police chief. There are bound to be a few good men on the force in Winter Cove,'' Kim said. She pulled her cell phone from her purse. ''Give me his number. I'll call and ask. Maybe we can double date tonight.''

"He's working," Emma reminded her.

"He gets a break. Besides, how hard can he possibly have to work? I thought Winter Cove was one of the safest towns in the state."

"Because the police chief takes his job seriously," Emma countered. "He doesn't date while he's on duty." At least she didn't think he did. Come to think of it, she had no idea what Matt's dating history had been before she'd returned for her father's funeral. For all she knew, he could have been involved in a torrid affair.

As soon as that depressing thought entered her head, she dismissed it. For one thing, she would have heard about it before now, especially if he'd dumped another woman fairly recently. For another, Matt was too honorable to sleep with Emma, if there was someone else in his life.

She realized Kim was regarding her with pity. "Obviously, you know nothing about the thrill of sneaking around just to steal five minutes in the back seat of a car with the man you love."

"No, I've missed out on that," Emma said. "And don't look so smug, Ms. Two-Dates-and-You're-Out. You don't sneak around, either."

"I would if I had a guy like Matt in my life," Kim retorted with certainty. "I would not waste one precious second of any opportunity to be with him." She gave Emma a pointed look. "If you're going back to D.C., you should remember that. The clock is already ticking."

Emma frowned at the reminder. Unfortunately, she couldn't deny that that damnable tick-tock sound was getting louder and more annoying by the second.

* * *

Matt was not having a good night. He was frustrated by Emma's refusal to even consider the possibility of staying in Winter Cove. Cramer had handed him a pile of messages the second he'd walked into the station, mostly from disgruntled locals who'd received parking tickets and fines and thought he ought to do something about getting rid of the meters in downtown, or at the very least extending the amount of time a driver could legally park without being ticketed. Two hours was not nearly long enough to shop, get a perm or have a leisurely lunch, they claimed.

"You gonna do something about the meters?" Cramer asked, following him into his office.

"Such as?"

"I don't know, maybe give those women the numbers for the men on town council and let them get hassled for a change?"

Matt brightened. "Now there's a thought." He handed back the stack of messages. "Do it."

"Why me? I had to calm 'em down, in the first place."

"Then they'll be really receptive when they hear the solution you've come up with. You'll be their hero."

"I'm not looking to be anybody's hero, which is why I've been perfectly content with desk duty in here all these years. And if I'd wanted to be a damn diplomat, I would have gone to work for the State Department," Cramer grumbled. "You don't pay me enough for this."

"I pay you to do what I ask you to do," Matt corrected. "Besides, you get a lot of perks."

"Name one."

"I know about the doughnuts that Sarah Davis

brings you fresh from the bakery the instant she takes 'em out of the oven," Matt said, watching as the sergeant's ears burned red.

"I pay for 'em," Cramer replied indignantly.

Matt grinned. "Never said you didn't, but you have to admit, no one else in town gets that kind of service, especially at five a.m."

"That's between me and Sarah. It is definitely not one of the perks of working around this dump." He gave Matt a speculative look. "Since we're talking about personal stuff and all that, what's happening with you and Emma these days?"

"We're friends. Always have been."

"And that's it?" Cramer asked, his skepticism plain.

"That's all I'm saying on the subject," Matt said firmly.

Cramer nodded slowly, and then a grin began to spread across his face. "Whoo-ee! You finally made your move, didn't you? What'd she do, turn you down?"

Matt kept his mouth clamped shut.

"Or was she the reason I couldn't get you on your cell phone all last night?" Cramer asked, his expression thoughtful.

"You know, old man, I could fire your butt."

"But you won't," Cramer said with confidence. "I know where all the skeletons are buried around this place, including a few I'm sure you'd just as soon I not spread around town about you."

Matt scowled at him. "My life's an open book."

Cramer chuckled. "Then you've told Emma all about your little fling with Jennifer Sawyer a few months back?"

Matt winced at the direct hit.

"Didn't think so," Cramer said smugly. "And I imagine folks around town would love to know that you finally made your move on pretty little Emma. Everyone was beginning to give up hope."

"Who besides you has been speculating about the state of my love life?" Matt asked.

Cramer waved the wad of messages. "These folks, for starters. Soon as they finished grumbling about their tickets, they asked how things were going between you and Emma. I believe bets are being placed in some quarters."

Matt nearly groaned. He could just imagine how Emma would react if she found out that their relationship was such a hot topic. "I'd better not catch anyone at it."

"You gonna start arresting half the women in town in the middle of their perms?"

"If I have to," he said grimly. He was having enough trouble with Emma without a bunch of busybodies interfering.

Cramer wisely bit back a chuckle, then guffawed openly at something he spotted behind Matt. "Don't look now, boss, but your night's about to go from bad to worse."

Matt turned and saw Gabe and Harley being escorted across the room by a patrol officer. He frowned at them. "What have you two been up to now?"

Officer Juan Gomez tried to control a grin and failed. "Found 'em digging in the trash over behind the Yeager Building. One of the tenants reported hearing prowlers." He held up a zippered freezer bag containing what looked like an address book or a small date book. "They claim this is evidence in Don

Killian's death. Since the last I heard that case was closed, their claim made me suspicious.''

"I'll take it," Matt said. "Thanks, Juan."

"Should I book 'em?" Juan asked.

Gabe regarded him indignantly. "For what? Going through the trash ain't a crime. If it were, you'd be hauling the homeless in here every night of the week, to say nothing of those middle-class scavengers who like to roam around town to see what treasures have been left at the curb on trash day."

"He has a point," Matt conceded reluctantly. "Though I'm not above considering a charge of illegal trespassing with intent to create mischief, if I don't like the answers I get when I question them."

"So that's the thanks we get for finding Jennifer Sawyer's date book," Harley grumbled. "I doubt Emma would be as ungrateful as you seem to be. Then, again, I imagine you'd prefer she not get a look at it at all, what with your name likely to be all over the place in there."

Matt took a fresh look at the item in the plastic bag and realized that it was made of expensive leather. "You're sure this belonged to Jennifer?"

"Saw her with it often enough at the diner," Gabe replied, evidently sensing that the tide was turning in their favor. "You must not have been too observant when she was around, if you don't recognize it. Maybe your mind was on other things."

"Looks like a hundred other date books to me," Matt countered, tired of being reminded that he'd kept his relationship with Jennifer—brief as it was—from Emma. It was a mistake he'd better correct before it blew up in his face.

Gabe gave him a pitying look. "For a police chief,

you sure are lousy at picking up on clues. Look at the initials, right there in gold, plain as can be.'' He flipped over the bag to display them. ''J.S.''

Gabe leaned back with a satisfied look. ''Well? You ready to change your tune now? Is this critical evidence or what? Why would she ditch an expensive date book she used every day of the week, if there weren't something incriminating in it?''

Matt regarded the two men with surprise. ''You haven't looked inside?''

''Of course not,'' Harley retorted. ''That would be tampering with evidence. We're not fools. We didn't even touch it, except with a pencil to get it into that bag. Didn't want to mess up any fingerprints.''

''I see watching all those crime shows has paid off,'' Matt said. Gabe and Harley might be annoying the daylights out of him, but they definitely weren't fools. ''Okay, then, let's take a look and see what we find.''

He led a small parade into his office, retrieved a pair of latex gloves from his desk and opened the zippered bag. Gabe and Harley were all but breathing down his neck. He scowled up at them. ''Back off, okay?''

''We found it. Shouldn't we get to see what's inside?''

''How about I tell you if I find anything worthwhile?'' Matt countered. ''Sit. Both of you.''

He flipped to the date of Don's death, then began working his way back, noting that *F.D.*—Flamingo Diner, maybe—was written in the upper corner of every single page. He'd flipped through one week before he saw ''Don'' scrawled in a bold hand at 2:00 p.m. It appeared once a week like clockwork

from then all the way back to the first of the year.
There were dozens of Dons right here in Winter Cove,
but Matt had a sinking sensation in the pit of his
stomach that Jennifer's notations referred to Don Killian. On some of those very same dates, Matt's own
name was penciled in as well.

Could he have been wrong about the exclusive nature of their brief affair? Could Jennifer and Don have
been involved at the same time he and Jennifer were
seeing each other? Was that why she hadn't been that
brokenhearted when Matt called things off, because
she'd merely been using him as a cover for a relationship she wanted to keep secret? Was that why
Jennifer had left town? Had Don called an end to an
affair right before killing himself? Had Jennifer been
so distraught over the breakup that she'd run away?
Add in the flowers, which she claimed not to have
sent, and an ugly picture was starting to take shape.

Pinning Jennifer down had taken a back seat to a
lot of other things lately. Even Emma seemed to have
lost interest in pursuing the cause of her father's
death. Of course, maybe that was because he'd given
her something else to concentrate on overnight.

Still, Matt couldn't deny that the date book raised
some sobering questions about Jennifer's relationship
with Don, questions that he wanted answered.
Whether he shared those answers with Emma would
depend on what they were.

He was on his feet and heading for the door when
he remembered Gabe and Harley, who'd been waiting
patiently for him to comment on the date book they'd
found.

"You guys did good work tonight," he told them.

"But it's time to hang up your trench coats and put away your detective kits. I'll take it from here."

"Then there is something in there?" Harley demanded excitedly.

"A hint," Matt conceded. "Nothing more."

"But a good hint," Harley persisted.

He grinned. "Yeah, a good hint."

Harley turned to Gabe. "Well, I'll be damned. I thought we risked getting shot for nothing."

"Told you," Gabe said triumphantly. "I think maybe we should think about getting licensed and putting out our shingle."

Even the thought of these two in the private eye business made Matt shudder. "Forget it," he said fiercely. "This was a one-time-only adventure. Count yourselves lucky that you survived it. You mess around in another one of my investigations, you might not be so lucky."

"I still say—" Gabe ventured.

"Listen to me," Matt interrupted. "Go home, take a shower and go to bed. Your investigative days are over. Finished. At an end. Got it?"

Both men looked disappointed.

"Too bad," Harley noted.

Gabe nodded. "Yeah." He shot a pointed look at Cramer as he added, "It was a helluva lot more fun than going bowling, I can tell you that."

Cramer scowled back at him. "You'll get no arguments from me."

As far as Matt could tell, assigning a watchdog to the two men hadn't paid off, anyway. They were a pair of sneaky old coots. He had to admire that, even if he didn't want to deal with 'em ever again.

18

It was 10:00 a.m. and still there had been no sign of Matt at the diner. Emma tried to pretend it didn't matter, but she felt oddly bereft inside. He was always around for breakfast, and even though she'd expected to be vaguely uncomfortable seeing him here among all their friends and neighbors after what had happened between them, she'd also known that she hadn't wanted that night to change their routine. She'd begun to count on his solid presence to keep her grounded.

"You know," Kim said casually, "you'd probably make a lot more tips if you paid attention to the customers who are here, instead of worrying about the one who's not."

Emma frowned. "I am not worried about Matt. He can take care of himself."

"I wasn't referring to his physical prowess, merely his failure to appear," Kim countered. "Tell me you haven't noticed."

"Okay, I've noticed. Kill me."

"I think your mom's noticed, too," Kim said. "She's watching you watch for him and getting more curious by the second. I think the questions are about to start rolling off the tip of her tongue."

"Heaven forbid!" Emma said. The last thing she

wanted was for her mother to start making plans for the future that included Emma staying here with Matt. She didn't want to be responsible for another disappointment in her mom's life.

Kim propped her chin on her hand. "So where do you think he is?"

"On a case, I imagine," Emma said, though she had never before known a case that was big enough to keep him away from the diner all morning long. She was struck by a sudden thought. Gabe and Harley had been behaving like a couple of cats who'd gotten hold of a particularly tasty canary. She regarded the two of them with suspicion. They knew something. She'd bet on it. She grabbed the coffeepot and went to check out what they knew. If all else failed, she could always dump the hot brew over their hard heads to get some straight answers out of them.

"Okay, you two, what's going on?" she demanded as she refilled their cups.

"I don't know what you mean," Harley said, looking as innocent as a choirboy, or at least a choirboy who had a few years on him along with a grizzled face and a very guilty conscience.

"I mean that Matt hasn't been in this morning and I think you know where he is," she told them with exaggerated patience.

"Haven't seen him," Harley insisted.

"Least not since last night," Gabe added, then gasped when Harley's foot apparently connected with his shin. He scowled at his companion. "We ran into him last night. That's all I'm saying."

Ah, now she was getting somewhere. Another push or two and they'd crack. "Where?" Emma asked.

Gabe looked to Harley for help.

"Can't remember," Harley said.

"Yeah, right," Emma scoffed, plunking the coffeepot onto the table so she could lean down and get right up in Gabe's face, since he was the one with the loose lips. "You two may be a lot of things, but you are not forgetful, Gabe Jenkins. Where did you run into Matt?"

"Out and about," Gabe said, obviously pleased with himself for coming up with an answer that told her absolutely nothing.

"Where?" she repeated impatiently.

Harley heaved a resigned sigh. "At the police station, if you must know. He was working."

She began to get a very bad feeling. "And you were there because...?"

Gabe's face lit up. "To see Cramer."

"Exactly," Harley agreed, clearly delighted by his friend's quick thinking.

"When did you two get so chummy with Cramer?" she asked. "I've never seen the three of you together."

"Just lately," Gabe explained. "Matt—ouch!" He scowled at Harley.

"Okay, why were you really at the police station?" Emma asked again. When they remained silent, she drew her own conclusion. "You got picked up, didn't you? Where were you poking around this time? I'm not walking away from this table until you tell me, so you might as well get it over with."

"The trash Dumpster at the Yeager Building," Harley admitted, obviously resigned to giving her at least a small crumb of information to nibble on.

Emma's heart began to pound. "What exactly did you find?"

"A date book," Harley confessed.

"Whose date book?" She looked from one man to the other. "Was it Jennifer Sawyer's?"

They nodded, their expressions guiltier than ever.

"And Matt's with her now?"

"No telling where Matt is," Harley said. "The man gets around."

Emma whipped off her apron, tossed it to Kim and headed for the door. If Matt was questioning Jennifer without her, she was going to string him up from the nearest tree. There wasn't a jury in the world that would convict her once they heard how he'd gone sneaking around behind her back after promising to keep her in the loop about her father's death.

Matt had been cooling his heels in Jennifer's outer office for hours now. He'd had no luck at all tracking her down the night before, so he'd come here first thing this morning, expecting to find her behind her desk by seven, eight at the latest. There'd been no sign of her.

Cori had finally arrived at eight-thirty to find him pacing the corridor outside the office, getting more agitated by the second.

"Where the hell is she?" he'd demanded, following Cori inside. "She hasn't gone out of town again, has she?"

Cori had frowned at his tone, then led the way to the inner office—the very empty inner office—without answering his question. That had been an hour ago and she was still giving him the silent treatment. Since his beef wasn't with her, he'd let it pass. No point in riling up a pregnant lady, especially one whose hormones were reputedly swinging more wildly than a novice boxer.

As if she sensed that his sour mood was lifting, she glanced up from whatever she'd been typing into the computer and gave him a hesitant smile.

"You want some coffee or something?" she asked in an apparent attempt at a peace offering. "I was afraid to offer you caffeine before. You already seemed a little hyper."

Matt shrugged. "Sorry. It was a long night. As for the coffee, forget it. I'd prefer some information on your boss's whereabouts."

"That I can't give you," she said. "Sorry."

"Because she swore you to secrecy?" Matt asked.

"No, because I have no idea where she is. It's one of her character flaws. She sees no need to keep me informed of her plans."

"Helluva way to run an office," Matt commented.

Cori shrugged. "We're working on it."

Matt smiled despite himself. "Who's winning this little test of wills?"

"She called in once last week, so I figure that's progress."

"You haven't heard from her since last week?"

"Oh, she was in yesterday, but that doesn't count. I'm talking about the times she disappears without a word and there's nothing on her calendar."

Matt's antenna went up. "Does that happen a lot?"

"Often enough to drive me crazy, especially the last few months."

"You have any idea where she goes when she vanishes without a word? Is she with someone in particular?"

"I have my suspicions, but that's all they are." She

frowned at him. "And before you even ask, no, I will not share them with you. You can ask her yourself."

"Assuming she ever shows her face," Matt said with disgust. "Doesn't she lose money when she's not here to take calls and make stock trades?"

"She's not a broker. She's a financial adviser," Cori reminded him. "But she does keep a close eye on the market for her own portfolio."

"It's been a tough market. How's she doing?"

Cori shrugged. "As long as I get my paycheck, I don't care. I'm not about to gamble it away on stocks."

"Some say it's still the best way to make money," Matt pointed out.

"Also the best way to lose it," she countered. "I'd have about the same amount of luck playing the slot machines in Las Vegas, and at least there I'd get to see a few shows." Her expression suddenly brightened. "Not to change the subject or anything, but how are things going with you and Emma?"

Matt considered his response carefully and decided to stick with something neutral. "Okay, I guess."

Cori rolled her eyes. "Not so hot, huh? Have you talked her into staying in Winter Cove?"

"No, but I'm trying to show her all the advantages."

"You being one of them?" Cori asked, mischief brightening her eyes.

"The jury's still out on whether she sees me as an advantage or a disadvantage," he said, thinking of the way Emma had gotten her dander up the last time they'd been together. She might enjoy the sex but she clearly wasn't about to let it sway her decision to leave.

"Then you must be losing your touch. Have you considered concentrating on what the town has to offer?"

His gaze narrowed. "Such as?"

"I heard Mr. Mullins is thinking of selling that junk shop of his over on Palm Drive. Could be the perfect opportunity for a woman who's been working in an antiques store. There have to be some good pieces buried under the rubble in that place and from what I hear, Emma's got a knack for finding treasures. Don was always bragging about that."

Matt's brain kicked into overdrive. He jumped up and planted a kiss on Cori's forehead. "You're a genius."

"Tell it to Jennifer," she said, grinning.

"You let me know when she's back, and I will," he promised her. He tossed a card on her desk. "Use my beeper number."

"You've got it," she said. "And Matt…"

"What?"

"Good luck with Emma. I was sorry things didn't work out with Jennifer for her sake, but I always thought you and Emma belonged together."

"Me, too," he said, then spun around and ran smack into the woman in question barreling through the door with a full head of steam.

"You…you…" Words seemed to fail her, so she took a swing at him.

Matt caught her fist in midair and studied her intently. "Is there a problem?"

"You bet there is," she said, her eyes flashing with temper.

The instant he released his grip on her hand, she stepped up and poked him in the chest. "You promised me that I'd be the first to know if you found out anything.''

"But I haven't found out anything," he said reasonably, well aware of the fact that he was splitting hairs. He had seen the date book. He just didn't know what it meant.

"You're lying through your teeth," she accused. "I know about the date book that Gabe and Harley found."

He sighed heavily. "Of course, you do." She knew because he'd been too stupid to tell the men to keep their mouths shut. He'd assumed they'd know enough to keep silent, especially around Emma. Of course, maybe the fault wasn't theirs. She could be damned persuasive when she wanted to be. No one knew that better than he did.

"Well, then, what do you have to say for yourself?" she demanded.

Matt shoved his hands in his pockets to keep from reaching out and dragging her into his arms. He had a hunch this would not be the time to tell her how gorgeous she was when she was furious. Nor was the moment exactly right for kissing her senseless, though if she kept on yakking about that damn date book, he was going to have to do something dramatic to silence her. Cori was listening with avid fascination and he didn't want her sharing the entire conversation with Jennifer. He needed to catch Jennifer off guard with what he knew.

"Not much," he finally said.

"Not much!"

"You're shouting," he said, his own voice deliberately quiet.

"I am not shouting," she said in a tone that could

probably be heard two counties over. *"This is shout- ing!"* She upped the decibel level to one that could shatter glass.

"You're obviously upset. Why don't we go some- where and talk about this?" he suggested, latching on to her arm and steering her out of the office.

Emma dug in her heels. "I don't want to go some- where. I want to know what you found out right here and right now."

"Nothing."

"I want to know every little…" Her voice trailed off and she stared at him in confusion. "Nothing?"

"Nothing. Jennifer's not in. She hasn't been in. And I would just as soon not let Cori know anything more about the date book. She might feel it's her duty to fill Jennifer in."

Emma flushed guiltily. "Oh."

He shook his head and looked into her eyes. "Emma, don't you trust me?"

"Of course, I do. Or I did, anyway, till I heard you'd come over here without me."

"I came without you because I have no idea what anything in that date book means. I saw no reason to get you all worked up until I had more to go on."

"But there was something in the date book that made you suspicious that Jennifer knows more than she's admitted, wasn't there?"

"Yes."

"What?"

He saw little point in trying to keep it from her. "Your dad's name turned up a lot, once a week like clockwork, ever since the first of the year."

Emma turned pale. "What do you think that means?"

"I don't know what it means. That's what I came here to find out. But Jennifer's among the missing again."

"Missing?"

He nodded. "Cori says it's nothing out of the ordinary for her to take off without telling anyone. Cori will call me the second Jennifer turns up and we can see her together, if that will make you happy."

"I don't know about happy," she said. "But I do want to be there. For now I'll settle for seeing that date book."

Thankfully Matt had anticipated that she might want to do exactly that if she found out about it. "Sorry. It's evidence. I've got it locked up back at the station."

Emma regarded him suspiciously. "I thought this wasn't an official case."

"It's not."

"Then why did you lock up the date book? What else is in there that you don't want me to see?"

He debated spilling the rest of it now, but she was a little too riled up to be either understanding or forgiving. "Nothing," he assured her. "While we're waiting for a call from Cori, how about some lunch? I'm starved. I missed breakfast."

"I noticed," she admitted.

Matt could barely contain his smile. "Did you really? How fascinating. Maybe we should skip lunch and go to my place."

"Oh, no, you don't," she said. "I'm still mad at you."

"Because of this morning?"

"No, because of yesterday."

"We could talk about that, too," he said. "It's very

important to communicate. In fact, communication is the backbone of a good relationship.''

"We don't have a relationship. We're having sex."

"You say potato. I say po-tah-to. Same difference.''

She rolled her eyes.

Matt grinned at her. "Bet I could make you change your mind.''

"I'll bet you could, too, but what would that prove?''

"That there's better living through chemistry?'' he suggested.

Emma fought a chuckle, but it escaped, anyway. "You drive me crazy, Matt Atkins.''

He thought of all the things he wanted to do to her and with her. Driving her crazy was a start. He reached for her hand and held it as they left the Yeager Building. On the street, he met her gaze. "Good crazy or bad crazy?''

Her expression turned thoughtful as she considered the question, probably from every angle possible.

"A little of each, I suppose,'' she said finally.

"Well, there you go,'' he said triumphantly. "It all balances out.''

She laughed then and he swooped in and stole a kiss. When they were both hot and breathless, he leaned close to her ear and whispered, "Just so you know, you drive me crazy, too. Always have.''

Rosa looked up from the food order she was putting together and spotted Larry from her support group standing hesitantly in the doorway of the diner.

"Are you closed?'' he asked.

"Pretty much," she said. "But the coffee's still hot."

"Mind if I come in, then?"

"Of course not. How do you take your coffee?"

"Black," he said, walking over to the counter and sliding onto a stool. He looked around. "Nice place. I can't believe I've never been in here before."

"Not everyone gets to this part of town. A lot of people do their shopping at the malls, not downtown," she said. "What brings you by today?"

"You," he said, then looked uncomfortable. "I don't mean that quite the way it sounds. It's just that I've been so impressed the last couple of weeks with how well you're adjusting already, when it's been eight months for me and I'm still a wreck."

Rosa poured a cup of coffee for herself and went around the counter to join him. "Believe me, I am not adjusting well. I was a mess up until my friend Sylvia got me to that first meeting. Talking to all of you has helped." She studied him intently. He was a nice-looking man in his mid-forties, she supposed from the hint of gray in his dark brown hair and the lines fanning out from his eyes. "The thing of it is, you suffered two losses, not just one. Not only did your wife kill herself, but you lost the woman you'd been hoping to marry after the divorce went through."

"That didn't help, that's for sure." He looked into her eyes. "Some days, though, I feel as if I'm the one who should have died, you know what I mean? Being left behind to live with all the guilt is hard."

"But your wife's death was not your fault," she reminded him, realizing as she spoke so emphatically that it was much easier to see that when it was someone else. "You were honest with her and she couldn't cope with that. It's sad, but it wouldn't have helped if you'd told her you'd stay. In the end, you both would have been miserable. Don't get me wrong. I don't believe in divorce unless all other options have failed, but sometimes it's simply for the best."

Larry nodded, his eyes filled with misery. "I thought it was for us. We'd talked, we'd fought, we'd even tried counseling, but we still couldn't get back to the way we'd been when we were first married."

"Maybe it's wrong for anyone to expect that initial glow to last forever," Rosa said.

"We lost more than that glow. We had nothing left in common. We ate every meal in silence, then she went off to her sewing room and I read the newspapers and trade publications."

"No children?"

He shook his head. "She couldn't have them and she refused to consider adoption. I think that was the beginning of the end. I'd always wanted a big family."

"How sad for both of you," Rosa said.

"Eventually I started staying late at the office, having dinner out, just to avoid all that silence," he said. "Maybe if we'd fought about that, it would have shown me that she still cared about what I did, but she never said a word. When I asked for the divorce the first time, it wasn't because I was involved with anyone else. I was stunned when she flatly refused. That's when I sort of drifted into seeing other women, just to have some conversation. I'd missed that." He regarded her with a sorrowful expression. "Then I met Elaine, and it all came back to me, what a real relationship was supposed to be. That's when I really pressed for the divorce and my wife threatened to kill herself. I told Elaine and she said it was okay, that we could wait till she got used to the idea. In the meantime, I moved out.''

"That was probably for the best," Rosa told him. "Your wife needed to know it was really over and that you weren't going to be blackmailed into staying."

"That's what I thought at the time. It's hard to believe that now, when my wife died because I left."

"She died because she didn't want to take responsibility for her own happiness," Rosa told him.

A smile hovered at the corners of Larry's mouth.

"What?" she asked.

"I see why everyone comes to you with their problems," he said.

Rosa laughed. "We can always see more clearly when it's someone else's problems. It's our own that we can't always resolve."

He met her gaze. "Would you mind if I come back from time to time to talk?"

Rosa felt an odd sensation in the pit of her stomach. Anticipation? Dread? It was hard to tell, but she wasn't ready to grapple with a relationship that caused either one. She fumbled for words that wouldn't hurt his feelings. "I don't know," she began, but he cut her off.

"Not like a date," he said quickly. "Just to talk. I'd like to get to know you. I've stayed away from women since my wife died and Elaine left. Too complicated, I suppose, but I miss being around females." He grinned. "I like the way your minds work."

"If it's only my mind that interests you, by all means stop by whenever you're in the neighborhood." Suddenly Rosa thought of Helen. She might be the perfect match for Larry. So what if she was a little older? He could use a nice, steady woman with a quick wit and a generous heart. And it would please Rosa no end to play matchmaker.

He drank the last of his coffee and reached for his wallet, but she shook her head. "This one's on the house. Welcome to Flamingo Diner."

"Thanks, Rosa. I'll see you at group, if not before."

Larry was almost to the door when it swung open, barely missing him, as Jeff came charging in. His hair was a mess, his clothes disheveled and he had the distinct wild-eyed look of someone completely out of control. Larry took a step back inside and regarded Rosa with concern.

"Maybe I should have another cup of coffee, after all," he said with a pointed look in Jeff's direction.

Though she was grateful for his instinctive desire to protect her, she shook her head. "No need. I'll be fine."

"Are you sure?"

She was too embarrassed to admit that this was her own son, not when he was staring at Larry with such a sullen expression. "I'm sure," she said, and forced a smile.

He hesitated, then nodded. "Okay, then. I'll be going."

Only after he'd gone did Rosa draw in a deep, steadying breath and turn to face her son. "Are you drunk?" she demanded, hands on hips.

"No," he said, though his voice was slurred.

"Drugs, then," she said, her heart aching. "Why are you here?"

He faltered at the unmistakable chill in her voice. "Isn't this the family business?" he finally asked, his tone scathing. "Such as it is."

"It belongs to those of us who work here and keep it running," she corrected. "You've lost any claim to it the last few weeks. I thought you got that a while back, but evidently it's slipped your mind again."

He blinked hard at her dismissal of his rights and for just an instant she could see a scared boy buried inside that sullen, angry facade. She refused to let herself feel sorry for him, though. Pity wasn't what Jeff needed. He needed some straight talk and it was past time she gave it to him.

"Sit," she ordered. She poured him a cup of coffee and set it down in front of him. "Drink that."

"You're not my boss."

"We could debate that, but since you haven't been showing up for work, I suppose you're technically right. However, I am your mother and you will listen to what I have to say. Now drink that coffee before I pour it over your head to sober you up."

He looked as stunned as if she'd slapped him, but he took a long swallow of his coffee before facing her again. "Mom, what's happened to you?" he asked, sounding more hesitant.

"I've emerged from the fog and taken a good, hard look at what's going on right in front of my face, and I do not like it, Jeffrey Killian. I do not like it one bit."

"Mom—"

"Hush! I'm talking now. If you want to stay involved with Marisol, I can't stop you. If you want to hang around with a bunch of boys who are living in a drug-induced haze, I can't stop you from doing that, either. But I am here to tell you than I can and will stop you from coming in here when you're all doped up.''

''How?'' he asked, his expression belligerent.

She kept her gaze steady and her tone even. ''I'll call Matt if you show up like this again.''

''You wouldn't,'' he said, clearly shocked.

''I would,'' she said emphatically. ''And I can keep your brother or your sister from loaning you money to buy drugs. I can keep you from stealing it from the register by changing the locks if I have to.'' At his stunned expression, she nodded. ''Yes, I'm aware that you've done that. I may have been living in a fog lately, but I do pay attention to our finances these days. I have to.''

Her words obviously hit home. He looked shaken.

''Good,'' she said with satisfaction. ''At least you're not denying that you've stolen money from here.''

''It's my business, too,'' he said defiantly.

''Not unless you contribute something, which you haven't for weeks now, at least not without one of us all but begging you to pitch in. It's time to make a choice, Jeffrey. You're either a part of this family or you're going to destroy your life with drugs.'' She kept herself from reaching for him. Instead, she regarded him steadily. ''I love you, Jeff. So do Emma and Andy. If you need help to get off the drugs, we'll get it for you, but we will not enable you to go on like this.''

''I don't need help from anybody,'' he said defiantly. ''I can quit anytime I want to.''

Rosa knew better, but she merely nodded. ''Then it's time to make the choice. What is it?''

"You expect me to decide now?"

"Here and now," she confirmed. "Because I've had it. I knew you were hurting and I thought this stage you're going through would pass, but it hasn't. It's time to grow up."

"This from a woman who hid in her room for weeks," he said scathingly.

Rosa didn't even flinch. "You're right. I hid. I didn't want to face the likelihood that your father had taken his own life." The color drained from Jeff's face, but before he could speak, she went on. "You suspect that's what happened, as well as I do. It's why you've been acting like this. You're furious with him. So am I, but I'm here to tell you that this is no way to get even. The only person you're hurting is yourself."

"Dad didn't commit suicide," he argued, but there was little conviction in his voice.

"Yes, I believe he did, and the sooner we all face up to that the better. Your father is gone, but we're not. Life goes on whether you want it to or not. I decided it was too precious to waste."

He regarded her curiously. "Does this have something to do with that guy who was leaving when I came in?" he asked as if he was ready to make something dirty out of it.

"Absolutely not. He's in that support group I told you about at Saint Luke's, but that's it. In fact, I was thinking I might introduce him to Helen."

Her response clearly took the wind out of his sails. He stood up, then, swaying slightly. "I gotta go."

Rosa felt thoroughly defeated. "Do what you have to do."

He started away, then came back and gave her a fierce hug. "I love you, Mom."

Tears brimming over in her eyes, she hugged him back. "I love you, too." Only after he was too far away to hear did she whisper, "No matter what."

19

Matt took the first chance he had to detour over to Palm Drive to check out the junk shop Cori had told him about. He'd passed the store a thousand times without ever noticing it, probably because the owner hadn't spent a nickel on improvements in the last forty years. It stood out like a sore thumb, though. Every other shop on the block had windows that glistened and new awnings.

The junk shop's front window was coated with a dingy layer of grime. The once-gold lettering had worn away to make the store's name all but illegible. Not that it had been an inspired name to begin with. It looked like it might have been Mullins Junk, though the *M* was virtually gone and only part of the *J* and *K* remained of the second word.

He thought at first the store wasn't open, but then he spotted a dim light at the back and tried the door. It swung open on rusty, creaking hinges. Great place for a Halloween party, he thought wryly as he called out for Joshua Mullins.

"In the back," replied a voice that sounded every bit as creaky as the door.

Matt made his way through cluttered aisles that barely allowed room enough for him to pass. Brass headboards were piled against one wall. Old oak

washstands and dressers were crammed against each
other at odd angles. Cheap metal shelving on another
wall held an assortment of items that ranged from
dusty bottles in every color of the rainbow to china
teacups piled atop one another to a precarious height.
If there were treasures buried in here, it would be all
but impossible to discern them in the poor lighting
and even more daunting clutter.

Matt vaguely recalled Joshua Mullins from years
ago. He'd been a crotchety old man then. He must be
a million years old by now. One glimpse of the bent
figure maneuvering through the back room on a
walker seemed to prove his guess.

"Stay there," Matt called to him, envisioning the
man breaking his hip trying to cross the curling, yel-
lowed linoleum.

When he was closer, Mr. Mullins squinted at him.
"That you, Matt Atkins?"

"Yes, sir."

"Heard you were back in town. Guess you ain't
stirring up trouble the way you used to, are you?" He
cackled dryly at his little joke.

Matt grinned. "Not if I hope to keep my job."

"Always thought Don Killian would get you
straightened out," he said approvingly. "He was a
good man. Too bad about what happened to him."

"Yes, it is."

"His family doing okay? I've thought about going
by the diner to pay my respects, but I don't get around
the way I used to."

"I'm sure they understand. They're doing the best
they can."

The old man gave him a sharp look. "That include
the boy, Jeff, I think it is?"

Matt regarded him with surprise. "Why would you ask that?"

The old man sighed and leaned even more heavily on his walker. "Because that girl he's been hanging around with is my great-granddaughter, and she's out of control. I hate to speak ill of one of my own, but Rosa ought to get her son away from Marisol, if she knows what's good for him. The girl has a wild streak. Got it from her mama, who never bothered to marry my grandson. She had some cockamamy idea that marriage was the thing that ruined a relationship. If they'd let me talk to her, I could have told her a thing or two about marriage. I was with my Rachel for sixty years, and every one of those years was a joy."

Matt could hear the concern and the frustration in his voice. "Anything I can do to help with your great-granddaughter?"

Mr. Mullins cackled again as if it were Matt who'd made a joke this time. "I 'spect you're the last person I ought to be telling about what I think is going on with that girl. Her daddy'll handle it, once he gets his head out of the sand. Hard to do right when it comes to discipline when he's only in the girl's life part-time." He met Matt's gaze. "What brings you by here? You looking for something in particular? That room may look like a mess, but I can tell you every single thing that's in there and pretty much where to find it."

Matt grinned. "I imagine you can. Actually, though, I came by because I heard you might be interested in selling out."

"To the right person, maybe," he said. "You don't

strike me as the type to want to fool around with a
lot of dusty old treasures.''

''No, but Emma Killian might be. She was in the
antiques business up in Washington. I think she might
consider staying in Winter Cove, if the right opportunity presented itself.''

Mr. Mullins cackled again and gave Matt a sly
look. ''You saying you ain't enough to keep her here
on your own?''

Obviously the man's frail health hadn't hurt his
ability to tap into the Winter Cove gossip network.
''Maybe,'' Matt said. ''Maybe not. I figured it
wouldn't hurt to hedge my bets.''

''You bring her on by sometime. No point in wasting my energy discussing this with you, when she's
the one who'll have to decide.''

Matt laughed. ''Good point. Any time in particular?''

''I'm here most days. Most evenings, too, for that
matter, now that the street's getting all yuppified.
Once in a while somebody with a good eye wanders
in, but mostly it's young people with too much cash
and not enough sense to know they're supposed to
bargain with me. You say the Killian girl knows her
stuff?''

''So I gather,'' Matt said.

Mr. Mullins nodded, his eyes sparkling with anticipation. ''Good. There's nothing I like better than a
lively negotiation with a smart woman. Take note of
that, young man. A smart woman will never bore you.
My Rachel, God rest her soul, was a live wire till the
day she died. I couldn't put a thing over on her.'' He
grinned. ''Not that I tried, of course.''

"Of course," Matt said. "I'll bring Emma by the first chance I get."

In fact, he could hardly wait. He had a hunch that his future was in Joshua Mullins's gnarled hands. Something told him, also, that he couldn't find a better person to entrust it to. Some men were born with wisdom about human nature. Don Killian had been one of those. Joshua Mullins had learned it the hard way, from a long life, hard work and a good woman. Matt wouldn't mind following in his footsteps.

Emma took one look at her mother's pale face and worried expression and knew something had happened.

"What's wrong?" she asked when she found Rosa at the kitchen table staring into space, her expression almost as bleak as it had been in the day's after Emma's father's death.

"Nothing."

"Don't give me that. Is it Andy?"

"Andy's fine. He's got a date tonight. Lauren Patterson finally said yes." She forced a smile. "Seems to me you ought to have one, too, now that Kim's on her way back to Washington. Where's Matt?"

"I have no idea where Matt is, and stop trying to change the subject. If Andy's fine, what about Jeff? Have you seen him?"

"He came by the diner earlier," her mother conceded with obvious reluctance.

"And?"

"He's in trouble, Emma," she said, barely choking back a sob. She visibly steadied herself, then added, "I tried laying it on the line with him, but I don't think I got through. Maybe he has to hit rock bottom before he'll get it, but it breaks my heart to think of it coming to that.''

Emma would have shaken Jeff if she could have gotten her hands on him at that moment. Her mother had been doing so well lately. Now worry about Jeff was clearly pushing her back toward the depression from which she'd only recently emerged.

"Mom, we may not be able to fix this. He has to want to get better.''

Her mother regarded her with regret. "I know that. I blame your father. If he were here, he'd know what to do.''

"I don't think so. I honestly think Jeff was already headed down this path before Dad died. You said yourself he was already mixed up with Marisol and she's obviously part of the problem.''

"Don't be ridiculous,'' Rosa snapped, then immediately looked contrite. "I'm sorry. If I'm being perfectly honest, I know you're right. He and your father had fought about his new crowd of friends, which only made them more attractive to Jeff. Your brother had pretty much stopped coming around long before your father died. I tried to pretend it was just because he was in college and testing his wings, but it was more than that. Jeff's been struggling for a long time to figure out who he is. The only thing he knew for sure was that he didn't want to be his father, that he didn't want any part of Flamingo Diner.''

"And Dad couldn't accept that, could he?'' Emma guessed. Her father had given in with undisguised reluctance to her wishes, but Jeff was his son. There was a difference. Her dad wouldn't have given up on Jeff as easily.

"No,'' Rosa said. "It broke Don's heart to have

his oldest son reject the business he'd worked so hard to turn into a success.''

''And now Jeff feels trapped and guilty because Dad's gone and we've been pressuring him to pitch in,'' Emma said thoughtfully. ''Maybe it's little wonder that he's looked for a way out.''

''Well, he picked the wrong way,'' her mother said fiercely. ''And this is an emergency, not a commitment for the rest of his life. I am so disappointed in him.''

''Did you tell him that?''

''Yes,'' she said with no apparent sign of regret.

Emma regarded her with surprise. Her mother was definitely getting back to her old self if she wasn't hesitating to speak her mind. ''Good for you,'' she told her mother.

''I also told him I loved him and that it was time for him to make a choice about straightening out his life.'' She gave Emma a worried look. ''I know he needed to hear that, but what if I just pushed him further away?''

''Mom, all any of us can do is try with him. In the end, it's going to be his decision. It's not like he's misbehaving on a play date. He's too old for you or even me to go charging down to wherever he's hanging out these days and drag him home.''

Her mother smiled. ''Doesn't mean I'm not tempted to try.''

Emma gave her hand a squeeze. ''I know. Me, too.''

When Matt walked into the diner, Andy caught his eye and beckoned him over to the grill, where he had at least a dozen eggs cooking, along with a pile of hash browns, and a couple of pounds of bacon. He was beginning to look like a pro, though the expression on his face was too grim for a boy his age.

"You need help, kid?" Matt asked. He stood back and admired the way Andy deftly flipped an egg without breaking the yolk.

"Not till you learn to do this," Andy said with a grin that quickly faded. "I wanted to ask you about something else."

"Okay, what?"

"This is between you and me, right?" Andy asked worriedly. "As my friend, not as a cop?"

"If that's the way you want it," Matt assured him.

"I think something's going on with Jeff, something bad. Mom and Emma were talking till all hours last night. I went down to get a soda and I heard 'em mention Jeff's name. I didn't want to eavesdrop, but I could tell they were both upset."

"Has Jeff been around lately?"

"I haven't seen him." His normally cheerful expression darkened. "I hate him," he said in a fierce undertone. "I know he's my brother and all, but I really do hate him."

He waited as if he expected Matt to chastise him for his feelings. Matt merely nodded. "I can understand that."

"It's not like things aren't bad enough, but he has to go and pull a disappearing act and worry Mom. What kind of son does something like that?" Andy demanded heatedly.

Matt squeezed his shoulder. "One who's a little mixed up right now. Come on, Andy, you don't really hate him. You and Jeff have always been tight. He helped you a lot right after your dad died, didn't he?"

"I suppose," Andy said grudgingly. "But where is he now?"

"He's struggling to make sense of things."

"Well, I'm tired of it. I'm tired of being the only one around here to help out Mom and Emma. Hell, Emma gave up everything to come home because she knew we needed her. What happens if she gets sick of this and goes back to Washington? Who would blame her? Not me. Some days I feel like I could pack it in and go with her."

"I don't think you need to worry about Emma going anywhere," Matt said. "At least not right now. And your Mom is better and back at work. Even if Emma left, Flamingo Diner would do fine."

"Not without me," Andy retorted. "Not unless Mom hired somebody, and we don't have the money for that right now. And I've got school starting. What happens then?"

"Want me to have a talk with your mom?"

"No, I want you to find Jeff and kick his butt from here to Miami."

Matt hid a smile. "Okay, kid, I can do that, too."

"What were you and Andy huddling about?" Emma asked when the restaurant had emptied out and she could join Matt.

"Guy stuff," he said.

Her gaze narrowed. "He wasn't asking you about sex, was he?"

Matt laughed. "Interesting that that's the first thing that popped into your head," he taunted.

Emma scowled at him. "This isn't a joke. Was it about sex or not?"

"No, the only Killian with whom I discuss sex these days is you."

"Very funny."

"I thought so. Don't worry about Andy. He's got his head on straight, and as for sex, he's seventeen. I'm pretty sure he knows all he needs to know."

She sank down in a chair, grabbed Matt's saucer and set the coffeepot on it. "You don't seriously think he's fooling around, do you?"

"I was at seventeen," Matt said.

She frowned at him. "Yeah, so I heard. But you were street smart enough to avoid getting into trouble."

"Only because your father sat me down when I was fourteen and gave me a lecture and a box of condoms."

She stared at him. "At fourteen?"

He shrugged, looking a little too pleased with himself. "I was precocious."

Emma let that pass. "So you think he had this same talk with Andy," she surmised.

"I'd bet on it."

"Thank God. With Jeff spinning out of control, the last thing this family needs would be for Andy to get some girl pregnant during his senior year. He's finally got a date with Lauren Patterson. He's had this thing for her forever. I wouldn't want him to let his hormones overrule his head."

"I don't think you need to worry about that. Lauren's a very sensible girl. Besides, Andy has a good head on his shoulders. More than that, he's as aware as anyone of just how irresponsible Jeff is being. I definitely don't think he wants to follow in his big brother's footsteps."

"Maybe not, but every now and then, he must feel as if he's carrying more than his share of the load. Who could blame him if he decided to reach out to some girl for comfort?" Emma asked.

"The way you reached out to me?" Matt asked quietly.

"Something like that." She drew in a deep breath. "But I wanted more from you than comfort."

"Glad to hear it."

"I just don't know what quite yet."

"You'll work it out," he said confidently and without any evidence that he was in a hurry. He looked around the diner, then stood up. "I'll be right back."

She stared after him as he went to the front door and flipped the lock. "What do you think you're doing?"

"Closing," he said as he turned the sign on the door to the appropriate side. He came back to the table and straddled his chair. "Let's talk."

She eyed him warily. "About?"

"You."

"What about me?"

"Your color's lousy and you're clearly exhausted. I thought you were doing great, but now I'm not so sure. I'm worried about you."

"Thanks so much for the confidence booster."

"You don't need sweet talk. You need action." He stood up and leaned down, capturing her mouth.

She debated shoving him away, but the kiss felt too good. When her head was spinning, he stood up and studied her, then gave a satisfied nod. "Much better."

"Better?" She felt dazed.

"Definitely better."

"Better than what?"

"The way you looked when I walked in here. You're working too hard, Emma. You're pale. You're strung so tight, I'm scared you're going to shatter. Even just now, you looked as if you were expecting me to drop more bad news on you about Andy."

"I'm fine," she insisted, though her hand shook as she tried to pour his coffee. Maybe she had been anticipating the worst lately. She had reason to be jittery. A lot of the news coming her way had been pretty devastating. She was no worse off than anyone else would be under the same circumstances.

"I'm fine," she repeated to emphasize the point.

"Yeah, I can see that," Matt said wryly. "I know things have been rough around here, but you can't shoulder the whole burden alone. I thought you understood that, but apparently you need reminding more often."

"I'm not doing this on my own, not anymore."

He scowled at that. "Who's helping? Your mom's back, but her heart's not in it, not entirely, anyway. Andy's here, but he can only do so much."

"Is this about Jeff?" she asked. "I don't want to go down that road with you."

"I'm not specifically talking about Jeff. I'm worried about you and the effect all this stress is having on you."

"Don't," she said. "Besides, I have you."

His frown dissipated. "Thank you. Who else?"

"You already said it. I have Andy," she said.

"He'll be back in school next week. What then?"

"I'll manage. And despite what you think, Mom really is getting better. She's been going to some meetings and she's almost back to her old self."

"And Jeff?"

"Let's just leave him out of this," she said again, aware that she sounded a little desperate. She didn't want Matt digging too deeply into what Jeff was up to these days. Not that he didn't already have his suspicions, but she wasn't about to be the one to confirm them. She and her mother could handle Jeff. They had to.

"How can I leave him out of it?" Matt asked reasonably. "He's a crucial part of the problem."

"Come on, Matt, give him a break. This hit him hard. He's had to give up college in his senior year. Instead of graduating, he's back here. He had a job at the mall, but he lost it."

"Then where the hell is he? If he made all these sacrifices for the family, then why isn't he here pitching in?"

Emma frowned at the question. "It's not your concern," she said stiffly.

"I'm making it my concern."

"Why?"

"Because you're worn-out. You need help. Jeff is old enough to be taking up some of the slack around here. Apparently my last conversation with him didn't make that clear enough."

"Forget it. Mom and I can deal with Jeff. The only help I want from you is answers."

"That's not what you were suggesting just a minute ago."

She decided she had to go on the offensive to divert his attention from her brother. "Dammit, Matt, what have you found out about my father's business activities? It's been days since Jennifer's last disappearance. Have you tracked her down or not? Are you just sitting around waiting for Cori to call? I could do that much myself.''

The tactic failed. He merely regarded her with a tolerant expression.

''You're not going to change the subject on me so easily,'' he said. ''Let's finish talking about what you're going to do to ease up on the pressure you're putting on yourself.''

As far as Emma could tell the pressure wasn't going to let up until she had her family back on an even keel and she could return to Washington. Sadly, that seemed to be months away.

''No answer for me?'' he asked.

''Like I said, it's not your concern.''

He gave her a look that disputed that, then reached for her hand. ''Come on.''

''Where? I still have a load of dishes to wash and the floor needs to be mopped. Besides, I'm still waiting for those answers. If you're not going to give them to me, then I need to finish up here and go looking for them myself.''

''The mopping and the answers can wait,'' he said emphatically. ''We're going for a walk.''

''But…'' The protest died when she recognized the glint of determination in his eyes. ''All right.''

He grinned. ''Good answer. I think you're finally getting the hang of this communication business.''

''You only think that because I agreed to do what you want me to do,'' she grumbled.

''Exactly. Works out nicely, don't you think?''

''Do you really care what I think?''

His gaze locked on hers and made her tremble inside. ''It's the only thing I care about,'' he said softly. ''The only thing. Maybe it's time you remember that.''

20

After the first time he'd had to coerce her into it, evening walks partway around the lake with Matt started to become a ritual that Emma looked forward to. She felt at peace as the sun slid below the horizon and the air began to cool. Being with Matt made her feel safe, and for a time each day, the weight on her shoulders seemed to ease. Being back in Winter Cove didn't seem like such a bad thing.

Tonight they cut off the path halfway around the lake and headed for Main Street, stopping to peer in the windows of all the new shops that had opened in recent years. As he did every night, Matt kept up a nonstop monologue about all the changes in town. The window displays of art, jewelry, expensive gifts and the latest designer clothes lent credence to his argument, when he said, "Winter Cove's not the same sleepy little place it was when you left."

"Maybe not, but it's not Washington," Emma retorted, determined not to buy into his less than subtle sales pitch. She'd seen the changes, and while they were impressive, she was not going to allow them to sway her into making a decision she was sure she'd come to regret.

"Meaning you'd rather not be here," he said, looking vaguely disappointed. "I'd hoped…well, never mind that.'' He gestured toward an ice-cream parlor. ''How about a cone?''

Emma didn't want ice cream. She wanted to pick a fight, though she couldn't entirely explain why. Maybe it was the heat. Maybe it was general frustration. Frowning, she shrugged. ''Whatever. If you want ice cream, get it.''

''I'll take that as a yes for you, too,'' he said mildly, refusing to be drawn into a fight. ''There's a bench across the street. You want to come with me or wait for me there?''

Maybe if she waited on the bench, her temper would cool down. ''I'll be across the street,'' she told him.

He started to turn away, then faced her, tucked his hand under her chin and kissed her hard. ''Think about that while you're waiting,'' he suggested.

Senses still spinning, Emma crossed the street and sat on the bench. There was a line at the ice-cream parlor, so she had plenty of time to brood about Matt's determination to trap her here in Winter Cove. How could he do that, when he claimed to love her? How could he add to all the pressure weighing on her these days? He'd known from the beginning that her heart was elsewhere. He'd even claimed to understand.

She watched him come out of the store with two double-scoop cones, then carefully weave his way through the slow traffic. Her heart—her damn traitorous heart—lurched happily at the sight of him. The fact that she was crazy about him made her crankier than ever and more determined to make him understand that she was not, under any circumstances, going to stay in Winter Cove.

Practically before he'd handed her the chocolate chip cone, she resumed their conversation as if it hadn't been interrupted.

"I told you from the beginning that I had every intention of going back to Washington," she accused.

"I notice you said Washington, not home," he said. "Winter Cove is still home to you, whether you want to admit it or not."

"I love Washington. It is my home now," she said emphatically.

"Fine, then go back," he said as if it were a simple matter.

Emma frowned at him. "You know why I can't. Not now, anyway."

"But you will at the first opportunity, right?"

She nodded.

"Has it occurred to you that it might be easier on everyone if you went now?"

"How can you say that? My family needs me."

"I'm not denying that, but if you left, your mom would be forced to pick up the pieces of her life. She'd be the one worrying herself sick that Jeff is addicted to drugs."

Emma hated that Matt said it with such certainty. She hadn't been lying to herself. She knew all the signs were there, but hearing Matt say it so bluntly made her realize just how desperate Jeff's situation really was.

"Jeff is not an addict. He's going to be fine," she said, fiercely defending her brother.

"Is he really? If you believe that, if you're making excuses for him, then you're part of the problem."

She shuddered at the accusation, because it made her feel helpless. She'd felt that way far too often since coming back to Winter Cove. She'd taken charge of her life once and made the hard decision to leave Winter Cove and make Washington her home. She ought to be doing it again, but she couldn't seem to find the strength. She hated the part of herself that was feeling so damned weak and vulnerable.

"I don't know what you expect me to do," she said heatedly.

"Be honest, with yourself and with Jeff," Matt replied. "He needs help, Emma. More help than you or your mother can give him. The last thing I want to do is arrest your brother for drug possession, but I will if I catch him at it."

Emma knew he would have no choice, but it hurt all the same. And it frightened her for Jeff's sake, because she knew he couldn't see just how much trouble he was in.

Matt regarded her with sympathy. "I know you don't want to hear this, Emma, but arresting him might be the best thing. It would force him to face what he's doing to himself before he gets in too deep to get out."

Her temper flared at the pragmatic, insensitive statement. Weeks of frustration came pouring out. Even as she spoke she knew she was directing it at the wrong person, but she couldn't seem to stop herself. So many things had happened to her family lately, things over which she'd had no control. It was little wonder she finally snapped.

"You are such a sanctimonious pig," she said, lashing out at the messenger. "You think it's all so easy. Our dad's dead, but we should all just get on with the business of living without wasting one single moment grieving or worrying about why it happened or acting out in some inappropriate way.''

''I never said that,'' Matt responded, sounding hurt that she would accuse him of such insensitivity. ''I'm grieving, too.''

Emma heard the real pain in his voice, but she wasn't ready to let him off the hook. ''Well, you'd sure as hell never know it,'' she retorted, fully aware of just how unfair she was being. ''You haven't done anything to help the situation. Have you even done one single thing to help me find out why he killed himself? It's been weeks since I asked you to investigate. You've made all the right noises when I pressed you, but your actions have been pretty half-hearted. It was days ago when Gabe and Harley found that date book of Jennifer's. Have you tried to pin her down about it since you went to her office and she wasn't there?''

''She hasn't been around since then,'' he said stiffly. ''Cori promised to call as soon as she showed up.''

''So? Do you honestly believe her loyalty is to you, rather than her boss? Put out one of those all-points bulletins or something,'' she told him.

''Jennifer's not a fugitive. She's not even a suspect in a crime,'' he explained patiently.

Emma didn't feel like being reasonable. ''Is that it, or are you just not anxious to get to the bottom of this?''

''That, too,'' he admitted.

''Because once I know why my dad died, I'll leave?'' she asked, suddenly thoroughly suspicious of his motives.

''To be honest, that's one reason,'' he conceded.

His admission rattled her. She hadn't expected him to be so forthright about his motives. He'd also said that was only one of the reasons.

"What are the other reasons?" she asked, trying to keep her temper in check.

"I'm still worried that the can of worms we're likely to open will be more hurtful, than helpful. I told you that at the beginning. Do you think I'm not aware of how much your family could use that insurance money? Right now, you're entitled to it."

"I don't give a damn about the insurance money," she said. "I told you I needed to know, no matter what. You'll have to give me a better reason." Watching the flicker of emotion in his eyes, she thought she recognized worry and regret. "There is another reason, isn't there?"

Matt tossed the rest of his cone into a trash can and shoved his hands in his pockets. He refused to look at her. Emma began to get a very bad feeling in the pit of her stomach.

"Answer me, Matt. Is it really me you're protecting, or is it someone else?" The answer suddenly dawned on her. "You have some sort of history with Jennifer, don't you? Is that it? Are you protecting her?"

"I'm not protecting her," he insisted, but he didn't sound convincing. "I don't even know if she needs protecting."

"But you did have a relationship with her," she persisted, praying that he'd deny it.

Instead, he regarded her with an unflinching look. "At one time, yes. It wasn't a big deal."

Emma felt as if her last lifeline—her faith in

Matt—had been snapped in two. "I don't believe this. How could you not tell me that weeks ago?"

"Because I didn't think it mattered," he said reasonably. "It was nearly a year ago, and it didn't last long. I was still hung up on you, so the relationship died before it ever really went anywhere."

"But you feel guilty enough about breaking things off that you want to keep Jennifer out of this mess with my father, is that it?"

He seemed startled by her assessment. "Maybe that is part of it," he conceded. "I wasn't consciously aware that I was holding back because of our past, but you could be right. I have felt guilty ever since I broke it off. And then when it started to look as if she might have gotten involved with your father right after that, I suppose I felt responsible."

Emma's head was whirling. "Did she know you broke up with her because you had all these old feelings for me?"

Matt shook his head. "I only told her that there was someone else I cared about, someone I'd never gotten over. I never said it was you." He sighed. "But I can't deny that she figured it out."

"Probably because a lot of people in town guessed years ago that you had a thing for me," Emma said. "It wasn't much of a secret. So Jennifer could have had a motive to want to get back at me and my family."

"By doing what? Setting out to seduce your father? Don't be absurd, Emma. I don't care how furious you are with me, don't take it out on Jennifer by making crazy accusations. She's a decent person. She wouldn't have set out to deliberately hurt your family.

To be perfectly honest, I don't think she was all that broken up when I dumped her. We're still friendly.''

''Do you think she'd let you see how much you hurt her?'' Emma scoffed. ''Women have their pride, you know.''

''Of course, they do, but you're wrong about Jennifer. She's not like that. If you knew her—''

Emma cut him off. ''Stop defending her. She's mixed up in my dad's suicide and you know it, or you wouldn't be dragging your heels about finding her so I can confront her.'' She looked at him as if she'd never seen him before. ''I thought you were on my side. I really did.''

''I *am* on your side. I am always on your side.''

Emma shook her head. ''Not anymore,'' she said, her heart aching. ''I never want to set eyes on you again. Never!''

And then she stood up and walked away without looking back.

Well, he'd certainly made a royal mess of that, Matt thought, as he watched Emma leave, her spine rigid. She might think it was over between them, but he had other ideas. He would find a way to make this right.

In the meantime, he was willing to admit that he should have told Emma about his relationship with Jennifer at the beginning, just to put the cards on the table. If he'd spoken up back then, he could have made Emma see that the relationship had been too brief to mean anything. Now it had taken on an importance far beyond what it had originally meant to either him or Jennifer.

And despite what Emma thought, he was convinced

that none of what had happened to Don had been tied to the breakup. Jennifer was not the type of woman who would seek revenge on him by going after the family of the woman who had held his heart all these years. She was more direct than that. If she wanted revenge on anyone, it would have been him, and she'd have pursued it enthusiastically. Instead, they'd remained on friendly terms, at least until lately when his questions had put her on the defensive.

"Smooth move, Chief."

Matt jumped as Cramer sat down beside him on the lakeside bench. "Where the hell did you come from?"

"I always take Gwendolyn for a walk this time of night," the sergeant said. He gestured toward the dog that had sprawled across his feet, panting.

"Looks like she's really enjoying it," Matt said wryly. "Ever think she might prefer to lie around the house in the air-conditioning?"

"Hell, we both would," Cramer said with a note of disgust in his voice. "But the vet says she's gaining too much weight. We're on a regimen to knock off a few pounds."

Matt bit back a chuckle. "I see. I always wondered what you did with your evenings."

"If I were you I wouldn't look so blasted smug. It's not like your life's going to be all that exciting from here on out. Sounded to me as if Emma's furious with you."

"Were you eavesdropping?"

"I was passing by," Cramer corrected. "Heard things getting sticky between you two and decided I should wait it out in case you needed a shoulder to cry on."

"I don't," Matt said succinctly.

"Then you've got this under control?" Cramer asked, his skepticism plain.

"Not exactly," Matt admitted. "But I will."

"What's your plan?"

"I don't have one yet."

"Mind a suggestion?"

What Matt minded was having a nosy sergeant who thought he could go poking around in Matt's private affairs, but apparently he didn't have much control over that. "Go ahead."

"You need to get those two women in the same room and straighten this thing out before it gets out of hand. In my experience, women get more difficult the longer the wounds are allowed to fester."

"Is that so?"

"I'm telling you, I know what I'm talking about," Cramer insisted. He dug around in his pocket and pulled out a beeper. "By the way, this is yours. You left it at the station. Cori's been calling you all afternoon."

Matt grabbed the beeper and jumped up. "Why the hell didn't you let me know?"

Gwendolyn lifted her head and growled at his sharp tone.

"I beeped you," Cramer explained patiently, giving his dog an absentminded pat on the head. "Same as she did. That's how I found out this was sitting on your desk."

Matt scowled. "Well, hell." He looked at his watch even though he already knew it was after office hours.

"Cori said to call her at home," Cramer added helpfully. "The number's in the memory on that dang thing.'' He gestured over his shoulder. "Pay phone's over there."

Matt took off, only to have Cramer shout his name. He paused and looked back. "What?"

"I wouldn't mind finding one of them fancy coffees on my desk first thing in the morning," he said, grinning. "Working the day shift is throwing me all off-kilter."

"If this works out, I'll bring you coffee every day for a month," Matt promised.

The woman on the phone was talking so fast, her voice so choked with tears that at first Rosa couldn't understand a word she was saying.

"Slow down," she commanded gently. "Who is this?"

"It's Marisol."

Rosa felt her heart slam to a stop. "Something's happened to Jeff, hasn't it?"

All she heard on the other end of the line were sobs. She wanted to scream, but one hysterical woman was enough.

"Marisol, stop it this second!" she said sharply. "Tell me what happened."

"Jeff got really, really sick, and then he passed out. Hawk wouldn't let me call for an ambulance so I had to drag him to my car."

"Where are you now?" Rosa asked, surprised by how calm she was. There was no time for panic or hysterics, so she simply wouldn't allow either one.

"The hospital emergency room," the girl whispered. "They won't let me see him and they won't tell me anything because I'm not family. Can you come, please?"

"I'll be there in fifteen minutes," Rosa promised. "And Marisol, it's going to be okay. If there's a chapel at the hospital, go in there and pray. I'll find you when I get there."

Rosa hung up and grabbed her purse, then ran for her car before remembering that she'd loaned it to Emma earlier when she'd come back to the house looking as if she'd just lost her best friend. Rosa snatched her cell phone out of her purse and dialed Helen. She was closest. She could be here in five minutes, faster even than a taxi.

"Please be there," she prayed as the phone rang and rang.

It seemed like an eternity before Helen picked up.

"Helen, it's Rosa. Jeff's in the hospital and I don't have my car."

"I'll be right there," Helen said at once.

"Thank you."

Because she wanted all the prayers and support she could muster, she dialed Jolie next and told her what was going on.

"I'll call Sylvia," Jolie promised. "We'll meet you at the emergency room."

Even as Rosa ended the call to Jolie, Helen skidded to a halt at the curb. Her hair was in rollers and there were traces of night cream on her face. She was still wearing her slippers.

"Don't even say it," Helen said. "I know I'm a mess, but I didn't want to waste a second getting here. Now tell me what happened."

"I don't know for sure," Rosa admitted. "Marisol called. She said Jeff passed out or something and she took him to the hospital. They wouldn't tell her anything."

They exchanged a look, neither of them daring to say what they both feared.

"He'll be fine," Helen said firmly.

"I know that," Rosa agreed. "He has to be."

"Where's Emma?"

"I have no idea. She said she had somewhere to go and she borrowed my car."

"Have you tried her cell phone?"

Rosa shook her head. "I hadn't even thought of that. God, what is wrong with me?"

Helen reached over and squeezed her hand. "You're scared, that's all. But you don't have any reason to be. This could be a blessing in disguise."

Rosa stared at her, even as she tried Emma's cell phone number. "How can you say that?"

"Jeff will have to get help now."

Rosa sighed. "I suppose." She listened to Emma's phone ringing and ringing, then finally gave up. "I guess she turned her phone off."

"That's okay. You have me. I'll be there with you."

"Jolie and Sylvia are coming, too."

Helen smiled. "Of course, they are. We've had to do this kind of thing for each other too many times, though. I think it's time for our lives to turn around. We could use some good news for a change."

"Maybe Emma and Matt," Rosa began wistfully, then cut herself off. "I can't think about that now. I have to concentrate on Jeff."

"Where's Andy?"

"On a date with Lauren Patterson, thank goodness. He needs to have some fun."

Helen frowned at that. "He should be here."

"Not until we know what's going on," Rosa said

firmly. "He's had to shoulder too much lately. I can handle this. And you said it yourself, I have you to lean on."

"Anytime you need me," Helen promised as she pulled up to the emergency entrance. She gave Rosa's hand one last squeeze. "I'll park, do something with my hair, and be right in."

Rosa dashed inside, determined to keep herself together until she knew exactly what they were dealing with. Marisol sprang out of a chair and came to meet her, her face streaked with tears, her usual heavy makeup washed away. She looked exactly like what she was, a scared girl.

"I'm sorry," she whispered to Rosa. "I'm so sorry. This is all my fault."

Rosa gave her a fierce hug. "There will be time enough to cast blame later. Right now we need to concentrate on Jeff. Have you heard anything?"

Marisol shook her head. "They still won't tell me anything."

Rosa went to the desk and explained who she was.

"I'll have the doctor come out to talk to you right away," the nurse promised. "Have a seat over there."

Rosa kept her arm around Marisol's too thin shoulders and guided her back to the hard, plastic chairs. The girl continued to sob quietly.

Minutes later Helen and the doctor arrived at the same time. Helen sat on Rosa's other side and held her hand tightly as the doctor stood in front of them, his expression somber as he rocked back and forth on his heels.

"I'm not going to lie to you," he said. "Your son is in bad shape. God knows what combination of drugs is in his system. We'll have to wait for the toxicology report to know for sure. Whatever it is sent him into cardiac arrest.''

''Oh, my God,'' Rosa whispered, even as Marisol's sobs grew louder.

The doctor ignored Marisol and kept his focus on Rosa. ''We have him stabilized for now, but he's not out of the woods. We're going to get him into ICU in a bit and then you'll be able to see him for a couple of minutes.'' He scowled toward Marisol. ''Family only.''

''I understand,'' Rosa said.

The doctor continued. ''I wish to hell I did. I see too damn much of this kind of thing and it never makes any sense to me.'' He finally turned his attention to Marisol. ''I hope you're getting the message here, young lady. Keep it up, and you could be next.''

Marisol gulped back a sob and nodded. Rosa almost felt sorry for her.

After the doctor had gone back to Jeff, Rosa looked at her. ''Do you want to call your folks? Have them come and get you?''

''No, please. My family doesn't live here, except for my great-grandfather and I can't worry him. Besides, I have to stay here. Even if I can't see Jeff, I need to know he's okay. I want him to know I'm close by.''

Rosa couldn't deny her that. At least Marisol had had the presence of mind to get Jeff to a hospital. She'd probably saved his life, even if she had been at least partially responsible for endangering it in the first place.

Jolie and Sylvia arrived just then. Helen stood up and reached for Marisol's hand. ''Come along, honey.

Let's you and me go and get everyone some coffee.
I have a feeling it's going to be a long night.''

"Thank you," Rosa said, aware once more of how
well her friend knew her. As grateful as she was to
Marisol at this moment, she also wasn't sure she
could bear to be around her another second.

The instant the chairs on either side of her were
vacated, Jolie and Sylvia sat beside her. Jeff was going to make it, Rosa reassured herself, and as long as
she had her friends, she was going to make it, too.

Emma had grown weary of waiting. She'd left the
investigation into her father's suicide in Matt's hands.
She'd left Jeff to work out his own problems. She'd
been waiting and waiting for her mother to say she
was strong enough for Emma to leave again. She'd
been drifting along on a tide of guilt and grief and
self-imposed martyrdom. Well, she'd finally had
enough, especially now that she knew that Matt had
been deliberately dragging his heels.

Jennifer Sawyer had answers, maybe not all of
them, but enough to point Emma in the right direction. And there was no reason on earth that Emma
had to wait for Matt before talking to her. If Jennifer
was still out of town, Emma would simply watch her
apartment and her office until she returned. How difficult could a stakeout really be? It wasn't as if Jennifer were some sort of criminal. This was likely to
be more tedious than dangerous.

She had borrowed her mother's car earlier and
driven to the address she'd found in the phone book.
So far, so good. There was nothing to it. She had no
idea why Matt had been making such a big deal about
handling it on his own. Okay, that wasn't true. She

knew precisely why he'd been balking at pinning Jennifer down for an interview.

"Damn him," she muttered as she spotted the lights on in Jennifer's house. "She's probably been right here all along."

Spurred on by fury and a sense of purpose she hadn't felt in weeks, she cut across the grass, marched up the steps and pounded on the front door. She was going to get to the bottom of this tonight, and then she could go back to D.C. and pick up her life where she'd left off. She ignored the fact that there would be a huge hole in her heart that Matt had occupied these last few weeks.

She leaned on the buzzer, then stepped back when the door swung open. Her heart promptly climbed into her throat.

"You," she whispered, feeling even more betrayed than she had earlier.

"I figured you'd turn up here sooner or later," Matt said. "Come on in."

"I suppose I shouldn't be surprised that you rushed right on over to protect her," Emma said, her voice flat.

"I did not rush over to protect anyone. Cori called and told me Jennifer was back. I came over to see what I could find out."

"Without me."

"Like I said, I figured you'd find your way over here before long, anyway."

"Is she here?"

Matt nodded.

"And?"

"And nothing. I just got here myself."

"Well, isn't that just peachy," she said sarcastically. "We can get all those pesky answers together and you won't have to bother reporting back to me."

He winced at her tone, but he didn't respond. He merely stepped aside to allow her into the foyer. Only when she was about to go into the living room, did he latch on to her arm and pull her to a halt.

"After this, you and I are going to talk," he said evenly.

She frowned, her gaze steady on his hand until he finally released her.

"We will talk, Emma. It's not over between us."

She regarded him sorrowfully. "It never even got started."

He scowled at that. "Don't kid yourself, Emma. It started years ago."

"You're the one kidding yourself." She met his gaze. "And do you really want to have this particular discussion with Jennifer in the next room? There's no telling what she might do if she overhears us."

"Dammit, Emma! I—"

She ignored whatever he was about to say and swept past him. Tonight all she wanted was answers. Her feelings for Matt didn't matter. To think that she'd almost been ready to turn her life upside down for him. Well, that was over. She'd never allow her feelings for him to matter again.

21

Once she was actually face-to-face with Jennifer Sawyer, Emma's heart began to thud. She'd convinced herself that she wanted whatever answers Jennifer could provide about her father's death—that she *needed* those answers—but now that the truth was hers for the asking, she suddenly didn't want to know, after all. She wanted to stick her head in the sand and accept the medical examiner's report that her father's death was an accident, something tragic, but totally uncomplicated. Unfortunately it was too late now to take the easy way out.

Jennifer Sawyer was a gorgeous woman in her late twenties. She'd been a regular at Flamingo Diner since her teens, when she'd been trailed around by half the football team. Emma had been younger and very envious. Now, looking at her with her classic features, pale complexion and haunted eyes, Emma saw that the years had only enhanced her beauty. It was little wonder Matt had been taken with her. Had her father been, as well?

"Hello, Emma," Jennifer said. She glanced at Matt as if seeking moral support, then added, "I can't begin to tell you how sorry I am about what happened to your father."

"Thank you," Emma said politely, forcing herself not to blurt out an accusation she couldn't take back.

Now it was Emma's turn to look at Matt, silently pleading for him to ask the hard questions she'd been ready to hurl at Jennifer herself only moments ago before she'd actually crossed the threshold. His expression grim, he finally nodded.

"Jen, Harley and Gabe found your date book a couple of weeks ago," he began. "It had been tossed in the trash Dumpster behind your office building."

"The same Gabe and Harley who were prowling around outside this place? And before you ask, it didn't take long for me to figure out that's who it was, even though you claimed it was just a couple of people who were lost. The rumor mill was full of it by the next morning." She gave Matt a bemused look. "What were they thinking?"

"They were trying to help," Matt said. "They thought you might know something about why Don committed suicide and they were looking for proof."

"In my garbage?"

Matt's lips curved. "We're talking Gabe and Harley. They watch a lot of TV."

"And the bottom line is, they found something, didn't they?" Emma said, since Matt hadn't. "Matt says my father's name was in your date book over and over again the first part of this year." She drew in a deep breath, then blurted, "Were the two of you having an affair?"

"Oh, my God," Jennifer whispered, looking shattered. She turned to Matt. "Is that what you think? How could you, Matt? You know me."

He regarded her apologetically. "We're asking,

Jen, not making an accusation. Why was the date book in the trash?''

"Because I was afraid of something exactly like this. I was not having an affair with Don," Jennifer said, still indignant. "But having his name in there was bound to make people wonder." She faced Emma, her gaze steady, her cheeks flushed. "Not you, though, Matt, or Emma. I'm surprised by the two of you. First of all, Don was old enough to be my father. Second, he was a happily married man, which you of all people should know, Emma. There was nothing on earth he cared about more than his family. I can't believe you would think he would ever cheat on your mother."

The suggestion that she was the one who was demeaning her parents' relationship cut Emma to the quick. "If I'm wrong, I apologize," she said stiffly.

"Well, you *are* wrong," Jennifer said.

There was enough heat and sincerity behind her words to convince Emma that she was telling the truth, about that at least. "But you do know something, don't you?" she pressed. "If you'd been spending a lot of time with him, you must."

"I don't see how this will help," Jennifer said. "It will only be more upsetting. Don was my client. More than that, he was a good friend. I don't want to betray him. That was another reason I got rid of the damn date book, so I'd never have to say anything more."

"It's too late to worry about that. He's dead," Emma reminded her sharply. "Because of something that happened, we all think he killed himself. Put yourself in my place. I can't rest until I know why. If he was your client, then you must know that the family's finances are a mess. What do you know about that? I think there's a connection between that and his death. I think you believe the same thing. I think that's why you've been avoiding not only me and Matt, but my mother.''

Jennifer still looked torn. ''Okay, you're right,'' she said, resigned. ''There's no point in protecting him now, not if the truth will help you get past this. I'll tell you whatever you want to know.''

Relieved and terrified at the same time, Emma met her gaze. ''Start at the beginning. When did you start working for my dad?''

''Your father came to me a little over a year ago. He said he had some money to invest. Over the years he'd poured most of his available cash into the business. He was worried that his savings wouldn't cover the last couple of years of Jeff's college education, much less stretch to cover Andy's. He wanted to make some investments.''

Emma began to see where this was heading. ''In the stock market,'' she said flatly.

''Exactly. We'd been talking about the market in the diner, about the boom in technology stocks, about initial offerings that skyrocketed, even about how that sector was fading, so I thought he was pretty well informed about the risks. Nevertheless, I explained them to him again. I suggested some conservative blue-chip investments, but he wanted bigger returns.''

Emma still couldn't believe he'd been so irresponsible. ''Are you actually telling me that my father borrowed against the diner to invest in risky stocks?''

''Not at first. He used the money he had in savings. Despite my advice, he went a little wild speculating. When he needed to cover some losses, that's when he began borrowing against the diner. He was so sure that he was going to recoup that money and make a killing. He wouldn't listen to a thing I said. I finally told him I wouldn't handle any more trades for him. The odd thing was that the worse things got, the more determined he was to keep going. It was almost like an addiction, like he was a gambler at heart.''

Jennifer's description was so unlike the father she remembered that Emma was having a hard time making the connection. ''I can't believe it,'' she whispered, thoroughly shaken. ''He was always so good with money, so careful. I can't tell you how many times he lectured us on not going into debt, on never risking something we couldn't afford to lose. He didn't even have a credit card.''

Matt nodded. ''He said the same things to me. He said them so often, I almost wondered if it wasn't something he'd learned from bitter experience.''

''Me, too,'' Emma agreed, wondering if there was something in her father's past that he and her mother had never shared with her.

''All I know is that he went a little crazy,'' Jennifer said. ''When I tried to stop him, he found a broker in an office downstairs who didn't care how much he lost, as long as he kept making trades. I saw him on what I later found out was the day he died.''

''His name was in your date book for that afternoon,'' Matt said.

''He told me that morning that he had an appointment with his broker and that he'd stop by my office afterward. When he got there, he looked absolutely awful. I knew then that he'd suffered more huge losses, but he tried to joke about it, as if it were only money, no big thing. He had to be devastated, though. By then, there couldn't have been any question of having money for either Jeff or Andy's tuition. In fact, I had to wonder if he wasn't very close to losing the diner.''

"How was he when he left your office?" Emma asked.

Jennifer hesitated, her expression thoughtful. "I'd have to say sad. In retrospect, when I heard what happened, I couldn't help thinking that the look I'd seen on his face was the look of a man who felt he had nothing left to live for.''

"My God," Emma whispered.

"It upset me so badly that I started to question all the advice I'd ever given to any of my clients," Jennifer said. "I was already at my place in North Carolina, but I decided to stay there. I needed time to reevaluate the career I'd chosen.''

Jennifer regarded her with sympathy. "Emma, I can't begin to tell you how responsible I felt, as if I'd pushed him down that road. I'm so sorry, Emma. If I'd had any idea how things were going to turn out, I would never have taken him on as a client. I thought I was helping a friend.''

As badly as Emma wanted to hurl accusations and blame at Jennifer, she knew that her father had been responsible for his own decisions. No one had forced him to make those investments. He'd always been clever with money. Obviously he'd seen the stock market as one more financial mountain to conquer for the sake of his family's future. When it had gotten the better of him, he'd probably been too embarrassed to tell any of them what he'd done. As if any of them would have cared more about money than they would have about him. My God, what a waste! What a complete and utter waste!

"How could you have known what would happen?" Emma said, surprised to find that she was able to feel some sympathy for Jennifer, after all. "This was his fault, not yours."

"I am sorry," Jennifer said again. "You were absolutely right about one thing. I was glad I'd gone away before I heard the news. Once I did I stayed away even longer because I couldn't bear to look any of you in the eye. You, Jeff and Andy lost your father. Your mom lost her husband. And I lost someone I respected and cared about."

Emma didn't want to feel sorry for the woman who'd had a hand, however innocently, in her father's destruction, but she did. "Thank you for telling me," she said. "I know it wasn't easy."

"It was harder watching him ruin his life bit by bit," Jennifer told her. "Your dad was a wonderful man. Remember that, and try not to focus on how his life ended."

"One more thing," Matt said. "I asked you once before, but I want to ask it again. Were you the one who sent those flowers to the lake, the one with the card asking 'Why?'"

Jennifer shook her head. "No. I can't say for sure, but I think it might have been Cori. We never talked about it, but I think she had some of the same questions about my relationship with Don that you did and was trying in her own way to make sure someone looked into his death. She's too good a friend to accuse me of anything directly, but I think she was tormented by what happened. Don't forget she saw him that last day, too."

Unable to face Jennifer for another second, Emma

stood up without a word and walked blindly outside. Matt was at her side in an instant.

"You okay?" he asked, tucking a finger under her chin.

She nodded, not trusting herself to speak.

He started to reach for her, then held back. "Will you tell your mother what you found out?"

"I honestly don't know." She met his gaze. "It almost makes it worse that this whole thing was about money. How could he think that we'd care more about money than we did about him?"

"He wasn't thinking straight," Matt said. "That's obvious."

"But we must have failed him in some way for him to think that."

"That's ridiculous," he retorted. "None of you failed him. If anything, it was the other way around. When the chips were down, he opted out, rather than sticking around to face all of you and figure a way out of the mess he'd created. It's the only sign of weakness I ever saw in him."

For the first time since his death, Emma no longer felt so angry with her father. All she felt was pity for him and sorrow that so many lives would never be the same.

Matt watched Emma warily. She was pale as a ghost and she wasn't saying a word. She wasn't even complaining that he'd climbed behind the wheel of her mother's car after tucking her into the passenger seat.

Finally, he looked over. "Where to?"

She shook her head as if coming out of a trance. "I have no idea."

"You want to go somewhere for a drink?"

"No."

"Something to eat?"

"I'm not hungry."

"My place?"

That got the wry look he'd expected, if not the response he'd hoped for.

"Okay, not my place," he said. "Do you want to go home?"

"I suppose," she said without enthusiasm.

He drove back to the Killian house, rounded the car and opened Emma's door. She seemed startled to realize that they'd arrived. He was not about to leave her alone in that state. Once he'd made sure that Rosa was inside and capable of coping with Emma's distress, then he'd take off. Not a minute before.

But inside, there was no sign of Rosa or of Andy.

"I'll make some tea," Matt said.

"Fine, whatever." She trailed along behind him into the kitchen, like a scared kid who was afraid to be too far from the protection of an adult.

"Apple cinnamon or wild berry?" he asked, holding up boxes of tea bags from the cupboard.

"Wild berry, I guess."

He poured hot water over the tea bags, then set her cup in front of her and sat opposite her. "I think you need to sit down with your mom and talk this out," he told her. "Andy and Jeff probably need to know, too. Keeping this buried inside you will just put a barrier between you and the others."

She shook her head. "I don't want to destroy their image of Dad. They thought he was invincible. So did I."

"I think his suicide pretty much shattered that

myth,'' Matt said. "He was only human, Emma. He made mistakes. We all do.''

She finally met his gaze. "Matt, this wasn't some little clerical error. He gambled away almost everything. You have no idea. None of us care about inheritances just for the sake of the money, but he put Mom's future at risk. How could he do that?''

"He got in over his head. It happens. And sometimes it happens before a person even realizes just how bad things have gotten.'' He met her gaze evenly. "I got in over my head with you years ago.''

She almost smiled at that. "Hardly the same,'' she said.

"I don't know. I'd gamble just about anything to keep you.''

"I'm not a prize you can win in some high-stakes game,'' she said tartly.

"Believe me, I know that better than anyone.''

Her expression softened. "I do love you, you know. I love the way you've been there for me every step of the way since I got back here. I love that you're here right now, despite all the mean, hateful things I said to you earlier.''

"I deserved some of them.''

"You deserved all of them,'' she corrected. "But I forgive you.''

"And I forgive you for being pigheaded and stubborn about going back to D.C. when you know you could be happy here. *We* could be happy together.''

She frowned. "Maybe we'd better not discuss this right now.''

He grinned. "Whatever you say.''

Just then the phone rang. Matt looked at Emma,

who was staring at it as if there were no one in the universe she wanted to speak to.

"Want me to get it?" he asked.

She nodded.

He stood up and grabbed the phone. "Killian residence."

"Matt, is that you?"

"Hi, Mrs. K. Where are you?"

"Is Emma with you?"

She sounded upset. Matt immediately braced himself for bad news. "She is. What's up?"

"It's Jeff. He's in intensive care at the hospital."

"We'll be there in a few minutes," he said at once, his gaze on Emma who was regarding him with an increasingly worried expression. "How's he doing?"

"Just hurry, Matt, please. And if you see any sign of Andy, bring him along. I think he and Lauren Patterson went to the movies."

Matt didn't like the sound of urgency in Rosa's voice, nor was he crazy about the way the color was draining out of Emma's face as if she were already anticipating the worst.

"Hang in there, Mrs. K. We're on our way."

Emma was already on her feet by the time he'd hung up. "What happened to Jeff?"

"He's in ICU. Your mom didn't say why, but it's not good. We need to get over there. She said Andy went to the movies. She wants us to look for him on the way."

"Drop me off first, then you go and look for him," Emma said, racing ahead of him to the car.

"The theater's on the way," Matt reminded her, as he backed out of the driveway, tires squealing. He sincerely regretted not having his car, so he could head for the hospital with siren blaring and lights flashing.

As it was, he broke more than one law en route to the multiplex, where the early show was just letting out. Emma spotted Andy in the crowd and shouted for him. Looking puzzled, he loped over to the car, his date following more slowly.

When Emma didn't speak up at once, Matt said, "Hey, kid, we've got to get over to the hospital. Something's up with your brother and your mom wants you there."

For an instant Andy looked defiant, as if he might refuse, but then the reality of the situation hit him. He nodded at once and turned to the girl. "Lauren, I can drop you off first."

"It's okay," she said. "I can ride along, if it's okay."

"Good idea," Matt said. "Then I'll give you a lift home, after I drop Andy and Emma off."

They climbed in the back seat and Matt eased into the traffic now streaming out of the theater parking lot. Emma still hadn't said anything.

Andy reached over the seat and squeezed her shoulder. "You okay, sis?"

She forced a smile. "Of course," she insisted, reaching up to pat his hand. She even managed a smile for his date. "Sorry to spoil your evening."

The teenager waved off the comment. "I just hope Jeff's okay. That's all that matters."

Matt skidded to a stop at the emergency entrance and Emma and Andy piled out. "Emma," he said, drawing her distracted gaze back to him. "I'll be back in ten minutes, tops. Hang in there, okay? And give your mom a hug for me."

"I will."

He sat there, watching the two of them walk inside the hospital, shoulder to shoulder, holding hands. It was hard to tell who was comforting whom, but he was relieved that they had each other. If this was a drug overdose, as he very much feared it might be, they were going to need all the support they could get.

Rosa had seen Jeff for a total of twenty minutes on two separate visits to his cubicle in the ICU. Each time she'd been horrified by how pale and lifeless he seemed to be. Her boy had always had so much energy, so much spirit. If she were being totally honest, she knew it was more than the drugs that had drained that spirit out of him. Things had been bad, but not this bad until she'd forced him to face facts about his father's death being a suicide. He hadn't been ready to hear that, even if the suspicion had been eating away at him. In the end, maybe she'd done as much damage to him as the drugs.

She sat beside his bed and held his hand. "Jeffrey Killian, you are not running out on me, not like this. Do you hear me?"

She kept up the chatter for the entire length of her visit, alternately badgering him and telling him how much she loved him. When the nurse signaled that her time was up, she gave his hand one last squeeze.

"Emma and Andy will be here soon. I expect you to be wide-awake by then, okay? I love you."

She leaned down and pressed a kiss to his forehead. "I know things have been bad, my darling boy, but we're going to fix it. I promise."

She was at the door to his cubicle when she heard the raspy whisper.

"Love you, Mom."

Tears filled her eyes, but she blinked them away as she ran back to the bed to look into those precious dark brown eyes so like her own. "Oh, sweetie, you scared the daylights out of me," she scolded.

"Sorry."

"But you're going to be okay now," she said smoothing her hand across his brow. "We're all going to be okay."

He sighed and his eyes drifted shut just as the doctor came in to check on him.

"He was awake. That's a good sign, isn't it?"

"It's a start," he conceded. "Let me check him out and I'll let you know how things are going."

Rosa drew in a deep, relieved breath and went back to the waiting room. "He woke up," she announced to her friends just as Andy and Emma arrived.

"Mom, what happened?" Emma asked.

There was little point in trying to cover up the truth. Everyone here knew how much trouble Jeff had been in lately. And secrets had a way of leading to tragedy.

"An overdose," she said. "He had a heart attack."

"But he's just a kid," Andy said, clearly shocked.

Rosa reached for his hand. "And let that be a lesson to you about what drugs can do to you," she said fiercely.

He gave her one of those too-grown-up Andy looks. "As if I'd ever be dumb enough to try drugs."

"There was a time when Jeff would have said the same thing," she reminded him.

Andy caught sight of Marisol just then. "It's her

fault,'' he accused bitterly. ''What are you doing here? You have no right to be here. You're not family. Get out.'' He started toward her as if he intended to physically drag her from the waiting room.

Rosa understood his anger all too well, but she grasped his hand and stopped him. ''You can't blame all of this on Marisol,'' she told him quietly. ''Your brother is an adult. He made his own choices. And if it weren't for Marisol's quick thinking, your brother might have died tonight. She brought him to the hospital in time.''

Emma regarded the girl with surprise and went over to sit beside her. ''Thank you.''

''Andy's right,'' Marisol said, looking shattered. ''This was my fault. I just wanted to have some fun. I didn't know anything like this could happen from smoking a few joints.''

''You were doing more than smoking pot, or at least he was,'' the doctor said, apparently overhearing her as he emerged from the ICU. ''But he's showing some definite signs of improvement. I think there's reason for some cautious optimism.''

Rosa began to weep at the news, shedding the tears she hadn't permitted herself until now. Emma guided her to a chair, then sat beside her.

''I'll get you some more coffee,'' Helen said.

''Tea,'' Emma corrected. ''Herbal, if they have it.''

''I'll go,'' Andy said, shooting another bitter look at Marisol.

She returned his gaze with a defiant look of her own. ''I'll come with you. You can't carry enough drinks for everyone.''

He looked as if he might balk at the offer, but typical of Andy, he could never be deliberately mean to someone and his anger rarely lasted more than a minute. Rosa watched him with pride as he walked away.

"That child has had to deal with too much," she said. "It's a wonder he hasn't fallen apart."

"He's strong like you, Mama," Emma said.

Rosa squeezed her daughter's hand. "And like you. I don't know what I would have done without you these past months."

"You'd have survived," Emma said confidently. "Maybe if I hadn't hung around, it would have been better."

"How can you even say such a thing? I want you here. This is your home."

"Washington is my home now."

Rosa gazed into her daughter's eyes and saw the turmoil. "Is it really?" she asked quietly. She glanced up in time to see Matt coming into the waiting room, his gaze immediately going to Emma. "Are you sure you haven't found something here that's more important?"

Emma didn't answer, but she smiled at Matt when he sat beside her and put his arm around her shoulder.

My God, Rosa thought, those two were so in love, it made her heart ache. If only there were some way to make Emma admit it before it was too late.

Tomorrow, she thought wearily. She would worry about that tomorrow. Tonight she had just enough strength left to pray for Jeff's full recovery.

22

Emma could have slept for a week, but instead, she intended to open the diner right on time at 6:00 a.m. at her mother's insistence. She knew it had to be done. In fact, she knew better than anyone how critical every dollar was these days, but she would have given anything for even an hour in bed after spending most of the night at the hospital.

An icy shower helped to revive her, but it was the sight of Matt waiting for her in the driveway that made her pulse sing. He hadn't left her side all night. When he'd brought her by the house earlier to change clothes, he'd said he would be back and he was, despite her argument that he needed sleep. She could count on him to do exactly what he said he'd do. His reliability was something she'd come to prize, to say nothing of the way his touches could inflame her. She'd been trying hard not to dwell on that. It got in the way of doing what she knew she had to do.

"I told you to stay home and get some sleep," she scolded, even as she got into the front seat of his car. She had to fight not to lean back against the cushions and close her eyes. If she fell asleep now, she'd sleep for a month.

"I told you the same thing. Guess we're both stubborn," he said mildly. "I knew you'd insist on Andy staying home. Somebody has to help out at the grill. You can't do it all.''

"I could have managed," she insisted.

"But now you don't have to."

She gave him a grateful look. "Thank you."

"Anytime, sweetheart. You know that."

She did. Even when she'd been furious with him for not telling her he'd been involved with Jennifer, she had known that he would never in a million years let her down. Not really.

"I spoke to your mom a few minutes ago," he told her. "She says Jeff is doing better. He's more alert this morning and they're bringing him breakfast in a few minutes."

"Thank God for Helen, Sylvia and Jolie. They haven't left her side for a minute."

"That's what friends do," Matt said. "Especially in a town like Winter Cove."

Emma looked at him and knew that she'd found the same steadiness in him, and so much more. "I know," she said softly. "You taught me that."

For a minute it looked as if he might press the subject, but then they were at the diner and there were a million and one things to do to be ready for the breakfast rush. She was relieved not to have to deal with all the questions he was bound to have about their future. He deserved answers, even to the unspoken questions, but she knew he wasn't going to like them and she dreaded making him unhappy.

Thankfully, she had little time to worry about it. Every customer who came through the door that morning seemed to have heard about Jeff, yet not a one of them said anything judgmental. Emma wanted to cry at the concern they expressed. Even Gabe and Harley in their own gruff way tried to help.

"You need me at the grill, I suppose I can make eggs as good as Matt's," Gabe said, looking at the scrambled mess that had been made of his over-lightly order.

Emma laughed. "I'll keep that in mind."

"It's not like we come here just for the food," Harley added. "This place is home and you guys are family. I could make a big pot of gazpacho for lunch. Some cold soup might be just the thing on a steamy day like this."

Emma stared at him as if he'd just spoken in Swahili. "You can make gazpacho?"

"And a lot more," Gabe told her, regarding his friend with evident pride. "Before he moved here, Harley retired as an executive chef at one of them fancy hotels over by Disney World."

"My God, why didn't anyone here know that?" Emma asked. "Did you ever say anything to my mother?"

"No need to," Harley said. "Rosa and Don knew what they were doing. And you were doing just fine without me interfering." He gazed pointedly at the eggs. "Least you were till you let Matt get a spatula in his hand."

Emma's mind was whirling. "Would you be..." She shook her head. "Of course not. It's a ridiculous idea."

Harley regarded her with a curious expression. "No idea's ridiculous. Some just need a little fine-tuning."

"I'd have to talk it over with my mother, but would

you consider .pitching in here part-time once Andy goes back to school? I doubt we could pay much.''

Harley grinned. ''Have my doubts about that, too, but the truth is that I've missed having a crowd of folks to cook for. You think your mom would let me try out a few new recipes? Saw something with chocolate the other day that made my mouth water. No point in making something like that just for me. And I'll be darned if I'll get married again just to have someone around who appreciates my cooking.''

Emma laughed. ''Oh, yes. I think you just said the magic word. Mama's never turned down anything chocolate in her entire life. We've never had a fancy dessert menu, but I'll bet it would work with all the new yuppies in the neighborhood. If Mama agrees, we could stay open later. We'd be the place to go for coffee and dessert.''

''Well, then, you two talk it over and then we'll sit down and see what we can do,'' Harley said. ''I imagine I've still got a few good years of cooking left in me.''

Emma leaned over and impulsively planted a kiss on his nearly bald head. ''I think I love you, Harley Watson. And in case I haven't said it before, thank you for poking around till you found that date book.''

Harley's eyes turned even brighter. ''Then it did help?''

She nodded. ''It did.''

''That's all that matters,'' he said.

She regarded him with surprise. ''You don't want to know what happened?''

''Well, of course, we do,'' Gabe said testily, then quickly added, ''but we're not nosy.''

Emma laughed at that, then went back to pick up

more orders from the grill. She grinned when she saw the food on the plates. "You know, it's getting a little hard for me to tell who these orders belong to," she teased Matt. "They all look alike."

He scowled at her. "You want to trade places?"

"No," several of the customers at the counter said in a chorus.

Emma regarded them with surprise. "You'd rather have him cooking, than me?"

"Your food might be an improvement," Jess Davis conceded. "But the last time Matt had a coffeepot in his hand, he came close to spilling it all over me. I can eat eggs that are hard as rubber, but I ain't interested in being scalded by hot liquid."

"Same here," several others chimed in.

Matt frowned at them. "Talk about ungrateful."

Emma stood there listening to the byplay and felt something ease inside her. She wasn't quite ready to admit it yet, not to herself, and definitely not to Matt, but this really was home, and she was beginning to wonder why on earth she'd convinced herself that she belonged anyplace else. Sheer stubbornness, most likely. It was yet another trait she'd had in common with her father. Even as the thought crossed her mind, she realized with a shock that thinking about her father didn't make her feel quite so sad. Maybe the wounds were healing at long last.

Jeff was finally getting out of the hospital today, and it couldn't be soon enough for him or for Rosa. She shook her head as he complained about everything from the constant intrusions by the staff to the food.

"I want to get out of here," he grumbled yet again.

"As soon as the doctor signs the release papers, we're going," she reminded him.

"Well, it won't be soon enough for me."

"So I gathered," she said wryly, even as she gave his hand a quick squeeze.

Just then she saw Marisol standing hesitantly in the doorway. She'd been coming by a lot, but it seemed to Rosa that Jeff had been less and less eager to see her. His reluctance had clearly been apparent to the girl.

"May I come in?"

Jeff nodded. "We need to talk before I get out of here."

"Would you like me to leave?" Rosa asked.

Jeff shook his head. "No, you need to hear this, too."

Marisol looked him straight in the eye. "You're dumping me," she said with obvious regret. "I don't blame you."

"It's not that I don't care about you," he said hastily. He glanced at Rosa, then back to Marisol. "But I've got to make some changes."

"I know," Marisol said sadly. "Me, too. And it would be too hard to do it together."

Rosa regarded them both with surprise. Maybe there was more to Marisol than she'd given her credit for. As for her son, she'd always believed he was a good kid, but he'd shaken her faith lately. And, truthfully, she hadn't been expecting such evidence of maturity from either of them, but it gave her hope. "I think you're making a difficult, but very wise decision," she told them.

"Maybe when we both get our acts together, we

can hook up and see how it goes," Jeff suggested to Marisol.

"Maybe," Marisol responded, but she didn't look as if she believed it would ever happen. "I'm glad you're going to be okay."

"Yeah, me, too. And you're going to be okay, too."

She gave him a brave smile. "Yes, I am," she said confidently. "And in a way, it's thanks to you. I'm gonna stay with my great-grandpa for a while. He won't put up with me getting into any trouble. I'll be working for him at his shop, getting it ready to be sold. Stop by if you're ever taking a walk in the neighborhood. It's not that far from the diner."

Rosa regarded her curiously. "What shop is that?"

"Mullins Junk Shop on Palm Drive," Jeff answered. "You know Mr. Mullins, Mom."

"Well, of course, I do." She smiled at Marisol with genuine warmth for the first time. "He's a wonderful man. You tell him we don't see nearly enough of him at the diner anymore."

Marisol beamed. "I will. He's not too steady on his feet these days, but if I came with him, he could walk over. Would that be okay?"

Rosa gazed at her son and saw the hope in his eyes. "I think that would be fine," she said, then added, "In a few weeks."

Marisol nodded. "I understand. Well, I guess I should go."

She whirled around and left before Rosa or Jeff could even say goodbye. Rosa looked at her son. "Are you okay with taking a break from her?"

He nodded, though she thought she detected the sheen of tears in his eyes.

"It doesn't have to be forever, you know. I think she has some growing up to do and I think Joshua Mullins can help her with that. Then, who knows what might happen?"

Jeff met her gaze. "Have I told you what a great mom you are?"

She smiled at him. "Yes, but it's always nice to hear." She brushed his hair back from his face. "I wish I could make all of this easier for you."

"I know, but I got myself into this mess and I'm the only one who can do the hard work it's going to take to get out of it."

"Emma, Andy and I will be there for you, though."

"I don't deserve that, not after the way I bailed on all of you."

"Well, we'll be there just the same," Rosa said. "That's what families do, they stick together when things get tough."

And if God was merciful, things wouldn't get any tougher than they had been for them since the night Don died.

A week later, Rosa looked around the dinner table and thought how lucky she was to have all her children alive and well. She'd made Jeff's favorite, *picadillo* with black beans and rice. He was eating it with gratifying enthusiasm. In fact, he looked almost like his old self. The sparkle was back in his eyes and he'd even managed a joke or two during the meal. A week out of the hospital had made a real difference.

Andy seemed to be slowly getting over his resentment of his big brother and was eager to help Jeff get back on his feet. They were talking about shooting some hoops in the driveway after dinner. They sounded so normal, Rosa almost cried.

"No basketball," she said sternly and with regret. "Not for a few more weeks, Jeff. You heard the doctor."

"Then how about Monopoly?" Andy suggested. "I can whip you at that, even though you almost have that fancy business degree from college."

"As if..." Jeff retorted, making Andy grin.

Rosa smiled at them, then turned her attention to Emma. She and Matt could hardly keep their eyes— or their hands—off of each other. If those two didn't do something to solidify their relationship soon, Rosa was going to be tempted to propose on Matt's behalf.

Rosa was about to utter a sigh of satisfaction, when Emma carefully put aside her fork and regarded her with a look that made her very nervous. Dreading whatever her daughter was about to say that had put such a serious expression on her face, Rosa almost told her to keep her announcement to herself.

"Mama, there are a couple of things I think we need to talk about," Emma said in a dire tone that only increased Rosa's anxiety.

Rosa regarded her with concern. Whatever was up to make her daughter push aside her apple pie untouched couldn't be good news. Was this it? Was Emma about to announce that she was going back to Washington? If so, Rosa might be tempted to shake her until she woke up and looked around at all she had here. She had family and friends and a man who loved her unconditionally.

"What's on your mind?" Rosa asked, trying to keep her tone neutral.

"First, I'm not sure how you'll feel about this, but

I discovered something the other day I've been wanting to tell you about. I think it could be a solution to a lot of our problems."

Rosa noted that Matt stared at her with surprise. Whatever Emma was about to announce was obviously not what he'd been expecting. "Okay, I'm listening," Rosa said.

"Did you know that Harley was an executive chef in Orlando before he retired?"

Every single person at the table stared at her as if she'd just announced that the stuffy mayor of Winter Cove could tap-dance.

"You're kidding," Matt said. "Is that what the two of you were huddling about the other day?"

Emma nodded. "He said he'd be willing to work for us part-time, if you're interested. Andy's going back to school soon and Jeff will be, too."

"I don't know about me, sis," Jeff protested.

"You're going back," Emma and Rosa said simultaneously.

Jeff seemed startled by the fierceness of their responses. "How?"

"We'll find a way," Rosa said. "I imagine we still have some clout in the banking community in this town. It's your senior year. It would be a waste for you not to finish."

"The bottom line is you're going to need help at the diner, Mama," Emma continued. "It might as well be someone who's not only experienced, but someone who knows the diner's customers and us."

Rosa was still stunned by the fact that in all these years Harley had never mentioned the kind of work he did. Maybe he'd thought it would be too intimidating to a small diner's owners to know that one of their regulars cooked for a far fancier clientele.

"Can we afford him?" she asked. "I know our finances are in bad shape right now. It's one thing to take out a loan for Jeff's college expenses, but the diner's already in debt and I want to pay that off as soon as possible."

"I don't think we can afford not to hire him," Emma said. "And I got the feeling he wasn't looking for a lot. I think he's bored."

"I'll say," Matt said. "I don't think I can take him playing sleuth for me again."

Rosa regarded him with surprise. "What on earth was Harley investigating?"

Emma and Matt exchanged a look. Emma was the one who responded. "He was helping us try to find a motive for Dad's suicide. And that was the second thing I wanted to talk to all of you about."

Rosa suddenly felt sick to her stomach. She took a sip of cold water and tried to steady her nerves. She glanced from Jeff's suddenly shuttered expression to Andy's dismayed face. "I'm not sure—"

"Mama, you need to hear this," Emma said, deliberately cutting off Rosa's protest. "So do Andy and Jeff."

Rosa looked at her sons, who were nodding. "Okay, then, if you think it will help...."

"I do," Emma said. "You know that the finances for Flamingo Diner were a bigger mess than any of us imagined."

Rosa nodded. "It was so unlike your father to refinance the building without saying a word to me, to say nothing of refinancing this house. I can't imagine what he was thinking. Where did all that money go?"

"He was playing the stock market," Emma said. "Jennifer Sawyer filled us in. When he lost your savings, she tried to get him to stop investing, but she said it was like he was addicted to the game."

Rosa pressed her hand to her chest. "He was gambling?" she asked, her voice barely above a whisper.

"Mom, it was the stock market," Jeff began, but Rosa cut him off.

"It was gambling," she said emphatically. "He took money we couldn't afford to lose and bet it on stocks. He might as well have been playing roulette."

A million and one memories came flooding back, none of them good. There had been a time when Don had spent all his spare time in Miami either at the horse races or the dog track. Some weeks he'd do well and convince himself he was invincible. Other times he lost his shirt. They had fought about it over and over again. Her parents had warned her that she would be in for a very rough time of it, if he didn't give it up. Because she'd known they were right, she had forced the issue. It was the one time they had come close to calling off their wedding.

"Mama?" Emma said, regarding her curiously. "Are you okay?"

"I was thinking back to the months before your father and I got married. He was gambling too much. My parents saw trouble down the road if he kept it up. We talked, but he wouldn't—or couldn't—quit. I finally threatened to break off our engagement if he didn't give it up. It was touch-and-go for a while, like you said, as if he were fighting an addiction, but eventually he put our relationship first. As far as I know, he never gambled again. We never spoke of it again, but he knew what the consequences would be if he did.''

Emma stared at her, her expression dismayed. "What were they?"

"That I would leave him," Rosa said flatly, then uttered a gasp of dismay as she realized the implication.

Don had gotten in over his head in the stock market. He'd obviously been uncertain about how she would react if he told her about his investments. And when things had gone from bad to worse, he'd clearly feared she would make good on the threat she had uttered so many years before.

"Oh, Don," she whispered, tears streaming down her face. She gazed helplessly at her children. "If only I'd known what he was going through, I could have reassured him that the time when I would leave was long past." She looked at each of her children in turn. "Let this be a lesson to you. Nothing is more important in a relationship than communication. If your father and I had talked, really talked, maybe all of this could have been prevented and he would still be with us. I had no idea that such an old threat could weigh so heavily on him after all we'd been through."

Emma looked thoroughly shaken by the torrent of bad memories she'd unleashed. "Mama, I'm sorry. I thought you should know."

"You were right," Rosa said. "I'm not sure if it makes it easier or harder, but it was important to know what was going on in his head during those last weeks. It breaks my heart to think that he thought we couldn't weather such a crisis."

"Mine, too," Emma said.

Rosa blinked back tears and looked at her children. "Let's make a pact, all of us. From here on out, when we think of your father, when we talk about him, let's vow to remember all the good times, all the wonderful things he did for us and other people. Let's make tonight the last time we talk about how he died. If we dwell on that, we lose the best part of him."

Matt gave her an encouraging smile as he lifted his glass of iced tea. "I propose a toast," he said, meeting her gaze. "To Don, a good friend, a great father and a terrific husband. May his memory be with us forever."

"Amen," Rosa said, reaching for Matt's hand. "He was so proud of you, you know. Of all of you. I don't want any of you to forget that. And I think he's been watching over us since he died. I think he'd be proud that we've gotten through this terrible time. We're going to make it."

Though Emma's revelation had made Rosa heartsick, she felt lighter inside, as if all the pieces of the tragic puzzle had finally fallen into place. And now that the picture was complete, she could put it in a mental album, along with so many other memories, most of which were warm and wonderful. She wouldn't bury this one, but she could finally put it in perspective.

And wasn't that what getting on with life was all about, putting things into proper perspective? She'd have to ask Anne about that next time she went to her support group meeting at Saint Luke's.

"I have the feeling we're finally healing," Emma said as she and Matt took their evening stroll around the lake. It had been a long night and a longer day, but the walks always eased her mind. She turned to him. "But there's one more thing I'd like to do tonight."

He lifted her hand to his lips and brushed a kiss across the knuckles. "What's that?"

"I want to go all the way around the lake tonight. I don't want to turn back before we get to the place where he died."

Matt's expression darkened. "Emma—"

She cut off the protest. "It's all right. I'm ready now. I want to put it to rest, all of it."

"There's nothing to see," he told her.

"I know. That's why I want to do it. It's symbolic, I guess, of what Mom said earlier. The way he died really isn't the important thing. It's the way he lived, and he loved this town and the lake. He brought us here so many times when we were little. I want those happy memories back."

Matt sighed. "Then we'll walk around the lake."

She gazed up at his profile. "You've been such a rock through all of this."

He gave her a wry look. "People don't get involved with rocks."

She elbowed him in the ribs. "You know what I mean. Besides, I am involved with you, far more than I expected to be."

"Is it enough?" he asked.

"I don't know that yet," she admitted, knowing that the reply would hurt him, that in so many ways it was unfair. And yet, she had to be fair to herself, too. Maybe she'd blown living in Washington all out of proportion. Maybe she'd made it into a show of her independence, a demonstration that she was more than a small-town girl. She wasn't sure who she'd needed to prove that to, her family or herself. And now that she had, did it even really matter anymore? Those were questions she wasn't sure she could answer, not until she went back again, tested the happiness she'd found here against what she remembered of being on her own.

"You're leaving, aren't you?" Matt asked.

"You knew I would."

"How soon?"

"If Harley seems to be working out, soon, I imagine."

"I see."

"I have to do this, Matt."

He nodded. "I won't try to stop you."

She regarded him with surprise. "You told me once we'd slept together that you'd fight for me," she reminded him.

He grinned at that. "Never said I'd stop fighting, just that I wouldn't try to hold you here."

"How do you feel about long-distance relationships?" she asked.

A smile tugged at his lips. "Better than I used to."

Emma drew to a stop and turned to him. She reached up and traced the line of his jaw, the outline of his mouth. "I do love you," she whispered, just before she stood on tiptoe and kissed him.

Matt might have promised not to use words to try to stop her, but he threw everything he had into that kiss. Emma was pretty sure her toes curled and her knees melted. She was clinging to him to stay upright by the time it ended.

She was still leaning into him, feeling his heat and his love surround her, when she realized where they were. The mound of dead flowers and other tokens of affection were the giveaway. She sucked in a sharp breath at the sight and Matt's arms immediately tightened around her.

"I'm okay," she said, though her voice shook. She lifted her gaze to his, felt her nerves steady. "I really am okay."

"I know you are," he said. "But I like it when you lean on me just a little."

"Literally or figuratively?"

"Both."

Emma laced her fingers through his. "Then let's go to your place and I'll lean on you a little more inventively."

He grinned at the suggestion. "Anytime, darlin'. Anytime."

23

Emma called her old boss in Georgetown and asked if there was still a place for her at Fashionable Memories.

"You're coming home?" Marcel asked, clearly elated by the news.

Though she'd been stubbornly—defensively—claiming Washington as home ever since her return to Winter Cove, hearing that label from Marcel startled her. The description didn't fit as comfortably as it once had.

When had that happened? Emma wondered. When had she begun thinking of Winter Cove as her home once again? When she thought about it without her blinders on, she could see the truth. Winter Cove was where she mattered to people, where she was loved. It was where she'd discovered what it meant to be in love with a good man.

"I'm coming back to Washington," she corrected, not sure why it felt so important to make the distinction, even less sure why she didn't feel happier about it. She'd waited months for this moment, waited for her family to get back on track, waited to find the answers she needed to put her father's death to rest. She ought to feel ecstatic about finally being able to leave.

"I'll even pick you up at the airport," Marcel said, which for him was a huge concession. He hated driving in heavy traffic and there was no airport in the D.C. area where traffic was not an issue.

"That's okay. I'm not sure I can bear to listen to you grumble all the way back into D.C. I'll take a cab."

"Where will you be staying? You gave up your apartment, didn't you?"

"Yes, but it's not a problem. I'll stay with Kim until I find another place."

"There's an apartment above the store," he reminded her. "The tenant just moved out. It's yours, if you want it. You'd be right in the thick of things here in Georgetown. It's a great location for a young, single woman."

It was the perfect solution, but for some reason Emma didn't feel especially eager to grab it. "I'll take a look at it when I get there," she said, stalling.

"And when will that be exactly?"

"I'll fly up Sunday and be ready to go to work on Monday."

"Perfect timing," he said with gratifying enthusiasm, then spoiled it all by adding, "There's a sale I wanted to go to on Tuesday. I was afraid I was going to have to miss it."

Emma realized the old pattern was going to fall right back into place as if she'd never left. She would manage the store, while Marcel roamed the countryside.

But that was the way she wanted it, wasn't it? She liked being left in charge. She liked the responsibility, the persuasive negotiations with the interior designers.

Still, it might have been nice to be the one who got

to look for treasures once in a while, she thought irritably. Half of what Marcel sent back in the lots he bought was nothing but junk.

"Have you been missing estate sales the whole time I was gone?" she asked.

"No, I had someone who filled in when I couldn't be here, but it hasn't really been working out. She occupied space. She waited for the customers to make up their own minds, rather than planting the idea that they'd regret it if they didn't purchase whatever they were looking at."

"Couldn't you use this person one more time, so I could go to the sale with you?" she asked, hoping for an indication that things could change.

The request was met with shocked silence. "But I pay you to run the store," he said finally.

"You also pay me because I have a good eye for bargains that can make a huge profit. Wouldn't you be putting it to better use if I were at the sales?"

"I suppose," he said cautiously. "But then I'd have to pay someone else to be at the store. Let me think about it. We can talk it over when you get here."

Emma bit back a sigh. She could already tell that nothing would change. Marcel was too tightfisted and shortsighted to see the wisdom in what she was suggesting. For the first time, she ended a conversation with him feeling thoroughly frustrated and dissatisfied with her role at Fashionable Memories.

She wandered into the kitchen and found her mother fixing dinner.

"Something wrong?" Rosa asked, regarding her worriedly.

"Not really."

"Weren't you just on the phone with your old boss? You aren't having a problem convincing him to take you back, are you?"

"No, but it's on the same old terms," Emma admitted.

Her mother regarded her curiously, then asked as if she feared she might be treading on thin ice, "Did you want more money?"

"No, more independence to do what I do best," Emma explained. "I want to acquire antiques, not just sell them."

"And he won't agree?"

"He hasn't yet," she admitted, reaching for one of the cherry tomatoes in the salad and popping it into her mouth.

"Ever thought of opening your own business?" Rosa asked so casually that it was obvious that this was something *she* had thought about, probably often.

Emma stared at her. "Me? What would I use for money?"

"I imagine with your experience you could find an investor or you could get a traditional loan from a bank or apply for a loan from the Small Business Administration," Rosa said, offering yet more proof that she'd given this a lot of thought. "There are lots of ways to do it, if it's what you really want."

Emma had honestly never considered such a thing. She'd always thought she was too young to run her own business, but her mother and father had been younger than she was now when they'd started Flamingo Diner. Maybe she would look into it as soon as she got back to Washington. She gave her mother a kiss on the cheek. "Thanks, Mama. You've definitely given me something to think about."

Rosa let the subject drop, also proving that she'd contentedly planted a seed just as she'd intended. She was patient enough to wait for it to flourish. She did, however, ask, "You going out with Matt tonight?"

"He said he'd call once he knows what time he can break free."

"You two have gotten close these last few months, haven't you?"

Emma thought she saw where this was heading. "Don't get any ideas, Mama. I'm still leaving for Washington on Sunday. I already have my ticket."

"Tickets can be refunded," her mother pointed out.

"Not this one," Emma said, unwilling to even consider the possibility. She was going back to D.C. no matter what, even if she wasn't looking forward to it the way she'd expected to.

"Your decision," Rosa said readily.

"That's exactly right, Mama. It is my decision."

So, why didn't she feel a whole lot better about it? Why did she have this awful sensation in the pit of her stomach that she was going to be losing far more than she gained?

Matt sat at the counter at Flamingo Diner and watched Emma work. There was finally some decent color back in her cheeks and she no longer looked quite so defeated. Maybe that was because talking with Jennifer Sawyer had given her some closure when it came to her father's death. Maybe it was because her mother finally had her act together and actually seemed happy to be back at work at the diner. Jeff's behavior had improved dramatically since his brush with death. And Andy, well, the kid was back to getting all tongue-tied over girls, instead of trying to act like the man of the family.

As relieved as Matt was by the changes in these people he cared about, a part of him was filled with regret. Once again, he was going to lose Emma. The only difference was that he was going to have to sit back and watch her leave, rather than being the one doing the leaving. And now he knew just how much her going would cost him. She'd be taking his heart with her.

"You intend to let her get away again?" Rosa asked, sliding onto a stool next to him.

He whirled and stared at her. "I don't know what you're talking about."

Rosa looked as if she'd like to shake some sense into him. "Matt Atkins, I may have been in a daze these past few months, but I'm not blind. Nor am I stupid. You've been in love with my daughter for as long as I can remember. If anything, that old infatuation has grown stronger since she's been back."

He considered denying it, then decided not to waste his breath. "It doesn't matter."

She gave him a scathing look. "You can't possibly be that dense. Love *always* matters. Haven't you learned anything from Don's death? If he'd seen that, if he'd believed in the strength of our marriage, he'd still be with us."

"Emma wants to go back to Washington," he reminded her.

"So she says."

"She bought her ticket."

"Nonrefundable. I know." Rosa shrugged. "What's a couple of hundred dollars compared to a whole future?"

Matt stared at her. Had he missed something, something critical? "You think she doesn't really want to go?"

She smiled and patted his arm. "I think you could change her mind, if you put a little effort into it." She winked at him. "I hear that the junk store over on Palm Drive is for sale. I wonder if Emma's aware of that?"

She was talking about Joshua Mullins's place. Somehow he'd forgotten all about his plan to plant that particular idea in Emma's head. He grinned at Rosa. She'd always been one step ahead of him. "Think you can hold down the fort for an hour or two if I can get some things in order and get back here for Emma?"

"Haven't I been running this place for thirty years?"

"I'm glad you've remembered that," he said, suddenly serious.

Rosa's smile didn't quite reach her eyes. "So am I," she said softly.

Then her expression brightened. "There's Helen. I need to speak to her. There's somebody I want her to meet, a gentleman I met in my support group. It's going to take a lot of persuasion for me to get her to accept a blind date."

"You could be sneaky and just make sure both of them are here at the same time. That way there would be no pressure on either one of them," Matt suggested. "That's always better than a blind date with two people who are in a panic."

Rosa beamed at him. "What a wonderful idea! Any man that romantic should surely be able to figure out a way to keep my daughter right here where she belongs.''

''I'll work on it,'' Matt promised. ''Starting now.'' In fact, he already had a plan that he was pretty sure Emma wouldn't be able to resist.

''Look at us,'' Jolie said as she, Helen, Sylvia and Rosa were gathered around a table at Flamingo Diner after the lunch crowd had left. ''We are four of the most attractive women I know.''

''For our age,'' Helen said dryly.

Jolie scowled. ''For any age. We're smart. We're funny. We're nice. So why are we all alone?''

''Because there are no funny, smart, nice men our age available,'' Helen retorted. ''Besides, I thought you and that guy from the Italian restaurant were about to launch a steamy romance.''

''Only in my dreams,'' Jolie admitted. ''Turned out he was more than willing, but I discovered he already has a wife—his third, no less—and five little bambinos he'd neglected to mention. He'd acquired this wife after the divorce he told me about.''

Rosa gave her a sympathetic look. ''I'm sorry.''

''Don't be. It was just an infatuation,'' Jolie said with a shrug. ''I'll probably be in lust with a dozen inappropriate men before I actually find somebody worth dating.''

''At least you fall in lust,'' Helen said. ''There has not been one single man who made my pulse race since Harrison died.''

''Speaking of that,'' Rosa said, seeing her opportunity to mention that Larry would be dropping by shortly.

Before she could get the words out, the man in

question walked into the diner, looking tanned and healthy and attractive in the way that retired men who played a lot of golf tended to look. He spotted her and a smile spread across his face.

"I hope I'm not interrupting," he said. "You said this would be a good time to come by, Rosa."

"You're not interrupting anything more than girl talk," Rosa told him. "Larry, these are my friends."

She introduced them, then barely bit back a sigh when he automatically slid a chair in next to Jolie. Her eyes were already sparkling, her experience with the married maître d' forgotten.

"Anybody want coffee?" Rosa asked, resigned to seeing her scheme go completely awry. Why hadn't she considered the fact that Helen, with her quiet demeanor and understated style, always faded into the background when compared to Jolie's bright colors and exuberance?

"I'll help you," Helen offered, following her behind the counter. "Do you believe Jolie? She has the attention span of a fruit fly."

There wasn't the slightest hint of jealousy in Helen's tone. So maybe she and Larry wouldn't have been destined to be a perfect fit, after all, Rosa concluded. Obviously there'd been no bolt-from-the-blue attraction the instant he walked in. Maybe she should leave the matchmaking to somebody who'd had more practice, except when it came to Matt and Emma, of course. She was not going to let those two throw their lives away. She'd done some very satisfactory nudging earlier, though she couldn't imagine why Matt hadn't come back for Emma as he'd indicated he would.

"What's taking so long?" Sylvia asked, coming to

join them. "I feel like a fifth wheel out there. Those two have obviously made a love connection. I didn't want to watch."

"That's because right this second you're still at the I-hate-all-men stage of the divorce process," Rosa guessed. "That'll change. Are things going smoothly on that front?"

Sylvia shrugged. "Frank's fighting me every step of the way, but I'm not backing down. And I want you all to remind me of how it's been for the last twenty-five years, if you see me weakening for a second."

"That is definitely a promise I can keep," Rosa said, giving her a hug. "We are so proud of you for having the guts to walk away. It's hard to do at our age."

"It's hard to do at any age," Helen said.

"But somehow it's much scarier once you're in your forties or fifties," Rosa said. "Being alone seems unnatural or something."

"And there are so few men to choose from, unless you want to date some guy in his seventies who's just lost his wife and does nothing but play cards or golf," Helen added.

Sylvia forced a smile. "Gee, you two make it sound like so much fun."

"It's not," Helen said frankly.

"But it's better than a bad marriage," Sylvia reminded her. "You two had happy marriages, but I can testify about the other kind. I know all about what it's like not to get one shred of respect or consideration. I know all about living with a bully. I don't care how lonely I get, anything will be better than having to defer to someone else on every single thing I do or risk a battle.''

Helen looked thoughtful. "There is that. Maybe I should count my blessings.''

Rosa listened to them and wondered if she would ever get to that stage. Right now, Don was still too much a part of her life. She was getting better at concentrating on the good parts of their marriage. She made it a point to share her memories with Jeff, Andy and Emma, so that they could all start to heal. But a side effect of that was that she was nowhere near letting go and moving on. "I wonder if I'll ever get there,'' she asked sadly.

Helen and Sylvia regarded her with immediate worry.

"Are you okay?'' Helen asked.

"A little sad, but okay,'' Rosa assured them. "I suspect I'll miss Don for the rest of my life, but the hurt is easing more and more each day.''

"Do you remember the time he showed up at the diner on Halloween dressed like a vampire?'' Helen said, a smile on her face. "And none of the parents could get their kids to come in.''

"Probably because he insisted on serving a glass of tomato juice with every meal,'' Sylvia said dryly. "He even scared the dickens out of me that day. I wasn't entirely sure what was in that glass, so I made Helen drink hers first.''

Rosa chuckled. "I've never known a grown man who enjoyed Halloween so much, though that was the last year he got himself a scary costume. It drove away too much business.''

"Seems like Halloween's just around the corner,''

Helen noted. "Once Labor Day has come and gone, fall really flies by."

"And then it'll be time to decorate for Christmas," Sylvia said. "Somehow Thanksgiving gets lost in there. I expect all of you at my house this year, same as always."

Rosa studied her with concern. "Are you sure?"

"It's tradition," Sylvia insisted. "Who knows, I might even let my husband drop by, if he promises to be on good behavior." She looked at Rosa. "Do you think Emma will be home?"

"If I'm any judge of which way the wind is blowing, Emma will definitely be here," Rosa said.

"With Matt?" Helen guessed.

Rosa nodded. "He has a plan to keep her here."

"But I thought she was leaving Sunday," Sylvia said.

Rosa grinned. "That's *her* plan. Matt has other ideas. I'm putting my money on him."

"Do you know about this plan of his?" Helen asked.

"Not the details," Rosa admitted.

"Then how do you know it will work?" Sylvia asked.

"Because Emma's not stupid, and she loves him. I'm as sure of that as I am that we'd better get back over there before Jolie tries to seduce Larry right here in Flamingo Diner. She's got that look in her eyes."

"She always has that look in her eyes," Helen noted.

"Which is why I recognize it," Rosa said, picking up the fresh pot of coffee and an extra cup for Larry.

They all trouped back to the table and resumed

their places, even though Jolie seemed oblivious and Larry looked shell-shocked.

"Coffee?" Rosa asked cheerfully, then poured without waiting for a reply. "So, Larry, are you and Jolie getting to know each other?"

He blinked hard, then finally dragged his gaze away from the flamboyantly dressed Jolie. "What? Oh, sure."

Jolie smiled as if she'd just caught the juiciest canary in the aviary. "Did you know that Larry is interested in theater?" she asked as if that were an incredible revelation worthy of being reported in the Winter Cove newspaper.

"Isn't that interesting?" Helen said with amusement. "I believe you love theater, as well, isn't that right, Jolie?"

"I'm doing a local production of *Annie*," Jolie confessed, her cheeks turning a becoming shade of pink. "We open in two weeks."

"I'll bet you have the lead," Larry said.

Jolie's blush deepened, even as Sylvia and Helen rolled their eyes.

"The lead is a kid," Rosa pointed out. "An orphan."

Larry gave her a vague look. "I know that, but I imagine Jolie could pull it off."

"Why, thank you," Jolie said, clearly dazzled. "Isn't that just about the nicest thing a man could say?"

"The nicest," Helen said. "Larry, you'll have to come with us, when we go to see the production. We have tickets for opening night. I'm sure we can find an extra seat."

"Of course, I'll be there," he said at once, his appreciative gaze sweeping over the entire group. "What man wouldn't want to go out with four beautiful women?"

Rosa nearly groaned. She'd apparently let loose a monster. Maybe Larry was the kind of man who enjoyed having a lot of women in his life. After all, he had been running around on his wife, even if it had been during a time when he'd claimed to be trying to get her to agree to a divorce. Rosa wasn't taking any chances, though. She intended to warn Jolie to watch her step with him. And she needed to do it before things got any hotter between them.

"Everybody, I hate to cut this short, but I have to close up and be somewhere," Rosa said emphatically. "Larry, it was nice of you to stop by. Jolie, could you stick around? I want to talk to you about something."

That the something was going to be an attempt to nip this thing between Jolie and Larry in the bud made her feel a little queasy. It wasn't as if she could explain herself to Jolie, either. The things she'd learned about Larry had been expressed in confidence during their support group meetings. But she could make a general statement about the dangers of rushing into anything with a man Jolie didn't know all that well yet.

Helen apparently had some idea of what was on her mind, because she herded Larry and Sylvia from Flamingo Diner as if there were a fire somewhere that required their attention.

"What one earth is wrong with you?" Jolie demanded when they'd gone. Then a horrified expression crossed her face. "Oh, my gosh, was Larry supposed to be your date? I thought you'd just invited him over as a friend. If I was invading your territory, I'm sorry.''

Rosa saw little point in mentioning that she'd intended to fix him up with Helen. That particular ship had obviously sailed with no one on board.

''This isn't about me,'' she said. ''But don't you think you're jumping into something a little too quickly here? You barely know the man. That's a pattern with you. Just look at what happened with the maître d'.''

Jolie flushed. ''Larry isn't married. You know that or you would never have asked him to drop by. His wife committed suicide and his fiancée left him.''

''He told you that?'' Rosa asked, relieved, but not entirely satisfied.

''Well, of course, he told me. He's an honest guy. Anyone who spends five minutes with him can tell that.''

''But think about it, he had a fiancée while he also had a wife. At the very least, don't you think that calls for a little caution on your part? That's all I'm suggesting, that you take your time and get to know him before jumping into anything serious.''

Jolie regarded her with a perplexed expression. ''We've had one conversation. We're attracted to each other. We're not getting married tomorrow morning.''

''Heaven forbid,'' Rosa said with heartfelt emotion.

''Are you sure you're not jealous?'' Jolie asked.

''I am definitely not jealous. I'm just concerned.''

''Don't be.'' Jolie shrugged. ''Who knows, he may not even call.''

Rosa knew better. She'd seen the look in his eyes. "He'll call."

"I don't know why you're so sure of that, but I hope you're right. Stop worrying, Rosa. He's a nice guy," Jolie insisted. "Not like the others I've gone out with. I can tell the difference. He reminds me of Don a little."

Rosa was startled by the comparison. She certainly hadn't seen it. "How?"

"He's got that same wonderful streak of gentleness that Don had, the kind that lets you know he'd never do an intentionally mean thing."

Rosa bit back a reminder that Don had done the cruelest thing of all, he'd left her. "Take your time and get to know him, that's all I'm asking."

"I will. I promise," Jolie said. "I'm not the total flake you all think I am."

"We certainly do not think you're a flake," Rosa protested fiercely.

"I am when it comes to men," Jolie admitted. "Or at least I've been behaving like one ever since the divorce. I suppose I needed to prove to myself that I still had what it takes to attract a man. And you're right that I have set some very bad patterns, but I've learned from my mistakes. I really have."

Rosa gave her hand a squeeze. "That's all any of us can do."

"I'll call you if I hear from Larry," Jolie said. "I'll tell you exactly what he said and what our plans are. Will that make you feel better?"

A play-by-play of Jolie's love life? The thought boggled Rosa's mind. "I don't think you need to go that far."

Jolie left, looking happier than she had in a long

time. Rosa watched as her friend stepped outside. Larry promptly emerged from the shadows beside the building. Jolie smiled up at him as if he'd hung the moon. So much for caution, but if Jolie had her heart broken yet again, Rosa and the others would be there to help her pick up the pieces. That's what friends did.

24

Matt had intended to get back to Flamingo Diner that afternoon, but his plans had taken longer than he'd anticipated. In addition, he'd made the mistake of stopping by his office.

"Nice you could drop in, boss," Cramer noted, standing in the doorway and blocking any hurried exit Matt might have intended to make. "We've missed you around here."

Matt frowned at the sarcasm. "You knew exactly where to find me, if you needed me," he said defensively. "I've had my beeper with me."

"But has it been on?" the sergeant inquired.

Matt yanked it off his belt and stared at it. It was most definitely on. "Yes," he reported. "What the hell is wrong with you?"

"I've been fending off calls from various councilmen who are wondering why the chief of police is spending all his time flipping pancakes and burgers at Flamingo Diner," Cramer said. "I figured you wouldn't want me telling them you had the hots for Emma, so I got a little creative. I told 'em it was part of your new policy to display a police presence in the businesses around town. Just so I wouldn't be lying, I've got you scheduled to work at a library and on a garbage truck. Anything else you'd like to try to show the public how interested you are in protecting the community?"

Matt stared at him incredulously. "Have you lost your mind?"

"Nope, just trying to save your butt," Cramer said cheerfully. "The mayor got some bee in his bonnet about the time you've been spending at the diner. Said you were there more lately than you were here and it wasn't a good use of taxpayer dollars. I could hardly deny that you'd been there, since he saw you with his own eyes. Even ate some of your scrambled eggs, the way he tells it. Said they were lousy. He wondered if your cooking was indicative of the way you did other things, such as running this department."

Matt groaned. "I don't suppose it occurred to you to explain that I took leave to work over there?"

"Did you really?" Cramer asked, his expression confused. "Did you fill out the paperwork?"

Matt scowled. "You know damn well I didn't."

"Then you haven't got a leg to stand on. I figured the PR angle was the only way to go."

"But a garbage truck?"

"It'll make you humble," Cramer noted with a certain amount of glee. "I suggest you not ask Emma out for that evening, though."

"When am I doing that?" Matt asked, resigned to the inevitable. If Cramer was going to find a creative way to keep him out of trouble with the city fathers, then he supposed he had an obligation to do his part.

"That would be tomorrow morning at five," he said, struggling to keep a straight face. "It shouldn't be too bad. The temperature's only supposed to hit eighty-six tomorrow. And the weatherman says there will be a breeze. If you're lucky, it'll be blowing the right way.''

Matt bit back an expletive. ''You're really enjoying this, aren't you? Why the hell couldn't you have come up with something else for me to do?''

''I tried, but Flo over at the Twist and Shout refused to let you do a perm.''

Matt saw his time with Emma slipping away. ''I hope you didn't schedule that day at the library on Friday.''

''Nope, that's next week,'' Cramer told him. ''I thought I'd see about getting you something at the undertaker's next week, too.''

''Only if you want it to be your body I'm embalming,'' Matt said, barely restraining a shudder.

''Got it,'' Cramer said, grinning. ''No undertaker's.''

''And maybe you could put a hold on the schedule until I get back to you,'' Matt said. ''Not that I don't appreciate what you've done, but I think I'll try to wriggle off this hook on my own from here on out.''

''Whatever you say. I'd start with a call to the mayor, though, since he's the one who got the others riled up.''

''Believe me, I have every intention of speaking to the mayor,'' Matt assured him. He just had a few more important fish to fry first.

''What on earth has gotten into you?'' Emma demanded as Matt practically stripped her apron over her head and dragged her out of Flamingo Diner right in the middle of the lunch rush. He'd vanished without a word to her the day before and now he had the gall to come in here like he owned the place, like he owned *her?* She scowled at him. "There are customers in here, you know."

"Your mother has it covered," he said. "And I have something to show you."

"Can't it wait?"

"No," he said succinctly without adding one word of explanation.

Emma debated arguing, but with Matt in an oddly dangerous mood like this, it was probably easier to play along. She slanted a look at him and concluded that he looked a little edgy.

"Is everything okay?" she finally asked when they'd walked a couple of blocks and the tension in his shoulders seemed to have eased a bit.

"It will be," he said, his expression grim.

"Where are we going?"

"For a walk," he said, as if it should be perfectly obvious.

"But not a leisurely, relaxing stroll, I notice," she said dryly as she practically ran to keep up with him.

He regarded her blankly, then apparently caught on. "Oh, sorry. I was anxious."

"For what?"

"To show you something," he said impatiently, turning onto Palm Drive, a wide street with tall, royal palms lining the median. It was a short street that ran perpendicular to Main and for some reason, they'd never turned onto it on all their other walks, probably because Main led directly to the lake.

Emma was startled by all the changes, which were even more pronounced than they were on Main Street. The storefronts had been refinished with pink stucco facades and green-and-white striped awnings. The pawnshop she remembered was gone, replaced by an upscale gift boutique. A children's store next door had a window display of expensive baby clothes and the Mercedes-Benz of strollers. A few doors down from that was a jewelry store that boasted branches in Palm Beach and Palm Springs. That hinted that the customers were slightly more upscale than those she saw daily at the diner. She could imagine the clientele from Fashionable Memories coming into these shops.

She turned to Matt. "When did this happen?"

"Over the last five years. Winter Cove's become an attractive retirement community to wealthy northerners who don't want to live in Orlando or Tampa and prefer to live inland. If you drive a few miles west of town, there are some pretty amazing houses being built around a half-dozen man-made lakes and a very exclusive golf course."

"Why did you wait until now to bring me here?"

He shrugged. "It wasn't like I was hiding it from you. For all I knew you'd been here."

She frowned at that. He wasn't telling her the whole truth. She could see it in his eyes. "Come on. Spill it. Why are we here now?"

Before he could reply, she glanced over his shoulder and saw the For Sale sign in one of the windows. Just behind it was a cherry desk that would have fit right in at Fashionable Memories in Georgetown. The thrill of the hunt promptly gave her a shot of adrenaline. If the store was going out of business, maybe she could pick it up for a song. Marcel would be ecstatic. And there might be more treasures inside, though judging from the coat of grime on the window and the piled-up merchandise surrounding that desk, it was going to take a lot of excavating to unearth them, probably more time than she had between now and Sunday.

Suddenly suspicious, she glanced from the display to Matt. "This is what you wanted me to see, isn't it? This desk."

He nodded, hands shoved in his pockets. "I thought it might give you some ideas."

Something in his tone made her stop just as she was about to reach for the handle on the door. She searched his face, but his expression was neutral. "You mean something besides the desk, don't you? What sort of ideas?"

"Maybe not ideas, exactly. More like options."

Her heart began to hammer. "Come on, Matt. You're going to have to spell this out for me. I am not going to jump to conclusions. I want facts."

"Probably a first," he teased, then his expression sobered. "Let's take a look around inside and see if there's anything on display that interests you. I hear Joshua Mullins gets his hands on some really amazing things from time to time."

Emma still had a mile-long list of questions, but she decided none of them were urgent. Besides, she could hardly wait to explore the place. She pushed open the door and went inside, then came to an immediate halt when she saw Marisol behind the counter packing a box.

"Marisol?"

The girl whirled around and stared. "Hey, Emma." She avoided Matt's gaze, even as she greeted him with a mumbled hello.

"What are you doing here?" Emma asked.

"My great-grandpa owns this place. He has for years, but he's planning to retire as soon as he finds somebody to buy it. I'm helping him sort through some stuff.''

"That's very nice of you."

Marisol shrugged. "He's a great guy and he's been making sure I stay straight, if you know what I mean." She hesitated, then asked, "How's Jeff doing?"

"Good," Emma told her. "He's back at college."

Marisol's expression turned sad. "I'm really happy that worked out for him. I know he was really bummed about missing his senior year and not getting his degree."

"He was bummed," Emma agreed. "We're all glad it's worked out."

"So are you guys looking for something in particular?" Marisol asked. "Not that I'd be able to tell you where to look, but Great-Grandpa would. I can get him."

"No need. I'll just poke around for a while, if you don't mind," Emma said.

"Okay, then, I'll take this in the back and be back in a flash. Just holler if you need one of us before I get back." The girl picked up the loaded box as if it weighed nothing and disappeared through a curtained doorway.

Emma stared after her. "Looks as if she's getting her life back on track."

Matt smiled that slow smile that made her knees go weak.

"Lot of that happening lately." He tore his gaze away from her and surveyed the piles of junk. "So any idea what you're looking for?"

Emma was almost tempted to tell him she was searching for her future, but that seemed too whimsical to express. "Hard to tell," she said instead. "I'll know it when I see it."

"You could have it all," he suggested casually as she began sorting through a box filled with old silver tableware.

Her head snapped up. "What are you saying?"

"The business is for sale. It could be yours." His gaze locked on hers. "Unless you think you've got a better deal with Marcel."

"I promised him I was coming back," she said, even though a part of her was already wavering. Her own place? Wasn't that exactly what she'd been thinking about ever since her mother had planted the idea in her head? "No, it's ridiculous. I can't even think about buying a business."

Matt came up to her and tucked a finger under her chin. "But you're tempted, aren't you?"

She looked around at the spacious room, which could be turned into a wonderful showroom by someone with a little artistic flair and a whole lot of elbow grease. Her imagination kicked in at full throttle. The hardwood floors could be restored to a shine, the window washed and freshly painted with the store's name. Flamingo Treasures, she thought at once, something to tie it to the family business. She could have a bright pink flamingo with some sort of antique jewelry dangling from its beak as her logo.

"Okay, I'm tempted," she admitted. "But it's impossible."

"Nothing is impossible if you want it badly enough," he insisted. "Do you, Emma? Do you want your own business? Do you want to stay here in Winter Cove with your family?" His gaze searched hers. "With me?"

She felt herself trembling. "Exactly what are you asking, Matt?"

He returned her gaze with a perfectly innocent expression. "Keep poking around. Maybe the answer will come to you."

She stared at him, puzzled. Why wouldn't he just say it? If he was talking about building a future together, he needed to be more direct than this, she thought, exasperated with him and with herself for daring to start to dream.

Oh, well, if he was encouraging her to poke around, she might as well do it. There was nothing she enjoyed more. If he got bored waiting for her, too bad. She could always remind him that it had been his idea.

The box of silver was filled with good pieces that with a little polishing could be worth a fortune. There was a filthy old painting stashed behind a dresser that she was pretty sure was by a minor, but well-recognized, eighteenth-century French artist. Once it was cleaned she could be more certain. There was a matching set of Italian renaissance chairs in deplorable condition. And two or three good tables, one of them made of rosewood that she would love to own herself. All of the marked prices were at junk shop level. Obviously Joshua Mullins made no attempt to separate genuine antiques from the junk. It was a bargain hunter's paradise.

She was a little surprised that Mr. Mullins hadn't already emerged from the back to try to sell her something, but maybe Marisol had told him she was just browsing. Or maybe Matt had conspired with him to give her free rein to look to her heart's content in the hope of tempting her into buying not just a few items, but the whole shop.

Could she do that? She had the talent for it, the solid business instincts. And staying in Winter Cove under these conditions wouldn't feel as if she'd sold out. But where would the money come from? It always came down to the money. Even at these prices, to own the shop lock, stock and barrel was bound to cost more than she could readily lay her hands on.

She reached an old display case near the door to the backroom. She could hear the low murmur of voices and realized that Matt was back there with Marisol and Mr. Mullins. They were probably having a damned tea party while she was out here salivating over something she couldn't have.

She sighed heavily and leaned down to study the old estate jewelry in the case. There was a lot of junky costume jewelry mixed in with some Art Deco pieces that had increased in value in recent years. And in the midst of it all was a velvet jewelry box that looked brand-new. A card propped against it had her name on it. Her heart immediately began to race.

"Matthew Atkins!" she shouted.

He wandered in from the back, looking as innocent as any male she'd ever seen. "What's up, darlin'? Did you find something you can't live without?"

She pointed toward the display case, and was surprised to see that her hand was shaking. "What is that?"

Matt leaned down and stared at the box as if he'd never seen it before. "Looks like a jewelry box to me."

"It has my name on it."

He continued to peer through the glass. "So it does. Isn't that something? Wonder how it got here?"

Mr. Mullins emerged just then, barely containing a grin. Marisol peeked around the doorway, not even trying to hide her smile.

"Why don't I get that out so you can take a look?" Mr. Mullins suggested. He reached into the display case with his gnarled fingers and gently picked up the velvet box and the card. Before handing it over, though, he peered at her closely. "You are Emma Killian, aren't you? I wouldn't want to make a mistake about a thing like that."

"I am," Emma said.

"Maybe I should see some ID," he said, feigning worry.

Matt chuckled at Emma's obvious frustration. "I think I can vouch for her. I've known her most of her life."

Mr. Mullins nodded. "That's okay, then," he said, handing over the box and card. "I'll be in the back if you need me." He shooed Marisol back into the backroom with him, despite her protests. "Let those two have some privacy," he scolded.

Emma's hand shook as she held the box. "Matt, what have you done?"

"What makes you think I know anything about this?"

"It has you written all over it," she said.

He made a pretense of studying it. "Only thing I see is your name. You going to open it or not?"

"I don't know," she whispered. Once that box was opened, who knew what would be unleashed? One thing was for certain, a lot of her options would disappear. There would be no question of going back to

Washington if the box contained what she thought it did. She might be stubborn and hardheaded, but she wasn't an idiot. There wasn't a man in Washington who could hold a candle to Matt. Balance a lifetime with him against what she might lose by staying and it was no contest. She looked into Matt's precious face. She would gain so much more.

Finally, she drew in a deep breath and opened the card.

"Just wanted to see if you could spot the real treasure in here," it read. "Love, Matt."

Her eyes promptly filled with tears. "Oh, Matt," she whispered, throwing her arms around him. "The treasure's not in this box. If there's any treasure in this entire room, it's you."

He pulled back and grinned. "Want me to take this back then?" he asked, reaching for the velvet box.

"Oh, no, you don't," she said, stepping back and holding it out of his reach. "It has my name on it."

She flipped it open and found not the fancy, brand-new diamond ring she'd expected, but an antique ring with a setting so delicate and a stone so brilliant it made her blink. A ring this special, one that had endured the test of time, spoke volumes about the man who'd picked it out.

"Oh, Matt, it's beautiful," she breathed. "It's perfect."

He met her gaze, brushing away her tears with the pad of his thumb. "I want you to stay here and marry me. Hell, Emma, I've loved you for so long, I don't think I can figure out how to stop. I don't think I could stand it if you went back to Washington again."

He cupped her face in his hands. "But if that's the

only way you can be happy, well, I suppose there are plenty of openings for a cop up there, too.''

Emma's head was spinning. ''You'd do that? You'd go to Washington if that's what I wanted?''

''I'd go to the ends of the earth, if you asked me to.''

How had she missed the fact that this thing between them was inevitable? How had she not known that Matt's love for her was deep enough for him to put her needs first? She'd depended on him for months now. She'd cried on his shoulder so often she was amazed he hadn't demanded a new wardrobe of shirts. She'd even slept with him, but she'd missed the fact that *she* loved *him* enough not to ask him to go.

Maybe that was one more thing she should have learned from her father's death, that people tucked other people into familiar categories and simply accepted that things would go on that way forever. Nothing could be more wrong. It was important to pay attention, to dig beneath the surface, to look beyond the actions of someone close and see what was in their heart. It was important to be ready for change, to face it with excitement, rather than fear.

''You're not saying anything,'' Matt said, searching her face, his expression uneasy. ''I thought that things were different between us now.''

''They are,'' she said.

''But you don't love me,'' he concluded, looking shaken.

''No, it's not that,'' she said, touching a finger to his lips until she'd coaxed a smile from him. ''You just took me by surprise. My life has been in such a state of turmoil since I came back, I never stopped for a single second to consider whether we were ready to take this step. It's a huge step, Matt.''

His smile turned wicked. ''You missed the fact that we've been sleeping together? That was the huge step. This next one should be a piece of cake. We've been working our way toward it our entire lives.''

''I'm very aware that we've been sleeping together,'' she said, her cheeks heating as she glanced toward the back room to see if Mr. Mullins or Marisol might be eavesdropping. ''But that doesn't always lead to marriage.''

''It does when it's you and me,'' he said soberly. ''So are you saying yes or no?''

''I'm saying I care enough to stay here and try to figure it out,'' she said.

He nodded and tried to hide his disappointment, but she could read it in his eyes.

''Will you buy this place?'' he asked.

That much she was certain about. She was going to find some way to buy this junk shop and turn it into her own dream business where she would answer to no one. ''If I can get the money together to do it,'' she said.

''I could help,'' he offered. ''I have some savings.''

She shook her head. ''I have to do it on my own. It has to be mine, Matt.''

He nodded. ''That independent streak again. I'm familiar with it. Okay, then, you do what you have to do. Something tells me Joshua Mullins will work with you. Turns out he's a bit of a romantic.''

''He must be if he was willing to help you pull off this proposal,'' she said, looking deep into Matt's eyes. ''So can you be patient with me?''

"I've waited for you since I was twenty years old," he said. "A few more months won't make any difference."

"Months?"

"Okay, weeks."

Emma laughed at his impatience. It made her love him all the more. "How about a year?"

"Don't press your luck, Emma. I want babies. Lots of them, while we're both still young enough to keep up with them."

Her heart began to pound as Matt tucked a wayward curl behind her ear. "Babies," she repeated, a combination of wonder and panic in her voice.

"No need to panic," he soothed. "We can take this one step at a time. Business first, wedding second, then lots and lots of babies who look just like their mom."

Emma stood on tiptoe and kissed him. There was nothing scary about one tiny step, not when it was with Matt. He would never let her down. She thought of all the pain her father's death had caused her and measured it against this moment. She felt Matt's hand curve reassuringly around hers and decided that, like her mother always said, even the darkest cloud had a silver lining, if only you took the time to look for it.

SHERRYL WOODS

66955	ALONG CAME TROUBLE	___ $6.50 U.S.	___ $7.99 CAN.
66901	ASK ANYONE	___ $6.50 U.S.	___ $7.99 CAN.
66815	ABOUT THAT MAN	___ $6.50 U.S.	___ $7.99 CAN.
66600	ANGEL MINE	___ $5.99 U.S.	___ $6.99 CAN.
66542	AFTER TEX	___ $5.99 U.S.	___ $6.99 CAN.

(limited quantities available)

TOTAL AMOUNT $_____
POSTAGE & HANDLING $_____
($1.00 for 1 book, 50¢ for each additional)
APPLICABLE TAXES* $_____
TOTAL PAYABLE $_____
(check or money order—please do not send cash)

MIRA®